THE KEEPER OF THE
CRYSTAL BLADE

WINTERTHORN
BOOK THREE

NATHAN TAYLOR

THE WINTERTHORN SAGA

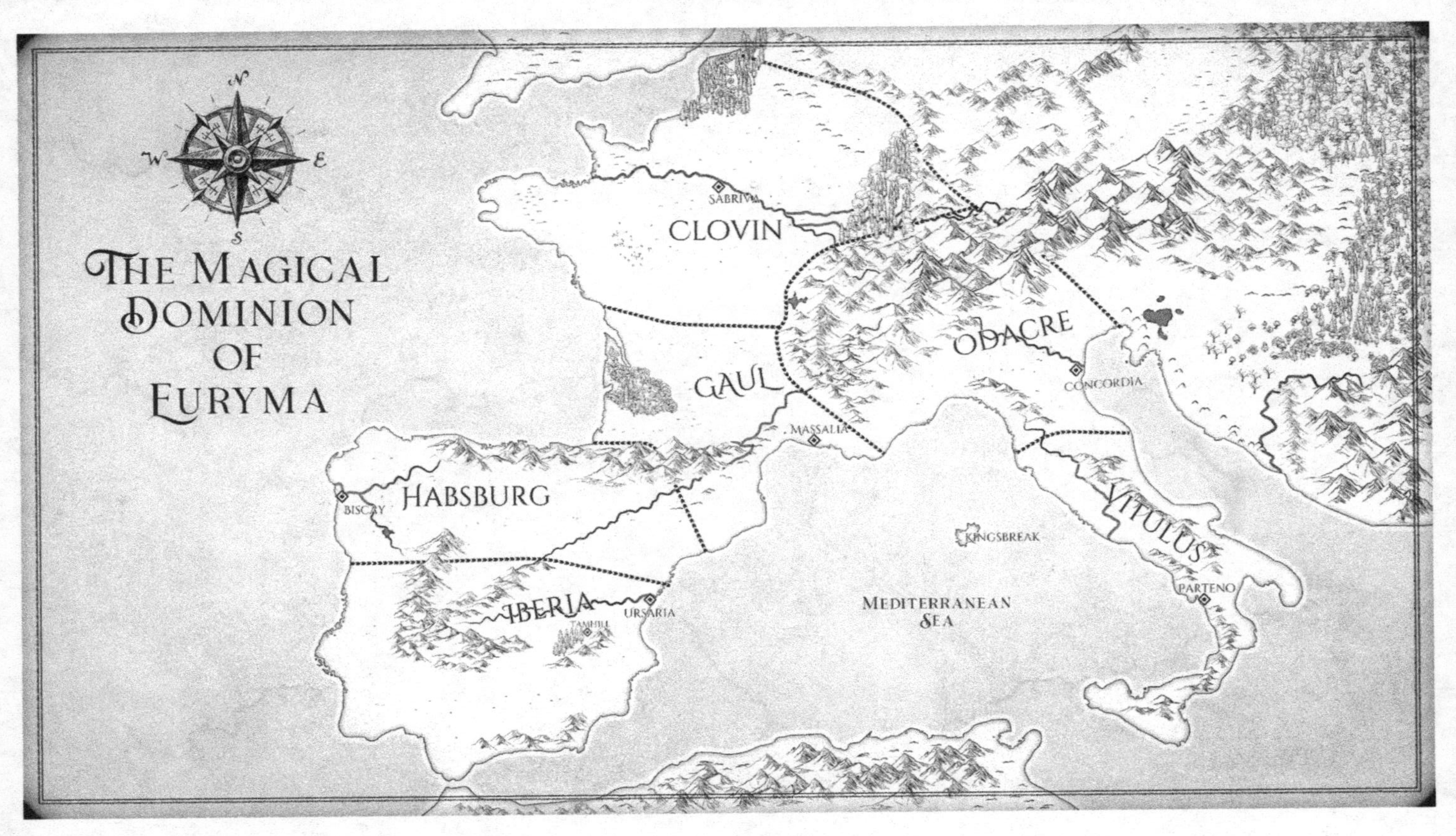

THE MAGICAL DOMINION OF EURYMA
CLOVIN
GAUL
OBACRE
VITULUS
HABSBURG
IBERIA
BISCAY
SABRIVA
MASSALIA
CONCORDIA
KINGSBREAK
PARTENO
URSARIA
TAMHILL
MEDITERRANEAN SEA

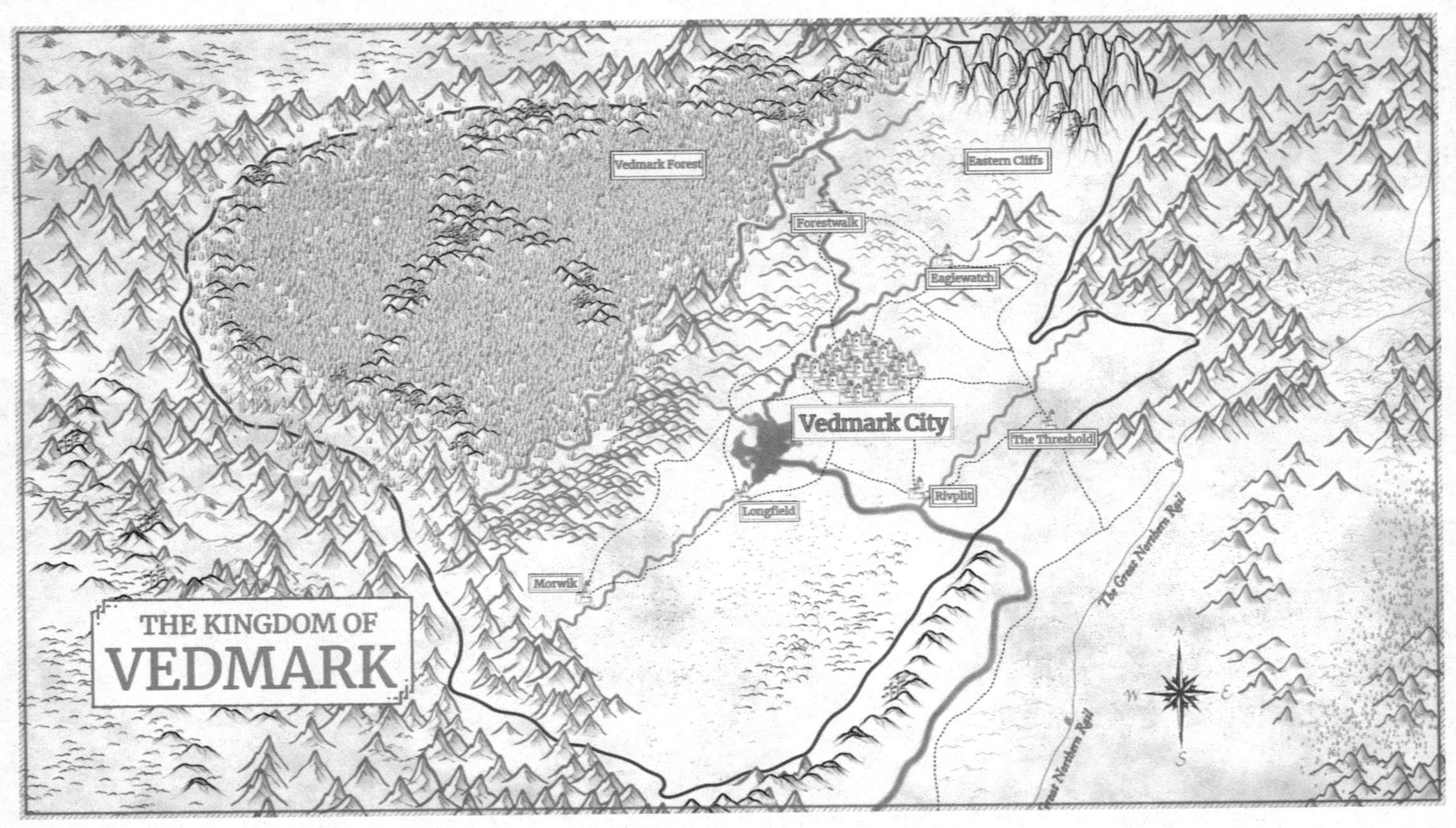

THE KINGDOM OF
VEDMARK
Vedmark Forest
Eastern Cliffs
Forestwalk
Eaglewatch
Vedmark City
The Threshold
Rivplit
Longfield
Morwik
The Great Northern Road
The Great Northern Road

WELCOME TO HISTORIC KINGSBREAK.

From the earliest days of Euryma's Founding, this small Mediterranean island has played a pivotal role in the legacy and history of our Dominion.

Once a seaside residence of the Fendragon Kings, Kingsbreak is now the site of Euryma's oldest and most prestigious college.

For nine months of the year, ten thousand students and staff call King's College home. Here, we combine the rich history of these halls with a cutting edge approach to manipulation, imbusion and mimicry.

As you tour our grounds and facilities, we trust you will enjoy the synergy of past and present that makes King's College the best Magical Education Institution in the world.

Kindest Regards,

Mary-Lou Nivin
Enrolments Officer
King's College

For John and Naomi

THE KEEPER OF THE
CRYSTAL BLADE

WINTERTHORN
BOOK THREE

NATHAN TAYLOR

CHAPTER 1
HORACE

The murder had been necessary.

When Horace thrust Winterthorn—the magical white dagger—into Arman Moore's heart, he had not just taken his life, but also the man's memories. Now, he was stuck in one of those moments. Living as two people in tandem. Horace Marley in the present, and Arman Moore from a thousand years earlier.

The memory balanced somewhere between reality and imagination. Distinct in the foreground; blurring to nothing on the edges. The sounds of the trees were muted, as if half forgotten, and a sense of foreboding hung over them. Arman was afraid. Horace felt the fear as if it were his own.

A crescent moon peeked between clouds, illuminating the forest clearing. Six paces ahead of him stood his brother, who now wielded a bloodthirsty army. One intent on destroying his home.

"Hail, Morkurik." The words felt odd as they spilled, unbidden, from Horace's mouth. These moments belonged to the past—he was only a spectator behind Arman's eyes.

1

The sensation took some getting used to. "You seek my audience?"

Morkurik closed the distance so they were face to face. The pair were obvious siblings—the elder shared Arman's straight nose and firm jaw—but the resemblance stopped at the eyes. Hooded brows hung over empty pits. If eyes were a window to the soul, Morkurik's was long gone.

Arman fought to hold his gaze, and lost.

"The Lucks of Iberia killed three of my Knights, *brother*." Morkurik spoke the last word with a hiss. "Now I discover you are their commander. You have betrayed me."

Ice spiked in Arman's veins, but he reined in the emotion at once. "I am not the aggressor here. You can guarantee your Knights' safety by returning to Vedmark. This is not war, it is slaughter. It must end."

Morkurik stared at him, his face a wax mask. Then he slid a curved blade from the scabbard beneath his cloak. The metal glinted midnight-purple in the moonlight. "Then we end it tonight."

Arman un-looped the axe from his belt as he stepped into a defensive stance. "What do you mean?"

"A duel of champions." Morkurik flicked the sword so it pointed skyward. "If you win, we will retreat. If I win, this land is forfeit to Vedmark. No lives wasted but our own."

He smiled, and Horace did not know if the shiver running down his spine belonged to him or Arman. "Where?" Anxious tension riddled Arman's body. "When?"

Morkurik's smile vanished. "Here. Now. Do you accept?"

Horace could not hear Arman's thoughts, but the blur of emotions gave him an idea of what the man was thinking. He knew he was outmatched, but the opportunity was too good to surrender. If he stopped his brother, he could stop the Knights. Horace's vision dipped as Arman's head tilted in the slightest of nods.

In a flash of movement, the midnight purple blade screamed overhead and caught Arman's axe in a shower of sparks.

"This land is mine." Morkurik's voice was a jagged glacier. Sword to axe, he pressed forward, eyes alight with wild fervor. Arman's feet pushed trails through the dirt until he spun free, swinging his axe head clean into Morkurik's armored chest. It sang like a struck anvil, but the blow left no mark. Arman raised his weapon to see a chip on the axe-blade's edge.

Morkurik peeled his breastplate loose—it fell to the ground with a clatter—then ran a hand over his sword. Green flames ignited along the blade's edge. "You cannot best me, little brother." He adjusted his grip on the sword's hilt. "Nor do you deserve to. You left. You abandoned our Kingdom to rot. Do not come begging now I lay claim to what is mine." He surged forward, moving with the grace of a deadly shadow. It was all Arman could do to stay alive. The sword weaved intricate trails of light in the darkness. It crashed against the axe, emitting white-hot flares.

Horace struggled to follow the fight. There was a maelstrom of emerald flashes before Arman leapt to safety. Agony erupted within the memory as the flaming blade sliced Arman's shoulder. The axe dropped from his hand. The scene blurred as Arman stumbled to regain his footing.

The flaming sword faded to a gentle smolder. "We could have done this together." Morkurik said. "We could have ruled this land."

"You would have killed me," Arman said. He staggered upright. "You would have killed me like you did Imond. Like you murdered our *father*." The pain in the word 'father' tore through the forest, carrying dead leaves away like a ripple in a pond. Arman looked down. Gleaming green light filled the fresh wound until the skin melded together. Horace gasped as if plunged into ice water. The immensity of Arman's magic was unlike anything he had ever experienced.

Arman drew himself tall.

"You dare use my power against me?" Morkurik hissed.

"This is not *your* power." Arman's axe leapt into his hand, the axe head bursting into green fire.

With a roar like a tumbling mountain, Morkurik threw himself forward. Weapons collided, and a blinding explosion of light engulfed the forest. When it faded, the scene transformed into a blur of color, too fast to follow. The sound of metal on metal thrummed and Morkurik flew backwards on a trail of emerald flames. He hit a tree—cleaved it in two—and landed smoothly on his feet.

Arman twirled his axe. "What would your Knights say if they saw you now? Morkurik the Mighty, undone by a lowly Prince of Vedmark."

Morkurik stiffened. Forehead creased, he gripped his sword with both hands. A strange energy pulsed from the handle, building like static in a storm. In one clean movement, Morkurik pulled his hands apart. Where once there was one blade, now there were two. The second sword—identical in shape and size—appeared to be made of solid light. "I will mount your head on a spear for children to spit on."

Arman threw his axe, but Morkurik rolled underneath it. Arman called it back. It reached his hands as they clashed again. The second blade was a viper, slithering through Arman's defenses, tracing cuts along his arms, dismantling him with fatal precision. Horace felt the pain, the desperation, the fear of imminent failure. The window had closed. Morkurik was gaining momentum. Even with Sila coursing through him, Arman had failed.

Morkurik pushed—methodical, meticulous—until they reached the edge of the clearing. With a feint and flurry, he ran the glowing sword through Arman's stomach to the hilt. A gasp tore free of Horace's lips. The luminous blade pinned them to a tree trunk.

"I told you," Morkurik said. "This land is mine."

Arman murmured a reply, too low to understand. His hair—matted with sweat and blood—was a mess across his face. He said something again, but Horace couldn't make out the words. Morkurik leaned closer, and Arman pulled the sword free, smashing the hilt into his brother's chin. Morkurik staggered back.

Arman's sense of failure reached its crescendo. In a blaze of light, the forest was gone.

Horace blinked. He was on his back, laying on a sandstone balcony staring up at the night sky. Arman rolled onto his side, and Horace watched the blood gush from his torso, bathing the terracotta tiles. "Maria," he groaned. "MARIA!"

A woman, dark-skinned and wide-eyed, ran into the adjoining room holding her colorful skirts aloft. "Arman!" She slid to the floor beside him. "What happened?"

"I couldn't stop him," Arman said. "He's too strong. He's—"

"Save your strength." She pushed a hand to his wound. Arman winced.

"His blade was pure Sila. I... I can't heal it."

Everything darkened. Their words grew quiet—as if lowered with a dial. Maria pressed both hands against

Arman's side. Blood leaked through her slender fingers and ran down her wrists.

The setting changed in the blink of an eye. It was daytime. Horace—or Arman—lay in an enormous bed with a cloth bandage wrapped around his torso. Skins of odd animals adorned the walls. Through a window, the Mediterranean Sea glittered as the waves caught the sunlight.

Beside him, the same dark-haired beauty from the previous memory worked at a small table. An intricate system of white and red tubes ran from the table's edge into Arman's arms. She turned to press a bone needle into a waterskin.

"Maria?" Arman murmured. Bright crimson liquid funneled through a tube into his arm. The woman spun at his voice. "What... what happened?" His gaze fixed on the curious contraption.

"You bled out." Maria straightened and checked the apparatus before settling by his bedside. She held his hand in hers. "I stitched the wound, but you lost so much blood. I had to come up with something." She waved to the water-skin. "I came up with this."

Arman's forehead creased. "Whose blood is this?"

"Swine blood," Maria said. "From the slaughterhouse." She shook her head. "I have been using Luck to clear it of impurities, to match it to your body."

Arman leaned back and winced as the tube in his arm shifted. "Thank Luck."

"You are not mad?"

He laughed. "I am alive," he said. "My enemies will create some excellent barbs when they discover I have swine blood in my veins, but I live to see another day.

Thank you." He took Maria's hand, and his gratitude gave way to concern. "What of the war?"

"Hush." Maria put a finger to his lips. "There has been no change. Rest, love. Do not burden yourself until you are strong enough to carry that weight. Sleep. I will watch over us." She intertwined her fingers with his. Arman closed his eyes, and again, the world faded.

Underneath a flickering fluorescent strip, Horace stirred into consciousness. He lay—drenched in sweat—on a thin mattress crammed in a glorified cupboard. To his left, a garment rack burst with Haberdeen's expensive dresses. To his right was an office.

Horace hated the memories. They clawed at him with a legion of razor-sharp hooks. Free at last, he poured himself into the surrounding nima. Ire Tides filled him, dulling their pull and numbing the pain. In a haze of purple light, the hooks lost their purchase.

Horace turned his attention to the photo of Haberdeen taped to the door. He allowed the image to manifest itself on his body. He dressed quickly, then entered his office. His desk was a mess of paper. Remnant Magic forecasts, refugee estimates, library catalogues of historical books. He had barely started organising the piles when somebody knocked on the door.

"Enter," he said in Haberdeen's sultry voice.

Benjamin Briggs struggled to close the door as he carried an armful of documents into the room. "Ophelia said you'd want these, Madam."

"What..." Horace faltered as the memories pulsed in his

head, threatening to drag him back. He took a controlled breath, then tried again. "What exactly are *these*?"

"Cave system surveys you asked for. Ophelia had me order them by square footage and ease of access."

Horace accepted the pile and flipped through the summary on top, scanning the list of caves. "Lombrives…" He circled the word in red ink as he said it, then glanced up from the sheet. "Lombrives it is." He rummaged through his desk until he found a manilla folder labelled 'Project Safehouse'. He added the list to the folder, then held it out to Benjamin. "Give this to Ophelia. It has everything she needs to get started. Tell her this is priority one. Am I clear?"

"Yes, Madam." Benjamin bowed his head, then left.

Horace leaned back in his chair. When he closed his eyes, he could picture a shimmering green ocean. Centuries of memories called to him.

Horace paved the swirling sea in Ire Tides until it gleamed purple. A thin shield of magic separated past and present.

Jump in.

Horace's eyes snapped open. A pulse of fizzling violet energy formed in his palm, but the room was empty. Outside, bleak grey skies loomed over downtown Biscay. "Who are you?" he asked.

I'm you, said the voice. It sounded familiar. *Or maybe me. Are we the same? I'm not sure.* Horace released the Ire Tides. The voice sounded like his father, but less… accusatory. "Where did you come from?"

I don't know. Perhaps I've always been here, and you just weren't listening.

Great, Horace thought. *Now I'm going mad.*

I'm not madness. I'm…

The voice never finished. Horace disregarded it and

picked up a list of texts from before Euryma's founding. These were the books that the real Haberdeen thought held the key to understanding Remnant Magic. All were accounted for, except one, highlighted in yellow on the page. *Oregin o Magi.* Horace stared at the words, as if he could summon the missing tome by force of will alone. Another document caught his eye—a report on the five hundred thousand people who had escaped Sabriva's destruction.

Do you really think you can hide that many people in one cave? Horace startled at the voice. The sheet fell to the floor.

"I have to do something." He leaned down to get the paper. "That's just the start of it. We need somewhere safe—"

The people don't need to be hidden in a hole. You just need to stop the storms.

"And how do I do that?" Horace paused, half-bent below the table, waiting for a response.

The answers are in the centuries living in your head. You just need to find them.

Horace frowned. He was combing the Dominion for a history book, when a millennium of Euryma's past resided in his head. *Could it be so easy?* A sharp knock shattered the thought, and he shook himself back to the present. *No. The memories are too dangerous.* The Fatesmiths needed him in the real world. Euryma needed him. Horace straightened in his seat. "Come in."

Ophelia entered, brandishing the manilla folder like a weapon. She slapped it on his desk and dropped into the seat opposite. "You can't be serious?"

"Perfectly serious. We need somewhere safe."

"You're asking us to build an underground city in days

so that we can start sheltering refugees in weeks... without magic?"

"Magic is what got us into this mess," Horace said. "We would be foolish to continue adding to the problem."

"It's impossible," Ophelia replied. "The logistics around food and water alone... How do you expect me to do this?"

"It's all in those plans," Horace said. "Engineers first, builders second. Pay them whatever they need. Then organize food, water and transport while they're building."

Ophelia flicked through the pages, her forehead creased as she read. "Half the suppliers you have on here were from Sabriva. They're dust now, Madam."

"Then find others," Horace said. "If they don't want money, tell them they're creating the means to keep their loved ones safe. Send word through our own ranks. Some of the LAMPs here must know how to use a hammer."

Ophelia's gaze softened. "I'm going to need help."

"Take Benjamin off flash-finding. We have plenty of other Fatesmiths to forecast storms."

"I don't mean *his* help," Ophelia said. "I mean *yours*, Madam. How long has it been since you've left this office?"

"Two weeks," Horace said. "Two weeks since Sabriva burned because of my failure."

"You can't blame yourself for that."

"I don't need your pity, Ophelia. I need you to keep Euryma's citizens safe. I'm not your project—the Lombrives cave is." Ophelia searched his face, but Horace gave her no emotion. "Half the Dominion is homeless," he said. "Until we can destroy the storms, that will only get worse. I don't care what it takes. I don't care how much of the Fatesmiths' coffers you use. It must be done, and you're the person I trust to do it."

Resolute, she nodded. "Yes, Madam." Ophelia gathered

the folder and left. When the door closed, the voice returned. *You are treating the symptoms. You need to stop the storms. They are the root of the problem.*

"By throwing myself into those cursed memories?" Horace whispered. "There are too many. It's a labyrinth. A death trap." He shook his head. "There must be another way." He picked up the sheet with *Oregin o Magi* highlighted in bright yellow. A desperate sense of hope flickered in his chest. "There has to be."

CHAPTER 2
DECLAN

DECLAN SAT on a fallen tree overlooking the endless canopy of Vedmark Forest. A patchwork quilt of moss cushioned the trunk underneath him, and he made a show of inspecting the various shades of green. Mrs. Winter waited beside him, wearing a black gown with a high collar. Neither spoke.

It had taken two weeks to return Arman's body to his cabin. Declan, Ava and Mrs. Winter had slipped through the towering walls of the Threshold under cover of darkness, threaded their way between the City and Eaglewatch and cut west into the forest.

After a frantic fortnight fleeing the Dominion, he was here. Sitting on a tree trunk. Delaying a funeral he did not want to acknowledge.

"I'm glad we brought him back." Mrs. Winter spoke with her eyes fixed forward. "He loved this place. I think it was the only part of Vedmark he considered home."

The silence returned, but now it carried an obligation to respond. Declan wet his lips. "This is not how things were supposed to happen."

"Perhaps," Mrs. Winter said. She turned her piercing gaze on him. "But that is irrelevant now. Here is where we are, so we will do what we can with what we have."

"Which is nothing."

Mrs. Winter arced a slim eyebrow, but said nothing.

"I'm sorry." Declan had not intended to sound so cold. Still, he couldn't deny his feelings. There was a hole inside him, and nothing that would even begin to repair it. He stared at his feet. "It just feels... hopeless."

"I understand it may seem that way," she said. "The night is always darkest before dawn. Rest assured, there are plans in motion."

Declan considered Mrs. Winter. As his homeroom teacher for a decade, she was a concrete representation of his former life. But she had known the truth about him the entire time. The duality of the woman bothered him more than he cared to admit. "What plans?"

Dry pine needles crunched behind them. Declan turned and his heart skipped a beat. Ava looked beautiful in a simple black dress. "Everything is ready," she said.

Mrs. Winter nodded, then met Declan's eyes. "Are *you* ready?"

Declan glanced back at the cabin where his grandfather's body waited. Dead. All because he was too weak to stop his best friend. "No," he said, standing. "But we should do it anyway."

They walked down to the clearing where Arman's cabin stood. From the outside, nothing had changed. His grandfather could be sitting inside, eating odd fruit or sharpening axes. The only difference was the grave they had dug on the building's left. A rectangular scar in the grass.

Declan's legs were poorly stacked towers of loose bricks. He wanted to say something, but he couldn't. A stream of tears was the only outward display of the grief that threatened to consume him.

Ava squeezed his hand. A weak smile was all Declan could offer. Mrs. Winter's fingers plucked the air like a concert harpist and the cabin door opened. A thick wooden panel drifted outside. Arman Moore's body lay covered in flower buds, with a peaceful expression on his face and his hands folded over his chest. Declan had worried the body might have started to decay, but his grandfather could have been sleeping. There was no way to know whose magic had preserved him, but it was a nice touch.

The board floated on an unseen tide. As it did, the buds bloomed, leaving a gentle trail of petals behind it. Rows of small animals—birds, squirrels, field mice—watched from the trees, while a line of armadillos—Lancelot included with his golden armor—bowed in reverence. Even the pines seemed to lean closer, as if bowing in respect. The body slowed to a halt above the burial plot.

A tangible weight hung over the clearing.

"It is a curious thing..." Mrs. Winter's voice cracked. She took a deep breath, then started once more. "It is a curious thing that just three of us gather here today to remember a man who helped the lives of millions." She dabbed her eyes with her shawl. "Of course, King Arman would not have cared that we are so few. That was not in his nature. He never sought to rule. He had power greater than any man in history and never sought to use it for his own gain. Arman understood hard work, duty, and sacrifice. He endured hardships we cannot comprehend in the name of what is right." She smiled at Declan. "Arman would not want us to grieve. He has returned to those he loved, and those he lost. We lay him to rest, and it is a rest well earned."

"A rest well earned," Ava repeated.

"A rest well earned." Declan's voice was less than a whisper. His heart ached, the pain of loss, of Arman and his parents and Amber and Ven and Dreyfus. It weighed on him like stone chains.

Mrs. Winter lowered her palm, and Arman Moore descended into the darkness. Tears blurred Declan's vision as his grandfather vanished from sight. From underground, green tendrils sprouted and climbed from the pit—joining, growing—they wove together to form two pillars that met in a perfect arch. As they connected, a kaleidoscope of flowers bloomed. An archway of braided vines spattered with color. A tribute to the King of Vedmark.

Mrs. Winter raised an eyebrow at Ava. "You did that with Luck?"

Ava's jaw hung slack. "I... I managed the arch. The flowers...." she trailed off, shaking her head.

"Amazing." Mrs. Winter considered the display. "This forest housed Arman for centuries. I suppose it has its own ways of saying farewell."

"He deserves it," Declan murmured. His throat felt like gravel.

"He did. Duty kept him here. Obligation to his people." Mrs. Winter smiled sadly. "Arman is free now. He is at peace."

Declan's stomach sank. *Now that obligation is mine.*

They stood in thoughtful silence for a long time. The animals retreated into the thickets of the forest; the trees creaked and straightened. Lancelot wandered forward as the other armadillos trudged away. His golden scales seemed dull as he curled up beneath the arch. Nobody said a word, but slowly, the weight of the moment lifted.

"Oh, I have something... I found it in the cabin." Ava withdrew a chain from her sleeve. A sapphire pendant hung from its end. She held it out to Mrs. Winter. "You gave me this, in the Knights' barracks, to find him. It's yours, isn't it?"

Mrs. Winter shook her head. "That belongs to the King." She looked at the grave and sighed. "Well, by inheritance, it now belongs to you, Declan."

Declan inspected the necklace. The metal was tarnished, but the sapphire sparkled in the afternoon light. "I'm not one for jewelry." He tried to grin. "You keep it."

Ava shook her head. "It's not just a necklace, though, is it?" she said to Mrs. Winter. "It helped me find him. Does it use Sila?"

"It may," Mrs. Winter said. "Does it work?"

Ava held the gem up to her eye. A brief pause and her shoulders slumped. "Nothing. Here. You try."

She handed Declan the pendant, and he peered through it. The trees, the cabin, the archway all became bright blue. Aside from that, nothing changed. Declan handed it back to Ava. "Keep it.".

A soft chime interrupted them. Mrs. Winter frowned as she dug a bronze device from her pocket. She opened it like a pocket-watch and sighed.

"What is it?" Ava asked.

"I am afraid I have been summoned to your uncle's hall."

Something like a growl rumbled in the back of Ava's throat. "Does he know what happened?"

"I expect word of Sabriva has reached his ear, but the only people who know of Arman's passing are the three of us and your friends from King's College." She directed the last statement to Declan. "Still, I fear time is running out. It only takes one Knight to cross the Threshold with Sila on hand to discover the barrier is gone."

"What are you going to do?" Declan asked. His stomach wound itself in knots at the thought of Vedmark's Knights realizing they were free to enter Euryma.

Mrs. Winter turned to the east. A breeze picked up, carrying her dark hair over her shoulders. "I am still deciding. If Rasporvin knows Sabriva has fallen, he will be eager to find the King. Perhaps we can buy a month or two of the Knights chasing ghosts in the forest. I do not know."

"What will we do?" Ava asked.

"Stay put for now. Rasporvin will not have forgiven you for releasing Haberdeen and breaking out of his barracks. Stay out of sight and wait for me." The bronze device chimed again. Mrs. Winter turned to Declan. "I will return tomorrow to finish our conversation. I know it feels hopeless, but I have a way forward." She tilted her head. "Walk me down the hill, will you Ava?"

Declan watched them go, then sat on the grass by the arch. Lancelot glanced up as he did, and Declan felt a fresh pang of sadness for the little creature. From what he understood, the golden armadillo was just as old as his grandfather. They had spent hundreds of years together, and now he was alone.

"I'm sorry," Declan said. He put his hand on the creature's shell as a new wave of tears rose up from the hole within. "I'm so sorry."

The sun dropped below a bank of clouds, casting liquid gold along their edges. Lancelot was gone, but Declan remained on the grass where Ava joined him. She held the necklace in her hand, and her eyes were swollen from tears. "Are you sure you don't want this?"

"No, it's yours." He stared at the archway; the blooms were the size of his fist. "I... I miss him."

"I wouldn't expect anything less," Ava said. "The Emissary will know more. Just... relax today. We'll have our chance to figure the rest out later."

Declan's stomach turned. *More chances to fail.* He lay back and Ava did the same. The wind plucked at the pines; a chorus of birdsong carried from somewhere distant. Time crawled by. Declan tried to find peace in the silence, to indulge in the memories with his grandfather, to enjoy Ava's company, but he felt... nothing.

"I feel like I'm cursed." He blushed at the words. They had escaped his lips without warning, and sounded so immature out loud.

Ava sat up. The sunset reflected in her eyes. "You're not cursed, Declan. Did you forget how you saved me? How you saved your friends from Kingsbreak? We wouldn't be alive if not for you. All you focus on are the terrible things that went wrong. Don't forget all the amazing things you have done." She waited for a response. When none was forthcoming, she sighed. "I'm going to start on dinner. I hope you like 'everything stew', because the Emissary told me to use up whatever's left so she can restock tomorrow."

"That sounds... wonderful. Thanks." Declan could see from Ava's expression that his tone was unconvincing. As she walked away, he took in the fading sky and felt like vomiting. He tried to contain the voice in his head, but it was too hard, too loud. *How long until she gets hurt like the others?*

"Enough," he muttered.

How long until you fail her too?

Stewed rabbit bubbled in a heavy pot inside the cabin. Declan could smell it from outside, and it smelled delicious. When he sat at Arman's simple table, he pushed the meat around for fifteen minutes before putting the bowl aside. Guilt still simmered in his stomach. Ava finished her own meal without speaking.

The fireplace burned down to embers that glowed in the darkness. Ava took the bowls and sat beside him. "Do you want to talk?"

No. Declan fought to calm his racing mind. Ava had been so kind, so patient. He had no reason to be angry with her, but...

"Declan. Talk to me."

He stared into the fireplace and took a long breath. "I grew up wishing I could do magic." As the words tumbled out, his eyes never left the glowing coals. "I watched my parents do everything with magic. I went to school and heard all about how my friends would one day go to college and learn to use it. But I wouldn't. I had to accept I would never have that, and as far as anyone knew, I did." He shook his head. "But that was a lie. I don't know why, but I never accepted it. I always wanted to have that power, and now..." Declan turned to Ava, her somber frown illuminated in orange. "I don't want it. I hate it. I just wish I'd left it alone."

Ava put her hand on his. "I know you feel that way now," she said. "But wishing away your gifts won't change what has happened. You need your Sila. We need it."

The words irked him more than they should have. "I don't want Sila."

"Dec—"

"Am I not allowed to feel sad?" he snapped. His grief boiled into anger. "Can I not be miserable about my dead family?"

Ava's mouth clamped shut. She inhaled a trembling breath through her nose and nodded. "It's not fair, Declan. I get that, but you can't allow the misery to win. Not now. You're on the edge of a precipice and I will not let you fall."

The anger in Declan's chest vanished in an instant. An odd sensation took its place—a sudden warmth in the empty. It felt good, as well as he had felt in months. Declan turned to Ava. That happiness couldn't be his, because there was no joy inside him. This foreign pleasure stuck out like a knife in his stomach. Wherever the feeling came from, it was not coming from within. "Don't," he whispered.

"Come on, Declan. We need you." Ava squeezed his hand. Dewdrops of sweat beaded along her hairline. Whatever she was doing was a herculean task.

The realization snapped into place. "Really?" He jerked his hand free. "You're using your Luck to cheer me up? On the day I buried my grandfather."

Ava's eyes grew wide. Her face colored. "I..."

"Don't you dare lie!" Declan stood. "Why would you do that?" The artificial warmth vanished, leaving emptiness and anger.

"Declan... I... I just wanted to—"

"To help?" Declan backed away from her. "Using your power to change how I'm feeling isn't *helping*."

"I'm sorry!" Her eyes shone in the firelight. "I didn't know it would upset you."

"You didn't know..." Declan trailed off. He shook his head, too angry to think. "You didn't know? Or you didn't care?"

He waited for Ava to reply. She stood—shellshocked—by the dying embers. "I'm sorry," she whispered.

Amidst the anger, Declan felt something new. A pull, as if he were a magnet and there was metal nearby. Without thinking, he embraced the sensation. A loud rip made Ava jump as the axes Mrs. Winter gifted him ripped free of his bag in the cabin's corner. They surged forward with a metallic thrum and he caught them on instinct. Ava's eyes expanded as he stood over her with the weapons. Declan stared at the grey-green wooden handles that vibrated in his palm. He turned and ran out the door, and into the black night.

CHAPTER 3
DECLAN

THE FOREST FELT different at night. Overwhelming silence amplified every footstep, rustle, and howling cry. Declan ran until he reached the river. An ancient willow tilted towards the water, and thick roots buttressed out around it. He dropped the axes and fell to the ground between the willow's roots, breathing in great gulps. Anger radiated off him. *How could she? We just buried him!* His clenched jaw hurt his teeth. He leaned against the tree and tried to relax.

There were no insect calls or swooping owls. Absolute silence crowded the night. Sheets of stars decorated the gaps in the canopy, and a crescent moon reflected off the slow-moving water. Slowly, the sting of fury dulled to disappointment and loneliness. Ava was his anchor. Or had been.

Something moved across the riverbank.

Declan dipped out of sight. The richness of the soil filled his nostrils. He reached out for his axes. Again, they responded to his call. A small part of him wondered how, but as he peeked over the river, the thought washed away.

A stooped man dressed in a pale grey robe strolled along the grassy bank. On occasion, he paused to inspect something unseen. The figure turned to face him, revealing a short beard and a familiar jaw line. Declan froze. *Impossible.* He stood slowly. It looked like... "Grandfather?"

The man stiffened and peered out from his hood. Declan staggered back. Those were not human eyes. They shone yellow, a pair of glowing topaz in the night.

Then the pain arrived.

Declan fell to his knees, dropping his axes as he reached to cover his face from the searing heat in those golden eyes. When that didn't work, he crumpled, hugging himself tight as he turned away. It did nothing. The creature's gaze doused him in scalding water. As a whistling shriek filled his ears, the world evaporated around him. The willow tree, the river, the forest, it vanished. Leaving him in empty white.

The burning sensation dulled to a persistent itch. Declan pressed his hand to an alabaster surface that felt like cold honey. He staggered upright, scanning the space. *Where am I?* There was no floor, no ceiling, no sky. Only endless emptiness. "Hello?" Declan called. "Is anyone here?"

There was nothing, and a sudden thought sent an icy chill through his veins. *You're in the Void.* Declan searched the emptiness for any sign of the creature on the river, then ran. With no frame of reference, it was impossible to know if he was moving or not. After a moment, minutes or hours, he hunched over to catch his breath.

"You have done well, Mage Ward."

Declan turned to the source of the sound. An amorphous white glob grew from the floor, like a candle melting in reverse. It stretched and split into four glossy figures—his parents, Haberdeen and Ward. Declan's tongue stuck to his dry mouth. He knew this scene...

"Your powers of persuasion are transcendent." Ward's cream lips curled in a smug grin. "The boy never suspected a thing."

Haberdeen nodded. "I was surprised with how quickly he agreed."

"I have fierised the prisoners. Where would you like them stored?"

"Melt them."

"As you wish." Ward gestured to the snowy statues of his mother and father. "And the boy's parents?"

I can't watch this. Not again. Declan tried to run, but it was pointless. When he glanced back, he had not moved a step.

"We have the boy," Haberdeen announced. "Melt them as well."

"NO!" Declan dived at Ward and passed straight through him. Despite its solid appearance, the waxy specter could have been liquid. He swung a fist into Ward's head; it splashed through it and Ward's smirk rippled back into existence. The wax bubbled and sank as his parents fused into a sickening puddle.

"No. No. No." Helpless, Declan crawled towards them as they dissolved into the floor and a new scene appeared. This time, a copy of him stood on a dais with the Grand Steward of Vedmark. His parents knelt on the ground between them.

"You have the Knights' Blade," Rasporvin said. "Now do it."

"I... can't." The glossy replica of Declan glanced up from the slender knife in his hand. "They are innocent."

"They are sacrificial lambs. Take your Sila. Do not be a fool, Declan Moore."

"I won't."

"It is your blood, or the world's blood," Rasporvin growled. "You cannot stop the storms without your Sila."

"They are my family!"

"That is why it must be them!" Rasporvin hissed. His lips curled, and he waved to an enormous Knight, who swelled from the floor. He approached from behind and pulled a sword to his mother's throat.

"Kill them, or we will."

"NO!"

Rasporvin slashed his hand in a cutting motion. The Knight obeyed. In a flash of movement, his mother's wax figure fell. Declan's heart wrenched as Angus Moore roared in anger. He knew the spectacle was fake, but his father's voice sounded so real.

The specter of Declan Moore rushed to his mother's side.

"There is no time for weakness," Rasporvin said. "The Knights of Vedmark will not tolerate it." He nodded to the Knight, who held the sword tip to his father's chest.

"Stop!" Declan's stepped between them. "I... I will do it."

Rasporvin's white lips bore a humorless smile. "Then do it."

The wax imitation turned to his father. "I'm sorry," he whispered. He leaned in and spoke in a whisper only Declan could hear. "They will pay for this."

He plunged the knife downwards. Declan closed his eyes, yet still he saw it happen. He watched himself kill his own father and take control of his own Sila. Hatred creased his face. Sparks flecked off his forearms as he glared at the towering Knight. "You are going to die for killing my mother."

"Ha!" Rasporvin spat. He clenched his fist, and Declan's raging form dropped to a knee. "You are powerless, Southern Knight." A victorious smile split his alabaster face.

The wax Declan trembled with the effort of raising his head. The flecks of energy faded as his magic extinguished. "I... don't understand."

"You should be more mindful of the weapons you use, puppet," the Knight said.

Rasporvin clapped his hands in perverse glee. "You have taken your Sila with an oath-bound blade, Moore. You are property of Vedmark now. You will do what we say, when we say."

A roar of anguish filled the Void, then cut short as the scene dissipated. Declan's stomach churned, and he searched for somewhere to empty it. He fell to the ground as another scene formed before him. Arman Moore moved lethargically, as if wading through treacle. A second figure emerged beside him, weaving between his grandfather's blows and stabbing at him with an ornate dagger. Horace.

"No," Declan whispered. "Not again."

The creamy figures danced around the emptiness of the Void, ducking below obstacles and navigating unseen terrain. At half speed, Horace's strategy was obvious. He kept Arman on a straight line, striking out any time he travelled too far either side. More than once, a window opened in Horace's defenses, but instead of attacking, Arman retreated, forcing Horace to follow him.

Not retreating, leading! Declan blinked in surprise. *Horace thought he was leading, but he was following.* Morbid curiosity colored his grandfather's final moments. *Where were you leading him?*

Arman swiped an open palm across his body and an axe landed on the ground where Declan had been hiding.

The curiosity became shame. Anguish crashed over Declan. *He gave me the axe. One last chance to earn my Sila. He orchestrated the whole thing and...*

A different Declan lifted the axe and hurled it in their direction. It cartwheeled towards his grandfather's chest, only to be swept from the air by Winterthorn. *I failed him.*

Horace plunged Winterthorn into his grandfather's heart.

The knowledge that he had failed his grandfather in his last moment was too much. "Why are you showing me this?" Declan screamed. He crouched by Arman's body. It, too, dissolved into the ground, replaced moments later by a new version of Horace standing amongst the ruins of a broken city.

"You've been a thorn in my side for too long." He drew Winterthorn from his cloak and stalked forward. As he did, Ava crashed down from above. They wrestled in the ruin. Ava had a dagger in each hand, but Horace stood ready. "ENOUGH!" he roared. Tendrils of white light erupted from his sleeves, wrapping Ava's wrists, and pulling her free of him. He dragged her closer. Ava's gaze flickered in his direction. "Help!" she wheezed.

"No," Declan whispered. Ava seemed to look straight at him. Only when he turned around did he see another version of himself, pinned to the ground.

"He can't help you," Horace said. "Declan Moore is well practiced in failing those he loves." He drove Winterthorn into Ava's stomach. A small whimper escaped her lips.

"Declan," she whimpered. Her last words hung in the air, then her head rolled to the side.

Declan was unsure if the cries he heard were from the vision or himself. Another scene formed. He tried to run, but no matter how fast he sprinted, he travelled nowhere. This world was empty, and he was trapped.

Horace stood over Ava, only this time it was amongst the remains of Sabriva Tower. He held her by the neck as he thrust Winterthorn into her chest. "Go away!" Declan shouted. He stumbled past them, but they followed. His legs ached. He was so tired. There was no escape. He watched Ava die over and over. Sometimes it was Horace, other times he was disguised as Haberdeen. Once, an unfamiliar woman stuck Winterthorn in Ava's back as she was about to plunge her own knife into Horace's heart. No matter who held the hilt, the result was the same. Ava died on Winterthorn's blade.

WINTERTHORN!

The words reverberated in Declan's brain, like the roar of an avalanche. He dropped to his knees, hands pressed tight to his ears.

BRING WINTERTHORN!

The voice was immense. A tremendous bellow that shook him with each word.

As Declan lay on the ground screaming, the scenes repeated. His parent's death. His betrayal. His grandfather's death. Ava's deaths. Repeated. Repeated. Every rendition was a searing brand on his failing heart. "Why are you doing this?"

BRING THE CRYSTAL BLADE!

Declan watched—helpless—as Winterthorn took Ava in the neck. He didn't know if it was the future, or some twisted concoction of his worst fears. He couldn't watch it.

Not again. He was exhausted, starving, thirsty, but most of all, broken. He sat—curled in a ball—on the ground as his parents melted to bulbous globs of creamy white. *You are not escaping.* Declan knew the words were true.

He was going to go mad here. He was going to die in the Void.

CHAPTER 4
SAMANTHA

THE TENSION in Samantha Winter's shoulders dissolved as the mountain path widened. She glanced back at the narrow crossing—bordered either side by a steep drop into stony crags—and rubbed the neck of her chestnut mare. The horse snorted in response. Few things made Samantha uncomfortable. Heights did.

Tall pines and wind-sculpted granite boulders rushed to surround her. When she reached a fork, she tugged the reins and started down a winding trail littered with fallen branches. An hour later, she arrived in a small cabin surrounded by well-tended gardens and green fields. A chorus of bleating greeted her arrival as their grizzled care-taker leaned on a post whittling a thumb of wood. Flakes of pine decorated his feet. "She's not here," Grigory said without looking up.

Samantha nodded. "I did not come here for her."

The old farmer continued to shape the carving. "Misha is in City running errands for an old man."

The question lay buried in the statement. Among Vedmark's many quirks, the taboo surrounding direct questions was most peculiar—and frustrating. Samantha frowned. "I am not here for him either."

"He will be sad to hear it," Grigory said. "Southern lands have captured his imagination."

"Just like Ava—those two could be siblings." Had she not been waiting for it, Samantha would have missed the falter of Grigory's blade. It was so tiny, she almost questioned it. Almost. "I think your *niece* should know."

Grigory grunted. "You speak nonsense."

"Then prove it." She rattled a small purse buried in her pocket. "I have mitka to trade."

The old man ignored her. He held his carved goat to the sky, frowned, then slipped it into his chest pocket. "Some knowledge is worth more than coin." He stabbed his knife in the post and met her eyes. "It would be a kindness if you kept your *suppositions* to yourself."

"Suppositions." Samantha smiled. "Misha and Ava are both Lucks, an ability passed through blood." She noted the slightest shift in his weight. "There are no Lucks in the Drakonov line... I'm sure you know where I'm going."

Grigory chuckled. "Luck would be most helpful on a farm. Luck would keep my goats safe, my fences sturdy. I can only imagine bountiful harvest from my garden." He shrugged. "Luck would be great blessing to me, if I had it."

"Your father once ran a reputable silwood yard." She relaxed against the wooden post. "That is a lucrative trade. He must have had some fortune to gain such an enterprise."

"No fortune in flames that destroyed Pa's business. No Luck in hard winters that followed." Grigory shook his head. "I hope you have not travelled far in search of secrets that do not exist."

He seemed genuine—genuine enough that Samantha felt a sliver of doubt. *It has to be him. There is no other link.*

Grigory's knife stood upright in the wood beside her. Strips of sanded leather wrapped around its hilt. She swallowed her second-guessing and acted.

"You are welcome to stay for—" Grigory cut off—startled—as the blade lodge in his chest.

Samantha held her breath.

The old man pulled the weapon free. It popped loose with a click. Scowling, he reached into his pocket. The sudden attack had ruined the front of his whittled goat, yet the carving had saved his life. "You could have killed me!"

Samantha exhaled. "But I didn't." She winked. "A lucky save. How... curious."

Grigory glared at her. "You—"

"I needed to know for certain," she said. "Things are moving faster than I would like, Grigory, and I am running out of people to trust." She spoke quickly, not daring to let him get a word in. "The Grand Steward has summoned me to his hall, and if I do not come back, I need you to pass on a message for me."

His knuckles were white on the blade's handle, and for a moment, she thought he was going to toss the knife right back at her. Instead, he slid it into his belt. "I will consider it, but only on one condition."

Samantha already knew what he was going to say. "I will not tell a soul about you, or the blood connection between your families."

Grigory relaxed. He dropped his arms to his sides and turned to the cabin. "Tell me your message."

<hr>

The moon hung high in a cloudless sky when she reached Vedmark City. An eerie quiet blanketed the streets, and a pair of guards waved her to stop as she passed one of the outer watch-houses. Samantha slowed to a halt as they rushed outside to meet her.

"Hail, Madam Emissary," said the older of the two—a broad man with a nose too small for his face. "Tell us what news you bring from Forestwalk."

The question in the statement caught her off guard. "I have no news from the northern settlements. I am here to hold counsel with the Grand Steward." She paused and wondered the best way to frame her request. "If you could explain why a report from Forestwalk is necessary, I could inquire further on your behalf."

"It's the Void!" A high tenor cracked in the younger guard's voice. He looked like a teenager grown too fast—a mess of limbs and freckles. "It spreads from the forest!"

"Hush, Orwin," the older man growled. He shook his head in obvious disappointment before returning to Samantha. "Just rumors, Madam Emissary. We presumed you may be investigating for Lord Drakonov."

"My mother lives in Forestwalk," the young guard whispered.

Samantha made a show of hesitating, as if deliberating on a moral dilemma. "The Void is a sore subject, but I will find out what I can." She smiled reassuringly. "And I will pass word to the night watch at first opportunity."

The guards bowed, appreciation shone on the younger one's face, and waved her on. She continued towards her meeting, already planning how she could best use their loyalty in her favor.

The Steward's Hall had changed—thin scars spread across the ceiling like forks of lightning. Samantha subdued a tiny smile. Declan Moore had left his mark, and not even the Knights of Despair could erase it. Not completely.

Rasporvin's gaunt eyes were practically glowing. It was a wonder his greasy hair had not caught alight. He sneered as she climbed the steps. "Tell me of the southlands."

Samantha inhaled her loathing of the man, let it dissolve in her lungs, and breathed out. "The Dominion is in shambles," she said. "Sabriva has fallen. The ruling High Mage is dead. The rogue Fatesmiths have seized power. Remnant Magic sweeps the inland corridor. Towns and cities have been erased from existence, hundreds of thousands killed in its wake."

"Good."

Samantha's eyes narrowed. "These were innocent people."

"They are trespassers in my land."

"Your land is Vedmark."

Rasporvin glared at her. "We do not erase our history here, *Emissary*. Euryma belongs to Vedmark, and Vedmark belongs to me." He slapped a slender hand on the Emerald Throne. It echoed off the cavernous ceiling. "If Sabriva is undone, the time has arrived. We must move south with all haste."

Samantha dipped her head long enough for a second calming breath. "Your army cannot pass the Threshold until the Deathless Demon is dead. You should send your Knights into the forest to kill him."

"I will not send men to die in that forest," Rasporvin said. "We will find safe land and we will wait until the Knights can use their Sila. We will be ready when the time comes."

"With respect—"

"No!" Rasporvin's voice rose with shrill fervor. "No. There is no time. The Void. It spreads. Morwik is lost, and still it grows." He slapped the throne again, this time with both hands. "We must abandon this cursed Kingdom."

"Then permit me to do my duty as Emissary," Samantha said. The madness in his eyes unnerved her, but she would not let it show. "I will barter peaceful passage with these Fatesmiths. You can protect Vedmark's people without hurting others. I just need time."

"Time is not our ally!" Rasporvin's lips puckered as if he'd tasted something sour. "Our weakest Knight wields powers beyond their comprehension. I do not need peaceful passage."

Samantha crossed her arms. "I am an Emissary for Euryma. I will not advise bloodshed against my people."

Hateful sparks glittered in the Steward's eyes, but before he could open his mouth, a door behind the dais opened. A servant dressed in a forest-green tunic rushed to the front, his gaze cemented to the floor. He dropped to his knees without utterance and held a small scroll above his head. With spidery fingers, Rasporvin unrolled the slip. As he read, his expression changed—from anger, to confusion, to surprise, to something Samantha did not recognize.

It's word of Arman's death. Samantha forced the thought aside. Her skin crawled in dread anticipation. "That message must be important for a servant to interrupt us." She kept a level tone, but her heartbeat pummeled against her chest wall.

"You may leave," Rasporvin said. His eyes moved like pendulums as they reread the words on the scroll.

Samantha was stunned. The Grand Steward hovered on the cusp of his life's ambition to invade Euryma. The Void had grown to swallow a settlement, and he did not want to discuss any of it. *What is in that note?* "Your Highness—"

"Leave my hall." Rasporvin's eyes narrowed as he

glanced up from the scroll. "Do not think I have forgotten your failure at the Knights' Barracks, *Emissary*. You tread thin ice. Go. Find these Fatesmiths. See what they can offer. But be warned—if I discover you are conspiring against me, the punishment will make you beg for death."

The Grand Steward's stare bored into her skull, but Samantha refused to give so much as a glimmer of a whisper of a hint that her loyalty could be questioned. "I understand." She turned and left—footsteps quiet, mind ablaze.

———

An hour later, Samantha rushed to fit the food she had purchased for Declan into her saddlebag. Her heart drummed in her ears. If the Void had moved that fast, they were out of time. As she mounted and started towards the gate, the gentle clop of hooves was enveloped by a crowd of armored men. Knights on stallions stepped out of the air.

A flat-faced man fell in beside her. "King Rasporvin awaits you at the Barracks, Emissary."

Samantha wrangled her confusion. "I have instructions to head south tonight. Urgent business."

"Things have changed," said the Knight.

Six Knights in full armor surrounded her. With an uncomfortable lurch of her stomach, Samantha nodded. "Lead the way."

The ride to the Barracks was short, but with every step, a pit formed deeper in her chest. They herded her in silence. Through the trade district, past the coppersmith's burnt husk, around a corner where poor children begged and into the looming structure that shadowed the entire street.

The Knights dismounted, Samantha followed. Insides

aflutter, face calm, she worked all the angles, creating arguments and counterarguments for any accusation Rasporvin might throw at her. *You'll be fine,* she told herself. *You've covered your tracks, you've thought through everything. Just keep your cool and you'll be—*

Some unseen power gripped her waist and pulled her into a square room. It slammed her against a wall with such force that a tall shield clattered to the stone floor. She opened her mouth but failed to speak. She tried to inhale and couldn't. When her spinning vision settled, her blood turned glacial. Knights of Despair lined the walls. Above them hung all manner of swords, pikes, axes and shields. She could not breathe, her lungs screamed for air. The spell vanished, and she dropped in a wheezing heap.

"Betrayer," growled a sharp voice to her right. A dead man's voice—one Samantha had never expected to hear again.

Green light smacked her face. She raised her arms, but her wrists snapped to her sides. Sila slapped her again and again.

"Enough," Rasporvin boomed. He sat on a wooden chair on an elevated stage at the room's far end. The assault stopped. Samantha struggled to her feet. Her cheeks were on fire; she tasted blood in her mouth.

Korvan Drakonov was as large as she remembered—a mountain of a man with eyes darker than a well pit. Long silver braids hung over shoulders so broad, they appeared to stretch his armor. A smug smile adorned his handsome features marred only by a scar running down the right side of his face.

How she wished he had stayed dead.

"I do not understand." Samantha looked to Rasporvin. His son's return from the grave explained his odd behavior, but not this barbaric treatment. Magic thrust her against the wall. She bounced off it and landed on a knee. Sila wrenched her upright by her hair—an involuntary whimper escaped her lips.

"Enough." Rasporvin waved a hand to Korvan. "Let her speak."

"She is a liar." Korvan's whisper was steel. "I would rather slit her throat than allow her to ensnare us with her serpentine words."

Samantha tried to glare at the silver-haired Knight. Her heart skittered against her chest. She shouldn't be here. *He* shouldn't be here. "I am not a liar," she managed. "I did not abandon the Kingdom. I did not carry Vedmark's sacred blade into the forest and vanish." She hoped the Knights surrounding her mistook the fearful tremble in her voice for anger. "We thought you were dead, but here you are. You accuse me of betrayal, but I have reservations of my own. I wonder where you have been all this time, why you didn't return to help fight the growing Void... but most of all, I wonder how Winterthorn somehow found itself in Euryma." Samantha turned to Rasporvin, a measure of confidence returning to her shaking body. "If you are relying on the word of Knight Korvan alone, then perhaps you should question who the real betrayer is."

Korvan's eyes burned black. He reached into his pocket and withdrew a single jade mitka. He flicked the coin toward her, leaving Samantha no choice but to catch it.

"I have mitka for knowledge. Are you willing to trade?"

Curse him. Samantha looked down at the coin as her analytical mind collapsed. A wave of panic gripped her tongue. She was trapped.

"Go ahead," Rasporvin said.

"I... I am willing to trade. This I know, unsullied by

untruth lest your mitka be spent." Her voice sounded so small. She was careening down a river—reaching out for a branch, or a root, and finding only slippery stone.

"Whom do you serve?" Korvan asked.

"The people of Euryma."

"Whom do you serve *in Vedmark*?"

"The King of the Emerald Throne," she murmured. Silently, she pleaded Korvan would take his questions no further.

Korvan's smile was more a sneer. A cruel, cold thing. One that knew it had its prey cornered. "What is the name of the King you serve?"

The mitka in Samantha's palm felt heavier than it had moments earlier. "His name is Rasporvin Drakonov."

"Very well," Korvan said. "That is all I ask. Seal your lie."

Samantha held the mitka up for the Knights to see. She flourished the coin, using the movement to create the only distraction she could muster. With her other hand behind her back, she gathered as much nima as she could manage. "I share this knowledge, true to my knowledge, let it show in green."

Rasporvin leaned forward in his seat.

The coin flickered. She did not wait to see it dull. She spun and pulled hard. A braided weave of air, wood, metal and kinetic energy hauled every sword, shield and axe from the walls with colossal force.

Green light filled the room. The weapons paused mid-flight, then crashed to the ground with a hideous din. Glowing Sila bound her hands and forced her to the floor.

The room was silent.

Rasporvin climbed down from his stage. He took a sword from the mess and held it to Samantha's cheek. "Betrayer," he whispered. "You are a traitor. A rat who has seen too much." He slashed upwards. Amidst an eruption of pain, Samantha's right eye went dark. Hot liquid rolled down her jaw. She fought to stay cognizant as shock set in. Rasporvin pressed the sword's point against her left cheek. "I told you that you would beg for death."

Samantha prepared herself to lose the other eye.

"And you will." Rasporvin lowered the weapon. "You will see Euryma destroyed. You will see the people you serve murdered like dogs. You will beg me to stop, and I will laugh." He waved a dismissive hand. "Take her away."

"Wait," Korvan said. Samantha wanted to cry. *What else could he want from me?* "This witches magic is weak, but she is not helpless. We must remove the rat's teeth."

Rasporvin pursed his lips and nodded.

Samantha tried to crawl away as pain ballooned in her palms. She glanced down in horror. Terrific heat engulfed her hands—fingers curled and sank like melting plastic until there were only two misshapen lumps. Before she could react, something seized her hair and dragged her from the room. Korvan followed to supervise as two Knights threw her into a cell. "Count yourself lucky, witch," he said. Every smug syllable made her hate him more. "I would have taken eyes, and arms, and legs." He rattled the bars, then left.

Samantha rolled onto her side. Clumsily, she bunched her shawl together and bit down through the pain. With nothing else she could do, she lay on the cold floor and cried.

CHAPTER 5
DECLAN

FLECKS of dry blood crowned Declan's fingertips. He had tried—and failed—to claw his eyes out amidst the carousel of terrors in the Void. He lay amongst the emptiness, aching for the reprieve of sleep.

There was only pain.

"Declan! Help me!"

Ava's desperation washed over him. She struggled to break free of Raul, who held her in a bearhug as Winterthorn cut her throat. A gurgle and she crumpled on the ground. No matter where Declan looked, her corpse stared at him.

"Please..." The words were barely audible. "Let me go." He had no way of knowing how long he had been here. His muscles ached, his mind ached, his heart ached. "I'll do anything. Just let me out."

THE CRYSTAL BLADE!

The voice was the burst of a derecho.

Declan jolted upright at the response. "Winterthorn?" His hoarse voice cracked as he yelled. "Is that what you want?"

BRING THE CRYSTAL BLADE!

"Yes!" Tears blurred his vision at the thought of release. "I will bring it!" Something sharp gripped his leg, piercing the flesh above his ankle. Declan kicked on instinct; he glanced down and saw nothing. Unseen claws dragged him backwards through the Void. "No! I said I would bring it! Let me go!"

BRING THE CRYSTAL BLADE!

The emptiness vanished, like removing a blindfold. Morning light warmed Declan's sweat-beaded face. The grey-blue river flowed beside him while birds twittered from their nests in the pines. With all his remaining strength, he craned his neck to find the source of the pain. A golden creature cleaned its paws on a patch of mossy grass.

"Lancelot?"

The armadillo considered him through marble-black eyes.

"You... saved me?"

Lancelot tilted his head, then gestured—as if in apology—to Declan's leg. Blood leaked from four punctures above his right ankle. Exhausted, Declan tore strips from his shirt to wrap the wounds, then fell back against the sand. "Thank you," he mumbled as bone-deep weariness over-took him. "You saved my life. Again."

He woke to find a large leaf atop his face, blocking the noon sun. Lancelot shuffled around, arranging a mound of fruit beside him. As Declan sat up, the armadillo nudged a small sky-apple into his palm, then held his tiny bronze paws to his mouth in imitation of eating.

A deep hunger awoke at the sight of it, and Declan

wasted no time. Lancelot rolled more into his lap. Declan ate in silence, and when the pile was only a stack of seeds and cores, he lay back on the sand once more. "How did you find me?"

No response.

"Okay. How did you get me out without hurting yourself?"

Still nothing. When Declan lifted his head, the armadillo was partway up the steep grass rise from the bank. "Hey! Wait up!" He staggered to his feet to follow.

At the top of the hill, they joined a narrow trail. Declan limped a pace back, grateful for the trees that provided constant support. They went slowly, and Lancelot stopped to wait whenever he fell too far behind. High above, the canopy stopped all but the most persistent beams of sunlight, keeping their way cool and dark. When they left the path for an overgrown section of forest, Declan could go no further. Pale bushes with prickly needles for leaves blocked the way. "You didn't happen to see my axes, did you?" Declan called into the thicket.

Lancelot emerged from underneath the nearest bush and, with a sudden motion, raised his front paws over his head. Declan had a momentary picture of the armadillo freezing partway through a star-jump. After an expectant pause, he repeated the movement.

"Oh," Declan said, realization dawning. "You want me to call them?"

Lancelot dropped back onto four legs and nodded.

Declan concentrated on the way behind him. He reached out, feeling for the same magnetic pulse he had sensed in Arman's cabin. He pictured their silwood handles and willed them to come.

A faint whistle arrived first, a percussion of breaking

wood followed. Then they were there, snapping to his palms as if they were extensions of his limbs. Declan regarded the axes curiously. "How did you know I could do that?"

Lancelot dipped his snout in a noncommittal gesture, then disappeared into the bushes. Declan cut a path to follow. Thirty-minutes later, they emerged from the tree line on the edge of a valley. A sloping clearing stretched below them. Knee high grass dropped to a creek threading between rocky hills. Declan followed halfway down to a large entrance dug into the stone. The armadillo gestured to the burrow. Declan shook his head. "I'm not sure I'll fit."

Lancelot imitated a ducking motion.

The creature had saved his life... multiple times. Declan nodded. "Lead the way."

He climbed down on his hands and knees to follow. As they crawled, the hole never got darker. The air itself seemed slightly luminescent. Twenty feet down, the burrow levelled out into a cave bordered by exposed granite walls. The dirt roof was just high enough that Declan could sit upright and his curls scraped the ceiling.

Other tunnels branched off the cavern, ranging in size from small to tiny. Lancelot ambled forward to the smallest tunnel and squeaked. Four baby armadillos stepped out. They eyed Declan warily. They had golden skin with no hard armor. Lancelot squeaked again and they snuffled to press their wet noses against the back of Declan's hand. A second full-grown armadillo emerged from a hole. It was slightly smaller than Lancelot, with a striped shell. It nuzzled into Lancelot's neck as they watched the little ones explore.

Declan grinned. "This is your family?"

Lancelot nodded. Their dark-shelled mother disappeared into one of the larger tunnels.

Declan stroked the soft skin of the nearest baby. "They're adorable." He let the tiny creatures roll over his hands and climb onto his knees until their mother returned, pushing a stunted sanarmelon ahead of her.

At a squeak from their father, the children climbed from Declan's lap and exited through a small tunnel. Lancelot's mate tilted her head to him and followed them out.

"You have a beautiful family," Declan said. The armadillo's shoulders slumped, and he pointed his snout to Declan's bloody ankle—the strips of his shirt were now soaked through—and nudged the sanarmelon against his knee. Declan cut it open with one of his axes and took a bite. The pain faded as he ate, and when he finished, he unwrapped the makeshift bandage to reveal four white scars. "Thank you," Declan said. "I... I'm sorry about Arman. I should have..." he exhaled and shook his head. "I don't know. I don't know what I'm saying."

Lancelot left through one of the larger passages. There was a clatter of movement and he returned with a pale slate board and a piece of charcoal. Declan's eyebrows vanished as Lancelot held the charcoal in his jaw and formed legible letters. The armadillo inspected the message, then raised it to show him.

Arman is free.

Lancelot's script was surprisingly neat. Declan's jaw hung open. "You can write?"

Lancelot tapped the word 'Arman' and it made sense. *A thousand years is plenty of time to teach a sentient armadillo how to write.* A lump formed in Declan's throat as he reread the words. "Yes. He is free now. I just miss him. He was the only family I had left. Now..." he trailed off as Lancelot started writing again.

Miss Arman too.

Declan nodded. Grief crept up his cheeks, but he forced a smile instead. "I'm glad I got to meet your family." He gestured to the cavern. "I was worried you would be all alone without him."

Lancelot scrawled a new message. *Have many families.* When Declan frowned, he erased the words and added more. *They not last.* The armadillo slumped forward at this, and Declan's heart ached for the little creature. Lancelot had lived for thousands of years. Like Arman, he must have watched every family he'd started turn to dust. "Was your life tied to Sabriva Tower as well?"

The armadillo shook its head as it wrote. This time, the script was shakier. *Magic in me.*

Declan did not know what that meant. Lancelot seemed upset by his confusion. He cleared the board and dragged it back through the tunnel. The slate scraped along the floor in a disheartening way. When he returned, he gestured to the exit leading to the surface and started towards it.

"Wait," Declan called after him.

Lancelot vanished from sight. Once again leaving Declan no choice but to follow.

The sun was balancing on the distant hills when Lancelot led him over the creek and back to the path leading up to Arman's cabin. When they stopped, Declan knelt and pressed a hand on the armadillo's armored shoulder. "I'm glad you're here, Lancelot. If you weren't..." he shrugged, feeling a pinch of embarrassment. "Well, I wouldn't be here without you. Thank you for saving me."

Lancelot nodded before ambling back the way he came. When the shrubs swallowed his golden armor, Declan turned back to the cabin. Ava would be inside, no doubt angry at him for leaving. He was angry at her. *Are you?* Declan stopped at the door. His feelings for Ava were a tangle of betrayal and relief that she still lived. Even free of the Void, when he closed his eyes, he saw her, dead on Winterthorn's blade. *Just forgive her. She just wanted to help you.*

He took a bracing breath and pushed the door open. The main room was empty, as were the others. "Ava?" Declan called. A note pinned to the dining table caught his attention. Ava's tight handwriting covered the sheet.

I am so sorry, Declan. Please believe all I wanted was to keep you from sinking into despair. I know I was wrong. Grieving for those we love is an important step in healing, and I tried to use Luck to take that away from you. I hope you can forgive me. I have gone to Ory's cabin to give you the time and space you need to grieve your grandfather. I will organize for The Emissary to wait with me here. Come and find us when you are ready.

Declan took the note to the seat by the mantle and read it again. It was a flawless apology. Everything he could have asked was printed on the paper, written proof that she cared. So why did he still feel so angry? Declan closed his eyes. An image of Haberdeen cutting Ava's throat appeared in his mind's eye. He pushed the thought away. Another returned. Ava's death, over and over, always delivered by Winterthorn's cruel edge.

Bring me the crystal blade.

The deathless demon's words whispered in the periphery. Whatever the creature was, it wanted Winterthorn—

and it wanted Declan to deliver it. He would not do that. *You've already unleashed one evil into the world.* Declan could not forget what he had seen in the Void.

There was no way to know if the visions were from the future, or his worst fears. *Does it matter?* If Winterthorn was a threat to Ava, Declan needed to destroy it. He would not lose Ava, not like he had everyone else.

As dusk fell and the cabin darkened, he made his decision.

Digging a pen from one of Arman's drawers, Declan turned Ava's note over and scrawled his response on the back. With stone-faced resolve, he pinned the message to the wall.

The fresh ink shone in the lamplight as he scanned over the well-intentioned lie one last time. "You'll thank me one day. I hope." Declan hurried inside to make preparations for the long journey ahead.

CHAPTER 6
AVA

EARLY MORNING FOG shrouded Grigory's cabin, leaving bulbous drops of water on the windows. Ava sat in bed—a blanket covering her knees—twirling Arman Moore's sapphire pendant in her palm. She had scrubbed it with a goatskin rag until the blue gemstone sparkled like the Mediterranean at the height of summer.

The gem fascinated Ava. Personal property of Vedmark's true king—a secret she could wear underneath her shirt. A silent protest against her uncle's fake claim to rule. It proved a pleasant distraction from the guilt of trying to manipulate Declan.

"Breakfast!" Grigory called from down the hall.

Ava slipped the chain over her head, tucked the pendant out of sight, and rushed to the kitchen. The aroma of a cooked meal was worth the icy sting of the cold floorboards on her bare feet.

"Misha found duck eggs in dam," Grigory explained.

"The scoundrel," Ava said. "How dare he!" Her mock indignation melted into a cheeky grin. "You know, you don't need to make an excuse every time we don't eat goat."

Grigory tipped two poached eggs, a thick slice of buttered bread and a handful of cooked tomatoes onto her plate, then helped himself to the same. "It is possible, but not likely." A scowl replaced his apologetic smile. "I sent Misha to collect new flint—and information."

Ava frowned. "Information... about the Emissary."

"Yes," Grigory's face darkened. "It has been two days now. We should have heard something."

The unpleasant lurch in Ava's stomach had nothing to do with her breakfast. "Let's hope Misha returns with good news." She bit her lip. Misha had not spoken to her since she'd left to help Declan. She steered a slice of fried tomato around the plate with her fork. "Ory, I need some advice."

Grigory eyed her warily. "I can give advice on farming goats, killing goats and cooking goats."

"I'm serious," she said. "Declan and Misha—"

"Are not goats." Ava rolled her eyes. Grigory sighed. "You feel strongly for Declan, but you have grown up with Misha. Last time pair met, they came to blows." He shrugged. "Misha is protective of you. You are older, but he feels duty to keep you safe. Understand his anger comes from kindness, and you may make more headway."

"Declan wasn't trying to hurt me."

"I know," Grigory said. "And Misha probably does too. But he is as stubborn as his father. I do not see him changing his thinking until you acknowledge it."

"He thinks Declan is dangerous."

Grigory nodded.

"Things would be much easier if there were no fool-hardy boys in the world."

"I agree." To Grigory's credit, he kept a straight face. Something clattered on the front veranda. "That could be him now." He leaned back to the window, then stood with a start. "Hide! Quick!"

Ava obeyed at once. Heavy footsteps creaked outside and finger tapped on the glass. Grigory hurried to open it. "Hail, Knight of Vedmark. Say what you need of me."

"Our King requested I check in," replied a dangerous voice. "He wants to know if you have had a visit from his niece."

Grigory's knees risked knocking together, yet he maintained an even tone. "I have the King's orders. The moment Mistress Drakonov visits, I will send word."

"Make sure you do," said the Knight. "We have caught her traitorous teacher."

Ava's stomach back flipped. *The Emissary!*

"Disgusting," Grigory said, layering thick disapproval in his tone. "I had suspicions that woman was a liar. All those from south are."

The Knight grunted his approval. "Send for us if you see anything. Vedmark relies on honest men like you."

Grigory bade him a formal farewell and—after a short time—closed the window. Ava counted to ten before exhaling. Goose pimples lined her arms. *They have the Emissary.* Grigory whistled to himself as he cleared the table, scrubbed the plates, and stacked them to dry. He puttered into the next room, then breathed a loud sigh. "You can come out now," he called. Ava stood slowly and placed her plate in the sink. Grigory returned to the kitchen. "This does not bode well."

Too right. Ava's skin crawled as she fell into a kitchen chair. "If they have the Emissary..." she didn't know where to begin. The woman had been her guiding compass for so long, now...

The door opened and Ava threw herself to the floor.

She crawled into a cupboard as Misha burst into the kitchen. His pale face scanned the room. "Rasporvin's got the Emissary! They're calling it treason! They say she's working with the deathless demon to destroy the Kingdom!" He paused in obvious confusion. "And you are on the floor."

Ava brushed her shirt off as she stood amongst the hanging cast-iron pans. "You dolt. I thought you were one of them!"

Misha's forehead creased in confusion.

"A Knight of Despair visited just now," Grigory said. "He asked after Ava. You would have passed him on the road."

"I... I saw no Knight," Misha said. He locked eyes with Ava. "If this Emissary business is true, we are going to be tangled up in it. I have mitka for—"

"Oh give it a rest," Ava interjected. "Just ask your questions."

"No." Grigory said. Ava opened her mouth in protest, but he shook his head. "The Emissary came by two days ago. She feared for her life and left messages with me in case she was discovered." He looked out the window, then closed the shutters. "We need to go find Declan. There we can speak freely."

Misha wasn't happy. He fiddled with Trevor's reins as the donkey—led by Ory—pulled them through the forest. "Why do we have to go see *him*?"

"Weren't you listening?" Ava said from between two stacks of goat skins. "A Knight dropped by unannounced today."

"I didn't see any anyone."

"That's even worse. What's saying he's not hanging around with the goats watching the cabin?"

Misha shrugged. "Then we use Luck to alert us if someone is nearby."

"I'm not wearing myself out all day keeping guard."

"It's better than going to *him*."

Ava fought to keep from rolling her eyes. Misha's hair stuck out in odd directions. He looked like a cornered cat. She took a deep breath and attempted to follow Grigory's advice. "You're right about Declan being dangerous when he's not in control. Nobody has taught him to use Sila and when he *can* wield it, he's not in the best frame of mind."

Misha stared out at the passing pines. "So why join him?"

"Because..." Ava let the words die in her mouth. Misha lived in blissful ignorance of the real king and his broken curse. How much did she dare reveal? "It's complicated.

"Complicated?" Misha shook his head. "He's a kid from Euryma."

"He's older than you."

"And you'd follow me to certain death?"

Ava clenched her fists. "There are bigger forces at work than you understand."

"Then tell me. Where did you go after you left with Haberdeen?"

"Unless you want to help, the less you know, the better."

"I don't want any part in Declan Moore's nonsense."

"It is not Declan's nonsense." Grigory held a gnarled stick in one hand and Trevor's lead in the other. "It is Vedmark's nonsense. And I expect we will all be swept up in it soon enough. Whether we like it or not."

Ava nudged her elbow into Misha. "You've known me

your whole life, Mish. When have I ever made any decision without a good reason?"

"That depends." His eyes narrowed. "Are you thinking with your heart or your head?"

The words were a slap in the face. Ava's cheeks burned; she ached to punch him in his stupid face. "You don't know what you're talking about."

"Every time you get involved with Declan, you nearly die. Use your head, not your heart."

Ava tugged on Luck and shoved his chest. Misha's balance faltered, and he fell onto the muddy road. "I am using my head!" Ava snapped. "I just wish you *had* a heart."

"Fine!" Misha scraped the mud off his arms. "Leave then! I'm going back."

"No, you're not." Grigory put a hand on Trevor's nose to halt their progress. "Come, Misha, get back on cart. Dark things call this forest home. You do not want to be alone with demons and wolves of night."

Begrudgingly, Misha climbed back into his seat. Mud dripped off the side of his face. Ava glared at him. "Let's swap," she called to Grigory without shifting her gaze. "I'll guide Trevor. You spend some quality time with your son."

<hr>

A half-moon illuminated the path up the last hill, and Ava was glad to see it. The cart wheels gave one last creak before falling silent. Grigory hopped down from his seat. "This is the place."

Ava nodded. The flowery archway marking the King's grave was a silhouette in the night. The windows were dark, no lantern in sight. *Something is wrong.* She handed

Ory the lead and rushed to the door. "Declan?" she called, then stopped dead.

A note was pinned to the front door. With trembling hands, Ava unfolded it.

Ava,

I am sorry you are reading this and not hearing it in person. I am leaving. My grandfather's death has robbed me of all hope. My parents are gone. My best friend is a murderer. Everyone I care about meets a terrible fate, and I can't bear to see that happen to you.

I am leaving Vedmark for a simpler life. I am not a King or a Knight. I'm an orphan with nothing left. Please do not come looking. You will not find me.

Thank you for believing in me. I'm sorry it was misplaced.

Declan.

"Ava?"

She ignored Grigory's gentle question. She re-read the letter more times than she could count. Shock turned to sorrow, then the sorrow soured to something bitter. *I would've followed you anywhere, and you abandon me? You abandon Euryma? You...*

She crumpled the paper in her fist. It was too much. She stormed inside, seized a chair, and threw it into the wall. *You idiot! You should have waited for me!* Ava wrenched on Luck, willing the ground to open beneath her, to give her somewhere to hide. The cabin started to tremble.

"Hey!" Misha grabbed her by the shoulders. "It's okay. You're not alone."

Sobbing, Ava slid to the floor, exhausted from the arguments, and the walk, and the sorrow. She felt like a light had been snuffed out inside her. "He's gone," she whispered. "Declan's gone. The Emissary's gone. What do we do now?"

Neither man answered. Grigory lit a pair of oil lanterns while Misha helped Ava into the chair she had not broken against the wall. The men spoke softly and Grigory went outside. Misha started the fire and made her a tea. She hugged the clay mug, wishing she could draw its warmth into her heart.

"It is done," Grigory said when he returned. "The cart is buried in brush down the rise, and Trevor is safe out back." He accepted a warm drink from Misha and settled into a comfortable squat. "I wish I could say it is time to rest, but there is much to discuss. Ava, tell us all you know about Arman Moore and destruction of Sabriva Tower."

Ava glanced up from her mug. "How do you know about that?"

"Your Emissary gave me short version. I want to hear it all now."

Ava took a deep breath and started talking. She told them everything—her imprisonment in Haberdeen's cell, the Emissary helping her escape, finding Arman, learning of his history, and the battle at Sabriva. Misha's jaw dropped lower as his eyebrows climbed higher. Grigory sipped his drink as Ava described the fight between Declan and Horace. As she relived Arman's final moments, she buried her head in her hands to hide the tears.

Misha stared into his tea. "So the Knights are free... and Declan left?" Disgust darkened his eyes. "What a coward."

Ava did not bother to argue back. They sat still for a long time, with only the crackle of the fireplace to hold back the silence. "What message did the Emissary give you?" she said at last.

For the first time in her life, Grigory seemed unbothered by the direct question. Firelight danced in his eyes as his gaze travelled between them. "She told me to send you both to northern remnants of Euryma."

"The Broken Empire?" Ava blinked. "Why there?"

"She said you were to go to a mountain village called Yabun where you would find some old friends who would help you raise an army."

"Old friends?" Misha frowned. "Did she give you their names?"

Grigory shook his head. "Your guess is as good as mine."

"And Declan?" Ava ignored Misha's tight-lipped scowl. "What did she say about him?"

"His instructions were to go south, to a place named Sabart. Though I have never heard such a name."

Ava placed the mug down and walked to the window. Moonlight cast a pallid light over the forest, giving the clearing a skeletal appearance. *So much has changed in just two days.* "I'm not going to Yabun." She turned to face Grigory. "I'm going to rescue the Emissary."

"What?" Misha asked.

"If Declan is gone, then the plan she left us to follow is outdated. Even if it wasn't, she saved me. I will not leave her to rot in the Knights' Barracks."

Grigory scratched the wiry white beard under his chin. "I have no love for your Emissary, but you make good argument. You both are blessed with the gift of Luck. Perhaps you are right not to give up on her so quickly."

"I owe her that much." Ava glanced at Misha. "What about you? Are you going to help?"

"I'm not sure I have a choice."

Ava rolled her eyes. "You always have a choice. I'm not going to force you to come with me."

Misha refused to meet her gaze.

"What is it?" she asked. "Come on. Out with it."

"Well... Is it so bad to let the Knights go? To open up new land for Vedmark? People in the City say the Void is growing. This could save our people."

Ava gritted her teeth to control the wellspring of exasperated fury within. "The Knights will murder millions. Women. Children. Families. You just want to give them a free pass because you're afraid of the forest?"

"No. Of course not." Misha's arms dropped to his sides. He looked at his father. "What will you do if I go?"

"I will ignore your questions and tend to my goats."

"What?" Misha shook his head. "After everything you just heard, you're going back to the farm? What about the Void?"

"Void is in forest, not my land." Grigory leaned back in his chair. "You go. Use your Luck. Save that wretched woman. Once you do, you can hide her in my cabin." His creased face split into a crooked grin. "But only if she likes goat stew."

CHAPTER 7
AVA

They left before sunrise. Trevor waited at the bottom of the hill while Grigory attached the cart. Ava scratched the donkey's nose and tried to ignore the cold, which somehow penetrated four layers of clothing. Her mind drifted to the Emissary and Declan, and a different kind of shiver ran through her. *You should have stayed.*

They rode quietly—ears pricked for the silence of the Void—and finding comfort in the creak of rusted wheels. Misha's lantern cast a small pool of light over the overgrown trail that shrank as the dawn strengthened. When they reached a crossroads, Grigory steered them to a stop. "It is time we part." Misha hopped down, and the men embraced. "Look after each other," Grigory said.

Ava nodded. "We will."

"We could use your wisdom," Misha said. "You could join us."

The old farmer smiled, but shook his head. "I am content with my choice." He held the donkey's lead to Ava. "Leave him at Eastern Gate stables. I will collect poor Trevor next time I visit City."

They waved their goodbyes. Misha didn't move until Grigory went around the bend and out of view. He didn't speak for a long time. When they reached the paved road to Vedmark City, he wiped his eyes with a dirty sleeve and turned to face her. "Do you have a plan?"

"I'm working on it," Ava said. It was a lie. Every time she tried thinking about rescuing the Emissary, the hopelessness of the situation set in. Her ideas collapsed like towers of twigs in a strong wind. "They'll be keeping her in the Barracks."

"I don't think the Coppersmith would appreciate us burning his store again."

Ava smirked at him. Blowing up a pile of copper to create a pillar of green fire had proved an effective distraction once, but she doubted the Knights would fall for the same trick again. "First, we need to confirm she's there."

"No," Misha said. "First thing we need are disguises. Rasporvin is looking for you. We won't be much use to the Emissary if we get tossed in the cell next door."

It was a fair point. Ava handed the reins to Misha and climbed into the back of the cart. It was a mess of farm equipment that smelled like manure. She tried an old seed sack, but it flaked to pieces at first touch. "This is useless," she said. "We have to find—" She cut short as she looked up and saw the City stretching below them. An exodus of carts and wagons trailed off away from it, flowing east like a colorful ribbon.

"What is that?" Misha asked. "Where are they going?"

"Euryma." Ava dropped the remains of the brittle fabric. *No. We need more time.* From their vantage point, there could have been five thousand vehicles curling along the road towards the Threshold. "They're going to Euryma."

"Good," Misha said.

"Good?"

"If everyone is leaving, the Barracks could be unat-tended—or less attended than usual."

Ava squinted down the rise, looking for any sign of the Knights' imposing horses. "I don't know. I can't see any Knights."

They continued south for three miles before crossing the stone bridge leading to the Northern Gate. The city's gatekeepers were gone, and a riot of movement flooded the streets. It gave the distinct impression of a wasp's nest hit with a well-aimed throw.

The cacophony of voices only added to the chaos, and Ava had to shout to be heard over the din. "We should circle around."

Misha steered the cart along a service path that skirted the city wall. As they approached an abandoned guard house, Ava squeezed his elbow. "Hold it."

She jumped down from her seat and climbed through an open window. The air was thick with the scent of old paper. Folders bursting with gatekeepers' records filled two enormous book cases. Leaning on Luck, Ava ducked under a desk to retrieve a box labeled 'uniforms'. Delighted, she tossed it down to Misha.

"I hope you like playing dress-up."

Five minutes later, they were a pair of guards in matching tunics. Misha brought the cart around to the western entry. The hum of activity was distant here. Trevor pinned his ears against his neck as he tiptoed through the empty streets. The cart's wheels squeaked ominously, and Ava held her breath—waiting for an ambush that never came.

They reached the Knights' Barracks without drama. Misha stopped a block early alongside a cobbler's storefront. "Okay," he said as he tied Trevor to a post. "Let's hear it."

"Hear what?"

"The plan," Misha said. "How are we going to save the Emissary?"

Ava took a brushed-leather helm from the uniform box. It was oversized for her head, but she put it on anyway. "We're guards, right? We just need to deliver a message—a fight has broken out at the Eastern Gate. Once they dismiss us, create a distraction and I'll slip inside. Take Trevor to the garden alley behind the Steward's Hall and we'll meet you there in an hour."

Misha appeared unconvinced. "Just like that?"

"Sometimes simple is enough," Ava said. "Come on."

The Barracks' towering oak doors were open. As they drew closer, it became clear their plan was unnecessary. The building was empty. Misha relaxed visibly at the sight. "Well, that should make this easier."

Their tentative footsteps grew louder as they searched the rooms. Ava tried Luck, but there was no chance to manipulate. The Knights of Despair were gone, and the Emissary with them. When they reached the dungeons below ground, Ava found a torn black shawl in the corner of a cell. She picked it up and felt a cold spike in her chest. "She was here."

"You think they've taken her with them?"

Ava nodded. She didn't dare entertain the alternative. *She's alive. She has to be.* "The entire City is evacuating—things are going to be messy. It's the perfect chance to play on Luck and steal her away under Rasporvin's nose."

They wasted no time rushing back to the cart. Trevor's ears twitched at their arrival and they were soon clopping down the cobblestone road leading east. As they passed the

Knights' Barracks, Misha pulled on the reins, a confused scowl creasing his features.

"What is it?" Ava asked. "We don't have time to waste."

"The stables." Misha gestured to the open-roofed building on the other side of the barracks. "They're full."

Atop their raised seats, they could see through the wire windows. Tall stallions packed the long booths, shifting in their pens. Ava chewed on her lip. "If the barracks are empty, but the mounts are here... where are the Knights?"

"I guess we're going to find out." Misha flicked the reins, and the cart creaked towards the crowd headed to the east.

———

They reached the Threshold after sunset. Thousands of wagons crowded the road's edges, and beyond that, a constellation of campfires illuminated a city of tents. Misha had not exaggerated. Vedmark was fleeing the Void.

They left the cart in the first free gap they saw, then continued towards three enormous buildings that appeared to have sprung from nowhere. As they got closer, Ava realized the structure was actually one gargantuan travelling court. It was a twenty-foot tall exercise in exorbitance. Jewels the size of pumpkins adorned the trimmings of three domed peaks, while precious metals, masterfully bent into artistic swirls, decorated the wooden walls. The whole thing sat atop an enormous wagon-bed. A handsome rail hinted at a high balcony illuminated by fire-lit torches. "Rasporvin has to be in there." Ava's soft voice did nothing to hide her disgust. Her mother had died a beggar, while her uncle built monuments like *this*. "Which means the Emissary probably is too."

"Yeah, with an honor guard of Knights," Misha replied. "How are we going to get past them?"

"Same way we always do," Ava said. "Distraction, then extraction. Come on."

They slipped through the crowd of people, unnoticed during the evening's bustle. A combination of anxiety and relief surrounded them. Despite smiles and laughter, these people weren't out of the woods yet.

The court loomed larger. Gatekeepers stood at attention thirty feet ahead of the stairs leading inside. The men wore identical uniforms to those they had pilfered back in the City. Ava nudged Misha. "Seems we chose the right outfit."

"About time something went our way," he muttered.

As he spoke, a flurry of excited voices rang out through the guards. They gestured upwards. Ava turned to follow their gaze. High on the horizon, something massive moved across dusk's curtain. "What is that?"

A monstrous serpentine form descended over the Threshold, soaring overhead like a midnight gale. The crowd cheered as leathery grey wings parachuted outwards and the creature landed atop the court's balcony. Beneath the torches, a beaked dragon—the same one engraved on the back of every jade mitka—reared on hind legs and roared.

"Drevsmok," Misha breathed.

A cheer rose from the camp. Ava could feel her pulse in her eardrums. "Drevsmok are real?"

The drevsmok bowed and a white-haired Knight dismounted from its back. As he approached the balcony's carved rails, Ava's racing heartbeat doubled in speed. Korvan Drakonov waved to a gathering crowd. *How is this possible?* Her cousin was supposed to be dead. He had been better that way.

"It certainly looks real to me." Misha whispered, his attention fixed on the pallid dragon. "Father used to tell me stories about them, but I never thought…"

Korvan disappeared from view and Ava focused on the beast. It was fifty feet long, with triangular wings folded tight against a sleek body. Its eyes were larger than her head, powder blue, and devoid of pupils. "What did Ory say about drevsmoks?"

"It's just drevsmok—even if there are more than one. Like sheep. You don't say sheeps."

"Fine. What *relevant* things did he say?"

Misha pursed his lips. The color had drained from his face. "They fly as fast as the wind, they have a sense for magical power. Oh, and they breathe starshards."

"Starshards?"

He shrugged. "Father's tales didn't come with pictures."

Ava took a deep breath. Nothing had changed. The Emissary was still held captive, and they were wearing the perfect disguise to infiltrate her prison. "Drevsmok or not, we need to get around those guards." She concentrated on those nearest to them. It would be easy enough to take their place—all they needed was for a pair to abandon position for a minute or two. Ava tested a thread of Luck to prompt one man to seek a bathroom break.

The drevsmok snarled and twisted its head over the balcony's edge. Mindless eyes locked onto her immediately. Ava couldn't move. The dragon's gaze clutched her spine in a vise grip. Misha spoke in her ear—his voice a muted garble—then dragged her out of sight. The pain vanished the moment the eye contact was broken. The drevsmok let out a piercing shriek, and the crowd fell silent.

"Are you okay?" Misha breathed.

"It knew." Ava's heart drummed in her chest. "As soon

as I reached out for Luck, it knew…" She tried a calming breath, but she couldn't shake the sensation of the drevsmok's terrible hold.

Misha looked back the way they came. "They… have a sense for magic… that must include… Luck." His shoulders slumped at the realization. "Great. So now we can't even use Luck to help us."

Ava leaned against a wagon. She concentrated on her breathing until her pulse settled. When it did, she peered back towards the balcony. "Well. That's our distraction then."

"Excuse me?"

"One of us hides in the crowd and uses Luck. That should drive that thing crazy and create enough commotion for the other to get into the court and free the Emissary." *Unless Korvan finds you.* She pushed that thought away before it could take hold. "Easy, yeah?"

"Easy?" Misha shook his head. "You're mad. No, you're suicidal. You don't know what's waiting for you inside that wagon, and the moment you try Luck, you'll have a drevsmok on your back."

"Mish—"

"Then there's the matter of the Knights. Who knows how many are in there? At least one—or did you not notice your long-dead cousin up there?"

Ava scowled. "I saw him."

"I can't imagine that would be a pleasant family reunion." Misha held her eye. "We can't stay."

"The Emissary is in there. We will not get another chance like this. We can't give up." She flashed her best smile. "Besides, there are two of us and only one dragon."

The crowd roared even louder than before. Ava and Misha glanced up in unison; a silver cloud blocked the rising moon. No. Not a cloud. Ava's heart sank. At least a thousand Knights on a thousand drevsmok soared towards them. The people of Vedmark screamed and hollered. Their safe passage had arrived.

"Well... that explains the horses," Misha said weakly. "You were saying?"

The applause grew deafening when the drevsmok landed on the other side of the traveling court. It did not cease until Rasporvin—wearing a crown emblazoned with emeralds—approached the balcony's rail. Those watching fell silent when he raised his hands.

"Citizens of Vedmark," he boomed. "Rest easy this night knowing we leave tomorrow to take back our land. Tomorrow, we rid ourselves of the Void that threatens this place. Tomorrow will usher a new dawn for Vedmark. New land, new cities, new riches. A brighter future for all."

The people shouted their appreciation. Korvan appeared at Rasporvin's side, his pale hair tied back behind his ears. Rasporvin placed a hand on his shoulder, before gesturing below. "My son has returned!" More cheers. "Korvan Drakonov has proven our Kingdom's savior. He has revealed the rat in my hall, and set us free of her treachery!"

A steady chant broke out among Vedmark's citizens. "Kill the rat! Kill the rat!"

Ava's stomach turned. Rasporvin motioned for the people to settle. "The rat of Euryma is caught," he announced. "You will see her death. But first, she must see the error of her ways. Euryma's Emissary will watch her homeland burn in Vedmark's light." He smiled. "More importantly, Korvan brings a glorious message. The Deathless Demon is dead! The Knights of Vedmark are free to liberate the land stolen from our forebears!"

The words took a moment to sink in; when it did, a

thunderous roar of approval filled the night. A stab of terror robbed Ava of breath. *He knows.*

"There are guards approaching to our left," Misha whispered. "We need to get out of here."

The scene was too much. Ava let Misha navigate the crowd as her worst fear became a reality. Rasporvin's voice followed them like a foul stench. "Prepare yourself to take what is yours. Tomorrow we leave. To conquest. To victory. To a greater Vedmark!"

Misha pressed his cheek to her ear. "Come. This way. We'll go back home and come up with a new plan to save the Emissary."

When Rasporvin retired, the camp transformed into organized chaos. Misha pushed Ava through it until they found Trevor chewing on a bag of carrots the donkey had liberated from an unattended wagon. As they started towards Vedmark City, Ava glanced back at the travelling court. *I will come back for you. I promise.*

CHAPTER 8
AVA

THE CAMPFIRES of the tent city shrank to pinpricks as they climbed the sprawling hills leading back to Vedmark. They had not rested since dawn, and now—as they crossed the East River—it appeared they would not stop for a few hours longer. Ava felt the weight of tiredness pulling at her eyelids. Misha dozed gently beside her, his soft snores the only sound in the otherwise dead silence.

She pinched her wrist hard. Fatigue was no excuse for losing focus, but as the night wore on, an uneasiness blossomed in her chest. At first, Ava disregarded it as anxiety, guilt, or both. Yet as the minutes passed, the feeling grew more urgent. With a healthy dose of caution, she shuttered the lantern's beam and searched their surrounds. Tall grass on her left, a steep embankment to her right, an empty road behind and a lone donkey ahead.

You're exhausted. It's making you delirious. Just keep going.

She would have believed it, had she not scanned the night sky. The faintest movement—high amongst the inky black—grabbed her attention. The tiredness evaporated in a burst of panic. Ava nudged Misha hard in the ribs. He woke with a start. "Wha—"

"A drevsmok is following us," she said.

"What?" Misha leaned out of the cart. "Where?"

"Left side, a hand-span above the horizon." She tried to formulate a plan. It felt like her mind was sprinting down a shale hill with no firm footing. A wild idea took hold of her. "On my mark, cut Trevor loose."

Misha nodded without question. He drew a short knife from his belt and positioned himself where he could sever the donkey's harness. Ava tore a strip of cloth off her sleeve and opened the lantern's shutter. She hoped there was enough manure residue in the back for this to work.

"When I say so, cut him loose. I'll need your help to get the cart started down the hill. Once it's moving, we hide in the grass."

"And then?" Misha asked.

"Don't get caught. Don't use Luck either, or it will know where we are." She rolled the fabric into a cylinder and poked it into the lantern. It caught alight instantly. "Now!"

Ava tossed the flame over her shoulder. The harness broke with a loud snap. A whoosh of heat ignited the night as a bright orange flare plumed upwards. With a startled bray, Trevor took off up the road. The cart jerked sideways and Ava heaved with all her strength. There was a moment of resistance, and it was off. Hurtling down the embankment with gravity at the reins.

"C'mon!" Misha hissed. She turned as he vanished into the high grass. She dove after him as a hideous shriek tore the night in two. A sudden gale poured over them. It wrenched the grass-stalks flat against her back, threatening to pull them out at the roots. Ava crawled on her belly, putting as much distance between her and the noise. When the drevsmok howled again, she curled into a ball—palms pressed to her ears—and waited for it to pass.

It didn't.

Three more times the tempest roared overhead—the last with a frigid blast. Ava peeked out from beneath her arms. The grass to her left was gone. Ground down to a long line of chaff. Had she been a body-length closer, she would likely be dead. Ava's heart stopped. *Where is Misha?*

Crawling like an infant, she staggered away from the shredded vegetation. There was another burst of wind, a spray of icy pain, and the drevsmok was almost on her. The edges of its destruction lay only inches from her feet. *You can't move fast enough on your hands and knees. It's going to get you the next time it comes around.*

Ava was moments from standing when the dragon shrieked once more. The echoing call of a second drevsmok responded. The sound sent goose pimples up her arms. *Run!*

Before she could push off the ground, something seized her wrist and dragged her through a hole that appeared from nowhere. Ava fell on top of Misha, then rolled onto her back. Overhead, the tunnel ceiling shuddered, freeing small particles of dirt that rained down on them. Misha sat up, shaking his head in disbelief. "What is wrong with you?"

Ava didn't move. The fall had knocked the wind out of her, and her mind struggled to comprehend what was going on. After a few ragged breaths, she sat up. "What?"

"I must have shouted your name fifty times!" Deep lines creased Misha's forehead. "I could see you! I was screaming at you, and you ignored me! Do you want to die?"

"I..." Ava's voice was barely audible over another rumble from above. "I didn't hear you." Her hands trembled as shock threatened to overtake her.

Misha knelt beside her. "Are you okay?"

"Just a few bruises," she said weakly. Ava took a deep breath and searched the tunnel. "Where are we?"

"Some underground road system," Misha said. "I fell into it trying to shelter beneath a rock. There are trapdoors everywhere."

The red-clay walls were rounded, as if carved by some giant worm. It was lit by a gentle golden glow that shone through an unfamiliar emblem every ten paces. She climbed to her feet and inspected the closest light. Thirteen half-circles connected to make a shape like a sun. "I've never heard of anything like this," she said.

"Well, whatever it is, I'm glad it's here." Misha glanced up as the roof shuddered once more. "I'll take this over the alternative any day."

It was hard to disagree, and after a lingering glance at the odd symbol lighting the gloom, Ava nodded. "We should get moving."

Misha led them north. When her surge of adrenaline faded, Ava felt even more tired than before. They seemed to walk for weeks with nothing but the golden symbols and the stale air for company. When Misha finally pushed through a circular stone doorway in the ceiling, they emerged less than one-hundred paces from the road to Eaglewatch. The village was dim in the distance, lit only by the high lamps marking the entry. Misha pointed west. "We can cut through there and be home before sunrise."

Ava stifled a groan. Sunrise would be a full twenty-four hours without sleep. Misha may have caught some rest on the cart, but she was running on fumes. The hills were mammoth walls of black in the night. Resigned, she gestured forward. "Lead the way."

The moon set an hour before dawn, leaving only a faint

glow on the horizon to guide their way. Ava used a pine sapling to pull herself up the steep climb. A bed of loose rocks slid beneath her and she lost a layer of skin holding tight to the tree. They crested the rise to see Grigory's well-kept farm below, and all thoughts of pain vanished in a wave of relief.

When they reached the cabin, everything was still. Ava stumbled—like some undead creature—down the hallway and onto her mattress, where she fell asleep instantly.

Ava woke to a clatter of movement and shouts. As she squinted into the morning light, Misha burst through the door. His eyes were wild with panic. "Father's not here!"

The words took a moment to register, then hit Ava like a runaway cart. "Are you sure? He's not out with the goats... or headed to the City for Trevor?"

Misha seemed to fold away. Ava pulled him into a hug before he could collapse, and the weight of his head pressed against her shoulder. "I've checked," Misha sobbed. "He never made it back. They... took him. The Emissary must have talked..."

"Just breathe," she whispered. Unpleasant thoughts filled Ava's head, but she refused to let them overwhelm her.

"Father was never coming back here." Misha sobbed "He sent us away to protect us."

"You're jumping to conclusions." Ava said gently. "Why would they want him? He isn't a part of this?"

Misha stepped back. A hard glint formed in his eyes. "This is all Declan Moore's fault!"

"No. This is Rasporvin's fault."

"We've lived with your uncle's tyranny our whole life," Misha said. "It wasn't until *he* arrived that everything started to go down the river!"

"Declan has been trying to do the right thing!"

"Like attacking you?"

"We talked about—"

"Like running away?"

"It's not like that!"

"You should have left Declan in Euryma!" Misha slammed his fist against the door. "You brought him here, and now my father is gone!"

Ava had no answer to that. She held out her palms in supplication. "Be angry if you want, but there is no proof anyone took Ory. He told us to leave Trevor in the City, so what's to say he hasn't gone to get him? What if he left before dawn—before we arrived—to make the trip there and back?"

Misha shook his head, his gaze locked on the floor between them. "There are fresh claw marks out front. Drevsmok-sized ones." He stomped out of the room without another word, leaving Ava with no choice but to follow.

Twenty-feet from the front door, four jagged scars cut through a section of grass. Ava knelt beside them and ran her hand over the prints. Misha was right. They were recent—half-a-day old at most—and deep enough that whatever left them had claws as long as her arm. The unpleasant thoughts broke through her defenses, and Ava had no way to repel them. The Knights had taken Grigory, and it was her fault.

Misha said something and went back inside. Ava followed shortly after. She felt numb, not in a pleasant way, but like she had been robbed of any interest in doing anything. Her stomach rumbled, but she wasn't hungry. With a head full of regret, she went back to bed, but nightmares of shrieking drevsmok punctured her attempts at rest. Twice she woke, drenched in sweat, before sleep enveloped her at last.

When Ava woke again, it was dark. She tried to relax, but no matter how she positioned herself, she could not get comfortable. Her mind leapt into action and when Ava couldn't turn the thoughts off, she ignited a lantern and slipped outside.

Legions of stars glittered in the sky; constellations long burned out—or moved on—with only a prick of light left to mark their existence. Ava tugged the pendant out of her shirt and wondered where Declan was now. The front door creaked open.

"I can't sleep either." Misha looked a mess, but Ava said nothing as he joined her on the front step.

For a time, they sat in silence. The breeze picked up as a row of clouds crept overhead, hiding the stars, leaving nothing but the glow of the lantern and the sound of the wind in the trees.

"Declan left because of me." Ava's cheeks burned at the confession, but the blush was lost in the darkness. "I didn't want him to be miserable, so I tried to use Luck to cheer him up, and he felt it. He knew. He didn't leave—I drove him away."

A gentle drizzle started around them. "You didn't drive him away. He chose that." Misha pulled her closer. Ava let her head drop onto his shoulder.

She wished she could believe him. "I don't know what I'm doing," she admitted. "I... don't think I can stop this. Rasporvin is going to take the Knights south. He's going to destroy Euryma. He's going to turn it into... this... Vedmark."

"Why do you despise this place?" Misha asked. "Any time you talk about Vedmark, you change. Do you really hate your home so much?"

Home. Ava grunted at the word. "My earliest memories of Vedmark are begging for scraps from Knights heading out from the Barracks. They would kick my mother into the dirt, laughing. I held her frozen hands as she coughed bloody spittle onto the stone. She died. My uncle is the Grand Steward, and he refused to look after his own sister." Ava's fingernails dug into her palms at the memory. "This isn't my home. I hate this place. I hate its stupid customs, its narrow-minded people, and its greedy leaders."

"And Euryma is the answer?"

"It's *an* answer. The first time I went south, I saw strangers work together for common goals." Ava paused to imagine what might have been. "I don't think my mother would have died in Euryma." Ava stared into the darkness. The drizzle was now rain that washed over them with a dull roar. "I don't know if I want to save Euryma because I'm selfish, or because it's the right thing to do... but I can't stay here." She turned to his dark silhouette. "I have to do something."

Misha did not respond immediately, and when he did, it was with a heavy sigh. "I just wish they'd left father alone." He picked up the lantern and held it between them, fixing her with a hard stare. "I'm with you Ava, but on one condition."

She raised a questioning eyebrow.

"Forget about Declan."

Ava rolled her eyes. "Mish—"

"I'm not following an army of dragons to go chasing a

boy the first time we hear his name. I'll follow you to save Grigory, and the Emissary, but if Declan shows his face, I'm gone." His unblinking gaze never strayed from hers. "That's the deal."

A small part of Ava wanted to argue the point—to explain that Declan was a Warlock, and still their best chance of stopping the Knights of Despair. *But he left.* She clenched her teeth and nodded. "Deal."

He visibly relaxed at the word. "So... what do we do then?"

"We do what Grigory told us," she said. "We'll give the Knights a few days to clear out of the Threshold, then head to the mountains bordering Euryma to find Yabun... wherever that might be."

"Do you have any clue which friends we're expected to meet?"

"Not the slightest." Ava thought about the Emissary's cryptic message and shrugged. "Maybe people from the Directive? I really don't know. But she did. The Emissary had a plan, and that's more than what we've got."

They sat without talking a little longer. For the first time since reading Declan's note, Ava felt a sense of purpose. Her body relaxed, and at once, she was ready for more sleep. Misha seemed much the same. He yawned and soon bid her goodnight. Ava followed him inside. As she climbed into her bed, she made a point of taking the sapphire necklace off and putting it away in the bedside drawer. As the heavy jewel hit the wood with a clunk, she couldn't help but feel it was a symbolic act.

You left first, Declan. I'm just returning the favor.

CHAPTER 9

KATIE

THE DEAN'S office was a study in silence. Through the window, a perfect sky gleamed over the college's handsome architecture. Inside, the mood was not so sunny. Katie had said what needed to be said. Now, her jaw was clamped so tight, she feared her teeth might break. She leaned back on the leather couch and tried to consider the situation from Laurefen's point of view. *Just imagine you're a stupid old fool with zero sense of accountability.* The thought rang true, but it did not help.

The reason behind her frustration sat behind his bleached driftwood desk. Laurefen's fingertips pressed together to form a triangle, over which his bright eyes seemed to stare straight through her. Katie refused to speak, and after two silent minutes, he sighed. "This is unheard of. Nobody has ever left the Directive."

"Declan did."

"No," Laurefen said. "The Directive left him. Removed from our records when we discovered his true nature."

Katie rolled her eyes. "I should have gone sooner. For some reason, I thought that almost getting killed by a giant storm of *Remnant Magic* might... I don't know... convince you that Remnant Magic exists." She shook her head. "If you won't accept what's right in front of your nose, then I am done here."

"You failed to consider our perspective."

"No." Katie stood over him. "Don't you dare put this on me!" Her voice rose with her temper. "I told you. I screamed it in your face and you didn't listen. What did you do?" She didn't bother waiting for his response. "You bound me in nima and left me to die. If Mary-Lou hadn't come back for me, I wouldn't be here." Her whole body trembled with the anger that had been building all morning. "I read the press release. I saw what you said. Your refusal to acknowledge the cause of these storms is disgusting! You should be ashamed." She met his gaze, unflinching. "I know I am."

Laurefen's expression was an institution in control. He leaned forward, and seemed to weigh his words carefully. With a flick of his wrist, a faint wall of condensed air surrounded them, sealing the silence. "There is more to this than you know. More than you are *allowed* to know." Despite the shield blocking any whisper of sound, Laurefen's voice dropped to a murmur. "Remnant Magic should not exist."

Katie almost burst with frustration. "You saw it! You saw it with your own eyes!"

"Of course I did," Laurefen said. "I am no close-minded fool, Ms. Hall. I saw the storm, but I did not see proof of its origin. You say *our* magic creates this destruction, but I have evidence proving otherwise."

"What evidence?"

"I cannot tell you."

Katie wanted to slap his ancient face. "Then I'm done."

She tried to leave, but the panel door would not budge. "Locking me up in another room?"

"You know the Directive exists to protect Euryma's interests. This is true, but it is not the whole truth. Our real purpose runs deeper. A secret known only by a select few." The wall of air vanished, and the door opened. "You are free to go, but if you do, you will not understand why we acted the way we did." He crossed the room so they were face to face. "But if you stay, you are bound to the Directive. What we guard is more important than you can imagine." Laurefen nodded to the exit. "The choice is yours."

Anger pushed Katie from the room, while curiosity kept her feet rooted to the ground. If she stayed, she would be stuck in the Directive's hamster wheel. She could walk out that door and be free of King's College forever. *Then what? Remnant Magic is destroying the whole Dominion. Where will you go?* For a full minute, she stood motionless. Finally, in barely a whisper, she spoke. "Did my mother know?"

A sad smile lifted the corners of Laurefen's lips. "She did."

She closed the door. More than anger, more than anything, Katie wanted to do right by those she had lost. Dreyfus. Amber. Her mother. She would not let their sacrifices be in vain. "Fine. You've caught my attention. What is the Directive's secret?"

"I don't think talk will do it justice." He reached into his coat and withdrew a small blue key. It looked to be made of ice, or sea-glass. It had a crescent moon shape at its end. "And even if I told you, you would not believe me. You need to see it for yourself."

. . .

He led her out of the college gates and down the sloping grounds where dew drops still clung to the grass. A pair of scholars—those of the handful who had returned seeking refuge after Sabriva fell—wandered towards the Village. It didn't take long for Katie to realize they were headed for the small cave on the hill. She raised an eyebrow. She had not been down this way since Declan Moore proved his worthiness to join the Directive. "Are we doing Approval?"

"That is unnecessary." Sunlight cast deep shadows in the creases of Laurefen's face. He looked like a weathered cliff. He vanished into the darkness and his voice carried out from its depths. "Come. There is more to this passage than Approval."

This better be worth it. The narrow passage was steep and twisted. Chilled air attacked every inch of exposed skin, and when she nearly lost her footing on the slick mud floor, she summoned a sphere of photonima to light the way. Exposed roots hung overhead. Laurefen's boot prints marked her path below.

He waited at a stone door decorated with seven circular white gems. Laurefen waved to it as she approached. "Welcome to Euryma's most closely guarded secret." He turned the key, and—with a chime like a glass bell—the gems changed color. Katie stepped back on instinct. They were the same fiery shade of orange of the storm that destroyed Sabriva.

"Don't be alarmed," Laurefen said. "It is safe within."

The door slid open, and he gestured for her to follow. Cautiously, Katie entered a round room lined with black bricks. They jutted from the walls, and their uneven placement created an odd ensemble of shadows. In the middle of the room, a stone wall bordered a circular hole. She peered over the edge and her jaw dropped. Fifty-feet down, a chaotic miasma of orange light bubbled and swirled. "What is this?"

"The Well," Laurefen said. "It is the fountain of Euryma's power. The magic that every witch and wizard has ever used flows to and from this place."

His words were a wrench in the whirring gears of Katie's mind. This *was* magic. Her entire life, she had taken her abilities for granted. They had existed as readily as electricity, or gravity. Now, she stared—speechless—at the source of the Dominion's strength. It rippled like the surface of a star.

"While it appears identical to Remnant Magic, it is not. The magic in the Well moves in a cyclical pattern. Magic is drawn from here to be used, and then returns after. The Ancellum is not protecting King's College. It is protecting this. The heart of Euryma's power."

"But..." Katie tried to arrange her thoughts. "But you said it yourself. Remnant Magic is identical to this. This is it. It must not be making it back!"

Laurefen pointed to a mark carved a few inches from the rippling surface. "See that line?"

Katie nodded.

"That is the level marker. Sometimes it dips by more than a foot, but never more." Laurefen turned his attention back to Katie. "If Remnant Magic was building up, we would see it. The Well would drop, even empty, but it does not."

Katie frowned. "How is that possible?"

"That's what we need to figure out."

"Are there other Wells?"

"None that we know of."

"That's why you wouldn't believe me." Katie's eyes

never left the light below. "This is why you were so convinced the Fatesmiths were lying!"

"We would check the level daily. Mary-Lou kept meticulous records. We had every reason to think it was a lie."

"But if it's not Remnant Magic, then what else can it be? It looks *just* like this." Fifty-feet below them, a flare erupted from the Well. It twirled about in a fiery whip that looped half-way up the bore and fell with an ominous rumble.

"It is a mystery. A puzzle we have been trying to solve for years." Laurefen stepped back from the Well and held her gaze. "We have tried searching texts from when this place was built. Books from the founding are scarce, and many are unreadable."

"Have you asked the Historians Guild? Or the Librarians at Ursaria? Someone must know!"

"We must be careful who we talk to," Laurefen warned. "Very careful with our questions. Scarce few know the Well exists, but a slip of the tongue seeking information could change that. There are those who would seek to destroy it."

Those words made Katie's stomach quiver. She had never considered that. "Laurefen... What happens if the Well is destroyed?"

"We can only guess, but nothing good. We may lose the ability to do magic. The storms could double or triple in size or frequency. There is no way to be sure."

Katie chewed on her lower lip and stared into the abyss. All the magical potential in Euryma gathered in one spot. It was like standing on the edge of a volcano. "Why didn't you tell me sooner?"

"This is the most dangerous secret in the Dominion," Laurefen said. "We must protect the Well at all costs."

That's fair. Katie would not admit it out loud, but this

changed everything. The Dominion she knew has been obliterated by a small key in a stone door.

For a long time, neither of them spoke. Katie surveyed the room and tried to absorb every inch of the place. As she did, something on the cavern floor caught her eye. A crescent moon shaped keyhole. "What is that?"

"That activates the Well's protection," Laurefen said. "I hope I never have to use it."

"It's familiar," Katie whispered. "It's like... I've seen it somewhere else."

Laurefen smiled. "I can assure you, there is no other key like this one, and no other keyhole to match it."

Katie knelt to run her fingers along the impression's edge. A distant recollection floated past the cusp of memory, just out of reach. "What does the protection do?"

"We're not sure." Laurefen sat on the wall bordering the Well, Katie's stomach lurched as she imagined him falling backwards. "We know the Well was created at the time of the Founding. We have fragments of documents from the archives explaining its purpose. The rest is lost from memory.

Memory. Katie's knit coat suddenly felt too tight. As the terrible realization grew, the warm cavern seemed to grow cold. "Horace has Arman Moore's memories... from a thousand years ago..."

"Brilliant, as always, Ms. Hall." His expression darkened. "You have identified our greatest concern. We do not know how Vedmark's white dagger works, but Horace Marley has those memories. He may already know more about the Well than we do. He may not. We have no way of knowing unless we take action." Laurefen's lips twitched. "Naturally, Mary-Lou and Michael sit on opposing sides of the issue. I expect you can guess their stances."

Katie nodded. "Michael wants to take the memories by force; Mary-Lou would rather extend an olive branch?"

"You know them well," Laurefen said. "Michael is gathering intelligence in Biscay, testing if it's even possible to mount an attack. Mary-Lou is trying to organize a meeting with the Fatesmiths."

A venomous hatred stirred in Katie's chest. Horace had killed her mother—killed Amber. "I don't want the Fatesmiths' help."

"We may not have a choice." Laurefen started to the exit. He motioned for her to follow. "I do not trust the Fatesmiths, but I will do what I must. So should you. Amber would not want Euryma to burn because of a vengeful heart."

Katie took one last look into the fiery depths of the pit. "And my mom?"

Laurefen stopped. "Lisa would be proud of you, Katie. So proud." He turned to face her. "We all are. Whether you trust us or not, I am glad you have decided to stay. Euryma will need you before this is over."

CHAPTER 10

DECLAN

THE NORTHERN RAIL WAS GONE, or at least, major sections had been destroyed or abandoned. After three weeks of hard travel, Declan had stumbled on a small line headed south. The rusted excuse for a train had taken him as far as Valentian—a quaint river-town on Clovin's northernmost border—before the stone-faced conductor announced they would go no further.

Declan stopped at a notice board at the platform's stairs. Valentian had once produced lace for the entire Dominion, but when the textile industry fell apart, it became a white picket haven for those tired of Sabriva's city-bustle. *A calm retreat for the soul*, said a poster in sky-blue text. A wry smiled formed on Declan's lips. The train station was chaos. Everywhere he turned, people were carrying bags, or children—or both—with the same fearful expression. The air stank of anxiety.

Declan flowed with the crowd, like a leaf on a river, until he came to a sprawling parking lot. Rows of red buses stretched out and around the corner. A man in a black coat directed a long line of people.

With no hesitation, Declan slipped between two industrial bins. He didn't recognize the man, but he recognized the silver emblem on his coat's breast. He was a Fatesmith.

As Declan edged closer, another Fatesmith—a flaxen-haired woman—motioned urgently to her clipboard and pointed to the bus-line. The man nodded and cleared his throat. "Please have all your belongings ready to board," he said. "Calm and orderly. Rushing will only slow us down."

Haggard individuals stepped onto the vehicle and the line advanced until the Fatesmith raised a hand. "That's enough, thank you. The next bus will arrive shortly."

The doors hissed closed, and the Fatesmith gave the driver a thumbs up. It rumbled out of the parking lot so another bus could take its place.

Declan moved closer to see dozens of Fatesmiths walking up and down the line. They ferried buses forward, speaking via radio instead of Looptap. *One of them will know where Horace is.* He considered trying to take one from the shadows, but it was impossible. They functioned as a unit, to the point any missing body would quickly be noticed. *They can't work forever*, he told himself. He slid to the ground to wait until his window opened.

"Are you alright?"

A teenage girl stared down at him. She wore ripped jeans and held a half-finished burger in her hand. It smelled delicious.

Declan shifted to hide the axes under his long coat. "Uh. Yeah. I'm just catching a break from the noise."

"Okay then." She dropped her burger in the bin. Declan's stomach protested the waste.

"Are you waiting in line?"

"Well, duh." Her smile revealed rows of purple braces. "Why else would I be here?"

"Where is everyone going?"

She squinted at him, and her grin faded. She tilted her head, as if he were a peculiar insect. "You really don't know?"

Declan wasn't sure how to respond to that. Outside of the disaster at Sabriva, he had been out of Euryma for over a year. He did not know what the people thought—or if they even knew—about Remnant Magic.

"Magic storms." The girl folded her arms. "Bloody wizards overusing their powers. Now it's coming back to bite us *Bonfires* in the back."

Declan frowned. "Bonfires?"

"It's what we call ourselves." Her smile returned. "A group of LAMPs makes a Bonfire." Her eyes–suddenly suspicious—darted to his hands. "You're not a wizard, are you?"

"Me?" Declan laughed. "No. I'm no wizard. Just... out of touch." He nodded to the people boarding a new bus. "Where is everyone going?"

"Lombrives City."

"Never heard of it."

"That's because it's brand new! A whole city, built inside a massive cave system in Gaul. The Fatesmiths made it to protect us from..." the girl's gaze wandered over the bins. "I've gotta go." She waved back to the buses. "Make sure you line up too. Auntie Eve says Lombrives is that last safe place left in the Dominion."

"Thanks," Declan said, but the girl was already walking away. He watched her join a pair of women near the front of the line. They shouldered backpacks and disappeared onto a bus. For a moment, Declan considered digging the girl's unfinished meal from the bin. He had not eaten much on the road. Before he could decide, the flaxen-haired Fatesmith handed her clipboard over and walked purposefully towards the parking lot exit. Declan gave her a thirty-second lead, then followed.

On the corner of a nearby intersection, the woman entered a brightly lit convenience store. Declan melded into the shadows of the closest building and unlooped one of his axes. The woman soon emerged with a coffee. As she passed, he stepped out and pressed the axe blade to her neck. "Don't move."

She didn't listen. Instead, the Fatesmith threw her coffee at Declan's face. He ducked the scalding liquid as the woman weaved her hands in an intricate pattern. Declan cleaved whatever nima she was manipulating with his axe and moved to block her exit. He stepped into the Lion form, pushing the woman to retreat against a brick wall. Declan stopped mid stroke with the axe an inch from her chest. "Do. Not. Move."

The Fatesmith glared at him. "Who are you?" She spoke with a clipped accent. "What is the meaning of this?"

"I have no reason to hurt you, but I need information." He lowered his weapon. "If you answer my questions, you can return to your buses unharmed."

"Are you threatening me, lumberjack?"

"I am explaining the situation. Now, who is in charge of the Fatesmiths?"

The woman's eyes narrowed. "What kind of question is that?"

Declan flicked his wrist. The axe spun in a perfect circle; the blade stopped at her neck. "Answer."

"It is Madam Haberdeen, as it has always been."

They don't know. Horace was still wearing her face. "Where is she?"

"I... I don't know. Biscay. All our orders come from Biscay. That's all I know."

"Do your orders come straight from Haberdeen?"

"No. All orders come from Mage Ophelia. She reports to Madam Haberdeen."

"And this Mage. Ophelia. She is in Biscay?"

The woman nodded. Quickly. Declan couldn't tell if it was because she was nervous or because she was lying. "What's the fastest way from here to Biscay?"

"Train," the Fatesmith said. "Though the Central Line..."

Declan didn't need her to finish. The Central Line was a direct run from Sabriva to the other capitals. It would be long gone. "Which lines are still running?"

"Western Coast is safest. Most storms track along—" The woman's gaze locked onto something behind him. The color drained from her already-pale face. Declan inched the blade of his axe until it touched skin.

"No tricks," he said. The woman didn't respond. He glanced back. Someone stood outside the convenience store in a hooded blue cloak. Stranger still, a raven perched atop the mysterious figures' forearm.

In a flurry of movement, the Fatesmith knocked the axe aside and rammed her shoulder into his chest. Declan staggered off the sidewalk and onto the road. By the time he found his feet, the woman had rounded the corner, no doubt sprinting to the safety of the parking lot.

"You idiot, Declan," he whispered. He turned back to the bird woman, but she too was gone, leaving him alone in the street with only an upturned coffee cup for company.

When Declan tried returning to the parking lot, a group of blackcoats were waiting at each entrance. He watched them compare two men to a rough sketch before permitting entry, then started back the other way. He had all the information he needed. Horace was most likely in Biscay, off the Western Coast Line.

As night fell, the cold air grew fangs. Declan shivered as his empty stomach announced its displeasure. Halfway back to the station, a rowdy commotion forced itself out of a bar and onto the street.

Two men threw blind punches into whatever flesh they could find. A small crowd followed—jeering loudly. Bloody fists made meaty thuds until one of them—a square faced brute in a torn business shirt—caught the other by the collar and swung him to the ground. He knelt on the man and delivered a hailstorm of blows.

The onlookers cheered. The man on his back was unconscious, his bearded face a swollen mess., but the man on top did not seem to care. "What are you doing?" Declan shouted.

It was as if someone paused reality. The man in the blood-stained shirt stopped—his fist still in the air—and the crowd turned to stare at the ragged adolescent wandering the streets alone.

"He's a wizard," called a woman from the crowd. "He deserves it."

"He's getting his due," said the man with the bloody knuckles.

"Looks like he's had plenty." Declan gestured to the unconscious heap on the sidewalk. "You're going to kill him."

"Good. His kind have killed enough of us."

Declan pursed his lips. "I don't—"

"Get lost, kid," the man said. He threw the punch he'd been holding square into the man's nose. There was a crunch that made Declan's stomach turn, and a ruby stream flooded onto the road.

"Get off him."

The onlookers glanced at each other, then broke into a chorus of laughter. The man wiped his knuckles on his shirt, leaving a smear across his chest. He stood up and turned to face Declan. "What are you going to do about it? You're not a wizard too, are you?"

"I'm not a wizard."

"Then what's the problem?"

A small part of Declan could see the man was much bigger than he was. A bigger part of him refused to watch him murder a helpless wizard. The largest part of him just wanted an excuse to explode. The stewpot of pain, anger, misery, and frustration that had simmered inside him for the past week had found a worthy target. "I don't like bullies."

"Bully?" The man raised his fists. "Come on then. Or are you all talk?".

Declan willed his axes into his hands and poured his rage into an improvised Bull-Bear combination. In a surge of movement, the square-jawed man was on the road. His right wrist stuck out at an odd angle, and an angry purple bruised marred the side of his unconscious face.

"I think you should go," Declan told the bystanders. They exchanged uncertain glances; Declan pointed an axe at the man's motionless body. "Take him with you."

Like a herd of skittish deer, they dragged the man back into the bar. As they did, a middle-aged woman motioned to the wizard on the sidewalk. "Why defend them?" she asked. "If you're not a wizard, why would you care? They've burned our home to the ground with their magic."

The wizard she referred to was a mess of swollen cheeks and dry blood. "I... don't think he meant it. I don't think any of them knew about the storms."

The woman laughed at that, cold and unkind. "Didn't mean it? These mugs have had months to take the Fate-smiths' oath and stop using magic. They didn't. They don't want things to change. They care more about their magic than us LAMPs." She spat at the wizard's feet, then followed the others inside.

Declan returned his axes to his belt. The woman's words were a slap in the face, one that had torn down the curtains of his naïve worldview. *Is she right?*

Somewhere in the distance, sirens blared to life. Through the bar window, the LAMPs were crowded around a phone. Declan pushed his doubts aside and tore a strip from his coat. He wrapped the wizard's face as best he could, then leaned him against a wall. When a set of red and blue lights appeared down the road, Declan hurried in the opposite direction—but no matter how fast he walked, he couldn't escape the woman's words. *They don't want things to change. They care more about magic than us LAMPs.*

CHAPTER 11
DECLAN

EVEN AT NIGHT, the railway station was busy. Every arriving train was full to bursting with weary refugees clinging to hope. They would arrive, flood to the exit, and the platform would fall silent. Declan had extracted an unopened salad sandwich from a bin. It tasted like heaven. He ate as he watched the repeating cycle from the outdoor seating of a closed cafe.

After the fifth rendition—when the platforms fell silent once more—an elderly woman touched his shoulder. She wore an aging security uniform, but her smile was like a warm hearth. "You lost, son?"

Declan shook his head. "Just watching."

"Odd thing to watch." She tapped the neighboring chair with her iron baton. "Mind if I watch too?"

"Not at all."

"Thank 'ya dear." The guard eased herself onto the seat with a relieved sigh. "These old joints don't like standing for too long."

Declan smiled. "Looks like you've been busy. I've never seen so much foot traffic in a railway station."

"Refugees from the Head City. Sad business, those folks." She frowned as she scanned the empty station. "I'm Shurl, by the way."

"Declan." He held out a hand. Garish rings covered Shurl's fingers. Her grip was gentle, but strong. A loud chime repeated down the platform and another train arrived. A fresh flood of travelers disembarked. "Are they all going to the buses?"

"I expect so," Shurl said. "Fatesmiths have set up meeting points all across the Dominion, but none this side of Sabriva." A scowl stressed the deep creases in her cheeks. "Or at least what's left of it."

"Is anyone getting *on* the trains?" Declan asked.

Shurl shook her head. "A few occasionally on a southbound. Most lines run on a skeleton staff nowadays. Hard to find workers when the world's falling apart. Smokes, I'm only here cause I've got grand babies to feed."

The flood of refugees drained, and the station became quiet once more. Declan finished his sandwich. As he stood to toss the plastic container, a newspaper caught his eye, or rather, a photo of Laurefen Ember. He pulled the paper from the trash and laid it on the table. He read the headline out loud. "King's College Doom Dominion." Then looked sideways at Shurl. "Do you know anything about this?"

The old guard nodded. "It's a sore topic."

Declan scanned the story.

While Magical Storms continue to wreak havoc across the Dominion, the administration of Euryma's most prestigious college refuses to take the Fatesmiths' Oath. Dean Laurefen Ember describes the storm as 'an unprecedented phenomenon', but so far refuses to acknowledge the role wizards and witches of the Dominion play in their existence.

"They're the reason we're in this mess." Shurl tapped

the picture beside the article—a portrait of Laurefen, over-laid by a smaller photo of Sabriva's ruins. "They learned everything at their fancy schools, except how to be accountable."

"I... I know them," Declan said. "They didn't believe in the storms."

"Didn't believe?" Shurl pursed her lips. "Or didn't care?"

Four men appeared either side of them. LAMPolice in standard officer navy. Shurl's demeanor was unapologetic. "Your description matched the fella that beat a man half to death down on Prunswick," she explained. "Won't be a problem if you're innocent."

The lead officer pointed a rectangular metal device at Declan's chest. "Stand up and raise your arms."

Declan did as he was told. Two policemen patted him down. When they reached the axes, they stepped back. "He's armed," one said.

Shurl frowned in obvious disappointment. For some odd reason, Declan felt a surge of guilt.

"Drop the weapons," said the officer in charge, his curious device still aimed at Declan's chest. "Don't think of trying anything, or you'll be twitching on the floor before you can blink."

The other officers raised their own weapons. They looked like the electric razors his father would use to trim his moustache.

Declan considered his options. The consequence of attacking uniformed police would be much worse than injuring one angry LAMP. Even if he overpowered them, he doubted he could escape without hurting Shurl. She may be the reason he was in this predicament, but he couldn't fault her for doing her job. In the end, Declan eased the axes from their loops and placed them on the tile floor.

"Smart kid," said the officer. "We move. West exit. Two on back, chargers ready—just in case. Timmons, you bag the weapons."

"Good luck with your grandkids," Declan said to Shurl as he passed. The woman nodded in reply.

The officers led Declan up the stairs, ascending from the platform to the raised walkway leading back to the street. Blue and red flashing lights reflected off the entry signs. They would need to go down one more flight, and that would be his chance. He just hoped—

Something enormous swooped from the ceiling and buried its talons into the lead officer. He screamed and two whipcracks exploded, whizzing over Declan's shoulder with an electric hiss. Amongst the shouts of the officers and the crack of their chargers, Declan dropped to his knees and crawled to the wall. A massive raven circled the men, diving at them, then retreating out of range. Ahead of him, a blue hooded figure thrust a finger at the fire exit opposite. Declan nodded his understanding and ducked into the pandemonium. Amidst shouts, he kicked the door open. Halfway down, he closed his eyes and called the axes to follow. The weapons clattered down the metal-grate stairs before reaching his hands.

Panic pulsed through Declan's veins. He squeezed through a hole in a chain-link fence and rushed towards an empty alley. Rendered concrete walls rose high on either side of him, reducing the sky above to a narrow rectangle of dim stars. Something overhead threaded between the buildings. The raven was following him.

Declan ran. His loud footsteps echoed about him. The raven dived for him. The noise of wingbeats awoke terrible memories of Vedmark's eagles, and Declan stumbled onto the asphalt. His axes clattered on the hard ground.

Instead of dragging him to his death, the raven extended its wings to land on a sideways trash can. It tilted its head to stare at him. Then, with a soft caw, it released something at Declan's feet. The bird took the cylinder in its beak, then dropped it by Declan's hand.

"For me?" Declan asked.

The bird cawed again, then leapt into the sky. In three flaps, it was gone, leaving Declan alone with only the oddly wrapped item.

It was paper, rolled tight and tied by a length of blue ribbon. When Declan unrolled it, the message was just two sentences long.

Catch a bus to Lombrives. More instructions to follow.

Declan read it, then—when it made no sense—he read it again. The words created more questions than answers. *Don't get distracted,* he told himself. *You need to find Winterthorn. That's your focus.* He slipped the note into his pocket and lay back on the road. His body hurt, the air was ice, and he was just too tired to stand.

Declan crawled behind a stack of shipping pallets and leaned against the rough wood. As far as he could tell, he was on the wrong side of midnight. His large coat was back at the train station, and the air was only going to get colder. As he began to shiver, he felt the strange connection to his axes stir. Declan opened his hands and the weapons slid across the ground to reach him. Their wooden handles felt warmer than they should have been, and Declan smiled grimly at the words carved into the bottom. "Burn bright," he read aloud.

The axe heads ignited like a noonday sun. Declan dropped them in surprise. Brilliant white light cast shadows on the opposite wall and Declan rushed to hide their glow under his shirt. The glowing iron had a pleasant warmth, like a ceramic dish left too long outside. He pressed both axe heads against his skin and savored their heat. *How many tricks did you hide in these axes, grandfather?*

Again, he whispered. "Burn bright." The axe light extinguished in an instant. Declan repeated the act in three different ways. Thinking the words did nothing, but if he spoke—even in the slightest whisper—he could control the light. *You should put them out,* thought the most sensible side of himself. *Someone might see you.*

That was true. To anyone peeking down the lane, he would appear as a gently glowing beacon, and somehow, Declan didn't care. His eyelids were as heavy as millstones. He leaned against the warmth of the enchanted axes, and let exhaustion take him.

The train station was even busier in the morning. Declan stood opposite the entry wearing a torn curtain as a makeshift cloak; he waited for the anxious mass to vacate the stairway leading inside. Uniformed LAMPolice were dotted throughout, watching with alert eyes. There was no way to know if they were looking for him—it was entirely possible they were simply there to maintain order—but Declan had no desire to test his luck.

He tucked a mud-stained curl under his hood. *You can't wait forever.* Doing his best impression of an elderly man, Declan hobbled across the street. He was the only person moving against the crowd, and he immediately felt the officers' gaze on him. Careful not to break character, he tried to get past them quickly, but a broad-chested man moved to block his way.

"Excuse me, uh, sir," he said.

"Yes, lad?" Declan croaked. It was a terrible attempt at disguising his voice.

"If you want to get into the station, you'll need to use the entry on Fallmark. Over the bridge. This side is for exiting only."

"I cannot." Declan had already surveyed the station's designated entrance. There were twice the amount of officers at the gate. "My hip. These stairs are pain enough. I... I can't..."

"We don't make the rules, sir." The man turned to his fresh-faced partner. "Why don't you organize a squad car to drive this gentleman around to the other side?"

Declan didn't know what to do. A crowd of new arrivals flooded down the exit and Declan sidestepped so he caught the shoulder of a man carrying a suitcase in each arm. With a cry, Declan fell backwards. As soon as he was below the officer's line of sight, he ran for the stairs.

"Sir? Come back here!" The pair of officers navigated their way through the stream of people. A third officer appeared ahead. He held a radio in one hand and a charger in the other. He pointed the small rectangular device at Declan. "Stop there!"

Declan opened his make-shift cloak and swung an axe upwards. The blunt top hit the device. It sparked like crossed wires, throwing the man backwards. Declan climbed the last steps two-at-a-time and scanned the signs fixed to the ceiling. The Western Coast Line left from platform five.

A fourth officer rounded a corner. His eyes widened as Declan hurled himself into the man, knocking him off balance. As Declan raced down the stairs, two station guards waited for him. In a flurry of movement, he pulled off the filthy curtain and tossed it over them. As the men fought free of the fabric, Declan hopped a handrail and dropped to platform four.

"Stop him!" one guard shouted. More officers swarmed around him, chargers at the ready. A chime played, and a screen above him announced an inbound arrival on platform five—the Western Coast express.

Declan stepped into the Armadillo. A dozen buzzing wires sparked off the shield of spinning iron. The LAMPolice scattered as a loud whistle sounded through the station. Declan leapt onto the tracks as a sleek red train hurtled towards him. There was a screech of brakes and he threw himself onto the platform. The train took the rubber off his boots as he rolled to safety.

"There he is!" shouted a familiar voice. Shurl hobbled down a nearby flight of stairs, three officers at her side. The automatic doors opened and a flood of refugees poured into the station, all in a hurry to beat the rush. The old security guard was caught in the crowd, waving her hands with her wrinkled face creased in frustration.

Declan rushed into the nearest compartment, then hurried to the back of the train. By the time he sat down, they were moving. He dropped into a chair—breathing deeply—as Valentian became a blurred procession of busy streets and empty storefronts. A steady vibration built as they accelerated into Clovin's open plains. *You did it.* Declan exhaled and waited for his thumping heart to settle.

He was headed to Biscay. To Horace.

To Winterthorn.

CHAPTER 12
HORACE

SOMEONE HAD LEFT the heating on too high. The dimly lit conference room was sweltering. Ophelia droned on—flicking through a variety of complex graphs—while Horace tried to maintain focus. His neck itched. He ached to remove the jacket that felt like a tailored sauna. Ophelia clicked her remote and a colorful map of the Lombrives cave system appeared on the screen.

"The yellow is where the engineers can extend. We can create fifty feet of space each day without magic, or quadruple that with magic."

"No magic," Horace said.

Ophelia pursed her lips and switched slides to a spreadsheet. It was a mess of numbers and food items. As she described the logistics of feeding thousands of refugees, Horace drifted. The infinite ocean of memories lapped at the corner of his mind's eye.

You're wasting your time here.

Horace nodded. He'd grown accustomed to the voice, and spoke to it often—though only when he was alone. Ophelia continued, but she had lost his attention.

Hiding in caves won't stop the storms. You're treating the symptoms, not the disease.

"How do I stop them?"

Ophelia stopped mid-sentence. The slide now showed the different transport programs leading to Lombrives City. "I beg your pardon, Madam?"

Horace waved Haberdeen's manicured fingernails. "No, nothing." He arranged his face in what he hoped was a smile. "Just talking to myself."

You have to find the magic.

Horace frowned. The words made little sense... Magic was not hard to find. Even now, he could see the tiny threads of nima permeating every inch of the room.

You have to find the magic, the voice repeated. *It is in the memories. Find where it starts and you can stop it. The caves are a waste of time. Find the magic.*

Ophelia stared at him, as if waiting for an answer. "Sorry," Horace said. "I was distracted. Please, repeat that."

Ophelia placed her hands on her waist. "I asked what you wanted to do when we reached capacity. Do we wait for more cavern space? Or do we pack them in like sardines?"

"How long until we max out the existing area?"

Ophelia's lips thinned, and she flicked back to an earlier slide in her presentation. "In its current state, Lombrives City should hold five hundred thousand refugees. At the rate our buses are moving, we reach that number in two weeks. More beds are being built daily, but without magic, we are going to run out of room faster than we can make it." She turned back to face him. "What do we do when that happens?"

You're wasting your time.

Horace ignored the voice. "Keep building in the caves.

When the room is exhausted, begin construction on the surface—close enough so we can move them underground if a storm is coming."

Ophelia scrawled something in her notebook. "And how do we decide who stays where?"

"First come, first served. People who have been above ground longest get priority when cavern space becomes available. Otherwise, all new arrivals start outside and wait their turn."

Ophelia closed her book. She switched the conference room lights on and took a seat beside him. Concern creased her freckled forehead. "Are you alright, Madam?"

Horace wondered what she would say if he told her the truth—an immortal king's memories were tearing him apart from the inside. He was wearing a face that wasn't his, and constantly spoke to a voice in his head. "I'm fine, Ophelia. I admit, I am tired. We all are. We can acknowledge that, but we can't let it interfere. You are doing wonderful work with Lombrives City. You are keeping the Dominion safe."

Ophelia's expression didn't change, but her eyes beamed a note brighter. "You're the mastermind, Madam. I'm just following orders."

"We are a team," Horace said. "Hundreds of thousands of people owe their lives to you. But now is not the time to be complacent." He nodded to the door. "There is still a long road ahead of us before Euryma is safe."

"Understood, Madam." Ophelia took the hint. As she stood to leave, someone knocked on the door. She crossed the room and poked her head outside. After a pause, she opened it for Cameron Matthews—head of communications—to enter. Beads of sweat glistened off his bald head as he bowed.

"Yes?" Horace asked.

"You asked us to contact you if we ever caught wind of Declan Moore." Cameron stood a little taller. "We have. He attacked one of the bus rally points in Valentian last night. This morning, he boarded a Western Coast express. He's headed south, possibly this way."

"You're sure?" Ophelia said.

"We have security footage from the station. He got past a dozen uniformed officers with a pair of axes."

Horace hid a smile. His childhood friend had always been fast on his feet. "Put a watch on all Biscay stations on the connecting line. If he gets off within fifty miles of here, I want to know."

Cameron Matthews nodded and left, and Ophelia followed. She stopped at the door. "Why would Declan Moore come here?"

Because I killed his last remaining relative. Horace shrugged. "People make odd choices when they're convinced they are doing the right thing. Moore could be of use to us, but he needs to come to grips with reality. He's been living in a fantasy world for far too long."

She shut the door and Horace leaned back. Arman Moore's death had declawed Declan. Barring an emotional crisis capable of unlocking his Sila, he was as dangerous as a rock.

Rocks can be dangerous... in the right hands. Horace did not know if that was his thought or another's. He stared at the panel ceiling and ran a smooth hand through Haberdeen's hair.

You're wasting your time.

He closed his eyes. The endless green ocean beckoned. A thousand years of memories, of secrets, of solutions. He feared it. "No. There is too much in there. I don't have enough time."

I will guide you.

"And if I can't get out?"

I won't let that happen. Trust me. This is how you stop the storms. You are chosen, Horace. Chosen to save Euryma. Trust your destiny.

Cautiously, Horace stepped into that infinite sea, and at once, it rushed to meet him. There was a fit of noise—like a thousand shattering glass panels—and then silence. Horace squeezed his eyelids closed as a parade of colored lights flashed by him. Whether real or imagined, he could feel himself being steered through lifetimes. When the glimmering hues faded, a salt breeze tickled the back of his neck. Horace stood in a cavernous sitting room. It was an exhibit of white brick walls, lavish couches, and terracotta tiles. Behind him, an arch-shaped door framed an azure sea. The Iberian coast stretched out to the north and south. The village below bustled with movement.

"Leave it on the table, Arman," cautioned a regal beauty. "You are going to drop it."

"I will not drop this."

Horace turned as Arman Moore dropped a small grey totem on the floor. It tinkled like glass, but it did not shatter. In every other memory, Horace had existed as if seeing the world through Arman's eyes. Now, it was as if he was watching a live performance. "Whose memory is this?"

The question was directed at the mysterious voice in his head. It did not answer.

"You *will* drop it." Maria of Iberia's full lips twitched. "I told you, you silly old bull."

Arman smiled in apology and wrapped a strip of cloth around his hand. "Now we know it is sturdier than the last one." He picked up the totem and quickly placed it on a marble table, then pulled the fabric away as it started to smoke. The cylinder appeared unharmed. "It is searing hot. This vessel struggles to contain the power."

Maria held her hand close to the object. "What is stronger than wolframite?"

"Perhaps we need more." Arman scratched his chestnut beard. "Or we are looking at it the wrong way."

Horace leaned over Maria's shoulder. The 'vessel' was a five-inch cylinder covered in intricate carvings. Up close, it appeared as polished stone with a metallic sheen. Horace could feel the heat radiating off it from three feet away.

"What do you mean?" Maria asked.

"Sila lives in me. Luck lives in you. What if this creation of ours is not suited to lifeless substances?" Arman's gaze never strayed from the totem. "We may need to reconsider a living vessel."

Maria's expression soured. "This vessel burns like hot coals. Our previous vessel exploded, taking part of a wall with it." She brushed a dark curl over her shoulder. "I am not sure it is wise to inflict such ailments on a living creature. Not yet."

"I agree," Arman said. "There is more we must learn." He used the cloth to drop the cylinder in a clay pot of gleaming gold liquid. It hissed and bubbled upon contact. "But time is not our ally. Morkurik will not wait for us to solve this riddle."

Maria picked up a heavy set of tongs. She fished the totem from the water and returned it to the table. Steam still swirled off its surface. She leaned in, and Horace worried the ornate pattern would brand her nose. "Our pattern is uneven," she announced. "Those on the bottom are deeper than the top."

Arman raised an eyebrow. "You believe that would make a difference?"

"Equilibrium. Symmetry. These things are important to Lucks." She shrugged. "Perhaps it is the same here."

"Very well. I will get the tools."

Arman left the room. As he did, it darkened. Horace considered following him to see if it would keep the scene alive, but something told him that this wasn't Arman's memory—or the one he was looking for.

Darkness enveloped him. Horace recalled a school excursion to an iron mine. Deep below the ground, their tour guide had instructed them to turn their flashlights off. The darkness beneath the earth was absolute. This place—between the memories—was just as black. It pressed against him, corporeal in its entirety.

As the moments dragged on, his pulse quickened. Horace had never feared the dark, but this was something else. In the blink of an eye, he stood in a sparse forest of stunted trees and yellow grass, once again watching the memories from the outside. Arman and Maria looked... different. Arman's beard was long and wiry. Maria's lips were thin.

They crouched either side of a curious symbol dug into the clay. The symbols—intricate, curved swirls—were similar to those carved into the totem from the previous memory, only much larger. A shovel stood upright in the dirt a few feet away. A scaled ball sat in the center of the pattern.

"Are you ready?" Maria asked.

Arman sighed. "One is never ready to be forced into a state of despair... but we are out of time. Go ahead." Kneeling, he placed a hand on the leathery ball. As he did, a curious head poked up and an armadillo unrolled. "I am sorry," Arman murmured.

He returned to the marking's edge, his shoulders hunched—as if the world were strapped to his back.

"Is it enough?" Maria asked.

Arman held out an open palm. A tiny green sphere—like a miniature star cut from emerald—rotated in his hand. "It is," he replied in a pained voice.

Maria pressed her hands together—squeezing and rotating as if forming a ball of dough—until she'd created a globule of golden light. While Arman's magic was marble-smooth, hers was a misshapen thing. As one, they knelt to the ground and released their power—green and golden—into the intricate channels.

Horace leaned forward. The emerald light rolled over the shallow trenches, leaving a trail behind it that glittered like stars. In contrast, the golden lump moved like a wisp of colored fog. It streamed through the channel, splitting into two, four, eight different parts.

In moments, contrasting light filled the pattern. The power surged through the maze, then doubled back on itself. It flowed towards the armadillo, who absorbed it like a sponge. The small creature curled into a tight ball and its brown scales glowed. It turned white, then green, then gold, then faded.

Neither Arman nor Maria spoke. A bell tower rang eleven distant chimes. A gust of wind rattled dry leaves from an alder tree. The silence persisted. Slowly, the armadillo uncurled.

"It survived," Maria whispered.

Arman dropped to his knees. Horace stood a step behind him. The armadillo's armor gleamed golden in the sunlight. It lowered its snout to the dirt.

"You amazing creature. You survived." Arman dug a handful of pellets from a leather pouch tied to his waist. The armadillo's tapered nose twitched. It hopped over the empty channels towards him. "You survived." He shook his head, as if he couldn't believe his own words. The armadillo feasted from his palm with a small snuffling sound. Arman smiled at Maria. "Send for the volunteers," he said. "We need to see if it works."

Maria hiked up her skirts and sprinted away. Arman stayed on his knees, feeding the golden-shelled creature, and adding more food to his hand whenever it ran short. Abruptly, Arman stopped, and stepped into the middle of the intricate trench system. "No," he whispered. "Johan. Come see this."

Horace did not know who Johan was, but it seemed he had solved the mystery of whose memories he inhabited. He jumped over the channels to join Arman at the center. Arman leaned over the spot where the armadillo had stood. Horace circled him to see what he was looking at. When he did, he froze in place.

"Could it really be that simple?" Arman murmured

There. The voice made Horace jump. It reverberated all around him, as if spoken from every angle. *That is the source of your woes.*

A small pool—six inches wide—had formed in a crater of dry earth. The pool was not water, nor was it green or gold. It was a swirling miasma of rich orange. The color of molten stone. The color of fiery sunsets. The color of Remnant Magic.

It was night when Horace opened his eyes. The lights were off, leaving the neon glow of the city to illuminate the conference room. He rose on shaking legs and stood at the window. Far below, between the reds and greens of the stoplights, a constant procession of buses moved Fatesmiths to every corner of the Dominion with one goal. Protect Euryma.

Now you can.

Not for the first time, Horace questioned the nature of the voice in his head. Was it Arman Moore, reaching through the veil to redeem himself? Was it a mix of Horace's righteous ambition and the old man's memories? Was it madness?

"Does it matter?" Horace muttered. The voice had steered him in the right direction. He closed his eyes and pictured the glowing orange pool. The notion that magic could be stored was absurd, and somehow true. "The storms have a source."

If you find it, you can stop them.

Horace considered the city. Low clouds rolled over the southern suburbs, reflecting the amber glow of the streetlights to create an effect resembling the burning horizon he'd seen at Sabriva. That storm had built over the hills like a wave. Horace imagined a similar tsunami surging towards Biscay. The thought turned his blood to ice.

If you cannot find the origin of the storms, you cannot stop them. Find the magic.

"Origin of the storms?" Realization became excitement. After months of plugging a leaky ship, he had stumbled onto a way to drain the ocean. "Origin of magic..." Horace rushed to the phone on the conference room desk. He dialed the room code. A monotonous beep repeated twice, then cut off.

"Madam?" Ophelia sounded groggy. "Are you okay? It's two in the—"

"Or—" Horace almost forgot to mask his voice. He started again in Haberdeen's sultry tones. "Oregin o Magi. Have we found it yet?"

"I... I don't know. I haven't asked. Is everything—"

"Everything is fine, Ophelia." Horace relaxed his grip on the receiver. "I need you to find out where that book is. Bring me an update in ten minutes. I'm in the ninth floor conference room." He hung up the phone and fell into his chair, but he couldn't sit still. Nervous energy raced through him, and by the time Ophelia arrived, he was pacing the room.

"What can you tell me?" he asked as she entered.

A yellow note stuck on Ophelia's fingers. She held it out to him. "As far as the archivists can tell, this is the location of the only registered copy left in the Dominion."

Horace took the note and read it aloud. "King's College." He smiled at the irony. "Of course it is. Who would have suspected the bumbling fools might prove Euryma's saving grace? Perhaps it is time we accept the Directive's invitation to meet."

"I would rather eat a toad," Ophelia said.

"That book is the key to stopping the storms," Horace said. "And I would eat a thousand toads to keep Euryma safe. Am I clear?"

Ophelia's scowl melted into a sigh. "I will contact Mary-Lou Niven in the morning. I suppose it is about time they did something useful." She smiled, and then her face slipped. As if remembering something, she dug a second sticky-note from her pockets. "Cameron Matthews sends word from the Western Coast Express. It came through this afternoon, but I didn't want to... bother you."

Horace raised an eyebrow. "Declan?"

Ophelia nodded. "He got into an argument with a ticket inspector. He refused to leave the train. He claims he has sick relatives in Biscay. He should be here tomorrow."

A Warlock on my doorstep. What are the odds? Horace made no effort to hide his smile. If magic was a product of Sila and Luck, Declan could be half the equation for solving the storms. *Maybe it is destiny.* "Then we had best prepare a warm welcome. Gather a team. We have a guest on the way."

CHAPTER 13

DECLAN

THE MAN in the blue jacket looked perfectly forgettable—except that Declan had seen him five times since leaving Biscay West Station. He was plain-faced, of average height, with short brown hair, and wore a confused expression. Declan had doubled back, climbed a fire escape, and found refuge in a cardboard box. From his vantage above, Declan watched three others join the man. They held a whispered conference. The man pointed at the walkway and they fanned out.

Good riddance. Declan guessed they were Fatesmiths. He unfolded a map taken from a tourist stand and traced a path to Ninety-One Bay Street. The blackcoats made no secret of their location—it was on the busiest road of Biscay's central business district. Finding them had been easy. The real challenge would be getting inside. Already, dozens of Fatesmiths wandered the city. Horace would be well protected. It didn't matter. If he needed to cut his way in with his axes, so be it. Winterthorn had to be destroyed.

Declan tucked the map away as something warm pressed against the back of his neck.

"No quick moves, champ," said a woman in black. "These things tickle."

The 'thing' was a charcoal grey version of the LAMPolices' 'chargers'. Declan froze. "I haven't done anything wrong."

"Nobody said you did. Come down. We'll sort this out on the ground." The blackcoat stepped backwards. "You first. Easy now."

With a charger on his back and no clear escape, Declan climbed out of the box and started down the ladder. Five more Fatesmiths materialized from the street to encircle him. He recognized one as the woman who led the charge at Sabriva. She had auburn hair, freckled cheeks, and olive-green eyes. "Declan Moore?"

"Why do you want to know?" Declan's fingers itched for his axes.

"My name is Ophelia Damrodel. Madam Haberdeen welcomes you to Biscay and invites you to meet in her office." The turn of the woman's lips made her position on the matter obvious. "We were sent to escort you to headquarters."

Declan tried to hide his surprise. "An invitation implies that I have a choice." He raised his eyebrows. "Do I?"

Ophelia's smile could have extinguished flames. "You must do what you think is right."

The four other blackcoats unclipped chargers from their belts. A high-pitched keen filled the air as they activated the devices. Declan wondered how much damage his axes could do before one of the chargers zapped him. Then he recognized the moment as a golden opportunity. He gestured to Ophelia. "Lead the way."

They accumulated an entourage on their walk, reaching ninety-one Bay Street with an honor guard of twenty-two

Fatesmiths. Declan stared up at the surrounding skyscrapers. The Fatesmiths' headquarters appeared identical to every other forgettable building in downtown Biscay. The lobby—beige walls and grey carpet—was just as sterile.

When they reached the elevator, Ophelia waved the procession away. The door chimed, and they entered. Neither spoke as they ascended, and the silence continued until the lift opened on the top floor. Declan stepped into a hallway, but Ophelia remained inside.

"Madam Haberdeen waits for you in the Green Room."

She pressed a button and the chrome doors closed. Declan considered his reflection. It was the first time he had seen himself in weeks. He looked awful. Matted long curls, gaunt eyes, and a shadow of stubble shaded his cheeks. The elevator stopped and the doors slid open.

A figure appeared in the reflection; a mirage in a maroon cloak. "Ah, you're here."

Declan turned as the illusion of Haberdeen shimmered away. Horace Marley nodded to an open door. "Come in, Declan. We need to talk."

The Green Room's walls were pastel moss, illuminated by a chandelier of acrylic cubes. Horace motioned Declan to a leather seat as he sat on the other side of a lacquered desk covered in neat piles of paper. His long hair was tied back, his skin was pale, dark bags hung under his eyes. "Thank you for accepting the invitation," he said at last.

"Invitation?" Declan laughed without amusement. "Let's not play games. Why have you called me here?"

"I know you think I'm the enemy. You probably think I'm a monster, but let me be clear—ever since these memories fell into my head—my goal has always been to save Euryma from Remnant Magic." Horace slid a manilla folder across the table. "And with your help, it might be possible.

"Why would I help you?" Declan took the folder, but did not open it. His first instinct was to blame Horace for his grandfather's death. He resisted the urge. Talk of Arman Moore was a powder keg that would likely blow any chance of negotiation skyward. "I know what you did with the holdhouses. You ordered thousands of witches and wizards to be melted down."

Horace leaned back in his chair, then shrugged. "I lost my temper."

"Lost... your temper?" The words left Declan in a daze. He shook his head. "You murdered innocent people. Thousands of them. You know that's wrong, don't you?"

His childhood friend dismissed the question with a wave of his hand. "Look at those documents. It will all make sense."

Declan put the folder back on the desk. "What happened to you?"

For a moment, he worried Horace might explode. He closed his eyes, and his knuckles paled in clenched fists. "You," he said. "You happened, Declan. You called me out of my home and into a Fatesmith ambush. You defierised me in the presence of Haberdeen, and when she struck out at me with her white dagger, I defended myself. She caught Winterthorn in her side, then ran away. I lay in the snow trying to make sense of the new memories jammed into my brain." He opened his eyes and his gaze held Declan like a vise. "I'm not the bad guy," Horace said. "I tried to do it right. I tried to stick to Haberdeen's plan. Fierise people, put them aside, wait for the storms to die down."

"You were abducting witches and wizards from their homes."

"A small price to pay for the safety of a million LAMPs," Horace said. "And then your pals—the Directive—showed up. They ruined everything. All those months of putting people in safe stasis undone. I couldn't let it happen again."

"You didn't have to kill them."

"I did," Horace said. "Look what happened when I allowed the High Mage to go free. Euryma's leader should have protected his people. Instead, he wasted time and resources working out how to target Fatesmiths. I took care of it. Then your idiot friends tried to use Sabriva Tower as a weapon against me." Horace's jaw tensed. "Every step I take to protect the Dominion gets undone by witches and wizards who can't imagine a world where they aren't above LAMPs."

"And that justifies murder?" Declan said. "You. Killed. Thousands."

Horace slapped his palm on the wood. His eyes flashed purple. "Every melted witch and wizard in the northern reaches owes their fate to you. Your choices brought me here, and their sacrifice will be for nothing if you don't pick up that folder and read."

"I didn't—"

"READ!" Horace slammed both fists against the desk. Declan flinched in shock. He opened the folder.

There were only three pages, all written in Horace's perfect handwriting. They were journal entries about a series of magical experiments. Declan's heartbeat accelerated as the words turned his world upside down. His hands trembled when he put the last page down.

"Do you understand now?" Horace asked. "Magic isn't natural. It's an artificial combination of Sila and Luck. Your grandfather tampered with powers beyond his understanding and now the Dominion is paying the price." He leaned forward, a hateful glint in his eyes. "Remnant Magic is Arman Moore's creation. I was right to kill the old fool."

Declan leapt to his feet. Two spiraling tentacles of purple energy erupted from the floor beneath him. Before he could reach his axes, they wrapped around his arms and chest and dragged him back to the chair.

"You're not going anywhere," Horace said. "As Arman Moore's final descendent, his burdens fall to you to fix. You are going to use your Sila to end Remnant Magic."

The coils of Ire Tides were warm. Not hot, but rigid as steel. No matter how he tried, Declan could not loosen them. Waves of anger pulsed through him. Horace had killed his grandfather and now had the nerve to insult his memory. *Remember why you're here.* Declan pictured Ava's limp body, hunched over a pallid blade. He took a deep breath, his heart pummelling the inside of his chest. "Fine. I'll help you stop Remnant Magic, but you need to do something for me first."

Horace raised an eyebrow.

"Destroy Winterthorn."

There was an extended pause as Horace reached into his cloak. Gently, he placed the white dagger on the table between them. Ornate carvings covered every inch of the weapon. "Why?"

Declan wondered if Horace's mastery of Ire Tides allowed him to see through lies. He thought back to the Void, and the creature that controlled it. "Something evil seeks to wield it. I want to make sure that can't happen."

Horace ran a finger over the dagger's hilt. "You don't think I can keep Winterthorn safe?"

"I think it's safer beyond their reach. Destroy the dagger and I'll help. That's the deal."

Again, the silence returned. Horace tilted his head, as if listening to somebody else, but it was only them in the room. Finally, he slid Winterthorn out of sight. "You're not in a position to make demands," he said. "These storms are the legacy of your blood. Your mess. So you're going to help me, whether you want to or not." He stood and turned to the window. The buildings outside blocked the afternoon sun. "You can use Sila, at least you can in the right conditions. Now where's your girlfriend? The Luck? I'm going to need you both."

Declan's heart stopped. A sickening sense of guilt rose inside him. He had seen Horace kill Ava repeatedly in the Void. Now, he wondered if his actions to destroy Winterthorn might have set them on a collision course afterall. "She's dead," he said in a rush.

Horace turned from the window. He leaned over his desk and stared into Declan's eyes. "No. She's not. You're protecting her."

An animal rage threatened to take control. It was closer to panic than despair, and Declan had to fight to maintain his composure. "I'm not going to help you. You can't stop the storms without my Sila, and if you force me to use it, I'll overpower you."

"You would let Euryma fall?"

"And you aren't doing the same? For all your talk, you won't trade my help for Winterthorn. You're a hypocrite, Horace."

In a flash of purple light, the lacquered desk exploded. Sheets of paper filled the room, wafting from side to side as they fell to the floor. A slithering violet coil wrapped itself around Declan's neck and tightened. "Everything I do is for Euryma!" Horace hissed. "You couldn't do what I've had to. You can't make the hard choice. You let your parents die, you let your grandfather die. When push comes to shove, you always pick yourself!"

"You don't know me," Declan wheezed.

"I've lived the memories," Horace said. "I was there when Angus and Miranda Moore were turned into a puddle. I was there when Arman begged you to kill him." He shook his head in disgust. "You have a chance to do something selfless, and again, you choose yourself."

Declan was suffocating. The green walls were fading; his vision shrank until only Horace loomed in the haze.

"I may be a murderer, but I am no hypocrite. When all of this is over, and the world can start again... tell me the ends don't justify the means."

As darkness took him, Declan whispered two words. "Burn bright."

Air rushed into his lungs as the room ignited in white light. Horace stepped back in alarm as Declan staggered upright. Horace thrust out an open palm as Declan caught his weapons. A bar of crackling energy lashed out of him. Declan caught it on the axe head. The force of it pushed him backwards, but he held firm.

"You're testing my patience," Horace said. The Green Room looked as if it had played host to a small tornado. Declan adjusted his stance as they stood face to face.

"You really believe you're doing the right thing?"

"I do."

"Then give me the dagger."

Purple light sparked around Horace's pupils. "I can't."

"Ace."

"No, Dex. You don't get to lecture me on how things are done." He cocked his head as if listening again, then nodded —resolute. "Winterthorn still has a part to play. I will not surrender it."

Declan gripped his axes. "I wasn't asking." He tried to push forward. Violet electricity filled his vision and he was on his back before the sound reached his ears. A thunderclap reverberated in his skull as he sat up. Horace's Ire Tides had thrown him clean through a closed door. The light of the axe heads winked out.

"I offer you an olive branch, and this is your answer?" Horace turned his hand and a fizzling purple sphere crackled in his palm. "I don't need you Declan, I just need your Sila. I have a thousand years of knowledge of its nature, and I will pull it from your dead body if it means saving my people."

"Your… people?" Declan wiped his mouth—he could taste blood.

A mad glint sparkled in Horace's eyes. "I was chosen to save Euryma. It is my destiny. I will not fail."

He raised the glowing orb. Declan waited until the last moment, then leapt aside. With a crash, the Green Room exploded in a haze of shattered plasterboard. Declan threw an axe to the other side of the room and ran in the opposite direction. The distraction seemed enough as an angry wave of Ire Tides obliterated the far wall.

"WHERE ARE YOU?" Horace roared.

Declan called the axe back. It thrummed into his right hand as he reached the stairwell. Two Fatesmiths turned in surprise. He lashed out before they could call for help. One toppled down the stairs, the other caught the blunt edge of an axe head on his chest and collapsed against the wall. Declan jumped both bodies as he hurried down the stairs. His mind was a pinwheel in a hurricane, and by the time he exited through a back-alley fire exit, he was hyperventilating.

He fell into a stack of broken crates and crawled out of sight. *Grandfather created the storms. Horace is going to kill Ava trying to stop them. Magic is Sila and Luck. You failed. Horace still has the knife.* His thoughts were like mice in a bucket—each one clambering to reach the top before another pulled it underneath. Declan pressed his palms against his eyes and concentrated on his breathing. When his aching body finally relaxed, he felt like he'd run a marathon.

An icy drizzle swept overhead. Bulbous drops of water ran down the wooden crates, soaking his clothes. Shivering and miserable, Declan crawled out to find a half-dozen blackcoats searching the other end of the alley. He retreated into the mess of broken ply and waited. He held his axes at the ready, but the Fatesmiths never came.

As night fell, the drone of the city dulled to a serenade of distant sirens. Declan sat cross-legged on the asphalt and wondered what he would do next. Horace would not give up Winterthorn willingly, and Declan was not stupid enough to try the same thing twice. A raven's call in the night awoke a recent memory. Declan dug a blue strip of paper from his pocket and considered the mysterious message. *Catch a bus to Lombrives. More instructions to follow.*

CHAPTER 14
DECLAN

THE JOURNEY to Lombrives City was not pleasant. Declan would compare the bus to a can of sardines, though he was certain the fish would smell better. Exhausted refugees pressed against every inch of the vehicle for the eighteen-hour drive from Biscay. The sun rose over empty plains of charcoal. Remnant Magic's legacy was a sobering sight. It created an air of misery on the bus.

It was past noon when they arrived at the cave city's staging ground on the Ariege River. Here, blades of grass poked through the burned earth. Along the river, hundreds of people worked on modular constructions. Some assembled pre-cut pine frames, others stapled plastic sheets to the wood, while children sat atop the almost-finished homes, stuffing them with fluffy red insulation. The row of simple houses stretched into the small, rocky hills.

"This way," called a stout Fatesmith. Her black and white hair made Declan think of a skunk. He slung a stolen backpack over his shoulders and followed the crowd towards a sprawling blue tent. A line zig-zagged from the double-door entrance along rows of pickets and bunting. Declan's group joined the back of the line.

"The registration wait is about two hours," the skunk woman said. "Have identifying documents ready to claim a house. No papers, no residence." She left before they could ask questions.

Declan felt stupid. He had come here because of a cryptic note dropped by a stranger's bird. He had no documents, only two axes in a stolen backpack, and a handful of coins. *What are you doing here?*

Beyond the tent, most people followed a sloping path leading away from the river. Declan guessed that was the way down to the main cave. He reread the blue slip of paper, now creased from being folded and unfolded so many times. *More instructions to follow*. But there was nobody there to meet him, no instructions to be given. He needed to get into the cave itself.

Thick cords looped through pegs held the registration tent upright. Declan turned to the middle-aged couple behind him. "Uh, I need to use a bathroom. Can you save my spot in the line?"

The pair appeared beyond exhaustion. The man nodded, but said nothing.

Declan thanked them as he ducked underneath the bunting and walked around the back side of the tent. With eyes alert, he took an axe from his backpack and frayed as many ropes as he could. He heard footsteps and pretended to tie his shoelaces. When eight of them were partially severed, he rejoined the line.

As they shuffled forward, an extended groan sounded, and the ropes snapped.

Enormous sheets of blue canvas rippled downward. Shouts of surprise rang through the mass of people. Most retreated from the collapse. The scene dissolved into chaos, while a half-dozen Fatesmiths rushed forward to help. As they did, Declan maneuvered through the stunned crowd and ran down the path. A printed sign confirmed his suspicions. Lombrives City.

Declan hurried down a flight of wooden stairs. There was a shuffle of movement and someone in black had his wrist twisted against his spin. "A valiant effort," whispered a grim voice in his ear. "Come. This way. We've been waiting."

They didn't break stride. Declan wondered how the Fatesmiths had caught him so fast. He could feel the pull of his axes, but they were stuck in his bag with his bent arm holding them in place. "Who are you?"

The man did not respond. Declan considered fighting free, but the Fatesmith directed him towards the caves, which is exactly where he wanted to go.

The stairs joined a metal walkway leading to a cavernous maw surrounded by greenery. More pathways branched off into the cave's entrance. A steady hum echoed from the opening—a combination of a thousand conversations, all amplified by limestone walls. Lombrives City was a mess of movement, and as they stepped inside, Declan marveled at what the Fatesmiths had constructed.

It looked like a busy street, except the buildings were carved into the stone. Stalactites protruded from anywhere too tight to build into. Wooden walkways crisscrossed between buildings. Something like a ski-lift—packed with people—carried travelers overhead in an endless procession. There must have been three hundred houses in the entry cavern alone, and more stretched into the distant depths.

Further down, groups of Fatesmiths dragged carts of

crushed rock along raised metal tracks. More blackcoats shoveled the gravel over the rough sections of cave floor, creating level ground. The entire thing was a masterstroke in engineering with no hint of magic in sight.

Strong hands steered Declan into a narrow doorway to their left. A sign above it read 'sewage channel', and putrid air assaulted his nostrils. He fought the urge to gag as the odor grew stronger. The tunnel was barely tall enough to walk upright, and his shoulders brushed against damp walls. The man behind said nothing, seemingly unbothered by the stink that made Declan's eyes water. A steady roar filled the darkness, which reached a crescendo as they entered a massive cavern illuminated by red lights. The smell here was overwhelming. A towering underground waterfall plunged into midnight-black depths. Everywhere, signs announced the presence of raw sewerage. Declan breathed into his collar.

The man walked him to a manual elevator. He wrenched on the gate, then pushed. "Down we go," the voice said.

"What?" Declan tried to turn, but the blackcoat held him tight. "I'm not going down there. It stinks."

"It'll pass."

Declan dug his feet into the ground. "You're kidding?"

"It's this, or I'll take you back up the hill to the iron-hands you were so desperate to sneak past."

"What?" Again, Declan tried—and failed—to look over his shoulder. "You're... not a Fatesmith?"

The man barked a bitter laugh. "I'd rather die. Now get in."

With more questions than answers, Declan stepped onto the elevator. The man pulled a lever, and they descended. It took all of Declan's concentration not to empty his stomach over the rail. Just as he thought he could hold it no longer, they dropped below the ledge and the sickening scent vanished—replaced in an instant by crisp, clean air.

"I told you it would pass," the man said.

Declan savored the purity of each breath. "How?" he whispered.

"Magic. It keeps prying eyes away."

Declan agreed. The illusion would have worked on him. The roar of the water swallowed the creaks of the elevator falling alongside them. "Where are you taking me?"

The man ignored him. When Declan tried to peer over the edge, the man gripped his shoulder. "Stop leaning about. These lifts aren't safety rated." His grim tone implied the warning was no exaggeration, and Declan froze in place.

The elevator touched down with a clatter in a smaller cavern whose floor was slick from the waterfall's spray. They entered another dark passage that led to a blank rock face.

"Lobsters' claws," the man announced from behind. "It's a dead end."

Declan blinked. "What?"

Again, the man ignored him.

"What do you mean?" Declan growled. "You led us here. How can you—"

On the other side of the wall, something turned. There was a click, and a sharp scrape, then the wall opened and light flooded into the tunnel.

Declan blinked into the brightness. They stood on the edge of a great hexagonal hall with arch-shaped doorways on every wall. Thirty-feet above them, a jagged quartz crystal protruded from the roof. Illuminated from within, the quartz cast a soft light over the surrounds. Hundreds of people bustled about the hall. Some carried books, others wooden staffs and shields inlaid with iron. Nobody seemed older than twenty-five.

"Where are—" Declan turned and froze. His mind emptied. Recognition became panic. He staggered away from the man to collide with a girl carrying a handful of wooden weapons.

"Hey!" she snapped. "Watch where you're going."

Declan didn't speak. He stared at the man—at the ghost. "I... You're dead... I killed you."

"You didn't kill me," John said. "Just the monster wearing my face." He stepped past him to help pick up some wooden swords.

"But..."

John helped the girl to her feet. "If Master Johannasberg asks why you're late, tell him I held you back."

"Yes, sir." The girl spared a glare for Declan, then rushed from the hall. John turned to face him. "I expect you have many questions. Follow me."

"Where?"

"To find the woman who has the answers."

A shadow swooped from the ceiling. A raven swept over their heads and circled the cavern before landing on the shoulder of a dark-haired woman.

John pursed his lips. "Or maybe she'll find us."

They crossed the hall, and the woman beamed at him and held out her hand. "Welcome, Declan Moore. We are thrilled to have you here."

Declan drew a blank. She spoke to him as if he were an old friend. "Um... thank you. Hi." He took her palm, which was cold, but soft. "It's... it's nice to be here."

"My name is Helen Harcross, though I expect you know

me as the Warmistress." She tilted her head to the midnight-black bird perched on her shoulder. "And this is Nox."

The raven cawed in response.

"Hi," Declan repeated. Contrary to her assumptions, he had no idea who the woman was. Thankfully, her attention swung to John.

"Any trouble surface-side?"

"Only the trouble this one started." John nodded to Declan. "He created havoc at the administration tent. Nobody even noticed us slip by."

"Sparkling." Harcross smiled. "I'll take things from here. Thank you, John. You may resume duties."

John bowed and left; the mysterious Warmistress beckoned Declan to follow. They weaved through a series of well-lit tunnels and soon arrived at a tiny cavern whose floor had been levelled and polished. Glowing glass jars illuminated an eclectic collection of old furniture.

Harcross settled behind an antique desk and Nox hopped onto a brass perch. She looked... familiar. There were creases at the edges of her eyes, but her skin was smooth. Depending on her lifestyle, she could have been thirty or sixty. Declan didn't ask which. She gestured to a wooden chair opposite. "Have a seat, Declan." Her voice was pleasant, almost musical, her eyes were ocean blue. "Tell me, what news do you have from my daughter?"

Declan's mind and mouth emptied of words. After an extended silence, he shrugged. "I'm... sorry?"

"My daughter."

A thin film of water ran along the cave walls, producing a steady drip. The small space amplified the noise, which now filled the silence. Declan swallowed. "I... I'm not sure I know who that is?"

Harcross interlaced her fingers as she leaned forward. "Samantha Winter. Her looptap is intact, but she has not answered or received messages in days. I can only assume —since you're here on our doorstep—that she sent you with important information."

"Mrs. Winter?" The revelation floored Declan. But now she had said it—dark hair, blue eyes—the resemblance was obvious. Declan thought back to when they had last spoken. "I... don't know," he said. "She was going to meet with the Grand Steward of Vedmark... I left shortly after."

Harcross's smile faded. "Then what are you doing here? How did you know to find us?"

"You invited me." Declan unfolded the paper slip from his pocket and spread it open on the table. "That was you, in Valentian, wasn't it? You gave me this."

Nox the raven cawed its approval.

The Warmistress considered the note. A sardonic smile stretched on her lips as she leaned back, shaking her head. "I was there on business when I saw you save a wizard. I helped you escape the LAMPolice at Valentian Station so that you could join us." Her smile faded. "But you never came, and we moved on to other things."

Declan pinched the bridge of his nose. *This is a waste of time.* "What is going on? Where are we?"

Helen Harcross studied him. "This is Sabart." She raised a hand as Declan's mouth opened. "Sabart is one of six colleges. Euryma's Mag-Ed system prepared students for the day-to-day life of Euryma's past. We now prepare witches and wizards for Euryma's future."

"Future?"

"For war." Harcross's face darkened. "My daughter knew Vedmark was coming, and she refused to wait and watch. This is the sum total of her efforts to prepare

Euryma to defend itself. This is the army that will stand against the Knights of Despair."

Declan didn't know what to say. Of everything he had expected to find in Lombrives, a secret wizard army was not one of them. "So... you're not here to help me?"

"Help you?" Harcross shook her head. "I thought you were here carrying a message from Samantha. I thought you came to help *me*. To help us." Harcross sat back in her chair. "We have been training every college-aged witch and wizard displaced by the Fatesmiths' attack on magic." Her forehead creased. "This is the home of the Sabartians. The Scholars of War. And you've just stumbled upon us like a drunkard in the streets. Unbelievable."

———

Warmistress Harcross walked him to a circular stone hallway. "You will find lunch down that way," she said. "Get yourself a meal. We have wrangled some of the Dominion's finest chefs to our cause, and we supply them well. I'll find someone to organize a shower and a change of clothes." She started in the other direction.

"You're not coming with me?" Declan's mind was still reeling.

Harcross shook her head. "Your arrival is most unexpected. I have matters to attend to before we go topside." She waved him towards the door. "Eat some food, get cleaned up. You look..."

"Terrible?"

"Well travelled." Harcross finished. "I'll see you soon." She left in a chorus of clicking boots, and Declan followed his nose down the passage.

The Mess Hall was a sight to behold. Rows of long

wooden tables covered a gleaming stone floor streaked with copper veins. But the cavern itself was nothing compared to the smells. Aromas layered like slices of cake. Caramel, butter, meat. It wafted around him like a warm embrace. It had been weeks since he'd eaten a proper meal. His stomach quaked with longing.

At one end, a food-laden countertop serviced two lines of people that ran along the wall's edge to a bench laden with ceramic plates, behind which a blackboard listed the lunch menu. Today's offer was slow-cooked apple walnut pork with smoked root vegetables, served with buttered sourdough.

Declan took a plate, napkin, and silverware, then joined the line. At the countertop, he heaped an enormous mound of everything onto his plate, and searched the cavernous hall for somewhere to sit. John sat halfway down an otherwise empty table.

Declan hurried to join him. "Mind if I sit here?"

"Nobody else is."

"Thanks." Declan tried a mouthful of pork and shook his head. "Wow," he said around his food. "Wow. Wow. Wow." The meat—a mix of smoky sweetness—dissolved in his mouth. He took another forkful, and another, and another.

"A little hungry, are we?" John asked.

"Ihavenoteatenindays." The words were a muffled mess. Declan swallowed. "Sorry. I haven't eaten in days."

John raised an eyebrow. "Makes sense."

Something in his voice didn't sit right. There was a sharpness that Declan did not associate with the John he remembered. *That wasn't John*, he reminded himself. But this man reminded him of Michael. The dark scowl, the burdened eyes, the anger. "Is everything okay?" he asked.

John scraped his plate with a half-buttered roll. "Just dandy." He tossed the bread into his mouth and stood. "See you around." He swept down the aisle before Declan could say a word.

"It would appear our fearless general is in a mood once again," said a voice to his left. Declan turned to the source of the statement. A gangly blond boy with a hawkish nose watched John leave.

"Is he always like that?"

"Only on days ending in 'y'," the boy said. He smiled and extended a bandage-wrapped hand. "Austin Samford"

Declan eyed the bandages. "Are you sure you want me to shake that?"

Austin inspected his hand. "Should be fine. You don't have to do clean-up duty if you're injured."

"Are you?"

"Well, I've got a bandage on."

Declan's lips curved upward as he shook Austin's hand. "I'm Declan Moore."

Austin's hand went slack. "You are? For real?"

"Yes..." The reaction left Declan confused. "You know me?"

Austin opened his mouth, but stiffened as a hand touched Declan's shoulder. A woman with crimson hair smiled at him. "How is your lunch?"

"Uh, delicious." Declan looked back at Austin. "I was just—"

"Warmistress Harcross asked me to show you to the showers," the woman interrupted. "She also wanted me to give you this." She dropped a cloth bag beside his plate. The intensity of her gaze made Declan think of a cat. Her hazel eyes settled on Austin. "Shouldn't you be on clean up, Samford?"

"Not with this nasty bruise." Austin raised his bandage, and the woman unraveled it with a flick of her wrist. His hand was devoid of injury.

"Your pretend wounds only work so many times. Go, or I'll have you on breakfast duty for the month."

Austin blushed. "Yes, Sephina." He stood to leave.

"See you later," Declan said. Austin waved as he walked, his shoulders slumped.

Sephina filled the boy's empty seat. "What did he say to you?"

"Nothing." Declan watched Austin collect used silverware. "He... knew me." He glanced back at her. "Do you know me?"

Sephina's face was unreadable. "The Warmistress will be ready soon." She nodded to his plate. "Finish your meal, then I'll show you to the bathrooms. We don't want to keep her waiting."

THE KEEPER OF THE CRYSTAL BLADE

CHAPTER 15
DECLAN

ONE HOT SHOWER LATER, Declan felt better than he had in weeks. He rushed to dress into jeans and a clean shirt before meeting Warmistress Harcross outside the Mess Hall.

A 'college tour' swallowed the afternoon. Sabart was an isolated subsection of the Lombrives system, a half-mile below the main cave. Three enormous caverns extended off Quartz Assembly, the central space named after the spectacular crystal chandelier that illuminated it. Each space used for one of three disciplines. Combat, magic and strategy. After touring the caves, Harcross showed Declan to an elevator—this one with no waterfall in sight—and a diesel-powered winch raised them to the surface.

"We have almost five thousand students." Harcross led him through a dim tunnel. "All living within Lombrives City under the guise of LAMPs."

"How do all these people sneak underground on creaky old elevators without the Fatesmiths noticing?"

"Not all the elevators are creaky." Harcross laughed. "We have over fifty entry points, and those who use them have relevant excuses to be near their entry. There is a labyrinth of tunnels branching off Lombrives City. Most of the population believes wandering into them is a death warrant. We don't get many poking around—but for those that do, we provide certain... incentives to turn back."

Declan recalled the vicious stench of the waterfall. "Like keeping your sense of smell?"

"Exactly." Harcross stopped at a well-lit exit. She scanned the adjoining walkway before gesturing him forward.

"How much do you know?" Declan asked.

"About what?"

"About everything." He kept his voice down as the walkway melded into a larger one. "Vedmark. Horace. Me."

Harcross raised a finger. "Whatever Samantha knows, I know," she whispered. "Enough talk. Loose lips are dangerous in top side, and even more deadly in the Cathedral."

"Where?"

"You'll see."

They joined a throng of people headed up to a cement platform. The elevated square intersected an underground chair lift running thirty feet above ground level. They stepped out to let a seat take them from underneath. "Welcome to the snail-rail," the Warmistress said. "It's not fast, but it runs twenty-four hours a day, and is much better than walking."

Below them, thousands of LAMPs whose lives had been upended by magic filled a myriad of walkways snaking around buildings. From the chairlift, the paths looked like a mess of dropped spaghetti. The seat groaned as it began a steep ascent, taking them up towards a triangular gap in the stone. When they reached the apex of the climb, Declan gasped. The new cavern was double the size and bursting with colorful markets. They stepped off at an exit platform, and Declan followed—gawking—as they made their way into the spectacle.

"The Cathedral," Harcross explained, "is the heart of Lombrives City. People sleep in the homes, but this is where they come to live."

Hawkers shouted their wares over distant music. A puppeteer performed for a party of children. They laughed as the comical buffoon attempted to fight an orange dragon. "It's..." Declan trailed off. It was a shock to find so much... joy... amidst the destruction of Euryma's surface.

Harcross smiled. "It's freedom. This is the first time these LAMPs have been able to enjoy life free from wizard's rule." Her expression turned somber. "The Dominion does many things well, but it has failed the powerless." She chuckled at the miniature theatre—the buffoon now rode the dragon—and gestured for him to follow. "Come."

They navigated a tangle of walkways and stopped at a narrow tent. It was empty, which seemed what Harcross wanted. Tiny lights decorated the walls, the menu listed a handful of drinks. The Warmistress ordered a tea, Declan asked for a glass of water. He adjusted his axes—he had brought them, just in case—as he took a seat. "What's so special about this place?"

"It's mine." Harcross stirred her drink. "A little side business, as not to arouse suspicion. Nobody will bother us here. There are spells sown into the walls. Most won't even give it a second glance." She leaned forward and levelled him with a no-nonsense expression. "Let us speak plainly. While your arrival here is unexpected, I want you to stay. Samantha always intended for you to come to Sabart when you were ready. Now you are here, there is much you can learn. I can organize a place for you to live. You can enroll in whatever disciplines you choose. No more roaming between damaged nations. You can make friends with people your own age. Eat delicious food, sleep in a comfortable bed, and prepare for what's coming."

Once, Declan would have cut off his own hand to be included in a Mag-Ed institution, no matter how clandestine. Now... Declan drank his water and thought. He had come to Euryma to destroy Winterthorn. He had come to Lombrives to find allies to help. He met Harcross's steady gaze. "I can't stay. Not yet. I have something I need to do first."

"What is it?"

Declan frowned. "It's personal."

"As you say." She took a long drink from her cup. The fairy-lights strung behind him reflected off her eyes. "This *thing* you need to do... what if we helped you?"

"It's an option." Declan took another sip of water, hoping the ceramic cup would hide his satisfaction. "Why do you want me?" he asked. "I'm not a wizard, and I'm not a Knight. I'm barely a Warlock. What can I do for the Sabartians?"

"The Knights of Despair are well named Declan." The Warmistress sighed. "If they attacked today, every student I have trained would die. We need someone who can withstand them. Someone who can use Sila." Her meaningful gaze left no doubt about who that was.

"I can't use Sila at will," Declan said. "Even if I could, I'm not sure I would want to. Whenever I touch green magic, bad things happen." He shook his head. "No. I'm here on a personal matter."

Harcross stared into her mug, as if piecing his words

together like a jigsaw puzzle. "You're after your friend. Horace."

Declan's cheeks flushed, and he knew he'd given the answer away. "I'm not after Horace. I'm after his dagger."

"Winterthorn?"

He nodded. "I need to destroy it, before..." His stomach somersaulted. He didn't dare voice his fears.

"Then let us help each other." Harcross leaned in. "Horace inspects the city every other month. Stay, Declan. Stay, and we'll help you infiltrate the blackcoats ranks next time they are underground. We will use all our resources to help you."

Declan paused. It was exactly what he wanted, but it felt too easy. "You'll help me? Just like that?"

"Just like that. You help us, and we help you." She smiled. "Aren't you ready to have a home again?"

The word *home* struck a chord in his chest. Declan opened his mouth when the ring of heavy bells erupted in the distance. It reverberated through the ground; the ceramic mugs trembled on the table. Harcross stood with a start.

"What is it?" Declan asked.

"The Bonfires have found a wizard... or a witch." Her face was pale. "Let's hope it's not one of ours." She rushed outside, leaving Declan to follow. He chased her through a dizzying array of corners and stairs until they reached a viewing platform. Declan hunched over to catch his breath. Men and women marched up the central walkway. A young woman staggered ahead of them. She had long blonde hair, clumped together with dirt and dried blood. Iron finger-cuffs bound her hands. As she passed, an eerie mania infected the Cathedral—a bloodlust that made Declan's hair stand on end. At the tail of the precession, someone carried a bell. It chimed with each step, and the crowd sang with it. "Kill the witch! Kill the witch!"

Declan turned—wide-eyed—to Harcross. "What is this?"

"They call themselves Bonfires," she said. "And they call *that* Big Bonny." She gestured to the brass bell. "That poor girl isn't responsible for the storms, but many of these people believe their revenge is well earned." She averted her gaze. "Witches and wizards are not welcome here. Our students have strict orders to avoid using magic outside Sabart's halls. We can't protect them. Not without endangering our cause." She nodded to the crowd gathering around a raised platform. It was a gallows.

Declan's jaw dropped. "They're going to *hang* her?"

"She would not be the first."

"And you're... going to let them?" Declan didn't bother to hide his disbelief.

"What would I do except get myself hung up beside her?" Harcross shook her head. "Better one than five thousand."

Declan stared at the girl. She was young, but her long hair, her impish features... they reminded him of another witch. One who had died. One he had failed. *Amber.* Declan started for the stairs. Harcross grabbed his shoulder.

"Don't." Her voice was stern. "You'll get yourself caught and killed just for trying to help. Who will stop Winterthorn then?"

He pulled away from her. "Simple. I won't get caught, will I?"

The Warmistress called after him, but Declan was sprinting through the maze of walkways. He followed Big Bonny's chime. Groups of people rushed past him, mostly families intent on taking their children as far from the scene as possible. The jeers from the crowd intensified. He was running out of time.

Around a corner, a wall of people watched with their backs turned. The gallows loomed above them. The girl already stood on the wooden platform. She looked barely sixteen. Tears wet her cheeks as she fought to keep a brave face.

A broad-shouldered giant with a mane of black hair stepped in front of her. A hush fell over the Cathedral. "A LAMP in the night sets a room alight..."

"But a Bonfire turns night to day!" returned the chorus of people.

The man raised his deep baritone. "A LAMP IN THE NIGHT SETS A ROOM ALIGHT!"

"BUT A BONFIRE TURNS NIGHT TO DAY!"

The cry echoed off the high walls of the Cathedral. The man turned back to the girl. He snatched her wrist and dragged her to the edge of the gallows. "A witch has been found in our midst! She has used her blasphemous power. That same power that scours our homes and kills our beloved!"

"Kill her!"

"Hang her!"

The voices in the crowd made Declan's stomach turn. The girl seemed to crumble, staying upright only because of the man holding her arm.

"The Fatesmiths have sworn an oath to abandon their foul arts," continued the man. "But this is no Fatesmith! She is a witch! And in her arrogance, she adds more magic to the storms. What do we do with her?"

"Kill the witch! Kill the witch! Kill the witch!"

Declan's heart raced. He loosened an axe in his belt and judged the distance. He was too far back, too low on the ground. An empty scaffold towered over the tents to his left. He rushed towards it and started to climb. It wasn't great, but it was better.

"For your crimes against Euryma," boomed the man. "I order your death by hanging!"

Declan secured his legs between the wooden rungs. He unlooped an axe and concentrated on where the rope attached to the top beam. The man looped a noose over the girl's neck. A hand gripped Declan's ankle.

"You cannot do this!" Harcross had climbed to a spot three feet below him.

"I will not let them hang her."

"My daughter has devoted half of her life to keeping you alive. I will not let you get yourself killed on the day we meet." She tried to tug him down, but Declan held firm. "Come down. Now."

Declan paused. He looked at the girl. It could have been Amber herself. She cried as the crowd roared their approval. He glared at Harcross. "Fine." Declan slid the axe back into his belt. "Move out of my way."

"Thank you." The Warmistress began her descent. When she was far enough down that she couldn't stop him, Declan willed an axe into his hand.

As the man gripped the trapdoor lever, Declan took his shot. With both hands, he hurled the axe towards the knot atop the gallows. The force of the throw almost cost him his balance. He grabbed the scaffolding as the axe head hit with a tremendous crack. With a terrible groan, the structure buckled in on itself. The girl fell through the platform. The Bonfires' leader leapt into the crowd, and the gallows collapsed.

As one, the gathered sea of faces turned to the source of the disturbance. Declan clung to the scaffold. The stunned silence lasted long enough for the axe to hum back into his waiting hand. Then a roar of fury erupted from below.

Declan reached the ground as a thunder of shouts filled the Cathedral. Harcross stared at him, somewhere between shock and anger.

"Find the girl," he said. "I'll distract the Bonfires and meet you back at the stinky waterfall."

She opened her mouth, closed it, then nodded. Declan slid the axe into his belt and ran.

CHAPTER 16
DECLAN

A DISORIENTED MESS of shouts echoed off the elevated metal walkway. Footsteps followed Declan down dirt roads, around corners and up stairs. A group of teenage girls screamed as he pushed past, the screams repeated when his pursuers did the same. When three Bonfires tried to cut him off, Declan hopped the handrails and dropped to the gravel below. He scrambled under the flap of a long tent and found himself in a storage area filled to the ceiling with identical blue tubs, each one labelled with stenciled white letters. He slid between the stacks as others entered behind him.

"He's not in here!"

"He is! I saw him! He went in here!"

"Right then. Search it!"

A clatter of plastic preceded the sound of breaking glass. A rough curse and a cry of pain. Declan peeked out of his hiding spot. There were two men. One rubbed his head, the other lowered a tub to the ground. Cooking oil pooled on the floor.

"Be careful. We need this stuff."

"How else are we gonna find him?"

Declan slipped to the edge of the tent. Silently, he took an axe and cut a long slit through the canvas wall. He stepped through it and found himself face to face with six unhappy-looking LAMPs. The largest had a red beard braided with gold beads. A sneer split his sharp face. "Lookie here."

Declan brandished both axes. "Don't say a word. Move out of my way and I won't hurt any—"

"He's out here!" bead-beard yelled. "The wizard is—"

Declan drove the side of the axe into his kneecap. The man screamed and Declan leapt over him. Someone seized his shirt; Declan thrust the butt of the handle under his armpit. There was a wet crunch, and he was free. He raced up a flight of stairs.

"We're gonna find you!" came a call from behind. "You can't run forever!"

Two groups of Bonfires swarmed either end of the walkway. The handrails shook as they chased him. Declan dashed for the lofty stage of the snail rail. He reached an intersection just as a blur of movement launched itself at him. In a moment, he was on his side—the wind knocked from his lungs. Declan's axes fell into the darkness below.

The source of the collision—a middle aged man with matted brown hair—wrestled himself on top and pinned Declan's forearms. He stank of overripe onions. "Nowhere to go now! Rodrick's gonna have your head, wizard."

"I'm not a wizard."

"Liar!"

To Declan's right, a group of Bonfires slowed to a walk. To his left, the path to the chairlift was empty. A bold idea came to mind, and Declan turned back to the man. "It's true," he said. "I *am* a wizard." He smiled. "And you're about to be a cloud of ash." Declan willed his weapons back to his hands. "Burn bright."

Far beneath them, two white spots blazed to life. The axe's glow reflected in the man's eyes. "What... what is that?"

As the lights surged upwards, the Bonfires backed away. The commotion distracted the man atop of him. Declan jerked an arm free and delivered a fist to his nose. The man flopped off him, and Declan stumbled upright, catching the axes as he ran to the snail rail.

"WHAT ARE YOU DOING? GET HIM!"

Declan jumped for the nearest chair. One of the Bonfires dived a moment late. He fell fifteen feet, screaming all the way. Declan turned back—three men crammed into the seat behind, with more following as well as they could. The lift meandered upwards. As Declan searched for an exit point, two of the Bonfires climbed up to hang off the cable between them. Hand over hand, they monkeyed their way towards him.

"Stop!" Declan motioned to the wire. "I'll cut it!"

The men paused. "You wouldn't," shouted the closer of the two. "You cut it and you're just as dead as we are."

"Magic will protect me," Declan shot back. "What's going to cushion *your* fall?"

The pair shared uncertain glances. There was a pause, then one shook his head. "The Fatesmiths' wards will block whatever magic you think you can do. Go ahead and try."

Something in Declan's face must have confirmed their suspicions, because they resumed climbing towards him. As the snail rail neared the next raised platform, four Bonfires waited to meet him.

The ground was thirty feet down, and the only thing

above were the steel wires fixing the lift to the cave walls. Declan considered them. A bad idea formed in his head. *This is stupidity.* He had no other choice.

He looped one axe in his belt, then stood on his seat with the other held ready. Adrenaline raged through him. The Bonfires were within arm's distance when Declan leapt from the chair. He swung the axe handle over the wire and caught it in his other hand. Holding tight, he slid down the wire—riding it to the wall like a zip line. The men watched, helpless, as they hung between seats.

As the wire levelled out, Declan dropped onto a walkway running between clusters of unpainted houses. He disappeared into the warren, not stopping until he reached the cave entrance. From there, he retraced his steps to the narrow passage labelled 'sewage'.

The waterfall smelled even worse the second time around. As Declan approached the red-lit cavern, two familiar faces peeked out from a gap in the stone.

"You idiot," Harcross said. "You absolute fool of an idiot."

"It's nice to see you too," Declan replied.

The blonde-haired girl stood behind the Warmistress with her nostrils pinched closed. As he got closer, he saw her eyes expand. "You!" she whispered. "That was you up there! You threw the axe."

A growl reverberated in the back of the Warmistress's throat. "It was. And it was a very risky thing to do."

"You saved my life," the girl said.

Declan nodded, then turned a glare on Harcross. "It was the *right* thing to do."

The roar of the waterfall filled the silence.

Harcross sighed. "It was. Well done, Declan." She shook

her head. "Let's get out of this stink and then figure out the mess you've made."

She herded them into the manual elevator. Declan took a deep breath when the putrid smell vanished. The girl blinked in confusion. "Where... where are we going?"

"Somewhere safe." Harcross's voice was ice.

The girl frowned at Declan. He attempted a reassuring smile. "Super safe," he said. "I'm Declan."

"I'm... Juniper," she murmured. "Juniper Reaves. Thank you... for saving me. I was so—"

"Enough," Harcross hissed. "You'll echo all the way up to the surface. Stay silent."

Juniper's lips snapped closed, and Declan winked as they descended into the blackness. Fifteen minutes later, Harcross herded them through Sabart's tunnels and into her office. There she paced. Three steps one way, three steps the other. Nox tracked her movement with one golden eye. Occasionally, she would mutter something under her breath, until at last she took a seat across from them. Declan and Juniper waited.

"You can't go back to Lombrives City," she said. "The Bonfires will be looking for both of you for the foreseeable future." She fixed Juniper with a flat stare. "Who were you staying with in the caves?"

"No-one," the girl replied. "They brought me here. I... I was lost and thirsty. They found me... drawing water from hydronima. They took me. I have nowhere else to go."

The Warmistress's expression softened. "Where did you come from?"

Juniper's gaze fell to the floor, where it remained. A moment later, her shoulders began to shake, as if she were holding in silent tears.

"Can we stay down here?" Declan asked.

"There are staff quarters behind the kitchens." Harcross pursed her lips. "At present, they are full. I'll try to move some workers up top." She shook her head at him. "I was hoping you would relieve some of my burdens, Declan, not create more."

Burden? The word irked Declan. The girl sat beside him crying, and Harcross was making her feel unwelcome. "Juniper did nothing wrong." He met the Warmistress's gaze with steely resolve. "But even if she did, I'd rather be a burden than a coward."

The implication was obvious, and Harcross frowned in response. "What you call cowardice, I call saving lives. You got lucky this time. I'm glad you did. Things could have gone much worse... for all of us."

"What will I do now?" Juniper asked. "What is this place?"

"Somewhere safe," Harcross said. "Even safer now that Declan has taken responsibility for you."

Declan raised his eyebrows. "What?"

"Juniper is here now, which means her only option is to join us. She can't just jump in with the other students. They've been here for months." The Warmistress smiled triumphantly. "That responsibility falls to you. Congratulations, Declan. You're a student-mentor."

"You're forcing me to stay?"

"That's exactly what I'm doing," Harcross said. "And you agreed to it the moment you upended the Cathedral to save her."

Juniper sat motionless, like a deer listening for an approaching predator. Declan clenched his teeth. "Fine," he said. "But our deal stands from earlier. You help me complete my task, and I'll stick around. Agreed?"

"It's a start." Harcross stood and walked to the door. "Come, Juniper. You look just like Declan did a few hours back. You need a good meal and a hot shower." She directed her attention to Declan. "And you..." The Warmistress shook her head. "I think you've created enough excitement for today. Go find some dinner and I'll organize sleeping quarters. Have a quiet night, Declan. For everyone's sake."

***

Sunrise did not exist in Sabart. In the utter darkness of his small bedroom, Declan slept for fourteen hours straight. He only woke when someone thundered on his door just before eleven o'clock.

"Are you alive in there?" It sounded like Sephina, the crimson-haired Sabartian who had run messages for Harcross the day prior.

Declan groaned in response. He fumbled for a glass jar on the bedside table and shook it. The chemicals combined, and a gentle light illuminated the room.

"Hello?" Sephina called through the door.

"I'm awake," Declan said. His mouth was as dry as parchment.

"Fantastic. Harcross wants you in Stone Hall in fifteen minutes. Better move fast if you want breakfast."

One hurried egg and chorizo roll later, Declan reached Stone Hall—the designated area for combat training. Thin black mats covered the center of a circular cavern surrounded by curved wooden benches on one side and weapon racks on the other. The whole place was lit by hundreds of glowjars hanging in rope nets from the ceiling. The Warmistress stood in the center of the room alongside a broad-shouldered brute with tangled brown hair that hung over his shoulders.

"Good morning," Harcross said. "How did you sleep?"

"Fine, thanks." Declan had worried that—between Horace's claims about his grandfather and everything Harcross had told him about Sabart—his mind would be running all night. He had been asleep before his head hit the pillow. After weeks of sleeping everywhere except a bed, a proper rest seemed exactly what he needed.

"Excellent." Harcross turned to her towering companion. "This is Master Marcus Johannasberg. You may know of his uncle Reginald, the late High Mage."

Declan nodded. Horace had all but confirmed that he was the one responsible for the High Mage's death. "I'm sorry for your loss."

Johannasberg bowed his head. "Thank you," he said in a baritone.

"Marcus is our weapons master. He has fought competitively across the entire Dominion and has two decades of experience with any weapon you can imagine."

"Okay..." Declan was not sure he liked where this was going.

"Samantha has told me you have some skill with an axe. Master Johannasberg has kindly volunteered some time between classes to evaluate your ability." Harcross smiled, and Declan could tell she was enjoying herself. "Wooden weapons only, of course. Our deal means little if you die."

"We should begin." Johannasberg strode to a rack of weapons before Declan had time to process what had been said. "We will start simple."

Johannasberg threw a quarterstaff across the room. Declan snatched it out of the air. As Harcross made for the door, he called after her. "Wait. You're not staying to watch?"

The Warmistress shook her head. "I would love to, believe me." She appeared to be struggling to contain a smile. "But I have plans with Ms. Reaves this morning. I will return when you're done to hear our weapons master's assessment." The grin broke through. "Good luck."

Declan didn't have time to respond. With a loud cry, Johannasberg lashed out at him. Declan dodged sideways. The rush of wind behind the staff lifted the hairs on his neck. *I thought this was practice?*

Master Johannasberg moved diagonally to cut him off. Declan tried to move into the Bull, but it was a mistake. The weight distribution was off, and Johannasberg closed the distance in a step. His staff whistled through the air...

Declan woke, flat on his back. Hanging lights dangled overhead. Johannasberg kneeled beside him, screwing a metal lid on a steel flask.

"What happened?" Declan's head felt like it was stuffed with cotton wool.

"I hit you in the head with a quarterstaff," Johannasberg boomed. His face split in a gap-toothed smile. "You left an opening, and I took advantage."

"You knocked me out?"

"All well. We are well stocked with sanarmelon elixir for such events."

Declan touched his temple. It was tender, but nothing more. "How long was I out for?"

"Less than a minute." Johannasberg pressed the fallen staff into his hands. "Shall we try again?"

Declan frowned. "Do I have to?"

The man laughed. It sounded like rolling thunder. "No."

Amusement shone in his inky eyes. "But it's the only way to get better."

Declan used the quarterstaff to stand up. He lowered his center of gravity and shifted his weight onto his back foot.

"Are you ready?" Master Johannasberg boomed.

Declan struck out in answer. Stepping into the long blows of Lion form. Johannasberg adjusted quickly, closing the distance to steal the sting from his strikes. Declan countered with Bear. Johannasberg feigned a side step, then rallied forward. The move caught Declan off-balance. He took a desperate swing for the head, bracing his arms to absorb the impact of the staff.

He missed.

Johannasberg dropped into a roll. Declan recovered in time to see the grain of the wood.

He blinked twice, then sighed. He lay on the edge of the mat. "I got hit in the head again, didn't I?"

"You attack well." Johannasberg offered a hand. "But you do not defend."

"I've never had to." Declan let the giant pull him upright. "As long as I kept attacking."

"An efficient strategy, until you meet a capable opponent." Johannasberg handed Declan his staff. "You have half of the equation. I will teach you to defend."

They spent the next hour on defensive footwork. The weapons master showed him where to put his weight so he could maneuver between offense and defense. They practiced while they sparred. Unlike lessons with his grandfather, Johannasberg was neither patient nor forgiving. He attacked with ferocity, always striking to immobilize. Declan needed reviving three more times.

Despite the bouts of unconsciousness, progress came

quickly. Declan was amazed by how much a shift in weight could affect his range of motion, or his ability to attack—or retreat—in an instant. During their final spar, he blocked seven consecutive strikes from Johannasberg's quarterstaff before the weapons master knocked it from his hands. Declan sprinted to the other side of the mats. Johannasberg tried to catch him, but couldn't. "You've done well, Declan." He laughed as he mounted his weapon on the rack. "You are quick on your feet, and a capable learner. You have an hour here before students start arriving."

"An hour? For what?"

"Now is your chance to be a capable teacher." He unclipped a smaller staff made from pale wood and pointed it to the door. Juniper and Harcross watched with broad smiles on their faces. Johannasberg extended the weapon to Juniper. "This is for you."

Juniper accepted, but held the weapon in front of her as if it were a deadly snake. She looked much better with the dried blood and filth washed out of her hair. "Why can't I just use magic?"

"In most situations, you will," Harcross said. "But magic is easy to disrupt. This class teaches you to be dangerous when your power is out of reach."

"Swords and axes are rare in Euryma," Johannasberg added. "But you can find a decent stick just about anywhere." He nodded to Declan. "You have one hour. Teach her well, as you were taught." Without a second glance, he joined Harcross, and they left.

Declan waited until the echo of their footsteps faded. "We don't have to do this," he said. "Yesterday must have been awful. We could—"

"No." Juniper stared at the staff in her hands. "Those men... they bound my fingers in clamps... I was helpless..."

she trailed off, then held the weapon out to him. "They're right. I need to be able to protect myself without magic. Where do we start?"

Declan was impressed by her resolve. "We start with your grip." He smiled as a welcome memory returned. He and his grandfather, alone in the forest. "You're holding it too tight. Hold it like you would a fish. You want it secure, but you don't want to choke the life out of the thing."

CHAPTER 17
AVA

THE MOUNTAINS between Vedmark and Euryma were barren and dangerous. Two weeks ago, Ava would have said they were empty too. She would have been wrong. Despite the harsh landscape, the Northern Remnants were home to thousands who lived lives untouched by magic, or who just wanted to escape it all.

"So this is it?" Ava asked.

"I hope so," Misha replied. He eased himself onto a small boulder to catch his breath. Luck had led them this far, but not without cost. "How are you doing?"

"I'll be better if this actually *is* Yabun." It was the seventh settlement they had visited in twice as many days. The mountain people did not trust outsiders, and getting anything close to directions from anyone required more Luck—and energy—than Ava cared to admit. She scanned the tents strung up along the narrow plateau. While identical in color—all a speckled earthy brown—they came in a myriad of sizes. The largest tent seemed to come out of the cliff face, and Ava wondered if the shelter extended into the stone. *Only one way to know for sure.* "There." She pointed.

"If we have friends here, that looks like a decent place to start."

Misha pushed himself upright. "I'd settle for a meal and a mattress."

They entered to find a makeshift bar—a sanded length of wood propped against two brick columns—with a half-dozen people hunched over it. It took a moment for Ava's eyes to adjust to the darkness. As it did, a short man holding a wooden club marched towards them. "Who you?" he demanded in a nearly unintelligible accent. "Why in Yabun?"

This is Yabun! Ava held out her open palms. "We are friends."

The man lowered the club. A yellowing smile split his face. "Friend!" He rushed to the far side of the bar and grabbed another man by the sleeve. After a brief pause, the larger man reluctantly followed him into the light.

"Well, I'll be a goat's daughter." Ava was not sure whether to laugh or cry.

A red-haired man with a straggly beard scowled at them. Mage Raul raised a clay bowl to his lips. Its contents smelled more like engine oil than alcohol. He held the liquid in his mouth, grimaced, then swallowed. "You've got a lot of nerve looking for us."

Ava's jaw tightened. "I didn't even know you were here, *friend.*"

"Friend!" The short man beamed and patted Raul's arm. "Friend, yes?"

Raul rolled his eyes. He leaned down and whispered something. The little man's eyes grew as he spoke. He shouted some foreign instructions, and the tent emptied. The small man left with a wide grin and a handful of copper coins. Raul gestured for them to sit. He took another swig of the foul-smelling brew. "Why are you here?"

Ava exchanged a glance with Misha, who swayed in his chair in an exhausted stupor. "We were told to come to Yabun, that we'd find friends here."

"Sorry, we're not interested."

Ava raised her eyebrows. "So, Haberdeen's here too?"

"Oh, it's Haberdeen now?" Raul chided. "No *Habby* when you need a favor, eh?"

"Are you listening?" Ava replied. "Someone told us to come. This is either the world's biggest coincidence, or you're the reason we're here." Ava tried not to let her frustration show. She was so tired. "If you don't know why, maybe Haberdeen does."

Raul's laugh held no mirth. "She doesn't want to talk to you. She wants to be left alone. So do I. We fled Euryma before the storms burned it to ash." He took another drink, tilting his head to empty the bowl. "We're done. Get outa' here, girl."

"We're not leaving until—"

"You've said enough," he said. "Go on. Get." Raul appeared older, more tired than she remembered. His hair was thinner, his eyes deeper. She relaxed and let Luck guide her words. "You can still save the Dominion from the storms." She held his gaze. "I thought you Fatesmiths stood for something."

In one motion, Raul's rough fist clenched around Ava's neck. Misha startled from his half-sleep and threw himself forward. Raul caught him by the collar. "I told you to get gone."

Bending Luck sapped the last of her strength, but Ava continued speaking. "The glorious Fatesmiths. Saviors of the Dominion." Her voice croaked as Raul's grip tightened on her throat. "All undone by a teenager?"

"Who?" Raul growled. "Declan Moore didn't—"

"I'm not talking about Declan," Ava wheezed, her words little more than a murmur. Tiny dots flashed at the corner of her eyes. Sunlight flooded in behind them as someone entered the tent.

"Raul!"

The pressure on Ava's neck vanished. She struggled to keep her balance and ended up hugging the barstool to stay upright. Misha's landing was much better. He swung for Raul's head. Raul caught his fist, then shoved him hard. Misha collapsed against the dirt floor.

"What are you doing?" Haberdeen wore a loose beige shirt and worn brown pants held up by suspenders.

"What we agreed." Raul glared at Misha. "Keeping you safe."

"From a couple of exhausted kids?" Haberdeen knelt to help Misha up. She stared at him, then at Ava. Her eyes expanded. "You!"

"Me." Ava massaged her tender throat—speaking hurt.

"Why are you here?"

"They're trying to pull us back in!" Raul snapped. "Back to Euryma to die."

"Someone told us we could find help here." Ava's words cut short amidst the pain.

Haberdeen considered them. The long scar winding from her mouth to her ear formed a crescent shape as she frowned. "Who told you we were here?"

"Samantha Winter," Misha said. "She is the Emissary for Euryma and Vedmark."

"Deena—"

Haberdeen silenced Raul with a finger. "Why?"

"She said we'd find friends." Misha glared at Raul. "Though you don't seem too friendly to me."

"You should have left when I told you," Raul said. "We got out, Deena. We escaped the Dominion. We're not going back to die."

"You don't get to make choices for me." Haberdeen's tone was level but stern. She helped Ava to her feet. "You are both spent. Come along. We'll get you sorted, then we can talk about our mutual acquaintance."

Yabun—a collection of tents and fallen boulders—lay on a flat between two sheer cliffs. Haberdeen's tent hugged the mountain side, and Ava was surprised when it extended into a shallow cavern. An assortment of ancient furniture filled the small interior.

Haberdeen beckoned them into seats, then vanished through a curtain door. Raul sat across from Ava, his face as hard as the bare rock beneath their feet.

Misha's tired eyes darted around the room; he gave Ava the distinct impression of a wild rabbit caught in a snare. She dropped her voice. "It's okay."

"The Emissary lied to father," he whispered back. "These people are not our friends."

Ava fell silent as Haberdeen returned with a platter of four different shaped glasses filled with the same amber liquid. She handed one to each of them. Ava arced an eyebrow.

"Moss punch," Haberdeen explained. "It will help with the tiredness."

Ava took a tentative sip. The punch was sour, but not unpleasant. Somewhere between apples and cranberries with a hint of ginger. Her body tingled, as if connected to a low-voltage battery. By the time she finished, the bone-numbing exhaustion had faded to weariness.

"How's your throat?" Haberdeen asked.

Ava swallowed and winced. "Sore."

Haberdeen turned a glare on Raul. His drink remained untouched. "I'm not apologizin' to them," he said. "If anyone is gonna threaten me, I'll do as I see fit. We came here to start over, didn't we?"

"We did." Haberdeen stared at the table. "But... I made a deal with Vedmark's Emissary a day before I got out."

"What?"

Haberdeen ignored Raul's outrage. She glanced up at Ava. "What exactly did the woman tell you?"

"I've told you," Ava said. "We would find friends in Yabun."

"Anything else?"

Misha cleared his throat. "The message said you have an army."

A rueful smile formed on Haberdeen's lips. "Not anymore."

"Enough." Raul's hard tone demanded answers. "Deena. What deal did you make?"

She turned to face him. "I traded freedom for the Fatesmiths. That woman promised to get me out of Vedmark, and I would order the Fatesmiths to her cause. She moved me from a crowded dungeon to a lone cell." She winked at Ava. "And our friend the Luck did the rest."

Plans on plans on plans. Ava's head spun in amazement. How had the Emissary known they planned to break her out of the Knights' Barracks? Had she known? Or had it been a coincidence? *Or Luck.*

"It was an easy deal to make. She knew nothing of my... exile... from the Fatesmiths, and now I'm free."

"So, how did she know we were here?" Raul growled.

"That, I cannot say." Haberdeen pursed her lips. "A

tracking spell, perhaps? We may need to go through our belongings."

"You're telling us you traded your life for an army of Fatesmiths... and now you can't deliver?" Misha banged a fist against the table. "We came all this way for nothing!"

Haberdeen shrugged. "It is what it is."

A dark scowl shadowed Misha's face. Ava said nothing. A seed of an idea grew in her mind. Ava opened herself to Luck and did something drastic. "What if we joined the Fatesmiths?"

Misha dropped his cup. He fumbled to catch it as amber liquid poured down the front of his shirt.

"That is your choice to make," Haberdeen said. "It has nothing to do with us. We are no longer part of that fight."

"That's the thing," Ava said. "We don't want *those* Fatesmiths. We want *your* Fatesmiths."

"Why?" Raul asked.

"Because there are other threats coming, and we need your help to stop them." Ava met his eyes. "If we can set things right—put you back in charge—you'll accept us as Fatesmiths. Together, we'll protect Euryma. From Remnant Magic and worse."

"Worse..." Haberdeen toyed with the word like a cat with a ball of yarn. "Vedmark?"

Ava nodded. "Their armies are on the move. A curse is engulfing their land. They are desperate to escape, to take Euryma as their own."

Haberdeen arced a slim eyebrow. "Why do you care, dear girl? Vedmark is your home. Why would you rise against it?"

"Home isn't about where you were born," Ava said. "Vedmark needs to be stopped."

"And where's your knight in shining armor?" Raul asked. "Where is Declan Moore?"

Misha shifted in his chair. Ava tried to assume an air of dismissiveness. "We don't know. Expectations grew too much for him, and he left."

"Coward ran away," Misha muttered.

Ava held Haberdeen's steady gaze with all the intensity she could muster. "We have nobody. It's true. We need your help, but you need us too. We know who the imposter is. We can take your army back. We can make things right." Ava flashed her most convincing smile. "Imagine what the Fatesmiths could do with a pair of Lucks at your disposal?"

Haberdeen turned to Raul. They stared at each other—unreadable in their silence—then she nodded to the pair. "That punch will wear off soon. When it does, you're going to want a bed. You make an interesting proposal. Give us time to discuss it."

Raul led them through the last vestige of dusk to yet another tent. While it looked a decent size from the outside, tall wooden crates cramped the interior. Two electric lanterns hung from the ceiling, filling the space with long shadows. "You can rest there." Raul pointed to a row of camp stretchers. "There are blankets underneath. Don't touch anything."

The moment he left, Ava exhaled. "That was unexpected."

"That's an understatement!" Misha turned on her. "I don't want to join the Fatesmiths, Ava. What were you thinking?"

"I was thinking that, unless I figured something out, we would have spent the last two weeks climbing mountains for nothing."

"We spent months trying to capture Haberdeen, now

we're pledging allegiance to her?" Misha inhaled through his nose. "I don't like it."

Ava didn't respond. She felt the same way.

They made their beds without speaking. The wind picked up, buffeting the tent, so the flaps flailed against the fabric. Soon, Misha started to snore. Ava was tired beyond description, but she could not sleep. The faint aroma of pine filled the air. It must have been the tall boxes filling the interior. Six feet tall, with fabric straps ratcheted around them, Ava wondered what was inside. The nearest crate had a sheet of paper stapled to the wood. It listed an address in Sabriva West.

Go to sleep. Ava lay back on the bed. She closed her eyes and tried to turn off her brain. It would not stop. The sounds of the canvas, the smell of the boxes, fears about the Emissary, Grigory, Declan, the fact their hopes hung on a Haberdeen shaped thread.

Ava stood and walked down the narrow aisle between boxes. Each one had a different address from somewhere in the Dominion. Concordia, Valentian, Jeltenham, Parteno. A sheet fixed to a box in the back corner made her pause. Tamhill.

Milworth Drive, Tamhill

Her breath caught. She read and reread the words again. Ava's heart thundered in her chest. The Emissary had given her that address. Fourteen Milworth Drive—Declan's house. The realization hit like lightning. *Why does Haberdeen have a crate from Declan's home?*

She grabbed it and pushed. It would not budge. She tried again, but the box seemed to be bolted to the ground. As Ava heaved against it, the wind carried a whisper of voices through the tent. Someone was coming towards them. *Oh no.*

She sprinted back through the boxes and leapt under the blankets. The tent flaps opened and someone kicked her leg. Ava pretended to stir.

"Wake up," Raul said. "There's a nasty storm coming. We need to get somewhere safer."

Misha covered a yawn. "Why?"

"In case Yabun gets blown off the mountain side." Raul took the nearest blanket and pillow and tossed it to Misha. "Hurry. We don't want to be here when it hits."

Ava gathered her things and followed. Thick clouds shrouded a starless sky. An icy wind whipped around them, whistling between the cracks of the mountain. Ahead of them, men and women hurried down a winding path. Some held lanterns, others held bedding. As they rounded a corner, Ava glanced back to the tent and wondered what Haberdeen was hiding in that box.

CHAPTER 18
HORACE

THIS IS A WASTE OF TIME. The voice seethed in Horace's head. *Kill her and be done with it.*

No, Horace thought in reply. *They have what I need.*

They are wasting your time. Just like the Moore boy. These people don't want to help you. They want to control you.

Horace fought to keep his expression level. They were in an empty office on the third floor of the building. Ophelia sat at the scratched plastic table beside him, while an older woman sat across from them. She had long, grey hair held in an intricate braid. Horace recognized Mary-Lou from stolen memories. He thought he had killed her at Sabriva Tower.

There is still time.

Horace pushed the thought away.

"Thank you for agreeing to meet with me," she said.

"But we didn't." Ophelia's voice was harsh. "We agreed to meet with Laurefen Ember. Not you. Where is he?"

Mary-Lou's expression faltered. "Dean Ember sends his apologies. Urgent business arose."

"Urgent?" Ophelia turned to Horace. "What could be more urgent than the fate of our Dominion?"

An icy tension crystallized between the women. The voice in Horace's head continued its tirade. He pinched the bridge of his nose and willed it to silence. When he could hear himself think, he arranged his face into what he hoped was a smile. "You requested a meeting, and here we are." His tone was harsher than he intended. "What do you want from us?"

"We seek to collaborate," Mary-Lou said. "We acknowledge our errors and want to help."

Ophelia pursed her lips. "It took you long enough."

Mary-Lou ignored her. "Remnant Magic is real, and we would like to do our part to protect Euryma. If we know what you know about the storms—their location, formation and all other pertinent information—we can assist you. Laurefen believes our expertise could be a valuable asset in stopping these disasters." She turned her attention to Ophelia. "You are right, Mage Damrodel. We were ignorant, but we cannot change the past." Mary-Lou nodded to Horace. "It is time to work together and save our future."

Kill her. A hot spark of Ire Tides fizzled in Horace's palm. He blinked. The voice had never done that before. He flexed his hand and let the spell dissipate. *How did you do that?*

The voice didn't answer. Horace waited, but it did not return. The Directive wanted information. He wanted their copy of Oregin o Magi, but he needed to be subtle. "Say we share what we know. What will you offer us in return?"

"You're not considering this," Ophelia interjected. "They're responsible—"

Horace raised a hand. Haberdeen's fingers were slim; her sunflower nails as bright as a luxury car. Ophelia fell silent as Horace rested his chin on his hands. "Will the Directive swear the bloodspell oath to stop using magic?"

Mary-Lou shook her head. "We will not bind ourselves with a blood oath."

Horace's mood darkened. "Then you are hypocrites. You come here asking for help with the storms, yet you're not even willing to give up the power that created them."

"I cannot speak for the Dean."

"Then the Dean shouldn't have sent you to the meeting." Horace glared at her. Maybe the voice was right. These were the same fools that had obstructed him every chance they got. A surge of rage flashed through him and he slammed his fist on the table. Both women jumped. "Don't you understand what I'm trying to do? Magic is *killing* Euryma. We can only hide so many people underground. We need to stop adding fuel to the flames." He pictured the wave of Remnant Magic washing over Sabriva. Over Massalia. Over Parteno. Millions were dead because those like Mary-Lou dragged their feet in the face of danger.

Kill her! If she won't take the oath, she can't be left alive. She's going to make things worse. She—

"SHUT UP!"

A pulse of violet lightning crackled from Horace's hands. The center of the plastic table collapsed in a mess of sticky, grey threads. The women stared at him. Mary-Lou was bone white.

Ophelia touched his knee. "Are you okay, Madam?"

Horace relaxed. He should have felt embarrassment. He should have felt... something. "I am fine." His gaze fell on Mary-Lou. "You have taken too long to come to your senses. Thousands are dead because you tried to ransack our hold-houses in the north, because you tried to destroy us at Sabriva." He jabbed a finger at her. "And millions are dead because you didn't listen to us." He shook his head. "If you want to save our future, take the oath. Swear to me you won't use magic. Otherwise, the Directive remain our enemies."

Mary-Lou leaned forward. "Magic may be causing these storms—"

"Is." Ophelia interrupted. "Magic *is* causing the storms."

"Fine." Mary-Lou gritted her teeth. "But magic is also necessary to help your cause. How can we investigate the storms if we are cut off from the source of their power?"

"No," Horace said.

Mary-Lou's back straightened. "You're excavating the Lombrives Caves using LAMP machinery. How long does that take? Weeks? Months? Magic could accomplish that same task in hours."

"That doesn't matter," Horace replied. "We will complete the work in due time, and the storms will not grow any larger."

"But—"

"There are no buts, no ifs, no maybes. There is the oath. Unless..." Horace trailed off. He considered his open palms as if weighing difficult options. The time had come to play his hand.

"Unless what?"

"We share information that does not pertain to magic itself." Horace frowned. "The storm at Sabriva destroyed many important tomes, including those from the time of the Founding. If King's College has copies of such books..." He feigned uncertainty. "Perhaps we could exchange them with no formal need for an oath."

Horace held his breath. *You can't trust her*, the voice whispered.

Mary-Lou smoothed her skirt over her legs. "It might be possible." Her eyes flickered to Ophelia and she frowned at Horace. "May we speak in private?"

Horace nodded. A shadow crossed Ophelia's face, but she did not argue. When the door closed, Mary-Lou leaned forward. "Horace Marley. Son of Jebediah and Candice Marley. Southern Tamhill Prep until your Potentiality Test, where you were advanced to Arman Moore's Preparatory School."

Horace waved a hand and the office door locked. He let the illusion of Haberdeen's face fade away. "Mary-Lou Nivin. Recruitment Officer at King's College, promoted from Head of Faculty in Manipulation. No children. No husband. Married to a job that no longer exists." He smiled. "Did I miss anything?"

"No," Mary-Lou said. "Everything you said is true, but I missed something about you."

"Enlighten me."

"You're a hypocrite."

Horace bared his teeth.

"You talk of oaths," Mary-Lou continued. "You can't manipulate some geonima to clear a cave, but you can disguise your face for months on end?" She shook her head. "All hail the great Horace Marley. The chosen one. No. You're a kid from the slums whose father openly despised all magical people. You rose to the top of the food chain, then killed half of the witches and wizards in the Dominion. Now you've dug a hole to keep LAMPs safe, while encouraging them to kill any witch or wizard not wearing your coat. Wouldn't dad be proud?"

"You're—"

"Do you think we're stupid?" she went on. "We can see what you're doing, Horace."

Kill her. The whisper was urgent now. Horace clenched his fists. "I'm trying to save Euryma."

"Is that what you tell yourself?" she said. "You're not trying to save the Dominion, Horace. You're trying to extinguish magic. You're trying to put LAMPs on even footing with wizards. No. You're trying to do what your father drilled into your head from the moment you were born."

You need to kill her. Kill her now! Kill her!

"Magic caused these storms," Mary-Lou said. "There is no doubt of that. But magic saves lives every day. It heals people who would otherwise die, keeps the rain falling on our farmer's crops, keeps Euryma's borders safe from our enemies."

"And it keeps LAMPs like my parents underfoot." Horace reeled at the revelation. Her words carried a weight he didn't realize existed. "You have no idea what it's like. You're a witch. You've lived your whole life in magical privilege. What do you have to show for it? A few million dead people who never enjoyed those privileges."

Mary-Lou stood up. "You're right." She stepped through the table's melted remains and stared hard at him. "So *help* us do better. Share your resources, your knowledge. Let us use magic to *save* Euryma and then change it for the better."

Kill. Her. Now.

Horace's hands grew hot. The voice was trying to take control. He fought to wrench his power back, then wondered why he had to. *She's wrong.* That wasn't the voice in his head. That was *his* voice—and it was true. Every terrible thing he had been forced to do would be unnecessary if magic did not exist. Horace met Mary-Lou's gaze and she stepped back. "No, Mary-Lou," he said. "The witches and wizards had their time. This is for the best."

A forked tongue of Ire tides lashed out of him. Mary-

Lou cried out in pain as she caught it on her forearm and stumbled to the floor.

Sparkling spheres burned in Horace's hands. They cast flickering shadows against the office wall. Mary-Lou retreated to the corner of the room.

"You're making a mistake, Horace." The tremble in her voice betrayed her. "If you truly want to save Euryma, you need us. We can help you." Her fingers tapped against her palm.

She's looptapping! Kill her! Horace needed no encouragement. He raised one of the flickering orbs and unfiltered sunlight flooded into the room. Something hit his back. Ire Tides caught his fall, but not before Mary-Lou leapt past him. Horace turned as an Opening disappeared before him.

"NO!" He threw the sparkling orb and the wall exploded. "NO!"

The door handle on his left rattled. "Madam!" Ophelia called. "Are you alright?"

Horace assumed his disguise as he flicked the lock. Ophelia spilled inside. "What happened?"

"The old woman attacked me!" Anger laced Haberdeen's sultry voice. "She hit me with a weave of air and escaped through an Opening. How did she use magic? We have wards to stop that!"

Ophelia directed a sharp glare at someone in the hallway. "I will need to investigate that oversight."

Horace clenched his fists. He could feel his nails biting into his skin.

I told you. The voice vibrated with fury. *I told you to kill her. You should have listened. You should have let me take control.*

Two hours later, Horace sat alone in his office. His brashness had cost him Oregin o Magi. While storms grew stronger through the inland corridor, he had chased away the only people who could help him.

I need to get to Kingsbreak.

A simmering hatred bubbled in his bones as he recalled Mary-Lou's escape. Magic was an abomination, and the Directive held the key to getting rid of it forever.

Why? You have the memories. Use them!

"No," Horace told the empty room. Escaping the memories—even with the voice's help—was growing too hard. Gone were the days when he could ignore the swirling sea of memory. Now, Ire Tides were his only weapon to keep them in check, and even with that, it was difficult to break free. "The memories are too erratic."

I will help you.

He shook his head. "Arman's past has given me enough. The book is the key."

Give me control. I will find the memories and bring you back.

Horace gritted his teeth. The voice had tasted freedom during the meeting. For the briefest moment, it had summoned a sphere of pure Ire Tides. Now it wanted more. "No. I don't need the memories. I need the book."

You should have killed her.

Horace dropped his head against the desk with a thud. His mind worked furiously on the problem. "What if I mount an assault on Kingsbreak? Take the book by force?"

The Ancellum will stop you.

The protective spell was an ancient thing of legend. Horace considered it. *Why would King's College have such potent protection? It is a school, nothing more.* He turned the thought over in his head. *What if it the Ancellum isn't protecting King's College?* Horace bolted upright. "That's where they're keeping it."

The Ancellum protects Euryma's magic?

"It has to be." Horace unrolled a map across his desk and jabbed his finger onto the tiny island. "Protected by the Mediterranean, smack bang in the middle of the Dominion. It's the perfect place to hide it! The magic has to be here."

You must go to Kingsbreak.

"How?" Horace's brow furrowed as he considered what he knew. "The woman was adamant that magic needed to be protected. We could use that against them?"

It would need to be a convincing lie.

"What about—"

A knock on the door cut him short. Ophelia peeked inside and scanned the room. "Apologies, Madam. Am I interrupting?"

Horace shook his head. "Just talking through some ideas." Uncertainty glistened in her eyes, and Horace was aware of how little it bothered him.

Ophelia nodded. "Our investigation of the missing wards... is complete." She closed the door behind her. "It appears Laurefen Ember was in Biscay today, after all."

"Excuse me?"

"A flashfinder saw a man matching Laurefen's description roaming the lower corridors. It is our assumption that he disabled the wards that allowed for the Directive's hasty escape." She placed a piece of paper on his desk. "Here is the full report."

Horace's heart pounded in his ears as he tried to regain his composure. The Directive were relentless. He wanted to tear the sheet to shreds and then tear Kingsbreak in half. "Thank you, Ophelia." His curt tone had a finality to it. She left without another word.

When the door was closed, Horace's eyes shone purple. With a wave of his hand, he could turn the entire room to dust, but that would serve no purpose. He let the power subside and returned to the problem at hand. "The Directive knows I have the memories. If they believe I know something significant, I can trap them like mice in a cage."

A daring plan, the voice said. *Do not rush it. It cannot come from us. Let it seep out, like ink in water, until it reaches their ears. Together, we will destroy magic and save the Dominion.*

CHAPTER 19
KATIE

MARY-LOU WAS IN BAD SHAPE. Whatever spell Horace used on her had left more than a mark on her arms. She lay on the couch—glassy eyes staring straight up—while Michael changed her bandages. The faculty room's open windows invited a cool sea breeze. It rolled off the starlit Mediterranean and into the room, ruffling the class timetables and safety procedures pinned to the corkboard—artefacts from a time when the world was normal.

"The bleeding has stopped," Michael said. "This will take time to heal. The Ire Tides somehow slice and burn at the same time." Laurefen crushed fragrant ingredients in a stone mortar, and Michael slathered a handful of yellow salve on the twin gashes. Laurefen dusted her arm with herbs and Michael quickly wrapped it with practiced precision.

"Okay, Kate." Laurefen gestured to the bucket in her lap.

Katie squeezed the water from the cloth and dabbed at Mary-Lou's face. She winced at the touch, but did not complain. Katie was not sure if she could.

"This is a disaster," Michael growled. "And it comes as no surprise. The Fatesmiths can't be reasoned with."

"A bit early for 'I told you so', isn't it?" Katie dropped the washcloth with a splash. Their near-death experience in Sabriva had erased her reverence—and patience—for Michael. She touched Mary-Lou's shoulder. "Can you hear me?"

The older woman tilted her chin. It was barely a nod, but enough. Her gaze shifted from the roof to Laurefen. "Books." Her voice was dry as sand. "Horace wanted books."

Laurefen plucked a folded sheet of paper from his coat pocket. "I suspected as much." He unfolded the page and held it out for them. It was a list of titles, with one high-lighted in fluorescent green. "This was on one of the desks I searched."

Katie squinted to read the text. "Oregin o Magi... what is that?"

In response, Laurefen stood and collected a wooden box from behind a seat. It creaked open, and he lifted a small leather-bound journal from within. "This is Oregin o Magi by J.W Avonacas." Laurefen placed it on the table. "And I believe Horace wants it."

"Why?" Katie leaned in as Laurefen opened to a random page. A waft of ancient paper filled her nostrils. The pages were covered in tiny handwritten script in a language she did not recognize. "What is so important about this book?"

"For starters, after the storm at Sabriva, this is the last copy in the Dominion." Laurefen continued flipping through the journal. "It is one of thirteen books preserved from before the founding, but unlike the other twelve, Oregin o Magi has a... mysterious... history."

Katie's eyes never left the book. The words *were* gibberish. No paragraphs. Just blocks of text. "Mysterious how?"

"It was written by King Fendragon's chief scribe, Johan Avonacas, in a complex cipher," Laurefen turned the pages as if they might turn to dust at his touch. "Soon after its completion, Avonacas awoke with no memory of what he wrote, or how to decode it. It is—in the most literal sense of the word—a mystery."

"Horace is after a book that he cannot read?" Katie frowned.

"A book that *we* cannot read," Laurefen corrected. "Remember, he has memories from the Founding."

"Oregin o Magi is proto-Hispanic," Michael said in a troubled voice. "It means Origin of Magic."

Katie's stomach dropped. "Do you think he's searching for the Well?"

Laurefen nodded. "That is what I fear. This text may hold secrets that Arman's memories lack."

With monumental effort, Mary-Lou turned to face them. "Horace wants to destroy magic," she murmured. "He believes Euryma is better off without witches or wizards." She sank back against the couch, and a tense silence overtook the room.

Laurefen thumbed through Oregin o Magi; his forehead creased as he scanned the minuscule print. He closed it and sighed. "It would appear that, for now, our core mission remains the same. We protect the Well."

Michael nodded solemnly, but Katie wasn't so sure. As she stared at the small journal on the coffee table, a thought occurred to her—one she knew Michael would not like. "What if Horace *is* trying to stop the storms? What if this book holds the key to locking Remnant Magic in another Well?"

Michael scoffed. "Nonsense. Mary-Lou said it herself. Horace wants to end magic. That is his goal." He turned to Laurefen. "We should burn the book. Keep the Well's secrets beyond his reach."

"No," Laurefen said. "I will not destroy knowledge. That is not our way." He frowned at Katie and his expression softened. "You have always seen things in a way that others don't, Miss Hall. Perhaps you can discover something in these pages that other scholars have missed." He placed the book back in its box and held it out to her. "If the key to stopping the storms is in here, you have my complete support to find it."

Speechless, Katie took the crate, then nearly dropped it as an electric wail filled the air. Michael and Laurefen raced to the windows. The evacuation alarm continued, blaring from the college speakers to fill the entire island. "What is it?" Katie shouted.

"I don't know." Laurefen's fingers danced on his palm. Mary-Lou's eyes were wide. They waited in tense silence for a looptap reply. When it arrived, Laurefen's expression darkened and he uttered a single word. "Storm."

Katie's heart sank. He didn't need to say any more. They all knew what he meant. A Remnant Magic Storm was coming to Kingsbreak.

"We have to leave," Michael said. "Cedrus. We must get to Cedrus before it gets too close."

Katie froze. *No. Not here. We are safe here. The storms bypass us.* Michael and Laurefen rushed around her. They lifted Mary-Lou into a wheelchair and pushed her to the door. Katie had not moved; she still held the wooden box. It suddenly felt so unimportant.

"Come on Kate! Now!" Fear cracked in Laurefen's voice. Katie dropped Oregin o Magi, and rushed after them.

Michael pushed Mary-Lou along the cobblestone path. Ahead of them, college staff and their families raced south. Between the shriek of the alarm and the shouts of people, the entire scene seemed so surreal.

Cedrus—the towering cedar—came into view, a massive silhouette against a faint orange glow. It could have been sunrise, if it wasn't eight hours early and appearing on the wrong side of the horizon. "How long have we got?" Katie shouted

Neither Laurefen, nor Michael responded.

Behind her, children started to cry. She turned to see one of the college gardeners with his twin daughters. She didn't know his name, but she knew his kindness.

Katie delayed her step enough to walk alongside them. "Good evening." She flashed a reassuring smile. "It's a bit late for a stroll, isn't it?"

One of the girls nodded. They both fell silent.

"Don't worry," Katie went on. "We'll find somewhere for you to sleep. We're on an adventure, aren't we?"

One of the girls glanced at her father.

"She's right," he said. "Just a little adventure, then back to bed." The man gave Katie a grateful nod. They continued up the hill and reached a small crowd milling about the stone wall surrounding the tree. Katie estimated about sixty people, with more coming behind them. Katie wound through them until she reached the Cedrus' base. Laurefen spoke to Michael in hushed tones.

"What's wrong?" she asked.

"Keep it down," Michael growled.

Katie glanced back. Almost everyone watched them in terse silence.

"Michael can't make an Opening," Laurefen whispered.

It took all of Katie's self-control to maintain her composure. The southern horizon was a swelling display of orange light. She stepped closer between them. "Is the storm too close?"

"It would appear so," Laurefen murmured.

"What do we do?" Katie failed to keep the panic from her voice. "Could we go to the other end of Kingsbreak?"

Laurefen shook his head. "It's too far from Cedrus to summon an Opening."

"Even if we could," Michael added. "We'd never get there in time."

"So we wait here to die?" Katie's voice cracked. Her heart thundered in her chest. She felt like she was back at Sabriva, and the memories of the awful sound—of the awful pain—gripped her by the throat. "We have to do something!" She was crying, she realized, and she wasn't alone.

Behind her, others were trying—and failing—to create Openings. On the edge of the crowd, Katie saw the twins and their father huddled together.

"There is one option," Laurefen said. "If the Fatesmiths are hiding in caves, we could do similar."

"The Well?" Katie's mind spun like a flipped coin. She seized on the idea. "Yes! We need to get everyone down to the Well," she said. "Underground. That's our only chance."

"We cannot reveal the Well's existence," Michael said.

"We don't have to," Laurefen replied. "We just have to get them into the cavern leading down."

Michael's forehead creased. Frustration flared in Katie's chest. "We don't have time for this!" She ignored him and faced the pandemonium. "The Openings aren't working!" she shouted. The noisy crowd fell silent, save for the sobs of the children scattered between them. "We need to get underground. There's a narrow cave on the island's eastern side. We have to go now. Leave any bags. Move!"

She turned to Laurefen. "Lead the way. I'll trail behind."

To her surprise, neither of them argued back. Laurefen started down the path. Michael rotated Mary-Lou's chair. She looked so frail, but she spared Katie a smile. Laurefen stopped to scoop up one twin while the friendly gardener picked up the other.

"Go!" Katie shouted, shooing the people at the back. "Leave it," she told a woman shouldering her backpack. "Hurry!"

She glanced back and her blood became ice. The storm was no longer a glow on the horizon; it was a swirling tsunami whose flares exploded skywards. "GO!" she screamed. "RUN!"

They thundered down the hill. A half-dozen older scholars could not keep up. Katie encouraged them as best she could, but they were not moving fast enough. *We're not going to make it.*

"Go ahead, Ms. Hall," said her old imbusion instructor, Mr. Barker. "We'll just slow you down."

"I'm not leaving you behind," she said.

"You have to." The old man exchanged a sad smile with an elderly woman who Katie assumed was his wife. "We have lived our lives. It's not fair for you to miss yours." He took her hand in his and squeezed it. "Go. Go on. It's fine."

Katie nodded, unable to speak. With tears streaming down her face, she rushed past them to catch the rest of the crowd. She turned back to see them huddled together underneath a burning sky.

No. No. No. No. No.

They would not make it to the Well. They weren't even going to make it to the Village. The speed of the storm was unfathomable. As she ran down the hill, she saw Laurefen and the others turn to face their doom.

The high-pitched whine of the tempest reached her ears. The sound took her back to Sabriva. Back to the certainty that she was about to die. She stopped running too. In a burst of clarity, Katie witnessed her insignificance. The storm rolled towards Kingsbreak. An unstoppable force that would clear King's College like a sandcastle in a tidal wave.

There's no Declan to save you this time, she thought. And then—not wanting that to be her last thought, she turned her mind to something else—*I'll see you soon Mom*.

An explosion of Remnant Magic hit the island.

There was a deafening chime, like some gargantuan glass bell. The ground jerked, knocking her to one knee, as the sky lit up in a patchwork quilt of light. A geodesic dome made of every color flashed into existence. Remnant Magic rolled overhead, like water dashing over a stained-glass umbrella. It coursed over them. Glittering. Sparkling. Protecting.

The Ancellum. Katie's heart almost burst from her chest. Tears of relief blurred her vision.

"It's beautiful." Laurefen stood at her shoulder. The endless rainbow reflected in his tear-filled eyes. "Regardless of what the Fatesmiths think, magic has saved our lives."

The words unlocked an idea; a crucial piece of a puzzle falling into place. "This is the answer," she said. Gesturing skyward. "The Ancellum is the answer." She gripped Laurefen's elbow. "If we can recreate this magic, we can protect the Dominion. We could keep our magic. We could save Euryma."

CHAPTER 20
AVA

WINDS HOWLED, thunder crashed, and jagged forks of lightning danced across curtains of rain. The storm raged for most of the night, then—as suddenly as it arrived—it vanished. With the clouds gone, the stars glittered overhead, lighting a path up the mountain trail. Barefoot, Ava crept through the silence. A combination of Luck and memory guided her back to the single-room storage tent. Her body begged for sleep, but she had to know. *What is in that box?*

A Velcro strap secured the front entry. Ava tore it open as quietly as she could, then slipped inside. Haberdeen sat on a lone chair with a book on her lap and a lantern at her feet. "It's about time," she said. "I was starting to think you wouldn't come."

Ava didn't know what to say. After an awkward pause, she shrugged. "You know why I'm here, then?"

"I do."

"How?"

"Mice always find the cheese." Haberdeen smiled. "And Lucks always sniff out what they're not supposed to."

For the second time in less than a minute, Ava had no response to the witch's words. Haberdeen did not seem angry. This all seemed to be according to plan. If she were not so tired, Ava might have tried to unravel the woman's motives. Instead, she opted for a direct approach. "What's in the box from Tamhill?"

Haberdeen placed her fingertip on her nose. Her grin was reminiscent of a child waiting for their parents to discover some minor mischief.

"Well?"

"A well-kept secret," Haberdeen said. She stood, and her demeanor changed. Cool confidence radiated off her as she led Ava towards the back of the tent. "You said you wanted to become a Fatesmith. That you and your friend would help me take my army back, and I would supply that army as thanks. Is that accurate?"

Ava nodded.

"I have a counteroffer." They stopped at the wooden box, and Haberdeen placed her hand on it. "Join the Fatesmiths as my right hand. Swear an oath to serve me until the Dominion is safe. In return, I will use the full might of the Fatesmiths to aid you... and I will *give* you this box."

The air in the tent solidified. Ava's breath snagged like knit fabric on a nail. She searched Haberdeen's face. There was no joke, no trickery. Only a genuine offer. Ava frowned. "Raul—"

"Isn't in charge," Haberdeen said. "I am."

Ava chewed her lower lip. The deal was tempting, but only if the box held what she hoped—a hope so fragile, she feared to say it out loud. "I... I won't agree to anything until I know what's inside."

"A fair request." Haberdeen opened the ratchet with a pop. "There are two people who know about this. Two people in the entire world." The strap fell to the floor. "If you are to become the third, you *must* keep it a secret. Do you understand?"

Nervous energy slithered in Ava's stomach. She stepped forward, but Haberdeen blocked her way.

"I asked you a question. This secret *cannot* leave this tent. Do you understand?"

"I understand." Hope burned in Ava's chest. With trembling hands, she dug her fingertips beneath the lid. The front panel tilted outward. She propped it against the box behind her. Ava took a deep breath, then peered inside.

Two figures glimmered in the lantern light. Iron sculptures of a man and a woman. Even in the dark, Ava could see the resemblance between the pair and their son. Her heart staggered, then beat twice as fast to make up for it. "They're alive," she whispered. *Declan's parents are alive. I need to find him. To tell him he's not alone.*

"You cannot tell him," Haberdeen said. Ava wondered if she could read minds. "Declan must not know. Nobody can know. Not yet."

"But... they're his parents." Ava stared at the iron casts. "He needs to know. He's miserable. He's—"

"A liability," Haberdeen finished. "The world believes Angus and Miranda Moore are dead. Most importantly, *Vedmark* thinks they are dead. If they discover otherwise, they will make Declan do terrible things. They will force him to destroy Euryma."

"He wouldn't." Ava shook her head. "He would never."

"He would," Haberdeen said. "He cannot know. Not while Vedmark's armies exist."

Ava tore her eyes away from the sculptures. "How?" she asked. "Declan watched you melt them. How did you bring them back?"

Haberdeen raised her palm, a clear indicator that she wasn't taking questions. "Enough. You wanted to know what was in the box. Now you do. My offer stands. The casts and an army for your oathbound loyalty. What is your choice?"

"What happens to them if I say no?"

"I keep them." Haberdeen closed the wooden panel. "They are a valuable bartering chip." She pulled on the ratchet. The wood creaked as the strap tightened.

Ava chewed her lip. A myriad of possibilities ran through her mind, and for once, the guiding bands of Luck were no use at all. Swearing the oath would guarantee her an army to bring against Vedmark and save Declan's parents. It would also put her in a cage.

You don't have a choice, she told herself. *You need that army.* "How long does this oath last?"

"Until the work is done."

Ava raised an eyebrow. "Can you be more specific?"

"When Euryma is safe from magical storms and invading armies."

"And I get Declan's parents?"

"Of course."

Ava stared at the box. She imagined Declan's face when he learned they were alive. *Think of the guilt it will take off his shoulders.* "Okay. I'll do it."

A tingle ran up her spine. A cold realization that comes with any life-altering decision. Haberdeen smiled, and Ava couldn't help but picture a cat looming over a cornered mouse.

"So... How does this work?" Ava said. "Do I just swear on my honor?"

"It's a little more formal than that." Haberdeen picked up the lantern and started towards the entry. "Come. There are a few more hours before dawn. I will send for you tomorrow. We can discuss the specifics then."

Ava did not wake until noon. When she did, a platter of cold toast waited beside her bunk. She ate while she walked back up the path to Yabun. She arrived to find the village in the middle of an enormous clean up. The storm had left its mark on many of the tents, and the people worked together to repair the damage. Ava spotted Misha clearing melon-sized stones from a small rockfall along one of the central paths. Sweat wicked his dark hair over his face, he paused mid-step when he saw her. "What's this? The sleeping princess awakes at last?"

Ava contemplated driving an elbow into his stomach, but knowing Misha, he'd drop a rock on her foot. "I needed the rest," she said. "Nice of you to help."

"It's better than hanging out with our *friends*." He motioned to the pile of stones. "Though Raul was smart to get us out of the storm. A fallen boulder crushed three of the tents. Can you imagine if we stayed?"

Ava flashed a smile. "I guess even a Fatesmith can get something right on occasion."

"I hope so," he replied. "I think you're about to become one." He nodded behind her as Raul marched towards them.

"The sleeping princess has awoken."

"Hah." Ava shared a sideways look with Misha. "Original."

"Haberdeen wants you." Raul pointed to Ava. "Just you. I'll help this lad clear the rocks."

Misha grunted. "Yay." He made no effort to temper his sarcasm.

Ava winked. "Don't you have too much fun without me."

She picked her way through the busy paths and entered Haberdeen's tent. All the furniture had been pushed to the side wall, save for a small table and two chairs. Haberdeen glanced up from a cast iron cauldron sitting atop an electric stovetop.

"Ah, the sleeping princess—"

"—is awake. Yep, I've heard it twice already." Ava nodded at the bubbling brew. "What is all this?"

"This is you coming good on your promise. A proper oath."

"I..." A swarm of butterflies took flight in her stomach. "What?"

"Magic seals our agreement so that no one can change their mind." Haberdeen offered a reassuring smile. "It's painless. A drop of saliva is all I need." She tugged a rolled scroll from a pocket and handed it to Ava. "This is the oath. Read it carefully, its binding."

Haberdeen returned to the cauldron as Ava unrolled the slip. It was written on some sort of animal skin. Everything stated was as agreed, but the prospect of involving magic left a sour taste in her mouth. "I agree with what you've written, but I have zero interest in that." She waved to the simmering liquid.

"This is how it must be," Haberdeen said. "Spoken oaths are for long dead legends. If you cannot bind it with magic, I won't be able to trust you. Are you planning to betray me?"

"No. Of course not."

"Then why should this matter?" Haberdeen switched

the heat off. "This protects us both from a last-minute change of heart."

Ava reread the scroll. The oath was sound. She gritted her teeth. "Fine. What do I have to do?"

"You sit." Haberdeen added a final pinch of something to the pot. The bubbles changed from murky green to sky blue. She nodded in satisfaction, then moved the cauldron from the stovetop to the table between them. "It's a simple process. I'll read the oath, then I'll add some saliva. Once that is done, you do the same, then toss the scroll in. When liquid goes clear, we each swallow a glass of the stuff."

"Ew." Ava scrunched her nose. "No offense, but I don't want to drink your spit."

"Nobody ever does." Haberdeen shrugged. "If it helps, the magic dissolves all bodily fluids. The whole thing tastes like tepid water."

"That doesn't help."

Haberdeen laughed, as if Ava were joking. "Are you ready?"

Ava was not. The entire thing had been thrust on her with no warning, and now, she had half a mind to leave the tent and never come back. *If only Declan's parents weren't involved.* She shrugged her shoulders. "As ready as I'm going to be."

"Fantastic." With a flick of her wrist, Haberdeen unrolled the scroll. In a clear voice, she started to read. "I, Deena Herb, bind myself to this oath. Ava Drakonov will submit her services to Deena Herb. Ava Drakonov will not speak of Angus and Miranda Moore to any who do not know of their existence. Ava Drakonov will use her power over Luck to aid Deena Herb in protecting Euryma." She took a deep breath. "Deena Herb will use her authority over the Fatesmith army to protect Euryma. Deena Herb will promote Ava Drakonov to a commanding position amongst the Fatesmiths. When Euryma is safe from Remnant Magic and the nation of Vedmark, Deena Herb will grant Ava Drakonov ownership of the casts of Angus and Miranda Moore. When Euryma is safe from Remnant Magic and the nation of Vedmark, this oath will be fulfilled, and all binding promises will cease. This I swear." She leaned over the brew and let a single drop of spittle fall. The blue liquid frothed and turned yellow. Haberdeen handed the scroll to Ava. "Your turn."

With her heartbeat drumming in her ears, Ava repeated the oath. Nervously, she spat into the cauldron. The yellow liquid became vibrant magenta. She held the oath over it. "Now this goes in?"

"Straight in the pot."

The liquid hissed as it engulfed the animal-skin scroll. For a moment, Ava worried it might overflow. Then it settled, and the bright colors vanished. It could have been a pot of water. Ava wondered what would happen if someone else drank it by accident.

Haberdeen used a mug to scoop a small amount into two glasses. "Bottoms up?"

Ava stared at her reflection on the liquid's surface. "This is so gross." Before she had time to second guess herself, she threw it back in one gulp. It didn't taste like tepid water. It tasted like something wrung from old socks. Haberdeen handed her a mug of moss punch. "Wash it down, girl."

"You said it tasted like water!"

Haberdeen swigged her own clear liquid and grimaced. "Sometimes it's better not to know what is coming."

Ava drank the whole mug. Even after the punch, the

memory of the foul oath water lingered on her tongue. "So gross!" She wiped her lips. "What now? Is it done?"

"Our oath is sealed." Haberdeen poured herself a second glass of moss punch. "Now, I need time to plan our advance into Euryma. You should take the next few days to rest and recover. It might be the last chance you get for a while."

Three days later, Misha lay on the floor, staring at the ceiling. "I can't believe you did that."

Ava continued packing her bag. Her paltry collection of items spread out on the bunk. The khaki green walls of their tent rippled as a gust roared through the mountain village. She had finally told Misha about the oath—or as much as she could tell him. He had not taken it well. "It's done now." She squeezed a tight roll of shirts into a side pocket. "You should pack. Raul said we'll be leaving soon."

"You might be." Misha didn't sit up. "I'm staying here."

Ava rolled her eyes. "Nothing has changed, Mish. We came to Yabun to find help. We did that. Now we need to get our army."

"And in the meantime, you became a puppet."

Ava wrenched on the bag's zipper so hard it tore at the top. "Stop being a child. I did what I had to. This isn't Luck training. It's the real world, and sometimes, the real world requires sacrifices." She exhaled a small measure of her frustration. "Remember what we're here for. Grigory and the Emissary." She dug a sewing kit from a side pocket and went to work repairing the zip.

After a long pause, Misha sat up. "You should have

spoken to me first. That's all. I thought we were in this together."

I don't need your permission to do what I have to do. Ava bit her tongue. The words wouldn't help. When the silence started to stretch, Misha stood and started to pack as well.

Ten minutes later, the roar of a car engine interrupted the quiet. Two loud honks startled Ava. She slung her bag over her shoulder. "I suppose that's the signal to go."

She exited the tent to find a rust covered truck with mismatched panels waiting for them. Haberdeen sat in the passenger seat, Raul hunched over the open hood, adding water from a plastic bottle. He closed it with an ominous creak as Ava approached. "A beauty, ain't she?"

Ava frowned. "That's one word for it." The truck was a two-seater. "Where do we sit?"

Raul jutted a thumb behind him. "I threw a few mats down in the back. If you stay low, the wind won't bother you."

"And if it rains?"

"It shouldn't."

"How long is the drive?" Ava's question came through clenched teeth.

"As long as a piece of string." Raul climbed into the driver's seat. "Havin' second thoughts?"

Misha froze outside the tent. He stared at the speckled truck. "What is this?"

Raul smiled. "The best there is."

"It's a pile of junk!" Misha shook his head. "Can't we use an Opening? This thing won't make it out of Yabun, let alone down the mountain."

"Euryma's a hive of stationary wards," Raul said. "The LAMPs are uniting and looking for blood. They see us using magic, they'll kill us on sight. We travel by road. We blend in."

Haberdeen rolled down her window. "Climb in."

Ava felt an odd compulsion to do as she was told. She guessed it was the oath in action. A morbid sense of curiosity made her ignore the instructions. As the seconds stretched, the compulsion to obey grew more urgent. It was like a hunger—not of the stomach, but of the mind.

Misha hopped onto the back of the truck. "Come on," he murmured. "Might as well get it over with."

Ava didn't move. Her mind screamed at her to follow. She wanted to see how far she could push the oath.

"What are you waiting for?" Misha asked.

All three of them stared, and Ava gave in. A wave of euphoria washed over her as she complied with Haberdeen's instructions.

"What was that?" Misha whispered.

"The oath," Ava replied. Her head spun from the pleasure of obedience. "I wanted to see if I could resist."

"And could you?"

"Kind of. I don't know. It's... weird. I'll try again later."

They fell silent as the engine sputtered to life. The clutch engaged, and slowly, the truck crept along the steep road leading down the mountain, towards the Dominion of Euryma.

CHAPTER 21

DECLAN

IT DID NOT TAKE LONG for Declan to fall into a routine. The days blurred by, and in the blink of an eye, three weeks had passed.

Today was his first lecture on magical warfare. While Juniper had attended a half-dozen of the classes, Declan had politely refused. Magic was not Sila, and he expected he could learn little from stern-faced Mistress Stokes. Yet here he was, seated next to Juniper, with Harcross's advice ringing in his ears. *Today's lesson could prove the difference between victory and defeat against Horace Marley.*

The low ceiling in Brass Hall made the cavern feel smaller than the others. Students filling it to bursting didn't help either. A buzz of chatter echoed and multiplied off the stone walls. Declan and Juniper sat in the first row. She bounced with excitement as Mistress Stokes strode to the marble bench at the front of the room. "She's here."

Declan grinned. Juniper treated Sabart's teachers like rock stars. It was hilarious, yet endearing.

Their magical warfare instructor was a tall, wiry woman with midnight black hair and the face of someone

196

forever caught in the moment of swallowing a lemon. Her eyes were obsidian pearls that seemed to catalogue every inch of the room. Declan could imagine her taking a roll of attendance with one sweep of her gaze. "It is now ten o'clock. Please be silent." The drone of conversation ceased. Stokes nodded. "Today's lecture will explore a new material capable of disrupting magical energy. It is a substance purchased at great expense. We hope that, by training you to use it, it will be worth the cost."

Declan leaned forward. This *could* be useful.

She lifted a five-gallon bucket onto the bench top. "Does anybody know what this is?"

Nobody answered. Declan glanced over his shoulder to see a room of faces as blank as his own. He turned back and tried to read the yellow label printed on the front of the tub, but the text was too small.

"Excellent," Stokes said. "Because if you did, I would assume you were a Fatesmith spy." She popped the lid off and held up a handful of charcoal sand for all to see. "It is called irofil. At an elementary level, these are tiny grains of iron, but that is only the beginning. Irofil has a unique structure, not dissimilar to a snowflake. This allows it to remain airborne for much longer than expected. Throw a pinch in the air and you can block any magical attack in a cloud of dust." She let the substance fall back into the tub. "Potent enough to disrupt a fierisation square."

At that, whispered conversations erupted throughout the hall. Declan leaned so far forward, he risked falling off his seat. Fierisation had been the Fatesmiths' greatest weapon, and now they could fight back.

"Does it work on the Knights of Despair?" Someone asked behind him.

Stokes shrugged. "We do not know. Not yet."

Declan surprised himself by raising his own hand. "What about Ire Tides?"

"It will dampen the effectiveness of Ire Tides, but from our limited tests, it will not stop them entirely."

Harcross had been right. It wasn't a perfect solution, but it was something.

Juniper raised a hand. "You said it was new. Where does it come from?"

"The Fatesmiths make it."

A murmur of disapproving whispers filled the cavern. Many—if not all—of the students at Sabart held little love for the Fatesmiths. Stokes waved her hands for silence. "While I understand your hesitance, this is a tool we cannot afford to ignore. We do not know how the Fatesmiths make it, but we would be fools to refuse a valuable resource because it is produced by our enemies."

"So we are paying the Fatesmiths now?" shouted someone from the back.

Stokes glared at the speaker. "Euryma is at war, Williams. In the grand scheme of things, money means little right now." Her expression softened. "If I must choose between riches and freedom, I will pick our Dominion every time." She gestured to the buckets. "Enough of that. I have described what irofil does. Now, I will show you. I want you to think of a spell. Something more dangerous than a slap on the cheek, but not so destructive that it will bury us alive."

The tension lifted as a ripple of appreciation rolled through the room.

"If I call your name, congratulations. You have permission to attack me." Stokes scooped a handful of irofil. "I will disarm the spell. You will observe how I do it. Pay attention to the quantity, and the manner in which I move." She waved her empty hand towards a girl in the second row. "Ms. Mayhew. What do you have planned for me?"

The girl stood as directed, smiling nervously. "Do I have to say?"

The students laughed. Mistress Stokes' expression never changed. "Not at all." She pressed her hands together, taking half of the irofil in each palm. "Let us see what you've got."

The girl moved like a cobra. Her left hand traced a zigzag while the fingers on her right were a blur that Declan failed to follow. Juniper gasped at something he could not see. Stokes blew a charcoal cloud into the space between them. She stepped into its safety, then pivoted on one foot to trace a circle of dust around her.

Surprised gasps filled Brass Hall. Declan could not see nima, but the disappointment on Ms. Mayhew's face was obvious. He turned to Juniper. "What happened?"

"The threads..." Juniper's eyes were saucers. "They curled up like ashes."

Stokes remained unharmed. "A bold strategy," she announced. "Most attackers would not strike from beneath the ground. Regardless, it was not enough to breach the irofil cloud." She took another handful from the bucket, then pointed to the back of the room. "You. Mr. Porter, yes? Come show us what you are capable of."

A boy with an ill-advised moustache accepted the challenge and fared no better. Stokes called more names.

A competitive air built in the cavern. The Sabartians wanted to best their instructor. They seemed embarrassed that simple dust rendered their magical powers useless. Yet no matter how they tried, none could beat the irofil.

"How about you, Ms. Reaves?"

Declan felt Juniper tense at the mention of her name. "Uh. Okay."

"Remember," Declan whispered. "It's not where you strike, it's *how*." He smiled encouragingly. Juniper made her way to the front of the room.

Stokes weighed a small mound of irofil in her palm. "Are you ready?"

Juniper's eyes darted from her hands to the tub. Her face scrunched in the same concentration Declan recognized from their strategy lessons. Suddenly, her expression changed. Declan raised an eyebrow. He knew that look—it was the one she had when she came up with a smart move —either on the cob board or the sparring mats. "I'm ready."

Stokes clapped her hands, and an iron cloud formed between them. Instead of attacking, Juniper slowly drew her fingers apart. Declan couldn't see what she was doing, but the approving murmur of the audience told him it was something they had not yet tried. As Juniper lowered her hands, the irofil fell like a curtain. As Stokes' face appeared, Juniper thrust out both palms. An opaque sphere of condensed air surged from her fingertips.

A loud slap echoed off the cavern walls, and Mistress Stokes staggered backwards. A shocked silence followed. Juniper's face burned bright red as Stokes regained her footing. She adjusted her jacket, shaking any loose irofil to the floor. The room waited with bated breath. "Well done, Ms. Reaves." Stokes motioned to Juniper and Brass Hall erupted in applause. Declan joined in, smiling from ear to ear. The cheers lasted a full fifteen seconds before Stokes waved for them to stop. "An excellent strategy," she said. "Irofil may resist magic, but it is still bound by natural forces. By increasing the surrounding gravity, you reduced my shield's effectiveness. Inspired."

Declan nudged Juniper as she sat down. "Nice work."

"Thanks."

Mistress Stokes screwed the red lid back on the bucket. "As I have demonstrated, the most effective method of general protection is a cloud. Solid barriers are stronger for more direct attacks." She retrieved a dust pan from behind the bench and started sweeping the thick carpet of irofil at her feet. She talked while she worked, pouring the collected powder into smaller cups. "Now, you have time to practice amongst yourselves. Aeronima attacks only, and nothing that will leave a mark. Pair up and take turns attacking and..." Stokes glanced up at the sound of footsteps. John strode down the side aisle, his gaze traveling down the rows until it settled on Declan.

"Can I help you?" Stokes asked.

"Him." John pointed at Declan. "Warmistress Harcross wants him. Now."

Stokes dismissed the interruption. Without a word, she waved a hand for Declan to go.

"What's going on?" Juniper whispered.

"Not a clue," Declan replied. He gathered his bag and nudged her again. "Awesome job today, that was amazing. Have fun. I'll find you at dinner in the Mess Hall."

Juniper smiled. John left without another word and Declan hurried to catch him. He heard the scuffles of a hundred Sabartians rushing to pair up as he left. "Hey!" he called. John was already vanishing ahead of him. "Wait up! What does Harcross want?"

Declan came around a corner and nearly ran straight into him. John didn't flinch. "Harcross's bird brought me a message for you to go to her office. You know the way. I've got things to do." He turned on his heel and marched down the passage. Declan stood in stunned silence. By the time he recovered, John was once again out of sight.

CHAPTER 22
DECLAN

DECLAN MET Harcross in her office. Her normally perfect hair was a mess of tangles; Nox the raven was nowhere to be seen. In the room's corner, a section of the wall did not line up with the rest of the rock face. "John said you wanted to see me?"

Harcross did not respond. With two hands, she slid the mismatched wall to the side. It glided smoothly open to reveal a hidden passage. When it was the width of her shoulders, she gestured for him to follow. "This way."

"Where are we going?"

"Shh!" she cautioned. "We can talk when we arrive, but for now, be silent. The echoes carry. Come on."

The tunnel ran straight at a slight decline until it reached a winding staircase that descended into complete darkness. The stairs were steep, and Declan held tight to a chain that guided his path. The clatter of their quiet footsteps echoed upwards into the distant heights.

After fifteen minutes, Declan broke the silence. "How long does this go on for?"

"Almost there. Stop talking."

Ten more minutes and they reached flat ground. Not stone, rather some sort of spongy substance. It felt like walking on a bed of moss. Ahead of him, a circular doorway glowed with dim orange light, the color of Remnant Magic. "What is that?"

"You'll see."

Declan bit his tongue and followed. When they arrived at the door, a sense of disappointment overtook him. He did not know what he was expecting, but a round room with a rack of plant pots seemed underwhelming. Overhead, a panel of grow lights illuminated the space. Declan turned to Harcross. "Umm, what is this?"

"Welcome to the garden," she said. A measure of expectation shone through her expression.

Declan arced an eyebrow. "The garden?" His parents had fallen in love over a passion for plants. Their home in Tamhill featured one of the best gardens in Euryma. His gaze wandered from the black pots to the plastic watering can on the floor. "It looks closer to a greenhouse, and a sad one at that. What are we doing here?"

Harcross tucked a dark tangle behind her ears. Her eyes glittered with anticipation. "We are here because one seed bloomed today. I planted them when you arrived, and now we've got a fruit." She beckoned him to follow her to the rack. At the far end, a single stalk protruded from one of the pots. On its tip was a spherical white berry. It looked like a Styrofoam ball balanced atop a blade of grass.

"Okay..."

Harcross glanced up from the plant. "Do you..." Her smile faded as she trailed off. "Oh no. You don't know what this is, do you?"

Declan shook his head.

"Samantha never told you about the garden? About the seeds?"

"No. Nothing."

The Warmistress seemed to deflate. "So that means you haven't learned to use the berries either?" She pressed her hands to her eyes. "Oh no."

"Use the berries?" Declan frowned. "With respect, I have no idea what you're talking about. Why don't you just tell me what this is, and maybe I'll remember something Mrs. Winter said."

Harcross inhaled deeply. "We are short on time."

"Then give me the quick version."

"Fine." She breathed a curt sigh. "At some point, your great-however-many-greats great grandfather figured out a way to store memories in objects, with the caveat that only he could revisit them himself." She waved to the plant. "The idea entranced Samantha. In her brilliance, she discovered that if Arman stored his memories in seeds, the fruit of those seeds would allow someone else to experience those memories."

The words took a moment to sink in. *Experience the memories.* Declan stared at the tiny white berry. "You're saying... that thing holds one of Arman Moore's memories?"

"That is precisely what I am saying. Over a period of years, Samantha collected thousands of seeds, a library of memory." Harcross's expression darkened. "They were all destroyed when Remnant Magic razed Parteno. When Arman found out, he vowed to recreate the seeds, starting with seven memories he deemed most important for protecting Euryma." She brushed her fingers against the pot. "Vedmark's rightful King is gone, and his memories with him."

"Arman may be gone, but his memories aren't," Declan said. "Horace has them."

Harcross nodded. "For now, *those* memories are out of reach. *This* memory, however, is within reach. It sprouted this morning, but the fruit will not last long, and it can only be used once."

A pit formed in Declan's stomach as the ramifications of her words dawned on him. "I don't know how to access the memories."

Harcross's shoulders slumped. "Does that ring any bells? Did Samantha say anything about any of this?"

Declan shook his head. "Nothing."

They stood in silence. Harcross stared at the plant on the rack. "Then I suppose we need to find answers, and fast. I have some of Samantha's journals in my office. We can start there. She may have recorded something about the seeds."

Declan leaned past her to peer into the blackness through the door. "Up the stairs and back again?"

"I'm open to ideas if you've got a better one." She fixed him with a no-nonsense look.

"Up and back we go."

The trip felt shorter when he knew what to expect. Still, even at a run, it took them forty minutes to get the books and back to the garden. Another hour passed with nothing to show for it. Declan sat on an upturned bucket, searching one of Mrs. Winter's journals. So far, they had proved more cryptic than useful. He found nothing about plants, memories, or berries. *This is pointless.* He closed the book with a snap. "It's a fruit, isn't it? Shouldn't I just eat it?" He glanced up. "That's makes sense, right?"

Harcross lowered a different journal. "It took Samantha months to make the seeds work. If it was just a matter of eating it, I can't imagine it would have taken any time at all."

"Well, I can't find anything." He stood up. "How about you?"

Harcross shook her head.

"How long does the berry last?"

"A few hours," Harcross said. "More if we're lucky. We have spent a lot of time down here. More than I would have liked."

"Why *is* it down here?" Declan scanned the tiny room. "The bottom of a stone pit is an odd place to put a garden."

"After Parteno, Samantha took no chances. This cavern is deep enough to keep Sabart's most important treasures safe."

Declan wanted to ask if there were *other* treasures down here, but the urgency of the situation demanded his attention. He leaned over the plant, so close that his nose almost touched it. The berry looked like a pearl with a matte finish. "It reminds me of Winterthorn," he said. "Smooth, white, memory-related."

Harcross closed her book and came to stand beside him. She tilted her head. For a moment, they stood in silence. Then she slowly nodded. "You're right. Not just the color, but the texture. Winterthorn absorbs memories through blood." She shrugged. "Perhaps you need to use blood to activate the memory?"

"That's something." Declan turned to pick up the journal off the floor. "I've been looking for mention of memories, but nothing about blood. If—"

"Declan." There was a spike in Harcross's voice that made his heart plummet. Her eyes were wide as they fixed on the berry. "We're out of time."

The white sphere was no longer perfect. Tiny creases

spider-webbed the fruit's skin. They grew by the second, making it look more and more like a dehydrated pea. Panic rose in Declan's chest. "What do I do?"

"I don't know. Something!"

The berry shriveled before their eyes. Declan plucked it and tossed it in his mouth. He bit hard against his lip and swirled the metallic-tasting blood around the berry. He swallowed, then staggered to a knee. Some unseen force hit him like a train. The cavern began to spin, and his head felt like a helium balloon. Somewhere in the distance, Harcross called his name, but she was so far away, and Declan was floating into the vortex.

Colors rushed about him. A never-ending ribbon of pinks and blues that roared like rain on the ocean. Declan hovered in a daze. Between the stream of hues, two vague figures moved back and forth. In a moment of clarity, Declan realized this was supposed to be one of Arman's memories.

Hello? The word came out as a thought. Declan tried to look down, but there was nothing to see. This wasn't the Void. It was his mind. His grandfather's voice pierced the white noise, but it was a garbled mess of sounds, as if he were speaking underwater. *This is wrong. I must have done it wrong. I wasn't supposed to eat the berry!*

The roar continued. The silhouettes moved just beyond the curtain of light. Declan willed himself forward, to see what was on the other side, but he couldn't. He had no body *to* move.

He fought the urge to panic and tried to listen. If he could hear the memory, perhaps it wouldn't be a complete waste. He ignored the dull roar and focused on each syllable. With intense concentration, he made sense of the words.

"Were we to combine our powers, we may stand a chance," Arman said. "Sila and Luck. Morkurik would have no answer to that."

A feminine voice responded, but it was faint. No matter how he strained, Declan could not understand her words. When she finished speaking, a long pause followed.

"I think that unwise," Arman said. "We need this power. It is our one hope."

The voice murmured a response.

"No!" Arman's voice was clear, and he spoke with bitter anger. The cascade of colors changed to a deep maroon flecked with yellow and orange. "I will not sacrifice our greatest weapon! It is folly, Maria. I will speak no more of it."

The streams of light blended into each other and Declan felt as if he were being sucked down a giant drainpipe. *I can't go! None of this makes sense! I need more!* His silent pleas were pointless. A shrill ring filled his ears as a falling sensation overtook him. Then he was on the ground in the dim orange glow of the garden.

"Declan!" Harcross knelt over him. "Are you okay?"

Either he had fallen in a very convenient location, or she had propped up his head on a stack of Mrs. Winters' journals. Declan attempted to sit up, but a rush of blood sent him back to the floor.

"Gentle now." The Warmistress pressed a finger against his neck. After a brief pause, she nodded. "Pulse feels strong. Just slow down. Did it work? What did you see?"

A torrent of guilt held Declan's tongue. Arman had left him seven memories, and he just wasted one. "It did, and it didn't. I heard part of a conversation, but I couldn't see anything." He shook his head. "I don't think I used the berry properly."

Harcross pursed her lips. "Nothing to be done about it now." In spite of her words, she appeared deflated. "What *did* you hear?"

Declan closed his eyes. The stream of colors returned, as if burned into his retinas. He ignored the flashing images and focused on what he had heard. "Arman was talking to someone—a woman—about combining Sila and Luck. She said something, and he got angry. I... I don't know what it was." If nothing else, the conversation confirmed the report Horace had given him. Magic was artificial. Declan had not thought about that since their meeting in Biscay.

"Was there anything else? Any minor detail?"

"Nothing. I'm sorry." Gritting his teeth, Declan pushed himself to his feet. The garden spun about him, but he remained upright. "But it proves something Horace told me. He said magic wasn't natural. My grandfather made it to resist the Knights of Despair."

Harcross picked up her daughter's journals and stacked it with the others. If the revelation surprised her, she didn't show it. She motioned to the remaining pots. "If that is true, perhaps these memories will teach you the nature of magic. A way to..." She spun to face him. Something glimmered in her eyes. "Maybe that's it."

"Excuse me?"

"If you learn about magic, maybe you could control it. If you could control Remnant Magic, you could stop the storms and destroy Vedmark in one blow."

The idea hit him like a lightning bolt. An unfamiliar sensation rushed down Declan's spine. Something he had not known in a long time. Something he had failed to recognize in Harcross's eyes.

Hope.

The feeling was short-lived. It fractured as he considered the six remaining pots on the rack. "Did you plant all the seeds?"

Harcross nodded. "Those were Samantha's instructions. Once you arrived, there was no reason to delay."

"When will they sprout?"

"It is hard to say. They are... unpredictable."

"That's why you wanted me to stay?"

A sad smile graced the Warmistress's lips. "Amongst other things, yes."

"Other things?"

"Everything in its time, Declan." Harcross motioned to the plants. "If these memories are the key to Euryma's salvation, we need to find Samantha before they fruit."

"Can you take the seeds out until I learn how to use them?"

She shook her head. "Doing so would risk the whole plant. No..." She drummed her fingers against the metal rack, her brow creased in concentration. "There is chemical energy running through the seeds that I can manipulate. That might slow their growth, buy us a few weeks, but I cannot stop them. Not now. That's the best I can do."

"How do we find Mrs. Winter?"

"If I knew, I would have done so already. I am connected to her looptap, but she does not respond. She could be in a state of slumber, bound in finger-cuffs, or something else."

"Can you trace the nima that connects you?"

"I can't, but a Luck could." The Warmistress raised an eyebrow. "We could really use your friend Ava right now."

The words were a slap to the face. Ava was the whole reason he was in Euryma, the reason he needed to find Winterthorn. "No," Declan said flatly. "I am not bringing Ava to Euryma while Horace has the dagger."

"Why?"

Declan clenched his jaw. The fact she would ask without sharing her own secrets irked him more than it should. "It's like you say—everything in its own time."

Harcross rolled her eyes. "We're talking about the fate of the Dominion."

"We are." Declan considered the glow lamps that shone like a Remnant Magic storm. "But what does it matter if everyone you care about is dead? I've lost enough people for Euryma. I won't sacrifice any more." He braced himself with steely resolve. "Nothing has changed. Winterthorn is my priority. When the dagger is gone, we get Ava. Then we find Mrs. Winter, use the seeds, and figure out how to control Remnant Magic."

"Simple as that?"

Declan looked out into the darkness, and once again, wondered if he was making the right choice. "As simple as that."

CHAPTER 23
SAMANTHA

A COMMOTION outside woke Samantha from an uneasy slumber. She lay in a heap on an unwashed wooden floor. Iron shackles bound her wrists and ankles; enormous bolts fixed the cold chains to the top of her cage. Laroa's ruins were three days behind them. Or was it four? Samantha had no way of knowing. Time had no meaning in her cell; it blended together in a mix of pain and hunger.

Someone arrived at the door. Instinctively, Samantha retreated to the corner. Keys jingled in the lock, and lantern light washed in. Rough hands seized her. Samantha didn't fight. How could she? Her fingers were gone, her right eye blinded, her spirit broken.

Unseen figures dragged her up the staircase to the balcony of the traveling court. Another door opened to blinding sunlight. Samantha squeezed her eye closed while someone bolted her chains to the floor. She could hear Rasporvin speaking to somebody. When she raised her head, Rasporvin watched her from a wooden throne. He wore a silver crown and a satisfied smile. Bile rose in Samantha's throat at the sight of him.

Samantha turned away. They were perched on the edge of a rise. On her left, Odacre's mountain ranges rose like a stone wall. Less than a mile below them, a sprawling riverside town was coming to life. A sea of fog blanketed the streets, hiding the traffic, but not the sounds of engines. The tops of buildings protruded like islands. The sun kissed the rooftops, painting them gold. It was beautiful. The sight made Samantha feel ill.

A line of buses broke free of the mist, heading west along the highway and shrank into the distance. *At least some of them will get away.*

"The rat arrives at last," Rasporvin said. "Come, as promised, to watch another nest burn." He leaned forward and spat on her. "Reports estimate this is home to ten-thousand southern vermin." Rasporvin smiled. "Knight-master Korvan says it will take him only ten minutes."

Samantha wanted to cry, to scream, to beg. But she wouldn't. Not today. She had done all three in Laroa, to no avail. Rasporvin enjoyed her misery. She would not give him the pleasure. Not again.

"I thought that too easy," Rasporvin went on. He spoke as if butchering thousands of innocent people was as normal as observing the weather. "I challenged him to destroy it in half of that." He took her chin in his oily fingers. "We will watch together and see how he fares."

The Grand Steward pushed her face away, and the chains rattled as Samantha fell against them. Rasporvin stood as the travelling court turned on the spot. Samantha's heart galloped in her chest as the sight below her registered.

A thousand drevsmok crouched at the ready. A thousand Knights waited in green armor. At the front, Korvan removed his helmet. His ivory hair fanned over his shoulder plate. He raised a fist in the air. A terrible silence hung over them.

"No," Samantha groaned. "These aren't your enemies." Every word burned against her parched throat. "Leave them. There are women and children down there. Families."

Rasporvin stood over her, his expression grim. "I told you what would happen if you betrayed me. You are responsible for this, rat. This is your doing, and you will watch every moment."

"Please." Samantha's chains rattled as she bowed low. "I'm begging you. Please, don't do this."

Rasporvin held her gaze and raised his fist.

A thousand drevsmok took to the sky in unison. A roar of thunder marked their ascent, and the gale coming off their wings pushed Samantha flat against the balcony floor. She wanted to turn away, to hide her face and cry. She could not. Sila held her eye open as the Knights descended like locusts on a field.

Waves of glistening silver sprayed from the drevsmok's jaws. Brick and mortar washed away like sandcastles. Screams filled the air, only to vanish in blood-curdling silence. A whine of engines announced a stream of vehicles fleeing the city. A group of Knights banked hard. In a burst of green, Sila erased the cars from existence.

Emerald flames poured from the sky. It burned the fog as it streamed between buildings. Samantha's stomach clenched until she vomited a pitiful mix of water, bile, and stale bread.

Rasporvin seemed delighted by the carnage. When a burnt husk was all that remained, the Knights returned.

The loss of life was too fast, too complete, too barbaric. Samantha had not known about the drevsmok. Rasporvin had kept that to himself, and now she could not imagine any scenario where Euryma could resist an army of such brutal power. They were a Dominion of twigs, and Vedmark was a wildfire. Samantha lay in her own sick and cried.

Korvan arrived as the servants unlocked her chains. He ignored her, save for a wrinkle of his hooked nose. A mix of ash and sweat dirtied his face. "My Lord." Korvan dipped his head. "I trust you marked time."

Rasporvin lifted a golden pocket watch. "Eight minutes, my son."

The Knightmaster flinched as if struck. "We have failed, my King." But his voice held no apology. No sincerity. Only ice.

"There will be other nests to burn," Rasporvin said. "Consider this a chance to learn." He turned a smile on Samantha. "For next time."

Korvan bowed. From the balcony floor, Samantha could see the humility was a ruse. Anger burned in those eyes, and those eyes turned on her. "I trust you enjoyed the performance, rat. Your weak countrymen make poor sport."

Samantha dropped her gaze. She hated the man more than words could describe.

"She will watch it all," Rasporvin said. "And when we have drowned Euryma in Sila's flame, she will beg for her life."

They wanted a rise from her. They were waiting to order her lashed for insolence. Samantha bit her tongue.

"The rat is as poor a sport as her kin." Rasporvin waved a hand. Someone wrenched on her chain and Samantha jerked upright. She almost fell down the stairs, barely finding her feet before a bald servant shoved her back into her cell. It locked with a resounding click.

One servant threw a half-loaf of bread onto the floor

and left. It was the closest thing to a meal Samantha had seen in days, and while her ruined hands made eating difficult, she managed it. Samantha cried as she ate, and when the stale bread was gone, she curled into a ball to wait for tomorrow's massacre.

It was afternoon when the noise began. At first, Samantha's stomach clenched at the thought of another town for the Knights to destroy. Then the volume increased. It sounded... different. Something unusual was happening outside the travelling court. Even through the thick walls, she could hear fear in the shouts.

Her door swung open. Two servants seized her under the arms and dragged her upstairs. Samantha squinted into the fiery horizon. An orange sunset cast tangerine light over the balcony. Rasporvin sat on his throne with down-turned lips.

Someone shoved her to his feet. When she rolled over, the Grand Steward glowered down at her. His false crown glittered on a brow creased with concern. "Tell me about your storms." The brilliance of the sunset reflected in his eyes, and only then did Samantha realize there was no sunset.

She turned around to see Remnant Magic surging towards them. Her heart back flipped in her chest. *It's over. The storm will kill them! Kill us!*

"Focus, rat." Korvan's spiteful voice had claws. She had not seen him standing behind the throne. "Tell us about these storms, or we'll feed you to a drevsmok."

"You—" She trailed off in a coughing fit. Rasporvin and Korvan leaned closer, and Samantha began to laugh.

"You came all this way to die. Your grand conquest undone."

The back of Korvan's hand filled her vision. Everything vanished in a slap of light and pain. "Tell us—"

"Or what?" She tasted blood in her mouth. It emboldened her. She bared bloody teeth in a mad smile. "You'll kill me? You don't have the time, you white-haired worm. We're going to be dead in minutes. I just hope I live long enough to watch you burn."

A second backhand knocked her to the floor. Even so, she could not stop laughing. Only when Korvan's boot forced the breath from her lungs did she cease. A shrill whistle carried on the wind.

"It is southern magic!" Rasporvin shouted, though he could not hide the tremble in his voice. "It is weak. You must stop it with Sila. Call your Knights."

There was a shout, a thud of wings, and an enormous drevsmok leapt into the air. Korvan jumped from the balcony into its saddle. "Knights to me!" His words—magnified by Sila—thundered over the storm.

Hundreds raced to the front of Rasporvin's court. The orange tsunami looked as it did in Parteno. Immense. Absolute. Inevitable. Samantha bathed in its glow. Flashes of emerald burst up from beneath them, each igniting into an enormous octagonal plate, locking together with its neighbor. Rasporvin sat on the edge of his throne. Samantha crawled back as the wave surged forward.

Sila rose over them, a towering wall of light. Remnant Magic crashed into it with the force of a hurricane. An enormous crack shook the travelling court as the storm coursed overhead.

Samantha's heart shattered. *No.*

"HOLD!" Korvan roared. The shield quivered as flecks of

green tore off it in brilliant shimmering auroras. "HOLD! FOR VEDMARK!"

Rasporvin and his servants watched in silence, completely transfixed by the spectacle. An idea tugged at Samantha, and she looked back at the long chain trailing down the stairs. Every single Knight was pouring every ounce of strength into their defense. Rasporvin's eyes were glued to the sky.

At that moment, Samantha did not exist to any of them.

Gently, she sidestepped the chains, then froze when they clinked together. She waited for a full count of five. Nothing happened. The storm held everyone's attention. Everyone but hers.

From behind the wooden throne, Samantha wrapped the iron links around her wrists. She breathed in through her nose and counted down. *Three. Two. Now.* In one rapid motion, she looped it over Rasporvin's head and pulled as hard as she could. Vedmark's leader tensed as the chain tightened against his neck. His arms flailed uselessly as his servants stood, transfixed, at the balcony's edge. Samantha braced her feet against the wood and heaved with all her strength. She couldn't see Rasporvin, but she could feel his panic. He thrashed against her, like a fish out of water.

"How does it feel?" she whispered. "To come this far, only to die at the hands of a one-eyed rat?"

The roar of the storm swallowed his gurgling protests. Samantha ignored her trembling muscles—ignored every-thing—until his limp arms collapsed over the throne's armrest.

Still, she did not dare let go. A full minute passed before she eased her grip. When she did, Rasporvin sat still. The self-appointed King of Vedmark was dead—choked on the chains of his own emissary. Samantha peeked over the throne, and her heart stopped. Korvan was staring up at her. Korvan was smiling. Samantha ducked, dropped the chain, and braced for death.

It never came.

"HOLD KNIGHTS!" Korvan shouted. The last vestige of the storm flared overhead. When Samantha checked again, his eyes were back on the wall of green. "IT IS ALMOST DONE!"

She considered Rasporvin. Empty eyes stared out from a thin, mottled face. She pressed a fingerless hand to his cheek. He did not move. He really *was* dead.

She pushed at him again, just to be sure. This time, his head tilted sideways. As if in slow motion, the silver crown tipped and fell to the ground with a heavy thud. One servant turned at the sound. Curiosity became confusion. Confusion became surprise. Surprise became outrage.

"Murder!" screamed the servant. The others spun in shock. "The rat has murdered the King!"

Vengeful hands seized Samantha, and she didn't bother to fight back. They would kill her now, but they could not change what had happened. Rasporvin had paid for his crimes, and that could not be undone.

"You will burn for this," the bald-headed servant growled. His fingers held her throat so tight she couldn't breathe. Three men kneeled over Rasporvin's corpse as they tried in vain to revive him.

They wouldn't. They couldn't.

Wisps of orange light swirled overhead. Samantha admired them, smiling as her vision darkened. *There are worse ways to go.*

The pressure vanished. Air rushed into her lungs as a white-haired figure loomed over her. Green tendrils curled around his arm. He considered Rasporvin's body. "You have murdered my father." A band of Sila lifted Samantha from the ground. She hovered over an army of Knights.

Venomous cries rose from a crowd she could not see. Their fury was a mess of curses that morphed into a hysteric chant. "Kill the rat! Kill the rat!"

Yes. Kill me.

Sila jerked her back against the balcony. It pinned her to the floor.

"I will kill the rat." Korvan's voice was deafening. "But not yet. Do not let anger cloud your mind. Death is the easy option, and this creature does not deserve death. Not yet."

The words made Samantha's skin crawl. The Knights fell silent.

"My father wanted the rat to know loss," he said. "We will honor this. We will bind the rat and make her wish she had *never* been born."

A manic ferver overtook the army below. Sila hauled Samantha up by her hair. Her scalp was fire as she hung—helpless—over the crowd. They jeered at her with hate in their eyes.

"Make her watch! Make her watch!" The chant rose like a tempest.

"She will watch Euryma burn!" Korvan tossed Samantha aside. She landed hard, and when she tried to push herself upright, he pressed a boot to her back. "King Drakonov sought to return Vedmark to its former glory. Tonight, we shall honor him with a feast. For the glory of Vedmark!"

"For the glory of Vedmark!" cheered the Knights. The fear of the storm combined with the rage of Rasporvin's death seemed to coalesce into a feverish bloodlust. The sound of the camp was deafening.

When the people had dispersed, Korvan hopped down

from the balcony's edge and directed the servants to take Rasporvin's body away. His face was unreadable as he watched them go. Free of his Sila, Samantha curled up against the chains.

Korvan knelt so they were at eye level. "Look at you," he said. "Cowering like an infant." He shook his head, and then he smiled. "You may think you have won some moral victory today. Perhaps you thought you had cut the head off the snake, or earned your death, but you have not. Nothing has changed. If anything—you have made your plight worse."

As his words sank in, an unsettling realization turned Samantha's blood to ice. "You wanted this, didn't you?" she whispered. "You saw me. You could have saved him. You didn't."

"All according to plan." Korvan's smile broadened. "But it is your word against mine, rat."

"You let him die."

"I did." Korvan turned his back on her and retrieved the fallen crown. He stared at it as he spoke. "And now—as heir to the throne—Vedmark is mine."

Samantha felt like she was going to be sick. Her only victory had been nothing but a move on a chess board. "He was your father!"

"That man was weak." Korvan settled the crown atop his head. "And now I am King, Vedmark is strong."

CHAPTER 24
KATIE

KATIE REMEMBERED when Mary-Lou's spacious living room felt like home. It had been her sanctuary when the Fate-smiths took her mother. Now, she felt out of place.

Mary-Lou did not notice. At least, she didn't show it. She had made a full recovery and now bustled about with a cracked tea-set, forever the gracious host. "They should be here soon." She filled two empty mugs on the coffee table. "Have you had any luck with the spikeshields?"

"No." Katie hid her frustration behind a polite smile. "I'm still missing something." She had spent the last two storms down in The Well, analyzing its reaction to Remnant Magic. Each time the Ancellum activated, the swirling orange mass plummeted like mercury in an ice bath, only to surge back up once the storm was gone. Her efforts to create something similar using Ava's bag of opaque shield spikes had been a parade of failures. It was as pointless as her attempts to decode Oregin o Magi.

The two impossible tasks were taking their toll, but Katie refused to give up. "The Well powers the Ancellum, that much is obvious, but finding the mechanism for the spell is... guesswork." She accepted a warm mug and set it on the table beside her. "I should be there now, Lou. I don't mean to be rude, but why am I here?"

Mary-Lou cradled her tea as she eased into a plush armchair. "Laurefen has news from the mainland, something related to Horace Marley."

Katie's hands tensed involuntarily. The wound that boy had left in her life would never heal. She took a calming breath as the last vestige of sunset lost its color. The door opened and two men entered through the hallway. Laurefen wore an emerald coat embroidered with gold thread. Mud and food stains covered Michael's collared shirt.

"What happened to you?" Mary-Lou asked.

Michael scowled in response.

"Our apologies for the delay," Laurefen said, and Katie's stomach began tying itself in loose knots. The seriousness of his tone did not bode well. "This is important." He gestured to Michael. "Go ahead."

"At first," Michael started. "I hoped it was a rumor. After spending a day in a Biscay bin." He tugged at his dirt-smeared collar. "I can confirm it is not. The Marley boy knows how to breach the Ancellum."

A soft gasp escaped Katie's lips. *No!*

Mary-Lou put her tea down. "How?"

"We can only assume he discovered something in Arman Moore's memories," Laurefen said. "It is what we feared."

"No, I mean, how does he intend to bypass the Ancellum?"

"He plans to use the original stonework of Sabriva Tower." Michael walked to the window and peered skyward. "A piece of the debris imbued by the light of a full moon will allow him safe passage to Kingsbreak." Michael turned to them. "From what I know about lunar cycles, we have two or three weeks."

"To do what?" Mary-Lou asked.

"To stop him."

"The sooner, the better." Laurefen added. "We either need to reduce the rubble to dust, or remove it from the site of its destruction."

Katie listened in silence. She teased the words apart, the way one would a knot. No matter which way she twisted, it made little sense. "I don't understand the connection between the Ancellum and the tower."

Laurefen nodded. "I share similar sentiments. The Ancellum predates Sabriva itself by a significant amount of time."

"Arman Moore," Mary-Lou said. "He cast the Ancellum, and that the tower was what kept him alive so long. They are connected through him."

Katie pursed her lips. "Have you considered it could be a trap? A ploy to lure us to Sabriva?"

"We have," Laurefen said. "And it is a real possibility. But Horace Marley has Arman Moore's memories, and if Arman Moore created the Ancellum... It is reasonable to believe his memories would hold the secrets of its undoing." He fixed her with an intent gaze. "What choice do we have?"

"It... just doesn't feel right. These *things* were created either side of the Founding. You don't make a lock and then wait to make the key a year later."

"Our knowledge of the Founding comes from scratches on the scrolls that managed to survive the last thousand years." Michael shook his head. "Are you suggesting we base the security of magic *itself* on the scribbles of some long dead scholars?"

"I... no..." Katie sighed. She had no way to explain the sour sensation in her stomach. "It feels wrong. That's all."

"We will take precautions," Laurefen said. "Your gut instinct and attention to detail have proven correct in the past, Katie. We will not make the same mistake twice." He helped himself to the teapot. "If Horace is drawing us out, we will be ready for him. If Michael's reports are accurate, we must destroy that tower. We have two weeks. How do we accomplish those goals in unison?"

"Are the Fatesmiths guarding the site?" Katie asked.

Laurefen sipped his tea. "We have no way of knowing. Openings no longer function in the vicinity of Sabriva's ruins. We suspect the storm damaged the surrounding nima. A physical expedition is our only option."

"What about above-ground portals?" Mary-Lou asked. "If we dropped flashbulbs from the sky, we could turn the stone to dust from a distance. We wouldn't need to be anywhere near the tower."

Laurefen raised an eyebrow at Michael. "Would that work?"

"I don't know." Michael ran a hand over his shaved head. "I haven't tried anything of the sort."

"Go and try," Laurefen said. He motioned to Mary-Lou. "How many bulbs do we have?"

"At least a dozen crates."

Katie nodded slowly. They could release and run. Even if Horace was waiting for them, he couldn't stop a thousand glass spheres falling from a hole in the sky. *But he could.* Katie pictured the boy cutting Sabriva Tower's ancient stone to pieces with pillars of violet Ire Tides and swallowed loudly. "If Horace spots the flashbulbs, he'll shatter them before they reach the stone." She took a deep breath as she dissected the problem. "We need a distraction to keep him occupied."

"I can do that, if it is required," Laurefen said. "We are fortunate to have caught word of this when we did. We have time to plan. We will protect Kingsbreak." He waved to Mary-Lou. "Go. Assign whichever staff will help to fill the bulbs. Michael, let me know how it goes with the Opening."

"We should move the flashbulbs," Katie said. Her voice was sharper than she intended, and Laurefen raised his eyebrows in response. Katie glanced outside at a slim crescent moon. "If Horace's goal is to get *here*, we would be stupid to create an Opening straight to Kingsbreak. Once the crates are full, we should transport them to a secondary site, and then drop them from there."

"You are definitely Lisa's daughter." A wry smile split Laurefen's wrinkled face. "Excellent thinking Katie. Now. Let's get to work."

Two days and twelve crates of flashbulbs later, Katie was back in the Imbusion Lab. She sat on the floor, examining the frosted spike. It could have been a massive icicle—the length of her forearm and thick as a coffee-cup—were it not for the uncanny warmth that emanated from within. Ava had referred to them as 'shieldshards'. Everything beyond their name was a mystery.

"How do you work?" she asked, turning the spike around in her hand. It seemed perfectly smooth, unless stabbed into the ground, where it produced a pale yellow hemispherical shield. She stood to grab some heavy tongs that lay alongside a stone container. After much convincing, Laurefen had allowed her to collect a single crucible of Remnant Magic from The Well. It had not been easy—she had destroyed more crucibles than she cared to say—but now, with a simmering pot of pure magic at her disposal, Katie had an idea.

Or perhaps experiment was a better word.

She clamped the thickest end of the shieldshard and lowered it into the glowing liquid. When the tip pierced the surface, a sudden crack—like footsteps on an icy river—echoed off the Imbusion Lab's tiled walls.

Heart racing, Katie extracted the spike and her breath caught. A jagged fracture marred its length. A gentle golden glow shone through the split. "What is this?" she whispered. As she leaned closer, the lab door opened.

Startled, Katie fumbled the tongs; the spike fell to the floor and shattered. Something like golden jelly poured out of the fragments. They pooled together and floated upwards, a wobbling helium balloon that popped and vanished when it reached the ceiling.

Mary-Lou stood at the entrance, her hand still gripping the door handle. "I'm so sorry, dear!" she said. "What *was* that?"

"I... don't know," Katie said. She poked at the mess with her foot. The shieldshard now resembled broken glass. "It wasn't Remnant Magic. It was... gold." She shook her head as she glanced up. "Is everything okay?"

"Things could be better."

"Meaning?"

Mary-Lou sighed. "Openings do not work. Not on the ground, not in the sky. It appears the whole of Sabriva is cut off from magic."

"How close can we get?"

"There's a railway town called Alastair, about fifty miles

west." Mary-Lou tugged the indigo shawl draped over her shoulders. "We are headed there today."

"We?"

"Michael and I. Laurefen has gathered some nimrods attuned to Sabriva. We want to see if they still function after the storm, as well as scout the tower's ruins."

Katie grinned as she pictured the pair waving the nimrods around. "You'll be a few storybook magicians with magic wands." Her smile slipped away. "Do you want me to come?"

"I came to invite you..." Mary-Lou gestured to the broken spike on the floor. "Until I saw this. It looks like you're making progress."

"Hah." Katie shook her head. "If 'breaking things' is what you call progress, then sure. Still..." She bit her lip as she turned back to the crucible of Remnant Magic. "I might have found a foxhole to explore."

"These shields stopped Ire Tides. If you can alter them to stop Remnant Magic, that would be an incredible tool to have at our disposal." Mary-Lou smiled. "Michael and I will be fine. You continue exploring."

Katie nodded, then frowned. "If you are going with Michael, what is Laurefen up to?"

A smile tugged at the older woman's lips. "The Dean is off stealing vehicles from Euryma's abandoned cities."

"What? Why?"

"If we can't get the flashbulbs to Sabriva by Opening, we're going to have to move them in from Alastair. Laurefen's already found a monumental railway shed, and now he is off filling it with pilfered vans."

"I didn't even know he could drive."

Mary-Lou chuckled and pulled her into a hug. Katie squeezed back.

"Be smart, okay?" she told the older woman. "No heroics. Find out what you need to know, keep Michael in check, and come home safe."

"Yes, dear."

Katie rolled her eyes at the reversal of roles. "I'm not kidding."

Mary-Lou winked. "Nor am I."

The older woman gripped her arm before leaving the way she came. When her footsteps faded, Katie knelt by the broken shieldshard. She moved the pieces with the tongs, then poked them with her finger. When she picked up a long fragment, it was ice cold to the touch. The golden substance inside it appeared to be the power source of the shield. Katie considered the crucible of fiery magic on the floor. "I wonder what would happen..." she mused aloud. "If I replaced the gold stuff with the orange stuff."

She put the jagged section of the spike down and retrieved a new shieldshard. As always, it felt like holding a warm bar of glass. She picked up the tongs and felt a wingbeat of hope flutter in her chest. *There is only one way to find out.*

CHAPTER 25
DECLAN

"To the mat," Master Johannasberg boomed.

Declan did as instructed. Almost one-hundred students sat around the perimeter of Stone Hall. They watched in anticipation. Johannasberg tossed a quarterstaff; Declan caught it.

"Today, we will begin with a demonstration of correct footwork," he said. A murmur of excitement rippled amongst the spectators.

Declan set his stance. In truth, he would have preferred to be in the garden, but as the Warmistress was confident she had slowed the seeds' growth—there was nothing to do but wait for Horace's next visit to Lombrives City.

"Are you ready?" Johannasberg asked.

"Are you?" Declan spoke with fake bravado. To his left, he heard Juniper laugh.

In a flash of movement, Johannasberg lunged forward with an overhead attack. Declan moved aside, stepped back to avoid the counter, then caught a third strike against his staff. The trick was to watch his opponent's torso.

"Declan already had extensive training with the axe,"

Johannasberg narrated while they fought. "Concentrate on his eyes. What holds his attention as we duel?"

A rhythmic volley of loud cracks echoed off the walls. Declan parried every blow and even pushed Johannasberg off balance with a feint-and-kick he'd been practicing in private. An unexpected cheer rose from the spectators as the weapons master retreated. He returned with a furious blur of consecutive strikes. Declan caught them all but the last, which swept his feet off the mat. Declan rolled to a safe distance and whipped his own staff into the weapon master's ankles.

Johannasberg ended up on his back beside him.

"YEAH!" Juniper stood, froze, turned bright red, then sat down. Everyone laughed.

Johannasberg leapt to his feet and extended a hand to Declan. When they were both standing, he dipped his head in approval. "Excellent, Declan. Thank you." He motioned to the Sabartians. "Where was he watching?"

Hands shot into the air. Johannasberg pointed his quarterstaff to a boy in the front row.

"Your stomach."

"Correct," Johannasberg said. "Weapons can play tricks on you, but your core cannot lie. When you learn to track your opponent's torso, you cut through their deception. The duel become less a fight, and more a dance."

"It's funny you mention dancing," called a voice from the back of the crowd. John stood, and every eye turned in his direction. "Because *that* demonstration looked almost choreographed."

There was a collective intake of breath, followed by shocked silence. John may as well have accused the weapons master of lying. Everyone waited for Johannasberg's response. "Skilled fighters often give that impression," he winked. "To the untrained eye."

That garnered some laughs, but John walked down the stairs, unphased. "Untrained, am I?" He stopped by a rack of wooden swords. "In that case, there should be no problem with me having a go. A quick spar before the lesson continues?" He slid two swords from their sheaths—sparring blades designed to hurt, not kill—and tossed one at Declan's feet. "Come along. Let's see this fancy footwork."

Johannasberg's face was stone. "Our demonstration is over."

"Then allow me to extend it." John flourished his sword. "To leave no question about the validity of your teachings."

"Sure," Declan cut in as Johannasberg opened his mouth. "I could go another round."

The weapons master stepped closer to take his staff. "You don't have to do this," he murmured.

"I know." Declan picked up the sword. "But I want to."

Johannasberg shook his head, but left the mat without argument.

The sword weighed less than the staff, which was lighter than the axe. Declan had little practice with—

John attacked. Declan caught the first strike on his blade, but John pushed off and followed with a series of vicious blows that forced them to the mat's boundary.

"Clumsy movement," John said. He lashed out again, and a chorus of loud cracks echoed overhead. Declan withdrew, but John gave no reprieve. He hounded him around the mat with an array of different forms.

While no swordsman, Declan's footwork allowed him to avoid any direct blows. Yet no matter how far he retreated, he could not find enough space to mount a counterattack. John controlled every move, herding him into the corner like a goat. Declan ducked a swing, but felt the wooden blade skim through his hair. *You need to change weapon. Fast.* He searched the walls for a staff—or axe.

"Come on, Declan. Where are your eyes?" John chided. "You're supposed to be watching my torso, aren't you?" He lunged forward, but this time, Declan closed the distance, ducking the thrust and driving a shoulder into his armpit. John staggered to the side, but recovered too fast for Declan to take advantage.

A flurry of blows followed. Declan parried every strike before meeting John in a bind. They leaned against one another, their wooden weapons creaking at the strain.

"Why are you doing this?" Declan asked.

"You know why," John growled. He slipped loose and struck at a higher angle. Swords met with a loud crack. Declan pushed forward until the hilts jarred together.

"What are you talking about?"

"You. Being here." John's face trembled with the effort. "You're not a—"

"That's enough!" In two strides, Johannasberg stood between them. "We are here for combat training. Not testosterone-fueled arguments."

Declan stepped back. "I—"

Johannasberg raised a finger. "No. Not now. Thank you for your demonstration, Declan. That is all I need from you today. You may leave."

John craned his neck around the towering giant. "A lucky save."

Lucky for you. Declan bit the words back. He dropped the sword and stormed out of the hall. Master Johannasberg's voice rang down the tunnel. "Enough entertainment. Our lesson is on footwork. Collect a weapon. Find a spot."

Someone shouted his name, and Declan turned as Juniper rushed after him. "What was that all about?" she asked.

"No idea," Declan said. "John is a moron."

"John?" Juniper blinked at him. "I was talking about Johannasberg."

"What do you mean?"

Juniper glanced over her shoulder. They were alone in the narrow passage. The distant chorus of wooden weapons echoed behind them. She leaned in and her voice dropped to a whisper. "John was talking to you and Johannasberg panicked. You didn't see his face?"

Declan raised an eyebrow. "I was a little busy."

An embarrassed smile split her cheeks. "That's fair." The grin faded, and her brow creased. "Have you ever heard of someone here called Samford?"

"I don't think so."

"Okay."

"Why?"

Juniper shrugged. "When you didn't show for dinner the other night, I... I heard some girls talking. One mentioned your name, and the other told her to shut up or she'll end up like *Samford*."

Samford. A vague memory of a boy wearing a fake bandage crossed Declan's mind. "There was someone... Oscar. No. Austin. Austin Samford?" He frowned. "I met him the day I arrived here."

"Can you think of why someone wouldn't want to end up like him? Did something happen to him?"

Declan thought back to their brief meeting. It had been

in the Mess Hall. "He knew me, or he knew my name. He seemed... surprised that I was there."

Juniper glanced back the way they came. Despite the empty passage, she spoke in a whisper. "Could Johannasberg be keeping secrets from you?"

"He might be. If he is, we know someone willing to share them."

"Your best buddy John?"

Declan rolled his eyes. "That might be an exaggeration. You're right, I just need to talk to him alone."

"Well lucky for you, I know exactly where he'll be." Juniper puffed up in pride. "Johannasberg was giving him an earful when I left. John's going to be oiling every weapon in Stone Hall while the rest of us eat dinner."

"How delightful." The last place Declan wanted to meet John was in a room full of unsupervised swords. "We might end up going for round two."

"Do you want me to come along?"

"No. You cover for me at mealtime. Make it sound like I went to bed early." Declan exhaled a long breath as they reached the Quartz Hall. If Johannasberg had secrets, this was the perfect chance to find out. "Come on. If I'm skipping dinner, I'm going to need an extra lunch."

Declan found John sitting amongst a pile of wooden weapons. He held a tin of linseed oil between his knees as he oiled a chestnut quarterstaff with a rag. The cavern was darker than normal, most of the glowjars at the ceiling were dim. The air smelled like an antique store.

"Look who it is," John said as he approached. "Here for a rematch? No Johannasberg to save your skin this time."

"I'm here to talk. That's all."

"I don't have anything to say to you." John returned to his work, leaving Declan standing outside the pile. After an awkward minute, Declan opened the supplies cabinet and took a tin of oil, a handful of rags. John's eyes narrowed as he returned. "And I don't want your help either."

"It's my fault you're here." Declan popped the lid off the tin; the aroma of the linseed oil made his eyes water. He examined a nearby sword. "I could've ignored your challenge and left you looking like a fool."

"Better a fool than a coward."

"Oh well." Declan smeared a small circle of oil on the pommel and spread it up the handle. John watched him a moment, then finished his quarterstaff and started on another. They worked without conversation. Every few minutes, another glowjar would extinguish. As the room darkened, the silence grew louder. When Declan had completed a quarter of the swords from the pile, John cleared his throat. "Why are you here, Moore?"

Declan oiled the central ridge of a longsword's blade. When it was done, he turned to face John. "You almost told me something today. It must have been important, because Master Johannasberg interrupted us and sent me away." He wiped his hands on the oily rag. "I came to find out what it was."

"Is that so?" The darkness of Stone Hall hid all of John's face, except for a wry smile. "So you weren't playing coy. You really don't know, do you?"

"That's what I'm here for."

John chuckled as he started a new staff. "Harcross, the snake. She didn't tell you Sabart was made for you? They built all these war colleges for you."

Declan could only stare. Of all the things he expected

John to say, this was not one of them. He sat in stunned silence, processing the words, but they didn't make sense. "What do you mean?"

"Euryma needs an army to stop the Knights of Despair, and every army needs a leader. Who better than the Warlock descendent of the last winning general?" John tilted his chin so darkness covered his face. "Even if he is a witless coward."

The insult wasn't enough to erase the shock. "I... I don't want an army."

John laughed. "Right. This is a cave side holiday."

"No. I'm not kidding. I came here for help to save my friend. I've agreed to stick around until that help arrives, but I'm not a general, I'm not a leader. I can barely keep myself alive, let alone thousands of others." He shook his head as it all sank in. *This is why Harcross wants you to stay. She wants you to lead the Sabartians.*

"That sounds like the first sensible thing I have heard you say." John waved a hand at the cavern's entrance. "March up to the dear Warmistress's office right now and tell her, because, as far as I can tell, you don't deserve to lead."

Declan's cascading thoughts ground to a halt. Despite spilling secrets, John had also jabbed him every chance he got. Was he jealous? Did he want to lead the Sabartians? "What's your problem?"

"You don't deserve to lead," John repeated. "The Knights' green magic means nothing if you don't have this." He put a palm over his heart. "Or this." He pointed to his head.

"You don't know anything about me."

"I know enough."

"Yeah? What's that mean?"

"You could have killed Haberdeen, snuffed her out, ended the Fatesmiths, and you didn't." Tempered fury trembled in John's voice. "I know about Anderma, about Sabriva. You had two chances to kill her. Why didn't you?"

Again, Declan stared while John's words sank in. "Anderma... I didn't know what I was doing, but Sabriva... That was someone else, wearing her face. You know that Haberdeen's gone, don't you? There's a guy named Horace Marley impersonating her."

"I know you could have killed her, and you didn't," John grumbled. "You're weak. Too weak to stop a witch, too weak to lead an army." After a long moment, he picked up another staff and started on the handle. Declan considered the sword in his hands, trying—and failing—to put the pieces together.

"Why do you want Haberdeen dead?"

Silence.

"I saw her a few months ago. They had her in Vedmark. She was a husk of a person. She can't hurt anyone—"

"She killed my father," John said. "She would have killed me too, if she didn't think I was already dead. When I made it back to Kingsbreak, the cowards didn't dare to challenge her. Dean Ember said it would 'tarnish his legacy', the fool." John's gaze never strayed from the cloth in his hand. "Who cares if she's lost her power? She needs to pay for what she did. You should have killed her, Moore. I would have killed her."

John didn't speak again. Over the next hour, they finished oiling the rest of the weapons. One by one, the final glowjars blinked out. By the time the last wooden axes were oiled, the room was as dark as a cloudy night. Declan stretched out and felt his spine pop. He put the linseed oil away and turned to the door.

"Thanks for your help," John called from behind.

Declan nodded. His head swam with the smell of the oil and the burden of knowledge. This was not the John he knew at Kingsbreak. This was a man obsessed with revenge, and that wasn't even the worst of his problems. Declan kept his hands in front of him, feeling his way through the darkness towards Quartz Hall. *If Harcross means for me to lead the Sabartians, she has a lot of explaining to do.*

CHAPTER 26

DECLAN

It was common knowledge amongst the Sabartians that the Warmistress's open-door-policy was more a sentiment than a reality. As far as Declan could tell, Harcross spent most of her time in Lombrives—either managing her tea shop in the Cathedral or supporting the students scattered throughout the cave city—or deep underground, tending to the garden. It took him three days to find her in her office, and when he did, she waved a sheet of paper at him in mock frustration. "For goodness' sake, I get five minutes to myself and you show up."

"We need to talk."

Teetering towers of paper covered Harcross's desk. Declan held his breath as she balanced one more sheet on a particularly tall pile. "Very well, Master Moore. To what do I owe the pleasure?"

Declan had no interest in being subtle. "Are the Sabartians supposed to be my army?

The steady drip of the cave walls filled the room. Harcross's expression gave away nothing. "Where did you hear that?" she said at last.

"Does it matter?"

"Was it John?"

Declan ignored her question. "Is it true?"

The Warmistress crossed her arms, as if his response confirmed her suspicions. The glint in her eyes eclipsed the glowjars on the shelves behind her. "If the truth is what you desire, it is yours." Her voice dropped. "But be warned, Declan. Truths are like cats. Once they're out of the bag, you can't go putting them back."

"I'm sure I can handle it."

"If you say so." Harcross laced her fingers together on the table and took a deep breath. "John was telling the truth. He had explicit instruction not to, but I expect you've seen enough of John to know the rules don't apply to him. At least not in his mind." She shook her head. "But he is right. Samantha didn't form the Sabartians for Euryma, or the High Mage, or the Fate-smiths. These students are *your* army. The students know this. The staff know this. Now you do too." Harcross motioned to a note on her desk. "Master Johannasberg wrote a report about your... adventure in Stone Hall last week. My best guess is John wanted to show everyone that he was more deserving of their loyalty." Harcross smiled. "Boys will be boys."

"Why didn't you tell me?"

The smile vanished. "I did not feel you needed the pressure of impressing every person in every cavern classroom while you were here." Her voice grew louder as she spoke. "If I lied, I did so for your benefit!"

Declan clenched his jaw. He knew he should take a breath, calm down, bite his tongue—but he couldn't. "What *benefit* has leaving me in the dark done? You sit here scheming. Like Vedmark, like the Directive, like your daughter!"

Harcross stared daggers at him. "Leave Samantha out of this."

"What good has it done?" Declan stood over her. "Two dead parents! A dead grandfather!"

Harcross slapped an open hand on the table. "Don't you dare blame that on me!" she snapped. "None of us are where we want to be! We are all doing our best in a broken world!" The cramped office hummed with tense silence. Then, unexpectedly, Harcross deflated against her chair; the tension went with her. "I never meant you harm," she said in a small voice.

Declan fixed the Warmistress with a stern gaze. "But a lie is a lie, no matter how you justify it. If you do it again, I'm done here."

"Done?"

"Done," Declan repeated. "With you. With Sabart. With Mrs. Winter." He leaned forward. "So, last chance. Is there anything else you want to tell me?"

The ensuing silence had a weight of its own. Declan waited, refusing to break eye contact until she answered his question.

"There is," Harcross said at last. "But there are some things you should understand. Before... this... nonsense..." She gestured to the mountains of documents on her desk. "I was the Chief Healer at St. Finnigan's Hospital in Sabriva. I dedicated my career to protecting people. Bringing life into the world. Preserving those on death's door." Her voice cracked as she spoke. "And now, I find myself leading a war college. It is with cruel irony that I spend my days preparing young people to die..." For the first time since Declan had met her, she looked old enough to be Mrs. Winter's mother. She considered him with weary eyes. "So believe me,

Declan, when I say that I take no joy in what I am asking you to do."

Declan said nothing.

Harcross let out a shuddering breath. "Horace Marley has used too many Ire Tides. He's become a force beyond control, and the key to our success. When I told you we would help you destroy Winterthorn, I omitted an important detail."

A tight knot formed in Declan's stomach.

"Horace is not your friend anymore. He's not a wizard. He is not even human."

"What is he then?"

"We don't quite know. Historians might call him a Reaper." She opened a drawer and slid a worn diary across the table. "Though there hasn't been a Reaper in Euryma for centuries. The last time there was, King Fendragon only survived the uprising by begging a Knight to help him. Considering the notes they left, a 'Reaper' is a plausible definition of what Horace has become."

Declan flipped through the pages—yellow with age— and his heart rate doubled. Names and dates he had memorized during his classes, all catalogued in a scribe's immaculate handwriting. A line at the bottom of a page caught his eyes.

Advancing beyond control of elemental forces, Lord Arthur possessed extreme power expressed as explosions of violet energy. Conventional methods of magical attack were unsuccessful in repelling the advance of the monarchists. They were defeated in the province of Tamhill in the hills of eastern Iberia amidst a period of unseasonal downpour.

"The Rainy Rebellion." Declan whispered. "That was where Arman made his stand. My grandfather stopped... a Reaper?"

Harcross nodded. "If the battle of Tamhill taught us nothing else, it's that a Warlock can defeat a Reaper." She wiped the tears from her bloodshot eyes. "We don't need you to destroy Winterthorn, Declan. We need you to use it to kill Horace."

Declan lowered the journal. "Why?"

"That knife absorbs blood and transforms it into memories. Do you understand what that means?"

"That Horace has Arman's memories?"

"That's right," Harcross said. "Winterthorn transferred your grandfather's blood and memories to Horace. Put that dagger in his chest and you will not only recover every memory we've lost, but you will shed Arman's blood. Your family's blood." She raised her eyebrows. "And then—"

"—I'll get my Sila," Declan whispered. Realization floored him.

Harcross dipped her head. "You will gain access to your Sila. You could resist Rasporvin or perhaps combine with Luck to defeat the Knights of Despair. If we play our cards right, the Sabartians might stand a chance. Do this one difficult thing, and Euryma could survive."

Juniper waved to Declan at a table in the Mess Hall. She gestured to an empty seat, and Declan was thankful for it. He felt like a mess himself. Harcross's words had blown a hole in his emotions, to the point that finding a place in the crowded cavern might push him over the edge. As he sat down with a plate of meat and vegetables, he realized they hadn't addressed the fact Sabart was his personal army. That conversation would have to wait.

"What'd she say?" Juniper asked.

It took a moment for the question to sink in. Thoughts flooded Declan's mind; he shook his head to stem the flow. "Where do I begin?"

"At the beginning, duh."

Declan considered the girl with the dirty-blonde hair. Juniper—now something of a little sister—had found a semblance of normality at Sabart. Telling her the truth risked shattering that peace, and that was the last thing Declan wanted. *Some things are better kept secret.* He opened his mouth to lie, when a little voice interrupted. *Don't be a hypocrite. This is how Harcross treated you.* Declan paused, open-mouthed, and Juniper laughed.

"That bad, was it?"

"Kind of." Declan uttered something between a grunt and a sigh. "She told me... everything." In whispered tones, he recounted their entire conversation. Juniper's eyes expanded with each sentence. When Declan finished, she put her silverware down and rubbed her temples.

"What are you going to do?"

"I don't know." That was no exaggeration. "Horace killed my grandfather, but I'm not sure if I can kill him. He was my best friend, and I'm the reason he's in this mess." Declan pushed a piece of potato around with his fork. "I have no idea what I'll do," he said at last. "Killing him may be the right thing to do, for the Dominion, but he's my friend. If there's a chance I can save him, I will."

"What about your Sila?" Juniper asked. "You're going to need it."

"That's something I need to think about." Declan forced a mouthful of sliced beef. It felt like chewing a sock. He swallowed it and pushed the plate away. "If we're lucky, the Knights of Despair are still in Vedmark, and we can figure them out later."

Juniper's lower lip quivered as she leaned close enough so only he could hear. Unshed tears shone in her eyes. "The Knights of Despair," she whispered. "What are they?"

"Warlocks," Declan said. "They have the same magic as me, except they can use it whenever they want, like you. Well, not magic. Sila. People here call it green—" Declan stopped as Juniper's face went pale grey, as if she was about to vomit. "Juni? Are you okay?" When she didn't respond, Declan put a hand on her shoulder. "Do you feel sick?"

Juniper shook her head.

"Do you want to talk about it?"

She shook her head again.

"Is it about... before?"

She nodded.

"Okay." Declan knew Juniper came from east Clovin, that she had no family, and that asking her about anything before her arrival at Sabart would make her retreat into herself, just as she had now. "How about I walk you back to your room?" he said. "Relax for today. We can skip afternoon classes."

Juniper nodded, her cheeks still white as bone. Amidst an orchestra of mundane conversation, Declan led Juniper through the Mess Hall and into the kitchen quarters. Neither talked until they reached her door, where Declan squeezed her shoulder. "Have a rest. I'll come check on you later."

He opened her door, but Juniper remained at his side. "What... do the Knights look like?" Her voice was so small. She peeked out through frayed hair. Her eyes were puffy. "What do they wear in battle?"

"Green armor," Declan said. "Dark green, almost black, overlapping scales that click when they move."

An involuntary sob escaped Juniper's lips.

Declan's stomach lurched. "Have you seen them?"

Juniper nodded. "I... thought they were rogue wizards. They..." her voice cracked, and she started to cry. Declan pulled her against him.

"You're safe here," he told her. "The Knights can't hurt you. They don't even know we exist."

Juniper sobbed into his chest. "They... they..." she shook her head, too damaged to say anything more. After some unmeasured stretch of time, she raised her chin. "I'm sorry," she said, wiping her bloodshot eyes. "You must think I'm such a baby."

"Not at all." Questions gathered like storm clouds in Declan's mind, but he knew she would not offer any answers. Not today. "You're safe. Have a rest. We can talk about it another time." She flinched, and Declan thought about the box of trauma he kept locked within. "Talking will help," he said. "Even if it's just a little."

"I'll... think about it." Juniper squeezed his arm and went into her room. When she closed the door, Declan returned to his own cramped quarters. Juniper's words were more kindling on a bonfire of events burning out of his control. *The Knights of Despair are in Euryma.* He had hoped Mrs. Winter could have stalled Rasporvin for another month or two. Declan's mind bubbled with a thousand thoughts, all funneling back to the same chilling realization —time was running out.

CHAPTER 27

AVA

RAUL HAD REFILLED the coolant reservoir with water about fifty miles back. By Ava's calculations, they were due for a stop. She leaned out and slapped her palm on the driver's door. Raul wound the window down. "What's the temperature gauge saying?" she called.

"We're pushin' it," he shouted over the engine. "If we can get through the rise ahead, we can ride the downhill to Laroa. We can refill and cool down there."

"And if we overheat before then?"

Raul didn't answer. Through the back panel, Ava watched him exchange words with Haberdeen. They were starting up a stretch of steep hills speckled with rocks and shrubs. They had come down the mountains well enough, but this would be the first time they had needed to climb. Raul waved his hand for their attention. "Deena said she'll pull some heat from the engine if it starts smokin'. We're okay."

Ava sat back. What should have been a three-day journey had taken a week. Raul's precious truck demanded one hour's rest for every hour on the road. She leaned closer to Misha. "We've got to find another vehicle in Laroa."

"We'd be better off walking at this rate," he said. "If it's a decent-sized town, there will be wards up. Do you think they'll be able to track Luck?"

"Who cares," Ava said. "If we keep on at this pace, Horace will die of old age before we get to him."

They passed a sign warning of rockfalls and the ascent steepened. The motor's whine joined the roar of the wind as the truck fought gravity. As the horrible harmony reached its peak, they topped the summit. An unimpeded view of the western plains filled their gaze. A blood red sun skated along a shimmering horizon. A burnt line blighted a huge strip of earth from north to south. Ava wondered if the storm that destroyed Sabriva had left that scar.

With an abrupt hiss, the engine seized. Ava groaned as she leaned forward to the driver's window. "Please tell me you did that on purpose."

There was no reply. Both Raul and Haberdeen were staring down the southern side of the hill. Misha stood on the back of the truck. He squinted in the same direction. "Is that supposed to be Laroa?"

Ava followed his gaze. Far below them lay a smoldering ruin of streets and buildings. The structures were spread out, as if a giant had crushed them underfoot. Fires burned in small sections, but otherwise nothing moved.

Laroa was gone.

Ava climbed off the back of the truck and tapped on Raul's window. He rolled it down without looking at her. "That's not Remnant Magic," she said.

"You don't say." Raul's tone was... bare. His snarky attitude swallowed by the sight.

"How do you know?" Misha asked.

"Because if it was." Ava pointed to the ruins. "It would be a strip of scorched earth and nothing else. You remember Parteno. The storms don't leave destroyed buildings. They don't leave anything."

"So what did it?"

Seriously? Ava turned from the destruction to raise an eyebrow at Misha. "Who do we know that's on a mission to destroy Euryma?"

"Vedmark," Haberdeen said. "So soon?"

"We should take a closer look," Raul said.

Misha nodded. "It's not like this excuse of a truck won't blend in."

Neither Raul nor Haberdeen smiled. Ava didn't either. She knew her uncle was coming. She had been there when they left. But seeing the absolute annihilation of a Dominion town hit her harder than she expected.

Euryma was under attack.

The Knights of Despair had arrived.

The first thing Ava noticed was the stink. It reached them before anything else, and it made her eyes water.

"Ugh," Misha pulled his shirt over his mouth. "It smells like goat meat left to rot."

The description was accurate, but failed to account for the potency of the stench. If Grigory let every goat on his farm to die and decay, it still wouldn't come close to the fetor of Laroa's ruins. She wrapped a scarf around her nose and followed Raul down through the northern entry.

When they reached the town square, Ava had to turn away. Not only were the buildings destroyed, but bodies littered the streets. All peppered in the same rash of scars. Ava only had to see it once. That was enough.

"It's like they've been run through a sandblaster," Raul said. He covered his nose with his jacket. "What kind of creature leaves marks like this?"

"Drevsmok," Misha said.

Haberdeen turned to face him. "Excuse me?"

"They're like dragons." Ava kept her eyes up, desperate to distract her lurching stomach from the surrounding nightmare.

"I know what a drevsmok is," Haberdeen said. "I *didn't* know that they still existed."

"The Knights have a legion of them," Misha said.

Raul ran his fingers over a fallen wall flecked with thousands of tiny dimples, like it had been sprayed with ball bearings. "You're sayin' we have an army of Warlocks who can not only command green magic, but also ride on mythical dragons that breathe..." He slapped the pockmarked concrete. "Whatever this is?"

Ava nodded.

Raul turned to Haberdeen. "The Fatesmiths can't stand against this."

"Not in their current state," Haberdeen agreed. She alone had not covered her face. "We cannot stay here. There is nothing here to see but death and disease."

"The engine might be cool enough by now to refill, but it's getting late—"

"We have to keep moving," Ava said. "If Vedmark has come through here, there's no knowing how far ahead they are. We should ditch that pile of junk and find something that can run for more than an hour."

"I'm not leaving it," Raul said.

"Then park it somewhere and come back for it," Ava

turned her gaze on Haberdeen. "I don't have time to wait on a broken engine. We have to get to Biscay, get your army, and start preparing. Before it's too late."

A bright flare erupted from the buildings down the road. Half a second later, an enormous explosion swept over the top of them. Ava dropped to her stomach as a nearby building crumbled and fell.

"What was that?" Misha was on the ground beside her.

"Something flammable," Raul said. "Fires are running amok. It's too dangerous here. We should get back to the truck."

"There is no way I am getting into that scrap pile," Ava said. "Not if we can find something better."

"Ava's right," Haberdeen said. She raised a finger as Raul opened his mouth. "Laroa is destroyed. The Knights of Vedmark are not likely to return here—nor is anyone else. Kairi's truck will be safe here, Raul, but we need to continue."

Kairi? Ava exchanged a confused glance with Misha.

A growl vibrated in the back of Raul's throat. "Fine." He jabbed a finger at Misha. "But if my truck gets damaged..."

"Damaged?" Misha laughed. "Have you seen your truck?"

Raul's hands balled into fists.

Ava stepped between them. "This is stupid. We're losing daylight and wasting time. Raul, why don't you and Haberdeen place some rubble on your truck? That way, nobody will think about taking it. Misha and I will use Luck to find something a little faster." She dug a flashlight from her bag. "Meet back here in an hour. Sound okay?"

"You will not leave without us," Haberdeen commanded.

An unusual sensation tickled the back of Ava's neck as the oath took hold. She nodded. "Wouldn't dream of it."

They split in opposite directions. The moment Raul and Haberdeen were out of earshot, Misha turned to Ava. "Who is Kairi? And why does she drive such an old truck?"

"Probably his wife." Ava shrugged. "Or someone important. You should ask him yourself."

"I thought..." Misha glanced over his shoulder.

A smirk threatened Ava's somber expression. "You thought those two were...?"

"They're always together."

"I don't think it's that type of relationship," Ava said. "They seem... obligated to each other. Who knows?" She shook her head to clear the thought. "Come on. We're losing the light."

She opened herself to Luck and examined the paths they could take. As she tugged on chance, she found some more pliable than expected. She followed the odds of finding a functional vehicle. "This way."

Misha nodded. They walked down what might have once been a quaint alley. Now, a splintered mess of wooden beams covered half the road, all pockmarked with the same small dimples of the drevsmok's breath. Luck led them to a partially collapsed garage, its roller door bent out at an odd angle, like something huge had been thrown into it. Misha pointed at it. "In there."

They climbed over a mound of fallen bricks and jerked the garage door back onto its tracks. It slid upward to reveal a yellow luxury car. A smile spread across Misha's face. "You think it's faster than Raul's rust bucket?"

Ava didn't answer. She could have sworn something had moved on the back seat. She pressed her nose to the glass and locked eyes with someone peeking out from underneath a blanket. They vanished in an instant. "There's a person in there."

"What?"

Ava knocked on the window. "Hello? We're not here to hurt you. We just arrived—"

The door shot open as a teenage girl launched herself into Ava's chest. A mess of frazzled apricot hair filled her vision. Misha rushed to help, but Ava waved him off. The girl was crying against her. "I thought they came back," she sobbed. "I thought you were going to kill me."

Ava raised an eyebrow at Misha, who appeared as nonplussed as she felt. The girl stepped back and bumped into the car. A wailing alarm shattered the silence. She ducked inside and the shrill howl stopped. When she emerged, her cheeks were bright red. "Sorry," she murmured. "I didn't mean to jump on you." Her gaze dropped to the garage floor.

"What happened here?" Ava asked.

"We came to stay with my grandparents after... Sabriva... and..." She trailed off as she met Ava's gaze. "You wouldn't believe me if I told you. I don't know if *I* believe me."

Ava frowned. "Was it dragons?"

The girl's left eye twitched. After a long pause, she nodded. "They called us into Laroa Square. There was a wizard with white hair." Her voice quavered. "A few of the local MLEA arrived. He scrunched them together like..." her face went pale and Ava squeezed her shoulder.

"You don't need to tell us the details," Misha said.

"Then what?" Ava asked.

The girl shook her head. "The dragons came after that. Everyone was screaming. Running. I hid with my sister. We were so scared." Tears streamed down her face as she stopped to breathe. "We... tried to leave the next morning. Those of us that survived. They came back. They flew over... we got separated. I came back here." The girl buried her face in her hands.

This was the reality of conquest. Families, lives, hearts, all broken for the *glory* of Vedmark. Ava felt like someone had punched a hole in her chest.

Misha cleared his throat. "Do you have any family? Anyone you can go to?"

"If they made it out, they'll be going south, to Lombrives City. It's protected from the storms. That's where we were going before..." her lower lip trembled as she fell silent.

"We are heading south too, to Biscay." Ava squeezed the girl's shoulders. "We can take you to this Lombrives place, help you find your family."

The girl sniffed, but nodded.

"You're safe now, okay? We're not going to let anyone hurt you. I'm Ava, and this is Misha."

"I'm Zozi," she said, offering a tentative hand. "Well... Zoe. My friends call me Zozi."

Ava took her hand and smiled. "It's a pleasure to meet you, Zozi."

Night came quickly. Zoe fell asleep in the back seat of the car. Misha followed soon after. His forehead—pressed to the side window—bounced off the glass with every jolt in the road. Zoe leaned on his shoulder and started to snore. Ava was glad to see the girl get some sleep. She deserved it after the horrors she had seen.

Ahead of them, the world existed in the beam of headlights. They cut through the night like a comet. Ava leaned into the headrest and tried to relax.

Raul broke the silence. "What are we doing?"

"What do you mean?" Haberdeen replied.

For a moment, Ava wondered if she should clear her throat to let them know she was still awake. Instead, she sat motionless in the darkness.

"You saw Laroa. This is above our pay grade, Deena. The Fatesmiths aren't equipped to deal with this kind of enemy."

"You suggest we abandon Euryma?"

"It wouldn't be the first time," Raul muttered.

"We were living a coward's life." Haberdeen locked eyes with Ava through her passenger side mirror. The edge of her scarred lips tweaked into a knowing smile. "We formed the Fatesmiths to save the Dominion. We made our oath, bound in a simple phrase. I trust you remember it."

Raul sighed. "To the end."

"And do you still live by those words?"

There was a long pause. "I do," he said. "But that end is approachin' faster than I like. I never signed up to fight the mythical Knights of Despair. How are we going to beat them and stop Remnant Magic? Do you even have a plan?"

Haberdeen's gaze darted back to Ava. "We've got something better than a plan," she said. "We've got Luck. Don't we?"

Ava rolled her eyes.

"Still awake, hey?" Raul turned his rear-view mirror to see her. "What do you make of this business? How do you kill a drevsmok?"

"Fire? Sharp items? The same way you kill anything else, I expect." Ava stared into the starless abyss. "We're getting ahead of ourselves. We need that army. How long to Biscay?"

"Driving straight, two days," Haberdeen said. "Add one more if you really think we should stop at this cave city."

Ava had made it sound like Luck was the reason for dropping Zoe to her family. In truth, she just wanted to help the girl. "It's called Lombrives. Have you heard of it?"

"Not of any city, but I'm aware of the cave system." Haberdeen nodded to herself. "If you were looking to hide a huge number of displaced LAMPs, that Lombrives cave would be an apt choice."

The car fell silent, and Ava's mind turned to the challenge before them. Raul was right. The Fatesmiths would not be enough. They needed someone who could match the Knights' power, and the only person Ava knew who could do that was Declan. *Where are you?* For all she knew, he was still in Vedmark. She wanted to pull on Luck, to test the chance he was in Euryma, but doing so felt wrong. Maybe it was her promise to Misha, or her oath to Haberdeen. Still, she had to find him. Declan needed to know the truth. "Why did you keep Declan's parents alive?"

The abruptness of the question appeared to catch them off guard. Raul's eyes narrowed in the mirror. Haberdeen turned to face her. "We're not butchers," she said. "Angus and Miranda Moore were guilty of using magic in a society reliant on magic. An understandable crime. They never opposed us, or tried to undermine our purpose. We froze them in stasis so we could deal with the storms. A minor punishment for a minor crime."

"You killed others."

"We eliminated those who sought to impede our work."

"Declan said you melted them down."

"A humane method. Painless. More gruesome in theory

than practice." Haberdeen sighed. "You want the truth? Here it is. Declan Moore is the linchpin of Euryma's destruction. The future I foresaw in the white-haired wanderer's memories is not pleasant for him. In that future, Declan becomes Vedmark's puppet. Forced to murder his own parents, driven mad by guilt, and used as a weapon capable of wielding Remnant Magic."

Ava's mouth went dry. "That's... impossible. You can't wield remnant magic."

Haberdeen pursed her lips. "That is what I sought to avoid by fierising him in Anderma. We hoped that if he chose to go into stasis, the fierisation might stick. He was too strong for us to force the matter, so I needed his parents to convince him." She turned back to the front of the car. "But when you plan to change the future, you give up the advantage of foresight."

"What do you mean?"

"We didn't know what would happen once we put him in iron, so we planned for the worst. Think, Ava. What would have happened if Declan lost control and destroyed his parents' casts with green magic?"

Ava's mouth went dry. "He would have gotten his Sila."

"We would have given him access to the same power we sought to withhold."

"So they weren't his parents," Ava whispered. "You kept them separate to protect yourself."

"We made a mold and cast them in common steel. A prop used to manipulate the boy."

"And it failed," Raul said. "And the kid turned your unhinged protégé to dust."

Ava thought back to the night in the snow, to Declan's description of events. "You mean the Mage? Ward?"

Haberdeen's shoulders fell at mention of the name. "It

was a mistake to elevate him to Mage status. He became too *fervent* in our crusade to undo the storms."

"He became a psychopath," Raul said. "Never trusted the lad."

"Did Ward know he was melting down a fake cast?"

"No," Haberdeen replied. "Only Raul and I knew the truth. We expected Vedmark had agents amongst us. We wanted them to believe the Moore's were dead, and Declan useless."

Ava considered the night streaming past them. Haberdeen had seen Euryma's destruction and tried everything she could to stop it. *Would you have done it another way?* "You really aren't the bad guys. Are you?"

In the rear-view mirror, Raul rolled his eyes. "Figured it out, eh? Took you long enough."

"Nobody is the villain in their own story," Haberdeen said. "Everyone makes decisions—be it noble or not—for a reason." She frowned into her own mirror. "Now you know ours."

CHAPTER 28
DECLAN

MASTER WERRIER—A balding man with a speckled beard—commanded Iron Hall with astute lectures on strategic thinking. Of the three instructors at Sabart, Declan liked Werrier the most, but right now, the old strategist was embarrassing him.

They sat on either side of a circular table on a raised platform in the middle of the octagonal cave with the maroon walls. Between them, small painted blocks covered an ornate wooden board. The iridescent shell pieces inlaid into the grid shone beneath the spherical glowjars hanging from the ceiling. The lights reminded Declan of an upside-down lollipop and—for the moment—they were a welcome distraction. The game was called cob, and he was losing.

Master Werrier picked at his thumbnail while Declan examined his position. Beside him, Juniper watched with rapt attention. Declan's red cubes were being forced into a corner. He had reserves at the bottom of the board, but Werrier's blue force had pushed him too far. The battle would be over before he could unite his army. Declan

261

searched his mind for any scrap of wisdom from the previous three weeks of strategy lessons and came up blank. "I think I've lost," he said at last.

"I am inclined to agree," Werrier said. He nodded to Juniper, who had taken to the game with surprising ease. "Where did he go wrong, Ms. Reaves?"

Juniper bent forward until her nose almost touched the board. After a moment of intense scrutiny, she straightened. "The same fatal error as usual," she said. "He took too long to combine his cubes."

Declan smirked. "Easy now."

"Declan should have fortified his position as soon as you anticipated his flank." Juniper smiled at him, as if to take the sting out of her critique.

"That may have prolonged the conflict, but he still would have lost." Werrier turned to Declan and raised a thick eyebrow. "Think. Where did you fail from the outset?"

"I'm not sure..." Declan considered the weeks of private strategy lessons. The sheer volume of things Werrier expected him to remember made his head throb, but one word in the question stood out. *Outset.* It prompted a memory from an earlier lesson, and Declan understood. "I split my force too soon. I gave you control of the center."

Werrier's lips cracked in a smile. "So the young man *can* learn." He gestured to the board. "But you have learned too late to win this match." Werrier pushed a platoon of blues forward, blocking any chance of victory. "Do you concede?"

Declan glanced at Juniper. "Can you see any way out?" Her timely advice had saved him on more than one occasion, but she was quick to shake her head.

"Not this time."

"Then I don't think I have a choice."

"A wise decision." With a bamboo rod, Werrier separated the cubes by color. He swept them into two matching cloth pouches. "Tomorrow, we will return to outsets. It does you no favors to forget foundational concepts."

"Yes, sir."

Werrier pulled the drawstring tight, then slid the bags across the table. "You can take these if you want to practice with Ms. Reaves."

"Two beatings in one night?" Juniper poked her tongue out at him. "That's a tad unkind."

Declan bit back his retort as the echo of footsteps interrupted him. He turned with the others as the Warmistress appeared at Iron Hall's entrance. She wore a long ivory cloak and a smile that did not reach her tired eyes. "Excellent," she said. "You're both here. I have news." Harcross's eyes flickered to Juniper. She frowned. "Apologies, Ms. Reaves, I need to talk to Master Werrier and Declan. May we have a moment in here?"

"With respect, Warmistress," Declan said. "I'm going to tell her everything you say once you're gone."

Harcross's lips pressed into a thin line. "As you wish." She swept into an empty seat. "Some friends hiding amongst the Bonfires send word about Horace Marley."

Declan's body tensed. "He's here?"

"No, but we know where he will be. They say that Haberdeen has figured out a way to bypass Kingsbreak's protective spell."

"The Ancellum?" A cold shiver ran down Declan's spine.

Harcross nodded. "The Bonfires are giddy about it—taking bets on how long until they get to hang Laurefen Ember in the Cathedral. They've built a new gallows with him in mind."

The icy dread continued until it reached Declan's stomach. The Ancellum was his grandfather's creation; Horace must have found something in his memories. "What do the blackcoats want with Kingsbreak?"

"King's College remains in staunch opposition to the Fatesmiths. The Fatesmiths are culling all who refuse to take their oath." Harcross leaned back. "At least, that's the story they're pushing."

"So we'll meet Horace at Kingsbreak?"

"Let me finish," Harcross said. "From what I have heard upstairs, the key to Ancellum is a fragment of Sabriva Tower collected under the light of the full moon. If this is true, that is where Horace will be. That is where you will meet him and do what must be done."

A lump formed in Declan's throat. He swallowed. "How long until the next full moon?"

"That is what I came here to ask our resident astronomy enthusiast." She tilted her head towards Master Werrier. "Do you know, Archibald?"

"I haven't been out for the better part of a month." Werrier gazed up, as if his vision could pierce Iron Hall's ceiling. "From memory, we are at the beginning of a waxing gibbous. You have a week, maybe a day less."

One week? The answer inspired a rush of butterflies in Declan's chest. The Warmistress had made her intentions clear, but until now, the prospect of killing Horace had been a distant question for a later date.

"Forgive me, Helen," Werrier continued. "It... doesn't sound logical. They built Sabriva Tower *after* the founding, but the Ancellum was created earlier. How could one influence the other?"

Harcross bit her lower lip. "You suspect this is a ruse?"

"It is hard to know." The glowjars cast deep lines in the creases of Master Werrier's forehead. "But a strategist questions everything."

"I'll see what I can find out." The Warmistress kept her gaze on Declan while she spoke. "But I fear time is a luxury beyond our reach."

"And me?" Declan asked.

"Give me two days to investigate these rumors," Harcross said. "That gives you forty-eight hours to make peace with what you must do. Euryma needs you, Declan. Whatever doubts you have—work it out."

———

Dinner was a creamy concoction of chicken, pasta, and tiny tomatoes cooked in a velvety sauce. It smelled divine, and Declan couldn't eat a bite. The drone of anxious conversation filled the Mess Hall, and based on the whispers loud enough to reach his ears, the topic on every Sabartians' lips was the imminent attack on King's College.

Declan ignored the chatter and continued steering a wedge of tomato around his bowl.

"Do you want to talk about it?" Juniper asked.

Declan did not. If he closed his eyes, he could see Horace—his closest friend—skimming rocks on the lake, laughing over a meal at Bluebell's pizzeria, or trading sentences for homework. The thought of killing him made Declan feel ill. The logical part of his mind accepted that it had to be done, while every other instinct screamed at him to run away. "The future of the entire Dominion rests on whether I will end a friend's life. That isn't fair."

Juniper sat in silence. When Declan's tomato completed two circuits of the bowl, she put her hand on his elbow. "Are you going to do it?"

"I have to."

"Why?"

"Didn't you hear me? If I don't, Euryma will be overrun by..." Declan paused. The last time he mentioned Vedmark's army, Juniper had shut down. He sighed and tried an alternative approach. "Once again, I have to make an impossible choice. I've done this before—with my parents, and my grandfather—and both times, I've gotten it wrong because I chose the easy path. I can't do that again. I have to stop Horace, and I need to do it before..."

Juniper's hand fell back to her side. "Before the Knights of Despair arrive?"

Declan nodded. "We don't have to talk about it. But they are coming. If I can't stand against them, who will?"

They slid into silence. Students filtered in and out of the hall. Kitchen staff refilled massive steel trays with more pasta, then a selection of desserts. As the evening wore on, Declan's appetite remained in hiding. Juniper took their plates and returned with two bowls of chocolate pudding. The rich sauce gleamed in the cavern's soft light. She ate hers and then raised an eyebrow at his untouched dessert.

Declan pushed his bowl across the table. "It's all yours." He tried for a smile, but it was an empty gesture. He felt like a chicken in a foxhole.

A crash of breaking ceramic shattered the moment. Declan leaned back to see John headed in their direction. He shoved past a group of students, causing another plate to fall. Declan stood to meet him.

"You need to come with me. Now." John stopped when they were face to face.

"Why?" Declan asked. The Mess Hall was only half-full, but every single face was turned towards them.

"Because I have news." John's voice dropped to a grim whisper. "It's about your pal, Horace. Come on."

"You're a bit late," Declan said. "I spoke to Harcross this afternoon. I know where he's going to be."

John leaned so close that his words were a breath in Declan's ear. "I don't care where he's going to be," he murmured. "He's here. Now."

Declan's mind went blank. "What?"

"Outside. Hurry." John started back the way he had come. Declan followed in a daze. While his feet moved of their own accord, his thoughts raced in a whirlpool of emotion. *Horace is here.* A symphony of whispers accompanied them out of the hall, but John didn't speak until they reached a small stone alcove far from any curious ears.

"Haberdeen is on the surface with two Fatesmiths and a teenage girl. They're at the registration tent."

"When did they arrive?" Juniper asked.

Declan glanced back at her. He did not realize that she had followed.

"About ten minutes ago. They're waiting in line, which should give us at least half-an-hour." John radiated impatience as he turned to Declan. "Is it Haberdeen, or is it Horace?"

"I..." Declan forced the hailstorm of emotions aside and concentrated on the question. "I don't think so. Haberdeen fled the Dominion months back. If this person has Fatesmiths at their side, it has to be Horace."

"Are you certain?"

"As certain as I can be. The real Haberdeen has no reason to be here." Declan shook his head. *It has to be Horace.* "Does Harcross know they're here?"

"Not yet." John did not meet his eye.

Declan considered him. "You wanted it to be Haberdeen. You were going to go after her, weren't you?"

"What of it?"

Juniper cleared her throat. "If Horace *is* here," she said. "Now is your best chance to stop him. You'll be able to get much closer up there than you will at Sabriva. You've got crowd cover and the element of surprise."

She was right, but it left a bitter mark on his soul. "I... don't want to kill my friend."

With two hands, John shoved him into the wall. The sudden blow knocked the air from Declan's lungs. He adjusted his stance to fight, even as he gasped for breath. Juniper threw herself between them. "What was that for?" she snapped.

"Him!" John thrust a finger at Declan.

"What?" Declan wheezed.

"You're being an entitled child. Stop it." John's eyes burned. "Who cares what you want? I don't. Quit moaning about your selfish desires and start thinking about what everyone else needs."

He's right. Declan's raised fists fell by his sides. He was stuck in a cycle that always ended for the worse, because he always picked himself. It was time to break that loop, even if it meant breaking part of himself. "I'll do it. You two find Harcross. Split up and search everywhere." He turned towards the Mess Hall and John grabbed his sleeve.

"Dinner's over." John jabbed his thumb over his shoulder. "Lombrives City is *that* way."

"I know where it is." Declan pushed John's hand away. "But if you want me to stop Horace, I need to get something from my room first."

"And what's that?" John appeared unconvinced.

"My axes." Declan did his best to appear stoic, but inside, he was a mess.

CHAPTER 29

AVA

AVA HAD NOT EXPECTED the cave city to be so busy. Hours past sundown, the campsite was alive with activity that rivaled Vedmark City's busiest market days.

An endless flood of new arrivals flowed into various lines. There were people taking bags, people recording addresses, and—underneath tall electric lights in the distance—people building tiny houses stretching in both directions.

Overhead, a dark crescent shrouded an almost-full-moon. Its glow was unnecessary amid the rows of light-bulbs strung between the trees and tents. A noisy generator rumbled to their left, while a frustrated Fatesmith grumbled beside them. "Why are we waitin' in line? You're the Queen of the Fatesmiths. We should just cut to the desk and be on our way!"

Ava hated agreeing with Raul, but this time, he had a point. They stood at the back of a winding line, Raul and Haberdeen at the front, Ava in the middle, and Zoe a pace behind. Misha waited with the car a half-mile north. She touched Haberdeen's shoulder. "It would be faster."

"It would be," Haberdeen agreed. "It would also be impolite." She gestured Ava closer, then lowered her voice. "Someone is watching us. Early twenties, bright red hair. Don't look now, but she's standing in the shadows on the western corner of the tent."

"I'll get her," Raul said.

"And cause a scene? Don't be a fool." Ava maintained a passive expression. They edged forward and—under the guise of adjusting her Fatesmith coat—she searched the spot Haberdeen indicated. A young woman with a crimson ponytail appeared to be repairing a ripped section of canvas on the tent, but every few seconds she would glance straight at them.

"Do you recognize her?" Haberdeen asked.

"Nope. It seems like she knows who you are."

"I am inclined to agree," Haberdeen said, making a show of scanning the line behind them. "Though she has made no effort to greet us. Her actions are more of a foe than a friend."

"Do you think we're in danger?" Ava locked eyes with the woman. She cursed under her breath and dropped her gaze.

"What is it?"

"I think she saw me."

Haberdeen's lips thinned. "Can you do anything with Luck?"

Ava opened herself to the golden bands, turned back to the tent, then faltered. The woman had vanished. "No Luck required. I must have scared her off."

Raul searched the crowd, his brow furrowed. "If she's run off, let's not waste time waiting for her to come back."

Ava nodded. It would be great if they could reunite Zoe with her family, but Biscay was their priority.

"Very well," Haberdeen said. "But eyes open and remain vigilant. For the time being, this is enemy territory." With regal grace, she lowered her hood and pushed through to the registration desk. Angry faces turned to meet her, then jaws dropped as realization hit. They left a litany of whispers in their wake as Haberdeen split the line like a knife through butter.

When they reached the front of the tent, Haberdeen placed a hand on Zoe's shoulder. "This young lady was separated from her sister, and I would like to reunite them."

The balding man at the plastic table was the definition of flustered. "Yes, Madam, of course, Madam." His hands shook as he hurried to grab a clipboard. "What is her... your, uh, companion's full name?"

"Zoe," said the girl. "Zoe Zillmere. My sister's name is Bethany. She would have been coming from Laroa, in Clovin's north."

The balding clerk nodded as he checked multiple clipboards. Ava didn't dare try Luck for fear of finding its bands immovable. She would not be the one to confirm Zoe's sister was dead. As the stack of lists grew shorter, Ava's heartbeat moved faster. She suddenly wished she was back in the car with Misha. Anywhere but—

"Ah. Here we are. Bethany Zillmere. Arrived late yesterday."

A tender gasp escaped Zoe's lips. "She's alive?"

"Alive and well. They've set her up in settlement sixteen. Down by the river. Would you like me to send someone to show you the way?"

"Yes." Zoe's voice was a grateful whisper. "Yes. Please. Thank you. Thank you so much!"

The balding man disappeared through a curtain. He

returned with an even older gentleman who bowed and held his forearm to Zoe. "Settlement sixteen, is it?"

A prickling sensation ran up Ava's spine. She scanned their surrounds, searching for the red-haired girl amongst the crowd of refugees. *No sign of her.* Even so, something wasn't right. With unexpected effort, she drew down on Luck. The probabilities played out ahead of her, and she watched as the echo of a shadow stalked them from the darkness. She leaned in to Haberdeen. "Someone is following us," she said. "And I'm guessing you're their target. Stay with Zoe and Raul. I'm going to see if I can catch them while they're focused on you."

"If you must," Haberdeen said. "But remember your instructions."

Ava nodded. The oath to protect Haberdeen felt like a hand at her neck. "I won't be far behind."

Haberdeen gestured for Raul to follow Zoe and the old man. Ava gave them a slow count of ten before melting into the mass of Fatesmiths and refugees.

Whoever stalked their steps had a talent for avoiding detection. They moved like a whisper between the massive oaks on her periphery. As the crowd thinned, Ava dropped even further back. A robust group of rambunctious teenage girls walked alongside her, singing badly, laughing loudly, and otherwise enjoying a carefree walk home. By the time they reached settlement sixteen, Ava was fifty feet behind the others.

Settlement sixteen was identical to the fifteen other housing units they had passed. The rows of modular houses were closer to upright coffins than places of residence. They were unpainted pine with a glossy sheen that smelled like varnish.

When they reached a stack of building materials, Ava

broke off from the teenagers and settled into a narrow space between bags of insulation. A smell like mildew and burnt honey invaded her nostrils. Ava covered her nose as their old guide stopped outside one of the homes. He gestured to the door, bowed, then started back towards the registration tent. Ava ducked a little lower as he walked by, and smiled at the sound of his merry whistle.

When she scanned the scene through Luck's lens, a mirage of Zoe knocked against the door seven different ways, and every time the same woman answered. Every time, Zoe threw herself at her sister in a heartwarming hug.

In every one of them, they were safe. Nobody fell from the roof, or leapt out from behind the building. Whoever was stalking their steps had no interest in Zoe Zillmere. *They want Haberdeen.*

That thought put Ava on edge. She was oathbound to stop that from happening. The golden shadows faded away as Zoe knocked and a young woman answered. "Zozi!" The shout carried down the settlement, a mix of disbelief and unbridled happiness.

"Beth!"

The girls jumped into one another's arms. Ava felt a small measure of satisfaction at the sight. Joy could still be found in Euryma, even while it collapsed around them. "I thought I'd lost you!" Zoe sobbed against her shoulder. Her shrill words echoed in the night. "I thought those... things... got you!"

"I thought they got *you!*" Zoe's sister pulled her back and pushed the hair from her face. "We watched them destroy Laroa. How did you survive?"

As Zoe dived into her story, Ava spotted movement. Someone was climbing the vast oak tree growing opposite the houses. They hid inside the shadows, to the extent that

Ava could see the faintest outline scrambling up the trunk and disappearing into the branches that stretched far over the path. The mysterious figure was positioning themself directly over Haberdeen's head.

A strange tension took hold of Ava's limbs. The oath she'd sworn to Haberdeen seemed to have a mind of its own. She tensed her muscles, wrestled back control of her body, and resolved to stay hidden. The mystery attacker wouldn't do anything yet. Luck had shown her that much. She just had to be ready.

When Zoe neared the end of her story, Ava closed her eyes for a count of ten. When she opened them, the darkness was a shade brighter, and the figure overhead a shade more distinct. The top of a head peeked out from a cluster of oak leaves partway across a long branch. It was enough.

Ava shifted her weight onto her back foot and slipped two daggers from between her coat's silver buttons. The stiff Fatesmith coat limited her range of motion, but it *did* have plenty of places for daggers. The figure in the branches shifted again, and now Ava could see a pair of shoulders. *Found you.*

CHAPTER 30
DECLAN

AMIDST A WALL OF LEAVES, Declan watched and waited.

Horace—shrouded in Haberdeen's guise—stood alongside the girl and her sister, relishing in their obvious reunion. A second Fatesmith lingered a short way behind them, hidden in the shadows. Declan was here for Horace, but if two blackcoats needed to die for Euryma, so be it. He would not get a better opportunity.

Are you really going through with this?

The thought had followed him through fifteen rows of houses. Declan hoped the sight of Horace might give him some sort of confirmation that his friend was beyond saving. Instead, he found him reuniting a lost girl with her sister. Indecisiveness clung to him like a fever that he could not shake. *I don't have a choice. Vedmark and Remnant Magic aren't going away. Winterthorn is a risk to Ava. I can stop it all, here and now.* He clenched his jaw. *And all it will cost is my humanity.*

Down below, one sister hugged Horace. There was a procession of 'thank you' and 'goodbye', and then the door closed.

Every muscle in Declan's body tensed. The magnetic sensation of his axes—embedded part-way up the tree—hummed in his fingertips. Horace gestured to the Fatesmith. They started down the road, talking in muted voices. As Declan reached for the pouch of irofil John had left him, his coat sleeve caught a loose twig. It snapped in the silence.

Horace raised a hand and they stopped. "Hiding in shadows, are we?" he said in Haberdeen's sultry tones.

Declan somehow tensed tighter. He had used every piece of Johannasberg's training to stay out of sight, and Horace had found him anyway.

That's your cue. Declan emptied the bag and jumped. Axes pulled free of the tree and thrummed into his palm. The force of their flight slowed his fall and a mist of iron enveloped him.

He hit the ground in a fighter's stance as Horace staggered—coughing—through the haze. Declan rushed after him. He dashed out of the irofil to see the glint of metal and ducked as something whooshed overhead. He rolled back into the cloud as massive arms seized him from behind.

Declan threw his head back with a bloody crunch, then swept his leg and knocked the attacker off their feet. The man landed hard on his back. Declan turned his axe to finish the blackcoat when something silver flashed past him. Whatever spells they were wielding had an edge. Declan dodged left and glanced back. Three iron hilts protruded from a tree,

That's not magic. Those are daggers.

He stepped into Armadillo form as a flurry of throwing-knives penetrated the irofil. They bounced off the protective shell as Horace crawled to the fallen Fatesmith.

With a thunderous crack, the clearing darkened. Declan

watched one of the mighty oaks tilt and fall towards him. He closed his eyes and let the axes do their job. Horace dragged his companion to safety as the Armadillo shredded the branches to nothing. Sawdust filled the air, creating a new type of haze, and Declan tried to find his bearings.

A blackcoat leapt out of nowhere, knee aimed at Declan's chest. He blocked the blow but lost one axe in the process. Declan lashed out with his other axe, but the Fatesmith ducked and vanished.

Declan retreated to level footing. He found his balance as the attacker returned. This time he was ready. A furious exchange of blows followed until the Fatesmith peeled free to face him. Declan flicked his axe in a tight circle. Sapphire eyes met his and widened. Declan froze, his blade inches from her jugular. Recognition rooted him to the spot.

"Ava?"

Ava lowered her knife—the one Declan had not noticed pressed to his stomach—and stepped back. "Declan?"

Declan didn't know what to say. His mind was a spinning gear cut loose from all resistance. Ava was here. With Horace. In a Fatesmith's coat. A flying purple alligator would have made more sense. "What are you wearing?"

Horace kneeled—unarmed and unprepared—over the Fatesmith on the ground. Declan raised his axe. Ava moved to block his path. She put her hand on the axe head. "She doesn't want to hurt you."

Declan arced an eyebrow. "Don't you know who this is? You were there, Ava! He's done something to your head! He's—"

"This isn't Horace," Ava said. "It's Haberdeen. The real Haberdeen."

Declan's hand tightened on the axe-handle. Simmering

hatred bubbled to life in his chest. "The one who killed my parents?"

Ava opened her mouth, but no words came out. She blinked in confusion, then shook her head—speechless.

"What is going on? Why are you wearing a Fatesmith's coat?"

Ava hesitated. She tried again to speak. "It's not..." she took a long breath. Each word seemed a marathon. "I'm... trying to help."

"How?" Declan growled. Haberdeen stood up, and a second axe rushed into his hand. "Stay there," he told her.

"Declan please." Ava wrapped her fingers around the axe handles. "You left, but the Knights of Despair didn't go away. Remnant Magic didn't go away. We needed an army, and the Fatesmiths were the only option."

"We?"

"Misha's here too."

Declan fought to keep from rolling his eyes. "Of course he is." He kept his weight on the balls of his feet—ready to move at a moment's notice. "So what? You offer your loyalty to the blackcoats in return for an army? Did you forget?" He nodded to Haberdeen. "She is not the one leading them."

"I didn't forget anything," Ava said, and now her voice carried an edge. "But you left, Declan. You abandoned Euryma, but we didn't. We are going to Biscay to kill Horace, so Haberdeen can take her place."

In his mind's eye, Declan saw Horace run Winterthorn through Ava's stomach; his eyes burned purple as he smiled triumphantly. Declan shook his head. "No. No way. You can't go anywhere near Horace."

Ava arched an eyebrow. A thin smirk on her lips. "Excuse me?"

Declan lowered his voice so only she could hear. "Ava, you can't go to Biscay. You can't go anywhere near Horace."

"And why is that?"

"Because he's going to kill you. I've seen it. I saw it. I saw it in the Void." He dropped his axes in his belt. "I watched my parents die, I watched my grandfather die, and I watched Horace run Winterthorn through you. That's why I left. To find him. To stop him before he could hurt you."

A bemused smile crossed Ava's face. "Declaaan." She stretched the word like she was lecturing an unruly child. "The Void is a curse. It's not a magic window to the future. It drives people mad—that's how it works. It makes people see the things that will break their sanity."

Declan shook his head. "You weren't there. You don't understand. You can't go near Horace. I'm not going to let you."

"Declan—"

"NO!"

Ava stepped back as a flock of something took to the night sky. Declan forced himself take three long breaths before speaking again. "I can't let you go." He took her hand in his. "I... I'm... not strong enough to lose you."

Ava's sad smile was a slap to the face. "I'm sorry Declan. I need to do this. Vedmark is on their way. We need an army, and we need it yesterday."

"You don't," Declan said. "Mrs. Winter prepared an army. They're here. There's a whole college of witches and wizards training to help us. You just need to leave Haberdeen. Come with me and—"

"I can't," Ava said.

Declan paused. Her stern expression drained his excitement. "What do you mean?"

"I swore an oath," she whispered. "I'm bound to her until our work is done."

"What work?"

"Vedmark. Remnant Magic. The Knights. Haberdeen's trying to save Euryma."

Declan closed his eyes, as if that would somehow dull the blow. "Why?" The words were weak. He wanted to give Ava the benefit of the doubt. He knew how smart she was. *But why would you do something so stupid?* "Why would you swear that oath?"

Again, Ava hesitated. Her jaw worked as if she was chewing an enormous piece of gum. She clenched her fists, and a frustrated growl broke the silence. "I can't tell you," she muttered—breathless. When she glanced up at him, there were tears in her eyes. "But you have to believe that I'm doing it to help."

"She killed my parents."

The well of sorrow of Ava's face made him pause. She looked as dreary as he'd ever seen, but still said nothing.

"And you've joined them. You've joined her."

"Declan."

"I... I don't know what you want me to say, Ava." A weight pressed against Declan's chest. It grew heavier as Haberdeen approached them. "This is your fault."

"I am not your enemy," she said. "Vedmark spreads through the Dominion like a disease. We must prepare."

"I am prepared," Declan growled. "You're not the only person with an army in their back pocket."

"Then join us," she said. "We've seen what the Knights of Vedmark can do. Euryma will need every able body to stand a chance."

"Release Ava of her oath."

"I will." The scar tracing from Haberdeen's lip to her ear wrinkled as she smiled. "When the Dominion is safe."

Declan turned to Ava. "Where is Mrs. Winter? Does she know about this?"

"It was her idea. She left a message with Ory, before... they took her. She wanted us to find Haberdeen."

"Who took her?"

Ava's shoulders slumped. "Rasporvin figured out she was deceiving them."

"What?" Declan blinked. "Is... she alive?"

"We don't know. I... I think so..."

"Where is she?"

"The Knights have her."

Declan gritted his teeth. Warmistress Harcross would want to know about her daughter, but that would have to wait. He could not let Ava waltz off to her doom attached to a Fatesmiths' oath. He had no choice. In a hum of iron, Declan attacked. Ava caught the axe head against a dagger —three inches from Haberdeen's neck.

Haberdeen didn't flinch. "A Luck is oath-bound to protect me," she said. "I would be a fool to throw that away."

Ava's eyes pleaded for him to stop.

"Then I'll release her myself." Declan spun, sweeping at Ava's feet. She retreated, and Declan swung for Haberdeen's chest. By some fluke chance, the witch stumbled away from him. The axe-blade split air. *Not chance*, Declan realized as Ava put herself between them again. *Luck*.

"Declan! Stop!" Ava held a dagger in each hand. "I can't let you hurt her."

"I know." Declan noted the change in her stance. "But that won't matter once the oath is broken."

"She's not who you think she is."

Over her shoulder, Haberdeen began to weave a spell.

"Burn bright!" Declan shouted. His axes blazed, swallowing the night as he ducked beneath Ava's arms, but tripped over an exposed root. He found his balance as Haberdeen leapt to safety.

Beads of sweat shone on Ava's forehead. That was a good sign. The more Luck she used, the more tired she would become. *I just need to draw this out.*

Declan reset his grip. Ava relaxed her stance. If he was fast enough he could—

White hot pain erupted in the back of his head. Then everything was gone.

AVA

Eight hours later, Ava was still angry. They remained long enough to make sure someone found Declan. She would have stayed longer, if she could. Oaths and obligations had other plans. She glared out the window. The barren plains —barely lit by the morning sun—hurtled past them in a charcoal blur.

We're going too fast. Most of what Raul did annoyed Ava, but this time, his masculine stupidity was a safety hazard. She waved a hand from the back seat; Haberdeen met her gaze through her sun-visor mirror. "Yes?"

"Can you tell your attack dog to slow down? We're not going to help anyone if we're wrapped around a tree on the side of the road."

Raul's eyes darted to his mirror. "We just pulled an eleven hour drive from the top of Clovin to the bottom. Now you tell me we have to go all the way back, and you want me to do it *slowly?*"

Misha managed a nod. He held the backseat handle in a death grip. "I told you what I heard." His voice was an octave higher than normal. "Horace will be at Sabriva Tower at the next full-moon."

"So instead of going to Biscay, where we know the damned fraud will be, we are driving back—almost to where we started—based on a rumor?" Raul turned to face them. "Have I got that right?"

"Watch the road!" Ava barked. She hadn't forgiven him for smashing Declan's skull with a branch, and truth be told, the back-and-forth across northern Euryma frustrated her too.

Haberdeen said nothing. Her fingers danced as she tapped against her palm. The car slowed—if only slightly—and after a few minutes, she turned to Misha. "It appears your information was accurate. Every looptap confirms the same thing. Horace is headed to Sabriva Tower at the next full moon. He plans to use a piece of it to breach the Ancellum."

"What does he want on Kingsbreak?" Ava asked.

"Nobody knows for sure. Perhaps he is weary of Laurefen Ember refusing to acknowledge the storms. I expect your friends are aware and making arrangements of their own."

"My friends?"

"The Directive," Haberdeen said. "I cannot imagine they would lie down so the boy could conquer King's College unopposed."

"If we can kill the kid first, they won't have to." Raul's gaze lingered on Ava through the rear-view mirror. "So zip it and let me get us to Sabriva while we still have time."

"There aren't any wards here. Couldn't you just portal us there through an Opening?" Misha murmured. His cheeks were bone white.

Raul shook his head. "Openings don't work in stormblight. Remnant Magic clears the nima. It'll take years before magic works there again."

"That's not true," Ava said. "I saw Horace flee through an Opening less than an hour after the storm happened."

"Ire Tides," Haberdeen said. "You don't need to rely on external nima when you're bursting with them from within."

Ava jolted left as they cleared a tight bend. Beyond the guard-rail, black emptiness replaced what should have been sloping green hills. It was as if someone had taken a blowtorch to the horizon. Her stomach tightened at the sight, but she did not lower her gaze. "Do you really think the Directive knows what Horace is planning?"

"They have eyes and ears throughout the Dominion," Haberdeen said. "Even if they didn't, I am sure they have enough allies amongst Lombrives City to warn them of the rumors."

Ava nodded. She had met the witches and wizards of King's College's clandestine organization twice now. While they had shown her a measure of kindness, the older ones were narrow-minded goats. The only redeeming member of the Directive was Katie Hall, who Ava considered something of a friend. For her sake, she hoped they knew what was coming, and they were prepared.

Ava wondered if she could test the odds of Katie knowing about Horace. She had never tried anything of the sort—her training with the Emissary had centered on events in front of her—yet as she closed her eyes to focus on Kingsbreak's safety, the bands of Luck were as malleable as an elastic band. She stiffened in her seat.

"What are you doing?" Misha asked.

Ava didn't answer. A vision of a possible future flickered to life ahead of her. The transparent mirage of their car turned down a dirt road. She gripped Raul's shoulder. "Stop!"

They slowed, but not by much. Raul glanced back at her. "What?"

"Slow down. You need to go left." She pointed past his ear. "Up there. We need to go that way."

"Why?" Haberdeen asked.

"Luck." Ava's gaze fixed on the shimmering illusion. "We need to go that way. It will take us to something we need."

Raul appeared unconvinced. "And what is that?"

"I don't know," Ava said. The corner was coming up fast. "But at this point, we should take all the help we can get."

Haberdeen turned back to face her. "Will this help us stop Horace? Be honest."

The oath's binding sensation tickled the back of Ava's mind. She nodded. "It will."

"Raul. Turn left."

They all pitched forward as Raul hit the brakes. "This better be worth it," he growled. Raul turned onto the dirt track and the engine roared to life. The wheels kicked up a thick haze as they accelerated. "How far do we go?"

"I'm not sure..." Ava blinked. A half-mile to the east, a tight-knit mass of vehicles travelled perpendicular to them at high speed. She counted six vans and three small buses driving in proximity. A long cloud of dust trailed in their wake.

"What is that?" Misha asked.

"Could be more refugees," Ava said, but that made little sense. Whoever it was, they were headed north—away from Lombrives City. She focused on Luck and saw the golden shadow of their car pull out in front of the convoy, forcing all nine vehicles to a halt. "Raul, you have to get to the crossroad before those vans do."

"Say that again, lass?"

"They will stop if you force them. You need to cut them off."

"What has this got to do with finding Horace?" Haberdeen asked.

Ava shook her head. "Luck knows. I don't. Just do it."

A piercing whine whistled through the engine, then the yellow sports car leapt forward, pressing Ava back into her seat. Misha reached for the passenger handle as mountains of dirt erupted around them. Ava did the same. *He's going to kill us. We're going to spin out and crash!*

As they got closer, Haberdeen turned to Raul. "Are you seeing this?"

Raul nodded, his face set in intense concentration.

"Seeing what?" Ava asked.

Haberdeen gestured to the convoy. "Most of those vehicles have no driver. They are all tethered to the one at the front with a braid of air and elastic energy."

Ava leaned forward for a better look. Haberdeen was right. A lone figure sat in the driver's seat of a silver van. The rest appeared empty.

"Hold on," Raul said through gritted teeth. After one last burst of speed, he hit the brakes and spun the wheel hard. The turn launched Ava across the car—half onto Misha's lap—as they drifted out into the path of nine larger vehicles.

Ava seized on the odds of the van braking in time and heaved on Luck with all of her strength. She hoped Misha was doing the same. A cloud of dirt and dust enveloped them, turning day to night. When it settled, the van's headlights rested an inch from the passenger side door. Ava peeked up and met the gaze of an elderly man with a twirled moustache. He was a portrait of astonishment.

She knew that face. It was the Dean of King's College.

"Ember!" Raul roared. He slammed his door open and leapt out of the front seat. Ava followed a second behind. Laurefen reversed in a hurry, smashing straight into a purple mini-bus, and attempted to drive around them. Raul raised his palms, creating a wall of solid stone to block the van's path. He wrenched on the door, but it held fast.

Ava rushed to his side. "What are you doing?" she shouted. When Raul ignored her, she turned back to Haberdeen. "We need him!"

With a piercing shriek, a tunnel of air raced towards them. Ava retreated behind the car door as the gale hit. Somewhere within the haze, an engine roared and something crashed. When the wind died, there was an enormous hole in Raul's barrier and a silver van speeding away from them. The other eight vehicles remained abandoned on the roadside. Raul staggered to his feet. His beard—caked in a layer of soil—was almost black. He dashed back to the car, but Ava barred his path. "What is wrong with you?"

"Those vermin kept me locked in a cage!" Spittle flew from Raul's mouth. "They tortured me for information and left me to sit in my own filth!" He reached out to move her aside, but Ava caught his arm and twisted it. Raul swore as she shoved him against the window.

"I don't care what they did," she hissed in his ear. "I care about stopping the storms, and stopping Vedmark. He could have helped us! We need help, and you scared him off. You are trying to *kill* our help."

Raul pushed off the car door. He twisted free and lunged for Ava, only to bounce off an invisible wall between them. Haberdeen looked at him, disappointment etched on her stern expression. "Ava is right."

"Those people—"

"Did terrible, mindless, unforgivable things." Haberdeen waved a hand, as if brushing aside the Directive's sins. "But we are outmatched. We require allies, and the enemy of our enemy *is* our friend. You can get your revenge when this is all over, but that is not yet. Can I count on you to put the Dominion's needs first?"

Raul glared at her, then nodded.

"Good." Haberdeen's gaze shifted to Ava. "Can you use Luck to track that van?"

Ava opened her eyes to Luck. She concentrated on the odds of finding Laurefen. As before, a mirage of the vehicle appeared in the distance. "I think so."

"Excellent." Haberdeen gestured for them to get back in the car. "Let the old fool think he's gotten away. We can follow at length and find out where he's going. Then, perhaps, we can try a more *civilized* discussion."

"Or we can put them in iron like we should have done from the start," Raul muttered. He climbed into the driver's seat and started the engine. Ava did as told, but froze partway through buckling her seatbelt.

"Where is Misha?"

Haberdeen and Raul turned in unison. Ava was alone in the back seat.

"I don't know." Haberdeen shook her head. "I never saw him leave. He must have slipped out."

Ava exited the car. The intersection split four empty fields, all bordered by simple wire fences, with only a sparse assortment of trees around them. The only place to hide was amongst the assortment of vans and buses on her left. *Unless...* Ava refocused her intentions to test the odds of finding Misha. The rigidity of Luck's bands made it obvious he wasn't there. She considered the predicament, then shook her head. There was only one explanation. "Come on. We better follow."

Raul stared at her. "What about your friend?"

"We'll meet him there," she said, smiling. "The little sneak snuck into Laurefen's van."

CHAPTER 32

DECLAN

DECLAN WOKE in a bedroom he did not recognize. Unpainted pine walls were split by a single window overlooking the tops of trees and a grey sky. His axes leaned against a chair in the corner. The space smelled like a blend of sawdust and varnish. Declan managed to sit up, but his head felt like a bag of nails. An old man stood at the door—back turned—rolling bandages into tight cylinders while he hummed to himself in a smooth baritone.

Declan cleared his throat and the old man fell silent. "Where am I?" Declan asked, his voice a dry scratch.

The man's fingers slackened, and the bandage between them unraveled. Without a word, he left the room. Through paper-thin walls, Declan heard him speak.

"The boy is awake. Where is Helen?"

Staying upright was an effort. When the small room started to spin, Declan lowered his head onto the pillow. Out the window, a noonday sun peeked through the clouds. He closed his eyes and tried to put the pieces together. The last thing he remembered was... something... a fight in the forest?

291

The door opened, severing the thought. Warmistress Harcross wore a plum cloak and a frustrated expression. "My daughter told me many things about you," she said. "But she never mentioned you were so foolhardy."

Declan blinked. Nothing made sense. "Where am I?"

"Settlement Thirteen. Some fellow Sabartians provided you a place to recover."

"How long was I out for?"

"Much longer than was safe," Harcross said. "You were lucky. Had we found you an hour later, you would have been beyond healing."

"What happened?"

Harcross shifted his axes and dropped into the armchair by the bed. "You were unconscious, lying in a pool of your own blood. Witnesses said you were arguing with two women when a Fatesmith man smashed a branch into the back of your skull." Harcross's expression softened as she leaned back. "You should have waited for us. We could have helped you."

The words created glimpses of events hovering on the edge of recollection. Frustrated, Declan pressed his hands to his eyes. "I don't remember."

"Transient global amnesia."

"What?"

Harcross sighed. "That squishy grey mass holding all your memories took a solid knock. Memory loss is not uncommon."

"Will... I get it back?"

"You should." Harcross shook her head. "But you need time to heal. Time we don't have."

"Why?" Declan tensed as a wave of nausea rolled through him, and with it, a ripple of images. *Horace is going to Sabriva Tower. He needs the ruins to attack Kingsbreak.* He clenched his jaw until the sensation lessened, then peeked up at Harcross. "When is the full moon?"

"Three days."

Declan didn't answer. It would take them at least a day to get to Sabriva, which left him forty-eight hours to recover his strength—and his memories. "Do we have any more sanarmelon juice?"

Harcross shook her head. "Samantha supplied the healing flasks, fresh from Vedmark Forest. We used the final dregs of it to heal your head when we found you."

Samantha. Vedmark. The words were an itch he could not scratch. He gritted his teeth and stared at the bare roof. No matter how hard he tried, he couldn't recall the night's events. Declan focused on his last memory—losing a game of cob to Master Werrier—but even that seemed hazy. A tentative knock at the door broke the silence, and a pair of worried eyes peeked inside.

"Declan!" Juniper rushed to his side and threw her arms around him. Declan winced underneath the hug.

"Hey Juni," he said weakly.

She straightened, and her relief faded to anger. "What were you thinking? You were supposed to wait for us!"

"I..." Declan shook his head. "I don't remember, sorry." He turned to Harcross. "What was I doing in Settlement Sixteen?"

Juniper raised her eyebrows. "What do—"

"Temporary amnesia," Harcross explained. "At least, we hope it's short term." Her attention fell to Declan. "You received a message last night that Horace was here. You went out to find him—alone—and you paid for your ignorance. Now, we are left waiting for another opportunity."

"Another opportunity?" Declan repeated the words

under his breath. He shook his head, rejecting her conclusion. "Are you saying I shouldn't go to Sabriva?"

"Correct."

"We're just going to let Kingsbreak fall?"

Harcross looked like she'd eaten a lemon. "I've passed word to King's College. Laurefen Ember is well aware of Horace's plan. They are making arrangements to defend themselves."

Declan sat up, though it took all of his strength to remain upright. "This is my chance to stop him. Isn't that what you wanted?"

"It *was* your chance," Harcross countered. "Look at yourself, Declan. You're sweating pebbles just sitting in bed. You are in no condition to do *anything,* let alone fight." She fixed him with a pointed gaze. "You need to rest. Allow your body and mind to recover. There will be another place, another time."

"Isn't there something you can do to help him?" Juniper asked. "You are a healer, aren't you?"

Harcross nodded. "I can, but not here. The Fatesmiths' warded the settlements, and you never know which LAMP is a Bonfire in disguise. No. When you are well enough to move, we will get you down to Sabart. I can speed up the recovery process there."

Declan wanted to say something, but he knew she was right. He had taken an opportunity to stop Horace and wasted it. Now he would have to wait. Declan lay back on the bed and a surge of exhaustion washed over him. Somebody pulled the curtains closed, shrouding the room in pleasant darkness. Declan tried to thank them, but his eyes refused to open. Somewhere ahead of him, the door clicked closed. A moment later, he was asleep.

This time, Declan awoke to an intense wave of agony shooting up his spine like a firework that exploded at the base of his skull. His body went rigid as an enormous hand covered his mouth.

"Don't scream," Master Johannasberg said. The towering man was carrying him down a steep flight of metal stairs. "If you do, you will bring unwanted attention to us. We must get you to the caves."

Another fiery torrent flooded Declan's mind. he squeezed his eyes closed, trying to bite back the pain. The white-hot sensation made it hard to take in his surroundings, but from what he could tell, it was nighttime and they were creeping down the central stairway into Lombrives City.

"Hurry," hissed a voice—distant, yet familiar. They moved as part of a dense group. Declan thought he saw Harcross leading the pack, but he couldn't dwell on it, not when he wanted to howl in anguish at every torturous step.

Eventually, they reached a dark passage. The putrid smell of raw sewerage barely registered on Declan's nose. Johannasberg held him steady on the elevator as they descended. Declan must have passed out as they did, because moments later he opened his eyes, drenched in sweat, laying on a camp bunk in the empty Mess Hall.

All the tables were empty except for one covered in an assortment of open glass jars. Harcross stood over him, plucking at invisible threads while a stream of liquids twirled through the air like semi-transparent ribbons. They braided together in a rainbow of color. Harcross pushed a hand to his chest. "Brace yourself," she murmured. With a twist of her wrist, the shimmering substance flooded his vision.

There was a rush of burning cold and Declan gasped as every muscle in his body tried to contract at once. The spell stretched somewhere between seconds and hours, but when it faded, the pain went with it. An inner warmth filled him, like warm molasses in an empty tin. Harcross turned to replace the lids on her jars. Declan sat up in his seat.

"What did you do to me?"

The Warmistress finished capping the liquids. "Give it a moment."

"Give—" the question died in his lips as an internal tempest rolled through him. In a sickening wave of clarity, the night's events came back to him. His stomach plummeted. "I remember!" he blurted. His mouth struggled to keep up with his mind. "It wasn't Horace. It was Haberdeen, and Ava. They've got your daughter. Vedmark knows Mrs. Winter betrayed them. They have her."

"Slow down," Harcross said, though her forehead creased in concern. "Who has Samantha?"

Declan took a deep breath as he tried to make sense of the memories. "Ava Drakonov is working with Haberdeen. She told me Rasporvin found out that Mrs. Winter was betraying them. The Knights have her... somewhere..." He closed his eyes. Images of Ava wearing Fatesmith black haunted his inner eye. "What... what did you do to me?"

"I wanted you to recover naturally, but my colleagues convinced me otherwise. Master Werrier noted that your missing memories may hold some important secrets, and Master Johannasberg agreed to carry you from Settlement Thirteen to Sabart. I'm sorry, Declan. The journey down must have been torture." Harcross sighed. "I hope the pain was worth it. Tell me everything."

Declan ran through the events of the previous evening. It didn't take long, but the Warmistress had lots of questions. She had him repeat Ava's plan to kill Horace and take control of the Fatesmiths three times before falling into an uneasy silence.

"What is it?" Declan asked.

"Things are moving faster than expected." Harcross's words were a shadow of a whisper.

"I... don't understand."

Face pale, eyes troubled, the Warmistress turned to him. Her gaze carried a weight that made Declan's chest tighten. "If Haberdeen kills Horace first, you will lose any hope of gaining your Sila." She sat at the end of the bunk. "We have no choice. You have to go to Sabriva. The Knights of Despair are coming, Declan. It's time to become who you were born to be." She frowned as she scanned the empty Mess Hall. "But you're going to need help."

"Why am I here?" John asked.

The Warmistress's office was ice. Small clouds of vapor accompanied every breath. John sat beside Declan, wearing pajama pants and a grey shirt. From the other side of her desk, Harcross crossed her fingers against her chest. She glared at both of them, making no effort to hide her distaste. "There is a full moon two days from now. Horace Marley will be at the ruins of Sabriva Tower. And I need you," she nodded to Declan, "to kill him."

"So why am I here?" John repeated. He sounded as thrilled as Declan felt to be there.

"Because Haberdeen will also be there."

John's eyes narrowed. His gaze jumped from Harcross to Declan and back to the Warmistress. "What?"

Warmistress Harcross's jaw tightened; her lips formed a line as thin as a strand of hair. "Haberdeen has returned from her self-imposed exile. She was here, and she has made her intentions clear."

John turned on Declan. "You said it was Horace." Fury seethed in his hushed tones. "You said Haberdeen was long gone."

"Declan had no way of knowing," Harcross said. John leapt to his feet. "Sit. Down." Harcross's voice was stone. "Getting angry now will only waste precious time. You want to kill Haberdeen? Avenge your father? Here is your chance. If you can stop her, that gives Declan more time to deal with Horace."

John didn't reply. He returned to his seat, though his eyes were daggers.

"I don't want him," Declan said.

"Want?" Harcross laughed. The coldness of it sent a shiver up Declan's spine. "You think I want to be living in a cave? You think I want to be opposing an army who holds my only daughter captive?" She scowled at Declan. "This is a war. The luxury of 'want' died with your grandfather. We are all making sacrifices. It is time you make yours." She stood so fast, Nox startled awake. The enormous raven hopped onto her shoulder. "I'm going to leave you now, and you're going to sort out your issues." Harcross swept past them and stopped at the door. "Don't come out until you've dealt with your egos."

Before either of them could protest, she slammed it shut behind them.

"Yay," John muttered.

Declan didn't speak. The weight of the Warmistress's

words hung about him like a lodestone. *We are all making sacrifices. It's time you make yours.* He ignored John as he thought of all the things he could have done differently. John seemed just as happy to ignore him.

The minutes stretched into hours before Declan finally broke. *What are you doing? Every minute you wait, Ava is getting closer to Horace. To Winterthorn. Stop being a child.* Declan gritted his teeth, then cleared his throat. "You were right about me."

John didn't move. "Which part?"

"You said I don't deserve to lead. That I'm... weak." Declan closed his eyes, thought of Ava, and put his pride aside. "It's true. I'm selfish, and that selfishness has cost me so much. My family. My friends. I could have saved all of them if I had accepted who I was." Thoughts he had bottled up—never to be shared—tumbled out of him and he couldn't stop. "Every time I try to do the right thing, it backfires. Every time I try to protect someone, they die." Declan stared at the chipped cavern floor. In his mind's eye he could see Ava, dead on Winterthorn's blade. "I am so terrified it will happen again. I just want to keep the people I love safe. I've lost so many. I don't want to lose any more."

John studied him in silence. "It sucks, losing your parents," he said at last. "It's worse when you feel responsible. My dad died saving me. He gave me the chance to get away from the Fatesmiths. Now, I live every day wondering if I'm doing right by his memory. Would he approve of me abandoning the Directive that abandoned him?" He shrugged. "I don't know."

"I'm sorry," Declan murmured.

John nodded, but said nothing. The walls pressed in.

"I know I need to stop Horace," Declan said. "I know it's

necessary for the Dominion. But he's only where he is because of me."

"What do you mean?"

"We grew up together. He was my best friend. I called him to help me and the Fatesmiths got him. I knocked that first domino over. Everything Horace is, every awful choice he has made is because of me. I have to kill my childhood friend because he came to my aid when I needed him." Declan met John's gaze. "How do I live with that guilt?"

The steady drip of water along the walls of Harcross's office echoed in the silence. John's face betrayed nothing as he processed the words. After an extended pause, he shrugged. "What other choice is there? You can't change the past, Moore. You can create a better future. You just keep fighting—through the pain, through the guilt. One foot in front of the other."

Declan shook his head. What John was suggesting was too hard. "How?" he whispered. "How do you deal? Because..." He took a trembling breath and blinked away the tears behind his eyes. "Because I'm not. I don't sleep at night, when I do I have nightmares. In the day I put on a brave face but... I feel... empty."

John leaned forward. "You don't deal. You endure. Like swimming in a stormy sea. At first, the waves are enormous, never-ending, and you fight to keep your head out of the water. As time goes on, the waves grow fewer and farther apart. The waves never go away, but you get to a point where you can catch your breath between them. You endure long enough to find a new normal." He held Declan's gaze. "But you don't find it wallowing in pity. You find it by fighting to stay above the surface." He wiped the corner of his eye. "At least that's what *I'm* doing."

They fell into a distracted silence. Declan squeezed the

nape of his neck. The muscles were tense with the ache of emotion. He had said too much, far more than he wanted to reveal to anyone, let alone John. Yet somehow, speaking his mind had removed a weight from his soul. He took a deep breath as he faced John, who appeared to be struggling with his own inner demons. "Every choice I've made has turned out so wrong," Declan whispered. "What do I do?"

John frowned. "You do what you must, to make up for your failures. You kill your friend and use green magic to save the rest of us."

"And you?" Declan asked.

"I'll kill the witch before she gets in your way."

CHAPTER 33
KATIE

THEY WEREN'T FINISHED by midnight, but they were close. Six women sat around the edges of a depleted bonfire, each working from their own cardboard box of empty glass spheres. In a practiced motion, Katie pulled a thread of fire from the glowing coals smoldering in the pit, and coiled it inside the bulb. She sealed it as she released the pyronima, then placed the miniature explosive in a black plastic tub.

"Here he comes," Mary-Lou said beside her. "What do you think? Good news or bad news?"

Katie glanced as Michael strode down the hill towards them. "If you expect bad news, you'll never be disappointed."

Mary-Lou closed her own glass bulb. They each finished two more before he arrived.

"How many?" Michael called when he was within speaking distance.

"This is the second to last crate," croaked Merida, one of the ancient staff members who had agreed to help. A lifetime ago, she had taught Katie history. Now, they made preparations to destroy one of Euryma's most revered landmarks. "That gives us twenty more to add. Another small bus load, perhaps?"

"We have six buses left to fill." Michael stopped in front of them. The glowing embers reflected off his dark eyes. "I will have a dozen more boxes of empty bulbs arriving within the hour."

"Will that be enough?" Katie asked. A ribbon of fire hovered above her fingers. The other staff continued loading nima in silence.

"I don't know," Michael said. "If it were regular stone, I would say we had more than needed. Sabriva Tower was anything but ordinary. We will have to wait and find out."

"That doesn't fill me with confidence," Katie said. That same sentiment described her thoughts about their plan in general. She finished the bulb and added it to her collection. "Am I the only one who thinks we are cutting this too close? We should be attacking tonight or tomorrow. Not the day of the full-moon."

"Every day buys us more flashbulbs, more vans. We get one shot. It's a risk, but so is moving too soon." Michael held out his palms. "I don't like it either, but you play the hand you're dealt."

"Have faith, dear," Mary-Lou said. "Laurefen is confident that whatever enchantments protected the tower ceased with its destruction. If we hit the ruins with everything, there will be no moon-kissed stone fragments for Horace to use."

Three weeks of planning and that was the best they had come up with. Fill a bunch of vehicles with exploding glass bulbs and send them all into Sabriva in one fiery swoop. "Horace destroyed Sabriva Tower with the palms of his hands." Katie capped another flashbulb. "We could have a hundred vans and that would be nothing to him."

An uneasy silence spread around the spent fire. The women filling flashbulbs concentrated on their work. Katie sighed and picked up another empty bulb.

"He is strong," Michael agreed. "But he can't be everywhere at once. Laurefen has found enough nimrods to create a sizeable distraction. We will also approach from all sides. If half of our fleet reaches the tower, we have a high chance of destroying it all."

Katie nodded, but still felt sick. The entire situation was a mess of uncertainty, and the ever-changing plans only made things worse. She pushed her reservations away and tried to appear confident. "What do we need to do?" Her voice was weaker than she liked, but it was all she could offer.

Michael motioned to the fire. "Right now, finish these crates. I'll start moving them to Cedrus, and I'll bring back the new bulbs when they arrive." He gestured to the circle of women. "And I'll bring coffee too."

Mary-Lou smiled. "Good news at last."

A murmur of appreciation rolled around the group, and Michael laughed. "You'll have to settle for packet brew." He began stacking tubs of flashbulbs into a neat stack. "I won't be—" A startled gasp stole his sentence as his face dropped. Katie's heart sank at the sight.

"What is it?" Mary-Lou asked, but Michael stood in stunned silence, staring at his hand like it was a venomous spider. "Michael?"

He glanced up. "Laurefen. His thread is gone."

There was a synchronized intake of breath as a sinking sensation emptied Katie's stomach. Looptap threads only vanished for two reasons. Fierisation, and death. "What do you mean gone?"

But Michael was already running up the path—headed towards Cedrus and the travelling grounds.

"Merida. Finish these bulbs!" Mary-Lou said. "Hurry Kate." The older woman was on her feet, and Katie felt like she was stuck in slow motion. Laurefen was a stubborn fool, but he was also kind and thoughtful. If he was... *No, don't think about it.*

"Kate! Come on!" Mary-Lou pulled her upright.

They ran as fast as they could. Katie's staggering step found a rhythm as adrenaline brought her tired legs to life. Michael was a dark shadow in the distance. When they reached the last rise to Cedrus, Katie's lungs were screaming. Ahead of them Michael formed an Opening. They were still fifty paces behind when it grew large enough to walk through.

"Wait!" Mary-Lou shouted.

Michael turned back to them.

"Wait for us! We're stronger together!"

Katie's chest pounded, and she couldn't tell if it was because of the sudden sprint or the idea that she might never get a chance to resolve things with Laurefen. When they reached Michael, his expression was grim. "We move on my lead," he said. "Stay close. Protect each other. Neutralize the most dangerous threat first. Ready?"

"Ready," Mary-Lou said.

They waited for Katie. All she could manage was a weak nod. Her thundering heart was beating in her throat.

"Three. Two. One. Go."

They followed Michael through the Opening. The night was dark. Clouds shrouded the waning moon, leaving only dim streetlights to guide them. They huddled on the corner of a four-way intersection with a warehouse across the street. This was Alastair, and that was the railway shed where Laurefen had spent weeks stockpiling vehicles full of flashbulbs.

"That's the last place he was," Michael whispered, nodding to the unpainted concrete building. "Follow me."

With silent steps, they crossed the road. A rusted metal door at the entry was half open, a severed chain lay on the ground. Michael pointed to the door. He tapped his palm, and Katie received an unspoken message. *Me first. Wait for the all clear.*

Mary-Lou nodded. Katie clenched her fists to keep them from trembling.

Michael stopped a step back from the door. He flexed his fingers, then vanished inside.

Silence. Katie held her breath, waiting for Michael's head to reappear. Something snapped on her hand—as if someone had flicked it with an elastic band. Mary-Lou stared at her own palm.

Someone had severed their looptap with Michael.

We're all going to end up dead before we can even get to Sabriva. Katie grabbed Mary-Lou's sleeve and they retreated behind a nearby tree. She wound Mary-Lou's thread across her index finger. *What do we do?* she tapped.

We need to find a different entrance. That one's being guarded.

Katie nodded. *Michael?*

Mary-Lou's shoulders slumped. *I don't know,* she replied. *We can't think about that now. We have to get inside that building and see what's happening.*

They waited another thirty seconds, then circled around. On the eastern face of the building, a small light flickered in a high square window. *Could we look through there?* Katie nodded to the glass.

Not unless you have a ladder.

When they reached the northern side of the warehouse, they found a push-bar door at each end. Mary-Lou pointed at the closest one. *Two of us. Two doors. What if we go through at the same time?*

It would make it harder to get the drop on two places at once, Katie agreed.

I'll go left, you go right.

They kept to the shadows as long as they could. A nerve-wracking fifteen feet across the vacant parking lot and Katie was there. She looked across to where Mary-Lou stood by her own door. *I'm here.*

Check the lock.

The door did not appear to have one. Katie considered the bar holding the door closed. Pushing it down would lower the pin and let her inside. A broken padlock lay discarded at her feet. *Mine is open. Yours?*

Unlocked. Are you ready?

Katie's fingers trembled, but she managed to looptap her reply. *Yes.*

Here we go. Three. Two. One.

Katie shoved the push bar down and the door swung inwards. Immediately, another snap stung her hand and Mary-Lou was gone. She looked left—a warehouse full of vehicles blocked her vision.

It's just you. Katie pushed the thought aside and ran. Her feet echoed off the polished concrete. She didn't care. Voices followed her, carrying across from the opposite side of the room. As they approached, she flattened herself on the floor and wormed her way underneath the van.

"There's one more in here," called a sickly sweet voice. A familiar tone that made Katie's insides turn. Horace—disguised as Haberdeen. *What is he doing here?* "They're hiding amongst the vans."

Katie wriggled on her stomach, then rolled under a black bus. Footsteps followed. Katie crawled in the other direction.

"Are you sure?" said a man's voice.

Katie prepared to move to the next row when movement caught her eye. Someone walked towards her, checking beneath each vehicle. They took a few steps, crouched down, stood up, and repeated. *I guess we're not going to stop anyone.* Horace would kill them, reach the Well unopposed, and magic would cease in Euryma. The greatest Dominion on the planet would fail. Katie clenched her teeth. *Not without a fight.*

"They're more mongrels from King's College. Directive people. Both of them!" shouted a hard voice from across the warehouse.

The Fatesmith searching the floor turned around. Katie took her chance. She crept out from underneath the car, gathered two coils of aeronima and thrust them into the blackcoat ahead of her. The young man cried out as the condensed air threw him into the nearest vehicle. Katie tied the weave off—pinning the man against the silver van door —and rolled to safety.

Footsteps echoed from the high ceilings. Katie moved in the opposite direction, travelling in zig-zags, tying off knots of kinima as she crawled. She hoped the minor explosions of kinetic energy would confuse her pursuers while she made her escape.

When she reached the last line of buses, she stole a glance at the closest exit and did a double take. Three iron casts gleamed in the muted light—Laurefen, Michael and Mary-Lou. A lone Fatesmith stood watch. Shouts of pursuit continued from behind her.

Katie fought to calm her racing heart. She needed to

distract the guard. Further along the wall, stacks of archive boxes covered a chipboard bench. Carefully, Katie sifted through nima until she found what she wanted. With a gentle tug, the box on top tilted and fell. It hit the concrete with a resounding thud and the Fatesmith pivoted to face it.

Katie slipped free. Formed two enormous spheres of aeronima and raised them high over the woman, then she turned around.

"Kate?"

Katie's jaw dropped. She stared at the young woman wearing Fatesmith black. The condensed air dissolved. It made no sense. This person. In this place. In that outfit.

"Ava?"

CHAPTER 34

AVA

Ava's feet refused to move. Katie Hall looked like she'd been rolling in dirt. Judging by her hiding spot, that's exactly what she had been doing. "Why are you here?"

Katie didn't respond. Her startled gaze fixed on something over Ava's shoulder. Ava spun as Raul spun a shimmering silver square into existence. "Stop!" She raised her hands. "It's Kate. We know her."

"I know we know her," Raul said. "I know, because her pals beat the spit out of me on their island."

"She's the reason you got off that island," Ava said. "Drop the spell."

Raul tilted his head, looking past her. "What are you doing here? No tricks."

Ava turned back to Katie. "You can tell us."

"Us?" Katie's gaze darted from Ava to Raul. "What is going on? Why are you wearing—"

She cut off as Haberdeen arrived with Misha, who limped while he rubbed his shoulder. He shot Katie a dark look.

"No more chances," Raul barked. "Tell us what's going on or you'll be a statue like the others."

Katie went white. Still, she appeared unwilling to speak, and Ava couldn't blame her. Her previous truce with Raul had been tentative at best. "We're trying to stop Horace," she said at last. "Horace is planning on breaking the Ancellum. He's going to attack Kingsbreak."

"We know that." Raul gestured to the crowded warehouse. "I want to know why you have a room full of vehicles burstin' with flashbulbs."

"It's our... plan." Katie grimaced. "We were going to drive them into the ruins and blast the whole thing to smithereens."

"*That's* your plan? Blow it up?" Raul shook his head. "I thought the Directive was made up of scholars, not Neanderthals."

Katie did not reply. She stood there, looking awkward and overwhelmed.

"Why is Horace seeking access to Kingsbreak?" Haberdeen asked.

"We've got something he needs."

Raul rolled his eyes, as if frustrated by the answer. "And what, pray tell, would that be? What is so important that this boy wants to destroy one of the most potent protective spells in existence to reach it?"

"A book," Katie said. "About the origin of magic. He thinks it's the key to stopping the storms."

"If Horace can end the storms, why not give him the book and remain safe?" Haberdeen asked.

"Because..." Katie took a deep breath. "We believe it will allow him to stop *all* magic. For good."

The words were a hammer, leaving a stunned silence as it hit. Ava felt sick. The Knights already outmatched Euryma's wizards. If they lost their power, they would be help-less against Vedmark's army.

Raul's fierisation square dissolved as he spun to face Haberdeen. "Is that possible?"

"I... don't know." The woman's frown stressed the narrow scar running off her lip. "If it is, it would put us at a severe disadvantage in the trials to come." She motioned to Katie. "How does Horace intend to destroy magic?"

"I can't say."

"Can't?" Raul growled. "Or won't?"

Oh, enough of this! "Does it matter?" Ava snapped. "They want to stop Horace. So do we." She smiled at Katie. "We're here because of Luck. It led us right to you. That means something, Kate. I think our best chance of success is working together."

"No!" Raul growled. "I'm—"

"—Being an idiot." Ava finished. "Kate is not our enemy. Horace is. Get that into your thick head before you ruin everything."

Raul huffed like an oversized toddler. Haberdeen touched his shoulder.

"Thank you." Ava was a mess of nerves, but she needed to project confidence. She smiled at Katie. "What do you think about a little truce? For old time's sake?"

Katie tore her gaze from the three iron casts by the wall. "What did you have in mind?"

"You want to destroy Sabriva Tower's remains to keep Kingsbreak safe, but that's just a short-term solution. If Horace wants to reach that island, he is going to find a way. What if we could offer a more... *permanent* solution?"

"You want to kill him?"

"We understand if you have reservations."

"No," Katie said quickly. "I don't. You can kill him and burn his ashes for all I care."

Ava blinked. "Okay..."

Something burned behind Katie's eyes as she turned to Haberdeen. "You may have put my mother in iron," she said, "but Horace was the one who had her melted. He murdered my mother. He murdered my best friend. If you can rid the world of Horace Marley, I will do whatever I can to help you."

"And these three?" Haberdeen gestured to the casts beside them. "Do they feel the same?"

Katie frowned. "I think so. If it means keeping Kings-break safe."

"Allow us a moment." Haberdeen gestured to Raul, and the two walked to the far end of the room, speaking in hushed tones.

Ava stepped closer and Katie surprised her with a hug. Ava could feel the tension bleeding out of the girl. "I thought I was going to die," Katie whispered. "I thought you were Horace, that he'd found us..." she stepped back, looking her up and down. "What is going on, Ava? Why are you working with them again? Where is Declan?"

"It..." Ava exhaled. "It's a really long story. Declan is holed up in Lombrives."

"The cave city?"

Ava nodded.

"What's he doing there?"

"I don't know," Ava said. "But Vedmark is coming. That's why *I'm* here. That's why I'm stuck with Habby and Red. There's an army of Warlocks sweeping the Dominion and I need help."

"And if Horace is dead, Haberdeen can take the Fatesmiths back. Then you'll have an army. Is that why you joined them?"

The restrictive oath tingled to life, restricting Ava to a curt nod. *No. I joined because Declan's parents are alive. If I help Haberdeen, I'll be able to save them.* Thinking the words were hard enough. Saying them out loud was impossible. Before Ava could respond, Raul and Haberdeen returned. Their expressions betrayed nothing, but a vein pulsed in Raul's neck.

"We are in agreement," Haberdeen announced. "I will defierise the Directive on the condition they aid us in stopping Horace Marley. If they refuse, they will be put back in stasis until the Dominion is safe."

Katie chewed on her lower lip. "Let me talk to them first. They will help. I know it."

"As you wish." Haberdeen swayed past them to stand before the casts. While Ava had witnessed more fierisation than she liked, she had yet to see the opposite of the process.

Haberdeen slid her right hand along her left wrist, tracing her palm up over fingers and down to her elbow. As she repeated the action, something akin to bubbling wax formed above her hand. Tiny spheres—opalescent pinheads—popped into existence, congealed into larger marbles, combining to form an ivory orb. When it reached the size of a watermelon, Haberdeen directed it towards the cast of the old woman.

The iron cracked like desert clay, and fragments flaked into the ball, as if pulled by a magnet. As it did, the white sphere darkened. When the woman opened her eyes, the orb fell to the ground. Collapsing like a ball of sand on the concrete.

"Lou!" Katie grabbed the woman's shoulders. "Hey! You're okay!"

"What is that?" Ava pointed at the deformed lump.

"Irofil," Haberdeen said. "The iron takes on a crystalline structure."

"Sells for a pretty penny," Raul added.

Ava leaned down. The coarse powder smelled like Vedmark City's blacksmith, but... also like the fight back at Lombrives City. "Declan used this stuff. Threw it around us to make it hard to see."

"It has useful anti-magic properties. Hence why we sold it to the Dominion at a steep cost." Haberdeen formed a new ball ahead of her. "How else do you think we funded our army?"

"I... I never thought of it."

The tall balding man—Michael—stumbled to his knee. Raul had summoned a precautionary fierisation square.

"It's fine," Katie said, standing between them. She locked eyes with Michael and held up her palms. "I'll explain everything when Laurefen is free. Don't do anything stupid."

Michael pursed his lips as his gaze settled on Laurefen's cast. "He's alive." He breathed a long sigh and his expression softened. "Are you okay?" he asked Mary-Lou.

"I'm fine," she said.

The last orb fell to the floor and Laurefen steadied himself against the wall. He blinked up at them and his eyes widened. "What is this?"

"This young lady has made a deal on your behalf," Haberdeen said. She directed a meaningful look at Katie. "I will leave her to elaborate." She motioned to Raul, and the pair strode away.

As Ava watched them, she noticed Misha sitting alone

in the seat of a silver van. She glanced back to Katie, but the Directive were deep in conversation, so she walked around and joined Misha from the passenger side. "What's up?" she whispered.

Misha turned to her. His eyes were swollen and blood-shot. Ava could tell he was fighting to hold back tears. "What are we doing here?"

"What do you mean? We're trying to stop Vedmark."

"We *are* Vedmark. We're not bad people. We're not the enemy. It's those Knights, and your damned uncle."

"Hey…" Ava reached over to squeeze his elbow. "Where's this coming from?"

"I… I don't know. I just want to find father and go. I don't want to get caught up in a grand magical war. I want things to go back to how they used to be." His lips curled into a barely contained sneer. "Before Declan."

It took all Ava's self-control to maintain her composure. "We are here now, and Luck is shining on us. If we can get Haberdeen her army, we are one step closer to saving your dad. Everything sucks right now, but we're close."

"If you say so."

Ava levelled a knowing glance at him. "We're gonna get Ory back. It will get better. We just need to put in the work."

Misha said nothing. He gripped the steering wheel, and while he made no sound, his shoulders trembled with emotion. Ava had dragged him from his home into a fight he wanted no part of. She opened her mouth, but she had nothing to say. They sat in miserable silence, waiting for the Fatesmiths and Directive to unite.

Ava, Mary-Lou, Misha and Raul sat around a plastic table at the warehouse edge. Misha had not spoken a word all morning, and for all Ava's encouragement, seemed intent on wallowing in pity. With the large roller door up, sunlight warmed the sections of the tabletop that weren't covered in maps.

"This plan is a mistake," Raul said. He had been sullen since the Directive agreed on a truce. Ava suspected he had secretly hoped they would refuse to help, allowing him to fierise them once again. Despite his foul mood, he wasn't wrong. They had discussed their options at length, but they only knew so much. Their strategy relied on more guesswork than Ava liked.

"It's the best we can do," Mary-Lou said. The old woman appeared exhausted.

"Well, I hate it," Raul said. Outside, Michael loaded crates of magical explosives into a yellow van. Ava did not appreciate how nonchalant the bald-headed man was about carrying multiple containers of flashbulbs at once.

"You want Horace. We want the tower destroyed." Mary-Lou sounded like she was instructing a child on how to get dressed. "This accomplishes both goals. What would you do instead?"

"For starters, I would not be using myself as bait."

"You're on distraction duty because it's you who wants the boy dead."

"It will take more than me to stop him."

Mary-Lou glanced up from her map. "You're an accomplished Mage. You can handle yourself."

They all turned at the sound of footsteps. Haberdeen held up a brown paper bag. "Not much on offer except packaged food." She handed it to Raul. "Breakfast. Alastair's finest."

Raul emptied its contents onto the table. Mary-Lou glared at him, then pushed a plastic-wrapped croissant aside.

Ava helped herself to a muffin. "How is Horace so strong?"

Nobody answered at first. Raul appeared torn between the banana bread and the apple cinnamon slice. He shrugged and took both. "I'm guessing he's in Reaper territory now."

"What is a Reaper?"

"A Reaper is what happens when you use too many Ire Tides for too long," Haberdeen explained. "Most people burn out before they get to that stage. Though there are rare instances where individuals have become stronger. Vastly powerful."

"And vastly insane too," Raul muttered.

"But why?" Mary-Lou asked. "Beyond the destruction of Sabriva, the boy has had no need to draw on such power."

"Carrying another's memories takes a toll on a person," Haberdeen said. "I used the white dagger sparingly. Horace's mind has..." she frowned at Ava. "How old did you say Arman Moore was?"

"A thousand years. Give or take."

Haberdeen swallowed. "So, he has at least ten lifetimes in his head, plus everything I had. Horace can't contain that. Nobody can. He needs something to blunt its edge, and the only magic we can manipulate from within are Ire Tides. I expect Horace draws on them daily." She shuddered. "They destroy your ability to reason, and when rationality cracks, the animal brain takes over." She frowned in Mary-Lou's direction. "We require more firepower than the four of us."

Ava nodded. She was one of that quartet, along with Haberdeen, Raul and Laurefen.

"*Our* focus is on destroying the tower," Mary-Lou said. "That protects Kingsbreak. When the vans are in place and detonated, we can provide aid."

"Why worry about destroying the tower when we can kill the one trying to use it?" Raul muttered. "We need everyone. All of us against Horace. That is our only hope. Otherwise, he's going to pick us off one at a time."

"He's not wrong." Laurefen stood at the doorway, Katie by his side with a bright red face. She hefted two massive bottles of water onto the table then wiped the sweat from her brow.

"How did the scouting mission go?" Mary-Lou asked.

"Fatesmiths still guard the perimeter," Laurefen said. "We could only get so close."

"Did you see him?" Haberdeen asked. "Is he here?"

"We couldn't tell," Laurefen admitted. There was no doubt who *he* was. "There is a well-defended tent south of the tower's ruins. We watched for as long as we dared, but we didn't see Horace."

"So what do we do?" Ava asked. The full moon was tomorrow night, and the pair had been gone for hours to gather information they needed. Instead, they had returned with nothing.

"Raul's right," Katie said. "If we try to destroy the tower, we'll be contending with a hundred Fatesmiths as well. We need to focus on Horace. He is the threat, and he's too strong for us to split into two smaller groups."

Raul nodded his agreement. "She's always been the smartest one of you lot."

Mary-Lou kept her eyes on Laurefen. "Our priority is protecting Kingsbreak. Our plan—"

"The plan was based on old information," Katie said. "Last time we faced Horace, we had Arman Moore and Declan. We still lost. We can't afford to repeat the same mistake."

"We must adapt our strategy," Laurefen agreed. "The Fatesmiths will not let us attack Horace by himself. We're going to need to keep them occupied."

It was the same puzzle they had been contending with all morning. Two objectives, multiple obstacles, and nobody in agreement about what to do first. Ava watched Michael reverse a bus to the door and begin loading more crates, and an idea came to mind. "How do you set those things off?" Ava gestured to the bus.

"The flashbulbs?" Katie shrugged. "Crack the glass. Once the vacuum breaks, the pyronima reacts with the air. Kaboom."

"If you bend light around those..." Ava pointed to the line of vehicles outside. "Will they still stay invisible when you reach Sabriva?"

Laurefen followed her finger. "They may."

"We need to find out for sure." Ava nodded as her plan took shape. She smiled at Misha, who sat brooding in the corner. He alone knew how audacious her plans could be. "I think I've got an idea that would solve all our problems in one kaboom."

CHAPTER 35

LAUREFEN

Alastair to Sabriva should have been a twenty-minute drive.

Moving sixty-seven photonima-concealed vehicles down roads of ash took significantly longer. Laurefen wished they had another month. The weeks had passed in moments, and now, time was up.

Eight hours later, the buses and vans were in position. Laurefen knew almost nothing about the pair of Lucks, but —true to their word—they had kept the Fatesmiths out of their hair. The girl had demonstrated remarkable talent. Laurefen hoped Ava's proficiency extended to their plan. The fate of magic itself depended on it.

As the sun balanced on the distant hills, Laurefen sat alongside his trusted colleagues, a frustrated protégé and some old enemies as they waited—with a bag of nimrods and irofil—to burn what remained of Sabriva Tower.

"When is the moon due to rise?" Michael whispered.

"Twelve minutes after sunset," Raul said. "Ava and Misha will draw the Fatesmiths away at last light. When Horace is alone in the ruins, we blow the place."

"And if some stay behind?" Mary-Lou asked. "Are you willing to sacrifice ironhand blood?"

"I trust Ava's power," Haberdeen said. "The Lucks of Iberia were once the only thing the Knights of Despair feared. She knows we need as many soldiers as possible for the coming conflict. Ava will get them out."

"And if she doesn't?"

"Collateral damage is a reality of war," Raul said.

Laurefen agreed. He noted Katie's silence. The girl was unusually quiet—her brown eyes pinned to the opposite side of the ruins. She seemed to sense his attention, because she turned to face him. "What if this doesn't work?" she whispered.

"We finish the job ourselves." Laurefen patted the bag beside him.

"Sacks of dust and nimrods imbued years ago?" Katie exhaled a shuddering breath.

"To worry is to rehearse failure," Laurefen counselled. He could not remember where he'd heard the line, but it was apt advice. He ran a finger along a transparent nimrod. "Follow the plan."

An uneasy silence settled atop of them as the last remnants of sunlight faded behind the hills. As it did, an enormous flare of yellow light curled and danced over the other side of the ruins. A half-second later, a booming whip crack echoed over them.

"That's one." Laurefen raised a brass spyglass to his eye. The Fatesmith tent erupted in a swarm of movement. Ironhands formed small groups that raced towards the explosion. Laurefen smiled. It was working.

A smaller cluster of flashbulbs burst into a brilliant cloud of light. Still a few miles off, but closer than the one previous. It rumbled like thunder. More men and women rushed to investigate.

"Six minutes," Raul growled. "They're not moving fast enough. That moon will be out any moment."

A cacophony of light filled the sky as a straight run of violent eruptions surged towards the ruins. A half mile away, an entire bus detonated in one massive blast that pushed dusk to day. Sabriva's scorched skeleton lit up like a noonday sun. The terrible noise shook the ground.

Darkness returned. Panic broke the stunned silence and the desolate husk of Sabriva Tower emptied as the Fatesmiths streamed out of the tents. Yet instead of rushing after their comrades, they ran in the other direction—in *their* direction.

"We need to move," Laurefen said, but as he did, two purple Openings formed ahead of them. Their blurred edges expanded until the doorways melded into an enormous oval which the Fatesmiths rushed through.

"What?" Michael turned, slack-jawed, to Laurefen. "They are evacuating."

Without speaking, Katie pointed to the distant horizon. A sliver of white appeared over the hilltops.

The moon was rising.

As ironhands flooded through the Opening, a solitary figure moved against the tide, a woman with long red hair.

"There he is," Michael said.

Laurefen's eye never left his spyglass. Horace swayed through the chaos wearing a sweeping black cloak. He stopped at a small pile of jagged stone and raised a crumbling section to the sky. Laurefen pressed the eyepiece so hard his cheek hurt. He appeared to be... waiting for something. *What is he doing?*

Michael cleared his throat. "Horace is in position. It's time."

Laurefen reached into his sleeve pocket and removed a glass cylinder wrapped in silk cloth. It was the size of a matchstick and tethered to a single crate at the center of the vehicles. All he had to do was crack it, and thousands of flashbulbs would erupt in a fiery chain reaction.

"Wait," Haberdeen said. "There are still Fatesmiths fleeing."

"This is our chance," Michael said. "Break it."

"He's not going to attack Kingsbreak in thirty-seconds," Haberdeen said. "Let them escape."

"If he portals out of here, everything is lost," Michael shot back. "Do it now!"

Laurefen gripped the cylinder. *Such a small thing, to create so much destruction.*

"Those are lives you're about to end!" Haberdeen hissed. "People just trying to protect their homes! *Our* home!"

Laurefen shook his head. "Protecting magic is our legacy." In one motion, he snapped the trigger in two.

Brilliant brightness, brighter than bright, engulfed the landscape. Laurefen covered his eyes on instinct. He could see the bones of his wrists and hands. Searing heat passed through him, like some demon made of fire, and there was a deafening crash, as if all the thunder in the world had combined into one destructive boom. Everything spun until the ground hit him, knocking the breath from his chest. Laurefen sprawled in the dirt, while a piercing whistle filled his ears. A city-sized ball of flame ascended over the plains.

The fireball rotated as it rose, a horrible blend of red and orange, illuminated by flashes of lightning that sent shivers down his spine. An overwhelming sense of awe and fear overtook him. The explosion was colossal beyond description. Laurefen staggered upright, then fell to a knee. Michael and Haberdeen attempted the same. Everybody else lay in stunned silence.

Minutes passed before Laurefen found the strength to try again. Slowly, the others stood. Michael helped Mary-Lou to her feet. The bag of nimrods and irofil had been flung aside, emptying its contents around them.

"Too many flashbulbs," Mary-Lou murmured.

Michael coughed a laugh, then grabbed his side.

"Are you alright?"

"Just a bruised rib or two," Michael replied. "I must admit, I'm looking forward to some rest."

Laurefen smiled. Despite the ravages of the blast, he felt a weight of relief. Nothing could have survived that. Not the stonework of Sabriva Tower, and definitely not Horace Marley.

"Laurefen." There was fear in Katie's voice. She knelt at the crest of the hill. "Up here."

Laurefen half-walked, half-stumbled to her side. He squinted down, but without a spyglass, he could see only darkness... and a small purple light. His stomach lurched. "What is that?"

Katie handed him a pair of binoculars. Laurefen searched for the ruins. There were none. The stone piles were gone, but a lone figure remained. Encased in a violet glow, holding a single piece of rubble to the sky. No longer disguised. Radiant in his fury. Laurefen's heart turned to ice. The boy had survived.

"How?" Laurefen had not noticed Mary-Lou joining him. She looked through a spyglass which trembled in her hand. "That explosion could have sunk Kingsbreak. How is he alive?"

"Ire Tides," Haberdeen said. She shook her head. "He has shielded himself in protective magic."

"Not just himself," Katie said. "A chunk of the tower too."

"We can't compete with this," Raul said.

"We don't have to." Laurefen handed Katie her binoculars and began collecting nimrods from the hill behind them. "We just have to get that stone out of his hand and destroy it."

"That boy has to die," Raul said.

Laurefen turned to Michael and Mary-Lou. The grim determination on their haggard faces gave him all the confirmation he needed. "If we can help you, we will, but we must destroy that piece of rubble. All our magic depends on it."

"So, we make our stand," Haberdeen said. "How?"

"He's moving," Katie called out. She kept the binoculars pressed to her eyes. "We need to get down there. Now!"

"Find a nimrod," Michael said. "Attack from all sides. Get the rock and destroy it. That's the plan."

Nobody wasted time arguing. Laurefen scooped up two bags of irofil to go with his pocketful of nimrods and rushed down the hill, hoping against hope that Horace wouldn't leave before they reached the bottom. An awful sense of finality curdled in his stomach. *This is it.*

Michael took the lead as the ground leveled out. A thick haze of ash fell around them, muffling their footsteps until they were within a hundred yards of the boy. Horace turned as they approached. A wicked smile split his pallid features as his eyes sparked purple.

"Iron!" Laurefen shouted.

Michael emptied a bag of irofil into the air. A second later, a violet flash ignited against it. The area lit up like lightning inside a storm cloud. Laurefen flourished a nimrod from his coat sleeve. The moment he was clear of the irofil, he thrust the wooden rod forward. A bolt of electricity erupted from its tip. Horace ducked the attack. Laurefen felt the wood splinter and disintegrate in his hand. He threw the spent nimrod aside and drew another. Horace retreated as a half-dozen attacks blasted in his direction.

He slithered between spells, but he could not stop them all. A gale of concentrated air tossed him backwards, and a second crackle of lightning caught him in midair. Horace's airborne figure went limp as he crashed into barren earth. Laurefen raised a rosewood nimrod—charged with pyronima—and held it ready as they encircled Horace's body.

A curtain of sleek black hair hid his face. Laurefen pointed the nimrod down at him, but Horace didn't move. By all appearances, he was unconscious.

"That's it?" Raul said.

Mary-Lou's eyes never left the boy. "It feels too easy."

"Good," Haberdeen said. "Then we finish this."

Before Laurefen could react, she stabbed her nimrod downwards. A spray of stone spewed from within it, only to detonate inches from Horace's head in a flash of purple light. Raul swung his own nimrod. A pillar of flames enveloped Horace's body for a full count of ten. When it faded, a shimmering shield remained. Horace opened his eyes and sat up.

Laurefen thrust his nimrod forward, as did Michael, Katie and Mary-Lou. Fire, wind, and electricity engulfed him. Haberdeen and Raul added two new pillars of searing hot air to the fray. When the torrent died down, Laurefen's stomach dropped. Horace Marley sat cross-legged—unharmed—with his hands in his lap.

"I was worried you would not come," he said. Horace clenched his fists and Laurefen felt something ignite in his sleeve. He tossed his last nimrod to the ground as it splintered in a flash of light. Michael did the same. Their only weapons crumbled to dust. "Thank you for coming," Horace said. The purple shield around him shimmered away, and he stood to face them. "So, who do we have here? The Directive, my old friend Mage Raul... and if it isn't the famous Haberdeen herself?" He shook his head in disbelief. "I thought I killed you. Oh well. I'll be sure to do it right this time."

"You son of—"

Horace raised a finger and Haberdeen grabbed her neck. Her eyes bulged as Raul lunged forward. He was immediately knocked onto his back. Haberdeen clutched her throat, fighting for air.

"Stop!" Katie cried. "Let her go!"

Haberdeen's eyes rolled back in her head. Raul roared like a caged bear as he fought to get off the ground. Horace tilted his head. "I know you. You're Amber's friend. Pity you couldn't save her. Could you?"

White-hot hatred burned behind Katie's eyes. "What do you want from us?"

"That is the question of the hour." Horace waved for them to sit. As he did, a monumental gasp escaped Haberdeen's lips. Horace frowned, as if confused by what had just happened, then a crooked grin split his thin cheeks. "Brilliant," he announced. "A bit of Luck to save your friend?" He clenched his fist and Haberdeen stiffened. A rasping choke cut off her gulping breaths. "Come out, come out, wherever you are. If you don't, I'm going to snap her neck."

Ava emerged from the darkness behind him. "I'm here," she said, palms held high. "Let her go."

Horace's smile sharpened. "Ava Drakonov. A pleasure."

Haberdeen's breath returned with another gasp as Horace summoned a seat from thin air. It took Laurefen a moment to realize he was forming it from the specks of dust that had been Sabriva Tower. Stone chairs formed around them in a small circle and Horace gestured for them to sit. "Let's get to it then," he said. "I have called you here because you have information I need. If you tell me what I want to know, you can swear the Fatesmiths' oath to stop using magic and be on your merry way. If you don't..." He slipped a white dagger from the depths of his black cloak. "I will take it by force."

"What are you talking about?" Michael asked. "We weren't called here. We—"

"I told Euryma's most talkative talkers that I intended to use Sabriva Tower to breach Kingsbreak. I revealed where I would be and when I would be there. I brought an army of LAMPs to look the part, and sent them to safety the moment you started doing whatever it is you thought you could do to stop me." Horace smiled. "I called, and you came. Like obedient dogs."

Laurefen's insides froze. Horace didn't know how to undo the Ancellum. It was all a ploy to get them here. *And we fell for it.*

Horace turned his attention to Mary-Lou. "I am delighted you came, Mary-Lou Nivin. Our last conversation ended so soon. How about we continue it now?"

Don't do anything rash. Laurefen thought. He wished he could looptap her.

Mary-Lou lifted her chin. "I've already said everything I have to say."

Horace raised the crystal dagger and stood. "So be it."

"Wait!" Laurefen said.

"Yes?"

"What information do you seek?"

Horace returned to his seat. "Remnant Magic is destroying Euryma, but magic is a finite resource." He tapped his head. "I've seen it. I watched Arman Moore create it. I need to know where he stored it, so I can destroy it and stop the storms for good."

Haberdeen looked back at Raul, still on the ground, but no longer struggling against his invisible bonds. Laurefen took another deep breath, delaying as long as he could to think of something. "How can magic be stored in Euryma while also causing Remnant Magic storms at the same time?"

"I don't care," Horace said. "Magic is the enemy. I am going to stop it at the source." In a flash of movement, he stood over Mary-Lou with the white dagger pressed to her throat. A red pinprick bloomed at its tip. "And if you don't tell me right now. I'm just going to take it." He turned back to Laurefen. "You see, I am tired of the games. You can't stop me, but you can save yourself and your friends. What is it going to be?"

Laurefen's whirring mind came up empty. There was no other decision he could make except the truth. "Alright. You've won. Put down the dagger and I'll tell you what you want to know."

An unnerving smile crawled across Horace's lips. It was inhuman. Less the smile of a man and more that of a monster. He flicked the dagger to Laurefen's chest. Its point felt like a shard of ice. "You know what I'm looking for?"

"I do." It took all of Laurefen's resolve to keep his voice steady. "And I'm going to tell you. Lower your weapon and we can talk."

"I don't need to talk," Horace said. "I just need to know who to kill without taking on any... unnecessary memories."

"You said—"

"I said what I must to save Euryma," Horace hissed. He shook his head and the calm smile returned. "I know how much your legacy means to you, Laurefen Ember. Rest well knowing your secrets will save the Dominion. Even if I must take them from your corpse."

Laurefen closed his eyes. *This is it.* There was no time to think anything else. Laurefen felt the icy blade pierce his skin. Amidst a flutter of movement, the pain vanished.

When Laurefen opened his eyes, Horace was on one knee with an axe lodged in his right shoulder. Dark blood seeped down his side.

Laurefen turned, and words failed him. Declan Moore stepped into the light; his eyes narrowed on his kneeling friend. Horace tried to grip the axe head. His left hand flickered like a candle, then extinguished, leaving a clean stump. "What type of iron is this?"

With a metallic hum, the axe cartwheeled back to Declan's hands. Horace slumped forward with the force of its departure. Declan held the axe ready. "You've gone too far, Ace."

With intense concentration, Horace re-summoned his hand. "No," he whispered, pressing a glowing fist to his shoulder. The wound burned shut. "I've gone as far as I've had to."

"I don't want to hurt you." Declan raised his other

hand. A second axe leapt into his palm. "But I will not let you hurt anybody else."

Horace's eyes glittered purple. "You're not going to stop me, Declan. You can't. Without your Sila, you're nothing." He staggered to his feet, and everyone backed away.

Everyone but Declan.

CHAPTER 36

DECLAN

HORACE THRUST a hand forward and a luminescent bar of energy lit up the night. Declan stamped his feet. Iron flakes erupted from his boots, shrouding him from view. The Ire Tides fragmented against the particles in flashes of purple. Declan gestured to Laurefen. "Go south! There's a silver truck. John is waiting for you." His gaze landed on Ava. "Get everyone out of here."

"We can help," Laurefen said.

"You're more helpful out of my way." Declan dug a fistful of irofil from his pocket and refilled his shoe. "Get as far from here as you can."

The violet blaze abated as Horace charged through the haze. Waving the others away, Declan took a defensive stance. Horace's eyes were blazing amethysts as he lashed out with Winterthorn, but his form was sloppy, his movements predictable. Declan responded with his axe and Horace retreated enough to send another blast of magic in his direction.

Declan spun and caught the torrent against an axe head. The purple beam deflected into the ground, spraying earth around them. He turned to make sure the area was clear as Horace charged through the dirt. They collided in a mess of limbs. Declan swung for his chest and Horace dashed behind a wall of Ire Tides that curved over Declan like ocean waves. He stepped into Armadillo and let the heat wash over him.

When Horace attacked again, Declan was ready. He ducked the slashing blow and drove the handle of his axe into Horace's shoulder—the same wound he'd inflicted moments before. With a roar of agony, a crackling ripple of energy burst free of Horace, and Declan barely caught it against both axe heads. The power of the spell knocked him onto his back.

"I should have killed you when I had a chance," Horace growled. A flickering ball levitated above his open palm. "My mercy has only put Euryma at risk. No more!" He hurled the sphere. Declan rolled to safety as Ire Tides exploded behind him. "You're messing with things you don't understand," Horace continued. Another purple orb appeared in his vision. Declan sidestepped it and lunged forward, but Horace thrust a bar of energy into the ground between them. Burned earth erupted like a geyser, throwing Declan backwards, burying him under a mountain of soil. He wheezed as its weight forced the air from his lungs.

A violet glow illuminated their surrounds. Horace's magic cast jagged shadows across his bitter face. He knelt to meet Declan's eyes. "It didn't have to be this way. You—"

Something hit Horace's sternum. In a flash of sparks, a dagger fell at his feet. Declan could not see who threw it, but his stomach sank regardless. He recognized the blade's handle. It was one of Ava's knives.

With a shout, she charged over the top of the dirt

mound and planted a knee in Horace's chest. He stepped back as she landed—weapon in each hand—and slashed out at him. Horace retreated, sending bolts of Ire Tides to cover his steps. Ava weaved through the flares of light that speared past her. The pair disappeared from Declan's view.

No! No! Ava's too close. Horace has Winterthorn. He's going to kill her. Declan thrashed around to no avail. Sabriva's burnt soil buried him to the neck. A mix of color lit up the night as Michael and Laurefen rushed forward. Blue flames erupted from nimrods, but the fire fizzled out when Horace knocked Michael off his feet. Laurefen vanished from sight.

Wild panic ignited within Declan. Things were spiraling out of control and he was powerless to help. He strained with all his strength to pull his arm free, to claw his way out of the dirt. His breath caught as Ava staggered into view. A blistering spray of magic spewed from the stump where Horace's hand should have been. Ire Tides split the ground with a piercing crack. When it faded, a white line remained burned into Declan's vision. In the darkness, he heard a woman's voice.

"Now!"

Mary-Lou and Haberdeen appeared either side of Horace. They flourished matching nimrods and a hailstorm of stone obeyed their commands. Declan stopped struggling. They were like twin conductors in an orchestra, using the dusty remnants of Sabriva Tower to seal Horace in a crude sarcophagus.

Katie arrived, wielding the pale copper nimrod John described as a 'gravity stick'. She thrust it out, and the rock molded into a misshapen lump that resembled a gargantuan cocoon. Declan tried to shout. He couldn't. The heavy earth still squeezed his lungs. The others stared at the makeshift stone casket.

"You alright?" Raul called to Katie.

"He's... pushing back..." Katie hunched forward, as if someone was pulling on the other end of the rod.

Raul joined her. He wrapped his hands around the nimrod. "We need help!"

There was a surge of heat and the sensation of being hit in the face. A shrill ring filled Declan's ears. His vision blurred, and the pressure on his chest intensified. He blinked until he could see, and when he could, his blood ran cold.

Everyone was on the ground except Horace, whose entire body was ablaze in towering purple flames, like something that had stepped out of a nightmare. Concentrated fury lined a face Declan no longer recognized.

Ava recovered first. Horace drew his bone-white dagger. Declan's heart rate tripled. "Run!" he rasped. The word stole precious air from his lungs. He was trapped, and every exhaled breath crushed him a little more. "Ava! Run!" The words were a whisper. Nobody could hear him. He was helpless. Forced to watch her die, as he had in the Void.

You're not helpless.

The voice was quiet, but stern. It came from the inky blackness of his mind. He tried to breathe in. He couldn't.

You're not helpless, the voice repeated. Horace screamed his fury. Ava barely dodged Winterthorn's blade. *But you have to fight for it.*

A circle of Ire Tides blazed around Ava, creating a wall of flame blocking her path. Her face dropped. Declan attempted to move, to create an inch of space so he could breathe. Ava's gaze darted about in panic, and—as unconsciousness enveloped him—their eyes met.

Fight for it.

One dizzying moment and he was there. The depths of

Declan's mind were a familiar haunt. He retreated here when his parents died. When his grandfather died.

Now he was there once more—when Ava died.

Did she die? Declan searched the darkness. *No! Ava can't be gone. This can't happen. Not again. I did everything I could to stop it!*

"Did you?"

Declan blinked. It was Declan's voice, but he had not spoken, had he? There had never been another here. He stared into the blackness as a wispy tendril of smoke appeared from nothing. It rotated in a column, gaining form until it was... him. Declan Moore. The same, but different.

Declan raised a hand, but no axe responded. The weapons didn't exist in his mind. "Who are you?"

The smoky imitation considered him. "I am you. Who else could I be?" It paused, scanning the darkness, as if searching for the right words. "No, that is not right. I am... you, but..." It smiled, but there was no warmth in that expression. "I am who you need to become."

A shiver ran down Declan's spine as he considered the specter. It looked... hard, callous, empty. "And what if I don't want to be like you?"

"Then people will die." He tapped his head. "You are soft, Declan. That softness killed all the family we have. It may kill everyone you love."

There was truth in those words, and Declan was tired of fighting against them. He pursed his lips while his desires and doubts wrestled. "How do I do it?" He waved towards the cloudy imitation. "How did I become like you? Like... this?"

The figure reached into a deep pocket and withdrew a dagger. Intricate patterns covered the blade and hilt. It was a perfect replica of Winterthorn, except that it glowed vibrant green. "You kill Horace." He offered the handle. "Kill your friend, and you'll be just like me."

Just like me.

Declan closed his eyes, and took his power.

Reality returned in a rush. Sila ignited his bones, and the mound of dirt vanished. Horace gripped Ava by her messy curls, with Winterthorn pressed to her throat.

No. Declan clenched his fists. An emerald explosion threw Horace sideways as Ava stumbled to a knee. He rolled to his feet and, in one neat throw, Horace launched Winterthorn forward. It split the air like a bolt from a crossbow. Declan's chest seized. He willed himself between them.

Sila dragged him over an impossible distance, right to where his outstretched hand caught the blade. The dagger impaled his palm, lodging to the hilt, and Declan dropped to his knees. Pain radiated through him—ice that burned. He gripped the handle and wrenched it free, but a frigid chill overtook him—pulling like the depths of an arctic pool.

Declan drew on Sila's wildfire until it filled every fiber of his being. The cold abated, then pushed back with a vengeance. The magic of Winterthorn seemed desperate to take hold of him.

"Help!" Ava's distant voice breathed life into the flames. Declan's muscles tightened as he dragged Sila through him.

Horace strode towards them—his face a mask of hatred. Ava threw one of her knives. It punctured Horace's torso, sticking out like a pincushion. He didn't flinch. Declan gasped as the iciness returned. It took all of his concentration to resist the weight of the inner avalanche.

Laurefen shoved past them, a nimrod raised. In one

motion, Horace plucked the dagger from his ribs and jammed it into Laurefen. Ava's gasp filled Declan's ear. The old man staggered backwards.

"Laurefen!" A distant voice screamed.

"Declan!" Ava cried.

Horace was five paces away, ignoring the blood pouring from his open wound. He reached for Winterthorn when Haberdeen careened into him.

Ava held Declan's face in her hands. "Declan. You need to fight it. I need you!"

As she spoke, a pulsing pressure built around his cheeks. The fire inside him trembled in anticipation. She pressed her forehead against his and a fantastic heat rushed through him, washing away Winterthorn's chill, setting his skin ablaze.

Ire Tides hurtled towards them. Declan drew them down into a fist-sized clump and sent the magic back. Horace retreated as it burst in an amethyst explosion. An Opening appeared behind him. He glared at Declan. "This isn't over."

No! Declan dashed forward, but Horace was already gone. As the floating door shrank to nothing, a cylindrical beam of light blasted through it—straight at Haberdeen.

Before Declan could react, Raul dived between them. He caught the blow in a purple flash and fell to the ground.

"RAUL!" Haberdeen stumbled through the ash. She grabbed his shoulders. "You fool! You stupid fool!" She lifted him onto her lap. Declan could see clean through the man's chest. Haberdeen—the heartless stone of a woman who had ordered his parent's death—screamed, a blood-curdling, throat-tearing sound that filled the night.

Katie knelt beside her. Raul blinked up at them.

"Kairi?" he rasped. His dying eyes narrowed as he stared

at Katie's face. Color bled from his pale features. "You're here." Raul smiled as he stroked her hair. "I found you…"

His hand fell away. It landed over his heart and slid down to rest on his stomach. Haberdeen buried her head against Raul's shoulder and howled. Uncried tears adorned Katie's cheeks. Declan watched in silence. Mage Raul had been there the night his parents were taken. For all he knew, Raul had been the one that turned them to iron.

Good riddance, Declan thought, but for some strange reason, he felt bad for thinking it.

CHAPTER 37

DECLAN

"Help!" Mary-Lou called from further back. She leaned over another body. "Declan! Get over here!"

Laurefen lay on the ground, Ava's dagger in his stomach. His pallid face could have been carved from marble. "Can you help him?" Michael asked.

Declan looked at his hands. Winterthorn's blade had left only a small triangular mark on his palm. "I... can't." Sila no longer burned inside him. It had vanished the moment Horace escaped.

"What about you?" Mary-Lou nodded to Ava, who stood at Declan's side. "Do you have any of your healing potion? He's bleeding out! Do you have any vials?"

Ava shook her head. "It's... no, I don't. I'm sorry."

"We need to move him," Michael said. "Somewhere with magic."

"There's a silver truck," Declan said. He pointed south. "Back that way. You can use that to get him—"

A crackling streamer of white light drowned his words. Scorching electricity hit the ground ahead of Haberdeen, sending her backwards in an explosion of dirt. John strode forward, nimrod in hand and murder in his eyes. Haberdeen scrambled away as John tried again. Ava leapt from Declan's side, throwing herself into John.

The second bolt of lightning surged over Haberdeen's shoulder. The smell of burnt metal filled the air. John ducked Ava's elbow and shoved her hard. She rolled onto her feet, but Haberdeen had a rod of her own pointed square at John's chest. "Move, Ava." She tilted her head as she considered John, and a surprised expression dawned on her face. "I know you."

"You should," John snarled. "You murdered my father. He will rest well knowing I was the one to stop you."

Haberdeen stared at him for a long moment. "Your father was a Directive agent. He killed eight Fatesmiths."

"They were turning people to iron!"

"We had no other choice! The Magistri wouldn't listen. The storms were real. The storms *are* real. You've seen what they can do. We could have stopped them..." She lowered the nimrod and looked to the others. "We are in this mess because of *you!* You *people* who thought you knew better. This death and destruction is your legacy. You should have listened to me!" Haberdeen's words echoed in the night. Her gaze fell to Raul's body. "He would still be alive," she said in a tiny voice. She dropped the rod in the ash. "Go on then. Do it."

John blinked. "What?"

"Take your revenge. Kill me. It no longer matters."

Declan scowled. *What game is she playing?* He wanted Haberdeen dead as much as John. Right as she was about Remnant Magic, she had killed his parents. She had bound Ava to her lies.

"It's what you deserve," John said. Still, he hesitated.

"It is." Haberdeen's face was solemn. "So do it."

"No," Ava said, her eyes were wet. "We made a deal! You promised me to help fight Vedmark. We need your Fatesmiths."

"Take them," Haberdeen said. "Use your power to rise to the top. I have nothing more to offer." She fixed John with a hard stare. "Well? What are you waiting for?"

A vein throbbed in John's jaw. He glanced down at the rod in his hand. Declan held his breath. "You deserve this," John whispered. He thrust the nimrod forward. A loud crack echoed in the night and it shattered in a burst of electricity. The explosion knocked John off his feet, but left Haberdeen unharmed.

Ava dropped to a knee, her face drawn as if she had run a marathon. Haberdeen scowled at her. "I said no."

"You told me not to *attack* him." Ava's gaze was firm. "We have unfinished business, Deena. You know what you owe me."

A frustrated cry broke their staring match. Mary-Lou waved for them. "Stop it!" Blood-wet strips of her dress bunched around the knife in Laurefen's chest. "We don't have time for this!" she shouted. "I don't know how you're alive, John, but Laurefen is going to die if we don't get him help. Declan, where is this truck?"

"South," Declan said. "Five minutes' walk."

John shook his head. "No. I've got to do it," he murmured, trying and failing to sit upright. "I've got to kill her."

"You'll take revenge at the cost of another's life?" Michael asked. He stood over John, his brow furrowed. "I knew your father well. I counted him one of my closest friends. He was a good man. Are you?"

A storm crossed John's face. "Don't talk about my father."

Michael knelt so they were at eye level. "You'll get your chance to make things even. Now is your chance to do what's right." He grabbed John's arm and pulled him to his feet. "We need to save Laurefen."

For a moment, Declan thought John might attack Haberdeen with his bare hands. Instead, he took a deep breath and noddeed. "Fine," he said. "The truck is this way. I can get you out of range and we can make an Opening."

"Thank you," Mary-Lou said.

"But I'll be back for you," he said, glaring at Haberdeen. "I swear it." John turned away from her and followed Michael. Together, they hoisted Laurefen off the ground. He groaned at the movement, but otherwise remained unre-sponsive.

"Where do we go?" Katie asked.

"Sabart," John said. "Beneath Lombrives City. I know a healer who can help. Come on, we need to go fast."

John and Michael shuffled forward with Mary-Lou close behind. Katie didn't move. "Are you coming?"

Declan shook his head.

"Why not?"

"Did Horace get a section of the tower?"

"No," Katie said. "It doesn't matter. It was a trap. He can't get to Kingsbreak. He was drawing us here."

He wandered to the spot where Ava had come within inches of death. The white dagger lay in the dirt, half-covered in ash. "Then he's headed back to Biscay." Declan picked Winterthorn up. It was ice cold. "I can't come with you, Kate. My job isn't finished yet."

Katie considered him for a long moment. "Kill him

properly this time. For us. For Amber." She nodded and followed behind Mary-Lou. Ava started after her.

"You're going with them?" Declan asked.

"No." Ava gestured in their general direction. "Misha," she explained. "The blast hit him hard. I left him somewhere safe."

"That blast lit up the sky," Declan said. "It's the only reason I found you when I did."

Ava smiled, but it was weak. "I'm glad you did."

As she walked away, Declan turned Winterthorn over in his hands. The dagger was heavier than he expected. He had accomplished his goal. He had the blade. *But at what cost?*

Ava returned soon after, half-carrying Misha, who appeared to have stepped out of a furnace. The full moon illuminated ashen cheeks, and his burnt hair stood up like a sheer cliff. Ava sat him down. He sat with a dazed expression, though he was lucid enough to send Declan a dark look as Ava walked over to him. "We've got a few vans left in Alastair," she said.

"What are you talking about?"

"You have a job to finish, right? So do we."

Declan shook his head. "You can't come with me. I'm going alone."

"Haberdeen has to be there when he dies," Ava replied. "If she's going to take back the Fatesmiths, the switch must be seamless."

"That doesn't mean *you* have to be there."

"Declan." Ava pursed her lips. "I swore an oath to protect her. I need to come."

"And why did you do that?" Declan fought to keep his voice level. "What reason could you possibly have to do that?"

Silence. Ava's mouth could have been welded closed for all she said. Eventually, she breathed a long sigh. "You'll understand one day. I promise. Just... trust me."

It was the same answer she had given him at Lombrives. "I hope so," Declan said. "I know you need an army, but I want nothing to do with *her*." He nodded to Haberdeen, who had not yet moved from Raul's side. "She killed my parents, Ava. I'm not travelling to Biscay with her."

Ava squeezed his hand in reply. "Then travel with me."

"Aren't you listening? I don't want you there either," he said. "You nearly died tonight."

"But I didn't. I'm here. With you." She pulled him towards her. "Don't you get that I just want to be with you?"

She wrapped her arms around his chest and Declan's mind went blank. The hug seemed to exist outside time. Her smell and the sensation of her body pressed against him was everything. He knew how he felt about Ava, but he couldn't tell her. If he told her, she would end up like his grandfather, like his parents. It took all his strength to push her away. "I can't lose you," he said. "You're all I have left."

Ava glanced up at him with her brilliant sapphire eyes. "And I can't lose you either! You keep throwing yourself into harm's way like you're invincible and it's terrifying. Half the time, I don't know where you are, or what you're doing. Why do I have to hide from the dangers you actively pursue? That's not fair."

Declan squeezed her hands. He inhaled and released a shuddering breath. She had a point, and he hated to admit it. "I've never thought of it that way."

"So take me with you. I'm oath-bound to Haberdeen until the job is done. Help me get it done! I will tell you everything. I will explain it all. And we can be together. No Horace. No storms. No Vedmark. Us."

A wave of heat rushed through Declan. He searched her eyes, took in the faint freckles lining her nose, and a nightmare came to mind. Her waxy replica died while he watched—helpless. "I..." Declan trailed off. Those words were too hard, so he changed them. "I need you to stay away from Horace until this is done. After that, I'll go where you go. But I have to do this alone."

Her shoulders slumped, and she dropped his hands.

"Ava, please."

"I'm not letting you leave me again."

"Ava..." It was a challenge to keep the exasperation from his voice. *Doesn't she understand? Haven't we been over this?* "Please. Stay here."

"She can't," said someone behind him.

Declan stepped back. Anger rose—mercurial—in his blood. "What are you doing here?"

"It is time we have a conversation," Haberdeen said. Tears had stripped lines through the dirt and ash on her cheeks.

"I don't want to talk to you."

"My brother just died!" Haberdeen hissed. For a moment, she lost her composure, leaving a feral thing in its absence. "Raul was my closest friend. My only confidant. Now, he's dead. I *should* be grieving him. I want to grieve him." Her voice cracked with the words. "But I can't. We made a promise, Declan Moore. To the end. We were going to save the Dominion. We were going to stop Remnant Magic, even if it cost us our lives. I can't break that. Not when he has given his life for it. So we *will* have this conversation, so that you can understand."

"Understand what?"

Ava touched his arm. "That the Fatesmiths are not who we thought they were."

Declan shook his head. He refused to accept that. "She killed my parents. She didn't weave the spell, but she ordered it done."

"There was no other way," Haberdeen said.

"YOU DIDN'T HAVE TO KILL THEM!" Declan roared. His voice echoed in the night. He wanted to wring the life from the woman. She couldn't stop him. Her magic was out of reach. *Except Ava. Ava is bound to protect her.* "They were innocent."

"They were going to make you kill them," Haberdeen said.

"What? Who?"

"Vedmark were going to find you. They would take you, and your mother and father. They would have made you spill their blood to access your green magic. They would have used you to destroy Euryma."

"You're lying," Declan said, but her words tied his stomach in knots.

"Why would I lie? What reason would I have to do otherwise?" Haberdeen held his gaze. "I saw it in the white-haired wanderer's memories. I saved you from a life of unimaginable guilt. I ordered the deed so that you wouldn't have to."

"No." Declan shook his head. "I would never..." He trailed off, because she was right. He had seen that future play out in the Void, watched it repeat with his own eyes.

"You would have been their Southern Warlock. The Knight that could use magic beyond Vedmark's borders. A wolfhound forced to destroy your homeland." Haberdeen raised an eyebrow. "What would you have done in my place?"

When their eyes met, something snapped inside Declan. In a flash of movement he had Haberdeen on the ground and Winterthorn pressed to her throat.

Ava grabbed his arm, but he didn't budge.

"Do it," Haberdeen said. Her gaze did not flinch. "Take my memories. I harbor many sins, Declan Moore, but I am not a liar. Go on."

"Give me one reason not to!" Declan growled. A flick of his wrist and he could avenge his parents, John's father, Dreyfus, and everyone else she had murdered.

"If you kill her, the Fatesmiths will never follow us," Ava pleaded. "Please, Declan. Let her go. Please."

With a cry of anguish, Declan tossed the knife aside. He staggered away from it, fell to his knees, and screamed again. Haberdeen remained in the ash. Tears rolled down Declan's cheeks. He didn't want to believe it. He hated the woman. She was his enemy.

"I did what I had to do," Haberdeen said softly. "But I am sorry for the pain it has caused you. There truly was no other way." She stood up. "And while I know you hate me, fate has put us on the same path. The Reaper must die."

"I don't need you," Declan muttered.

"Only a fool refuses capable assistance."

"We can't beat Vedmark if Horace is commanding the Fatesmiths," Ava said. "Let us help you."

Declan didn't know what to do. Haberdeen's explanation had turned his world upside down.

"We must get to Biscay," Haberdeen said. "Horace is weak. There is no time to lose."

Declan ignored her. He despised the woman more than he could describe.

"Please," Ava said.

Resigned, he got to his feet. The beautiful, insufferable

girl would not take no for an answer. "I hope you know what you're doing."

"I know we're better when we're together." Ava pressed Winterthorn into his hand. "I need you Declan, and—even if you won't say it—you need me."

She was right.

But he didn't dare admit it.

CHAPTER 38
HORACE

HORACE CLATTERED into his empty office quarters, knocking over chairs and piles of paper as he eased himself onto the floor. He breathed in shallow, staggered breaths as his myriad injuries overcame the raging adrenaline. The worst pain of all wasn't physical. He had failed.

He had been so close. Winterthorn in the old man's heart, and he would have known how to stop the storms. Horace waited for the voice. The sole companion in his tormented mind. The only partner on his righteous path.

What do I do?

No response.

Are you there?

Nothing. Horace was alone. Purple light crowded his vision and he screamed. The walls shook. Shelves tumbled over. When the office fell quiet, Horace slumped back, exhausted. The ocean of memory loomed everywhere, begging to swallow him. Horace didn't fight it. He let it drag him down into its endless depths.

In a flash of color, Horace was on a hill overlooking white stone cliffs that rose from an azure sea. Behind them, wild olive trees dotted the hills, stunted by the rocky soil. A broad-shouldered man with a mane of black curls stood beside him. "Are you certain this will work?" he asked. "The Council of Nations do not like this, Arman. Lord Odacre claims you will break the world."

Horace's vision dipped as Arman Moore nodded. As always, he was an observer with no control of the memory. His lips moved of their own accord as Arman spoke. "Is it better to be free in a broken land? Or a slave in a conquered kingdom?" He pressed his palm to the grass. Horace felt the blades of green poke between Arman's calloused fingers. "You ask me for certainty." He sighed. "I am certain my brother is coming. I am certain he is intent on our destruction. I am certain Hispania's Lucks are outnumbered. Of these things, I am sure." He stood to fix the man with a hard gaze. "And I am sure that this is our best hope. Our only hope."

"But will it work?"

Arman shook his head. "I do not know. Maria and I have built Wells that could service a mile or more, but nothing of this scale. If we had time, we would test. We do not have that luxury. Rome is gone. Caesar is dead. We are out of time, Arthur."

The man—Arthur—ran a ringed hand through his hair. He squeezed his neck and exhaled a long breath. "You ask a hard thing, General. When I agreed to lead the Council, I did not think I would be left to decide between the destruction of our people, or the destruction of our home."

"*Possible* destruction of our home," Arman corrected.

Arthur smiled. "The Council will fracture if you sink Sicily into the sea."

"The Council will die if Morkurik continues unchallenged." Arman gripped Arthur's shoulder. "Put those thoughts aside. Is it not better to have the living deride us than the dead sing our praises?"

Arthur chuckled. A rolling, musical baritone. "I do not know if that is comforting, or terrifying, but I appreciate your candor." His expression hardened. "Create the Well, Arman, with a reservoir as planned. Odacre and his subjects may be cowards, but I am not."

Arman Moore bowed. "It will be as you say."

This isn't enough, Horace thought. It only confirmed that magic was stored in Euryma, but not how to reach it. *I need to know more.*

I am trying.

The return of the voice caught Horace off guard, as an enormous crack—like a collapsing glacier—roared above them. The pair stood in serene silence. Whatever was happening, it was not a part of this memory. As Horace searched the sky, a wall of darkness swept towards him, but before he could react, he was somewhere else.

He blinked and tried to find his bearings. They were in a circular cavern deep below the earth, illuminated by flickering brass torches and constructed around a hole that appeared endless. Beside him, two men and two women waited. None looked happy.

"This is an abomination," hissed a reed-thin man with an even thinner moustache. "You go too far, Arman of Vedmark."

"Enough," said the dark-haired man from the last memory. Horace realized this was Arthur Pendragon. Euryma's first king. Hero of legend. He didn't look like a legend, or even like the proud man from the previous moment. He looked weak, weary, defeated. "The Well was created at my command," Pendragon said, staring daggers at those assembled. "And it is fortunate I did. Vedmark marches towards us. We need help."

"It runs deep," said a woman in a cerulean cloak. She spoke in clipped sentences. Her face was round, but her features were stern. "I've seen your *magic*. It is... volatile..." she pursed her crooked lips. "Can you vouch for its safety?"

Arman—and by default, Horace—shrugged. "I cannot."

"This is not a comforting answer."

"With respect, Lady Vitulus, we are past the point of comfort." Arman turned to each of them. "You know as well as I that Morkurik is coming."

"And what if your outlandish scheme tears the fabric of our kingdoms asunder?" Odacre barked. "What matters of war if we are crushed? Or collapsed into the fiery lakes beneath?" He waved to the others. "What is to say this *General* is one of us? He is of Vedmark. This could very well be part of Morkurik's plan!"

Arman said nothing, but Horace could sense the whirlpool of frustration and anger swirling within him.

"Quit your foolishness, Odacre," said a second woman in a voice as sharp as nettles. She had wavy white hair and wore an intricate golden gown that ran to her neck. "If Arman wanted us dead, it would be as he willed. He has sacrificed much to protect our nations. If you cannot keep your serpent tongue in your mouth, I will have it cut out."

Odacre's eyes flashed with indignation. "You dare to—"

"I do," the woman hissed. "Iberia pays for your dalliance in blood. I have tolerated enough. No more." Her expression left no room for argument. When Odacre fell silent, the woman gestured to Arman. "I would like to hear more about this... Well. How does it work?"

Appreciation for the woman rippled through Arman as he spoke. "As before, we will combine Sila and Luck and store it in the earth. The bore goes as far as my range of power allows me. We do not yet know how the combined power will react in such volume, so we have established an overflow. Sixty cubits down the Well breaks into a tunnel system. It splits three ways, then converges into a smaller bore to prevent any unexpected accidents."

"Where is this *second* bore?" Odacre asked.

"Ninety miles north," Arman answered without looking at the man. "We built it below Sicily's northern reaches." He turned to each of them. "When the Well is full, we expect every man, woman and child with magical potential to access this power. Our army will grow beyond Lucks, and perhaps we will have the power to force the Knights of Vedmark from our borders for good."

The circular cavern fell silent. The woman in gold nodded to herself. "Such power will attract attention. Have you given thought to how you will secure this place?"

"I have." Arman said. "It is an imbusion of the island itself. Similar to a Luck shield, but with the Well's power acting as its core. I call it an Ancellum."

Horace's eyes expanded at the words. *This is what we've been searching for.*

"And it will be enough?" The woman asked. "Enough to withstand Vedmark?"

"It will be impenetrable from the outside."

"And what of the inside?" Odacre asked. "Who could be trusted to protect such power? Surely not yourself, *General*." Lord Odacre said the word with barely-veiled venom, but Arman ignored the barb.

"I have built a task into the power of the Ancellum. One that will ensure the... character... of its guardian remains upstanding."

"What kind of task?" asked the tall woman. Horace had still not caught her name.

"One that stretches deep into the mind of its subject. It will pull out their deepest desires and force them to choose between desire and duty. Those with the strength to resist will gain the Ancellum's approval. They will be charged with the Well's protection."

Pendragon's lips twisted in an uncertain grimace. "You have done this test?"

Arman shook his head. "I cannot. I created the spell. I am bound to see through it, as any other of Vedmark. No. It must be somebody else."

"I see." Pendragon nodded to himself. "The Ancellum shields the island and also provides the means to locate a worthy guardian—a Wellkeeper."

"This is an impressive spell." Lady Vitulus said, tugging on her cerulean cloak.

"It had to be," Arman said. "And while I find distaste in the necessity, we have chosen to seal the Well and Ancellum with Blood Magic. There is nothing stronger."

"Can anything destroy the Well once it is created?" Pendragon asked.

Horace held his breath. *This is it.* Arman frowned. "The Wellkeeper's blood is the key to both Well and Ancellum. If the guardian remains in Sicily, there will be no way for any agent of Vedmark to breach its protection."

"Stupidity," Odacre said. "What if the Wellkeeper encounters an accident? What if they stumble on a flight of stairs? Or are wounded while hunting fowl?"

"Be at ease," Arman said. Horace could feel the man fighting not to roll his eyes. "The Ancellum is not bound by the blood of the guardian staying in their body." He gestured into the endless hole. "Provided they do not bleed into this pit, the Well will remain protected. As long as they don't leave their blood for one on the outside to possess, no enemy can reach this island."

There it is.

Horace startled at the voice in his head.

We found it.

Magic was stored in a Well on Sicily—what he expected was now Kingsbreak—and Arman Moore had been the one to do it. The key to the Ancellum—to destroying magic itself—was the blood of the Wellkeeper. *But who is the Wellkeeper?* He thought. The memory continued around him, but Horace no longer paid attention. *Who would be charged with protecting Kingsbreak?*

The highest authority on the island, the voice replied, as if the answer were obvious.

That would be… the Dean of King's College. Horace's mind ground to a halt. Laurefen Ember, the man whose blood spilled on his sleeve when he drove a dagger into his chest.

Horace vibrated with excitement. Everything he had done, everything he had lost… It had all led him to this moment. The key to Euryma's future was stained on his coat sleeve. It was fate. It was destiny. *I am the chosen one.*

With a herculean effort, Horace tried to will himself free of the memory. Nothing happened. The subterranean chamber remained the same. The conversation continued, oblivious to his struggle. Horace closed his eyes and imagined he was clawing his way upwards. It had worked before. It would work again. He just had to concentrate.

"Then let us hope that this will turn things in our favor," Pendragon said. "When will you fill it?"

NO! Horace's eyes snapped open to the unchanged cavern. *I WILL NOT BE CONTAINED TO THIS… THIS THOUGHT! NOT NOW! NOT WHEN I AM SO CLOSE!*

Despite his rage, the scene continued—constant as the rising sun. Horace opened himself to his Ire Tides. He let the magic fill him and willed himself free of Arman's past. Slowly, the voices started to fade. Horace gritted his teeth and drew more of the Ire Tides through him. The heat intensified until it felt like his blood boiled in his veins. His vision blurred amidst the agony, but he would not be denied.

A scream escaped his lips, and—not for the first time—he felt some sense of himself tear away, lost into nothingness like chaff on a wind. The pain reached its crescendo, and for a moment, Horace feared he might really be trapped within the confines of his mind.

Then the voices were gone, and he was rising. Out of the flickering stone cavern, out of the ocean of memories, and back to the Dominion he planned to save.

CHAPTER 39
DECLAN

THE VAN LURCHED at every bump along the partially ruined road. When it did, Ava's head bounced against Declan's shoulder. After exhausting her Luck opposing Horace, she was fast asleep. Misha snored quietly from the front seat. Haberdeen drove in silence, while Declan—head pressed to the cold window—watched the world pass them by. They hurtled across a juxtaposition of past and future. Lush hillsides one side and barren waste on the other, all lit by the same rising sun.

Nothing felt real. He should have been a year deep in a groundsman apprenticeship. Horace should have been studying at King's College, sending letters of his exploits whenever he had a spare moment.

Instead, Declan was headed to Biscay to kill him. The friend who had sat beside him in every class, spent weekends at his house watching terrible movies, stood in the rain to cheer him on during track meets.

It seemed so long ago.

Ace is gone, he told himself. *You're destroying what remains.* His eyes wandered to Haberdeen. Her red hair was tied in a ponytail that vibrated as they bounced down the road. She was responsible for so much despair. She had killed his parents, sent Horace past the point of no return. Regardless of how she justified it, Haberdeen didn't deserve to live.

Except... Ava thought she did. Declan considered the faintly freckled cheek pressed against his shoulder. Declan squeezed Ava's hand and turned his attention to what lay ahead.

"This was never my intention." Haberdeen watched him through the driver's mirror. "When the Stormcloud Agency started seeing anomalies in their readings, I tried to take it to the Magistri. I never imagined they would ignore proof from their own wizards. Every attempt fell on deaf ears. The Grand Mages ignored me. When I pushed to be heard, they had me banned from their chambers. Newspapers were told I was dangerous. Higher-ups fired anyone who believed me. The Dominion was built on magic. Undermining it would damage the fabric of Euryma." Haberdeen shook her head in obvious disgust. "That was the lie they told themselves."

Declan remained silent. He didn't want her reasons. There was nothing Haberdeen could say to excuse what she'd done.

"As things got worse, it became clear that a peaceful solution was impossible. The High Mage knew the storms were building, and he did nothing. So we devoted ourselves to saving the Dominion. We discovered inverted weaves and learned that a fierised witch could survive a Remnant Magic storm. After that, we set about fierising as many people as possible. A short-term fix that was better than nothing. I sent hundreds of letters to the High Mage." Haberdeen sighed. "When they fell on deaf ears, we grew frustrated. Frustration dulled our empathy. The Fatesmiths became violent and careless. We started to see normal witches and wizards as enemies. If I could do it again..." she glanced at him.

"You'd what?" Declan whispered. "You'd keep my parents alive? Keep my best friend from turning into some... Reaper... that killed my grandfather?" A fire smoldered in Declan's chest. "Keep your excuses to yourself. I don't want them."

Through the mirror, Haberdeen's eyes were slightly red. She said nothing more, and that suited Declan just fine. He leaned back and closed his eyes.

———

There was a massive bang and Declan startled awake—he did not even remember falling asleep—as the van jolted from side to side. Clouds of ash hid everything except the morning sun as they labored over sections of asphalt that looked like some enormous tractor had ploughed through it. Ava sat up beside him, clutching at his hand. Misha grunted a curse from the front seat.

"A storm went through here." Haberdeen's forehead creased as she navigated the ruined asphalt. "Only a small section, though. It should level out soon."

"Where are we?" Ava called, but the din died as the road smoothed out. The haze vanished behind them and Declan's jaw went slack.

A sparkling ocean glimmered underneath the morning sun. It framed Biscay's distant skyline. Between them and the city, the rolling hills were a patchwork of green and yellow. A row of buses passed them in the opposite direction.

"How long until we get to the city?" Ava asked.

"We will be there by noon," Haberdeen said. All signs of her emotional frailty were gone. "We should start making a plan. Horace will be somewhere at headquarters." She glanced at Ava through her mirror. "Can you use Luck to find him? Or could you draw him out?"

"We're too far away." Ava leaned forward. "How are you feeling, Mish?"

"Sore." Misha groaned. He winced as he turned to face her. "I'll try to help, but..." his eyes darted to Declan and his expression soured. "We'll see."

Ava raised an eyebrow, but didn't pursue the subject. She squeezed Declan's hand. She hadn't let go since they woke up. "What do you think? You know Horace better than all of us."

Declan stared at the distant city, remembering the last time he was there. "He has an office on the top floors. That's where he should be. If you can create some chaos downstairs, I can slip by."

"Do you have your Sila?" Ava asked.

Declan shook his head.

"You're going to need it. Your axes won't be enough."

"I'll have more than my axes." Declan drew Winterthorn from his pocket. "I don't need to beat him with magic. I just need to get close. I don't think he expects me to kill him. I don't think he believes I can."

"Can you?" Misha's voice grated with irritation. It was the first thing he'd said to Declan in months.

Declan put the dagger away. "I don't have a choice."

Haberdeen turned and looked over her shoulder. "This plan is full of holes and has far too many pinch points for my liking."

Ava shrugged. "Planning right now is useless. We need

more information. Get us into the city and we'll work something out. With two Lucks, a witch and a Warlock, we should be able to figure out something."

As they approached Biscay, the throngs of oncoming buses thickened. Hundreds of vehicles passed them, all headed in the opposite direction.

"Where are all these people going?" Misha asked.

"Lombrives, I expect," Haberdeen said. "Though I am surprised by the number."

"It's almost like an evacuation." Ava chewed on her lip and then shrugged. "Oh well. The fewer people, the better, right?"

A row of identical skyscrapers grew on the horizon, then fell behind trees and houses as they entered Biscay's outer suburbs. Every corner was a hub of activity, every parking lot was a collection point, and every one of them was crowded. Lines of buses waited at red stoplights and still the people came. From elderly adults to children in strollers, an endless procession filled every sidewalk they passed.

Further in, the streets became quieter. The crowds faded, then vanished, leaving an ominous emptiness. A noonday sun shone over vacant bikeways and abandoned cafes with 'closed' signs in the windows.

"Where is everyone?" Misha asked.

Nobody answered. An anxious bubble formed in the pit of Declan's stomach. Something was wrong. He lurched forward as the van squealed to a halt, barely avoiding slamming his head into the front headrest. Without a word, Haberdeen reversed onto the curb and exited in a hurry.

"Where is she going?" Declan asked.

Hiking up her dress, Haberdeen ran into a service alley

between two brick buildings. Ava unbuckled her seatbelt. "Come on. Let's find out."

Declan followed Ava into the alleyway. Misha limped behind them. A quarter of the way down, Haberdeen stood motionless. When they reached her, Declan understood why.

An incandescent spray of orange light hovered above the concrete. It was like a miniature fireworks explosion—the size of a beach ball—caught in an endless loop. Nobody spoke as they watched, transfixed by the hypnotic display.

"What is it?" Misha whispered.

Haberdeen turned to them, but instead of wonder, her eyes were pools of dread. "A stormflash."

Declan tore his gaze free of the spectacle. "What?"

"This is what we were looking for when we sent flashfinders across the Dominion. We don't know how they work, but they appear before a storm comes."

An icy shiver washed down Declan's spine. "A storm is coming?"

Ava's face paled. "How long do we have?"

"We send flashfinders to track their growth and spread. With that data, we can predict a storm within a day." Haberdeen frowned at the light. "Without data... It could be a week, an hour. Who knows? It's impossible to tell."

Declan frowned as an unpleasant realization dawned on him. "They know it's coming. It's why they're emptying the city. It *is* an evacuation."

"What do we do?" Ava asked.

"What we came here for." Declan patted the dagger in his pocket. "If a storm *is* on its way, I need to stop Horace before it does. If I don't have my Sila, Euryma is doomed."

Nobody had any response to that. With sullen faces, they returned to the van. Haberdeen pulled off the sidewalk and drove towards the box-like skyscrapers of Biscay's Central Business District. It had only been a few months since Declan had last been here, yet so much had changed.

They stopped outside the enormous glass doors of the Fatesmiths' headquarters. Haberdeen turned to face them. "What's the plan?"

Ava's forehead crinkled as she searched the empty street. After half a minute, she shook her head. "Something is off..." In one smooth motion, she climbed over Declan and out the side door. She jumped an orange traffic barrier and walked right up to the front entrance.

"What is she doing?" Misha said. "She's going to be seen."

But the doors did not open. Declan unbuckled and joined her at the window. He raised his hands to peer through the semi-reflective glass. The lights were off, the lobby abandoned. Empty seats, empty desks, empty couches. The Fatesmiths were gone. He tried to pry the doors open. They would not budge.

Haberdeen wound down her window. "What is it?"

Ava scanned the surrounding buildings. She searched the sky, as if hoping somebody might appear above them. "There's no Luck to draw on. Nothing to influence. There's nobody here. Horace. The Fatesmiths. They're gone."

CHAPTER 40
KATIE

THE CLOCK above the door said it was noon. It didn't feel like it. After their disastrous attempt to stop Horace, John's unexpected—and miraculous—return from the dead, and the chaotic sprint to an underground city, the last twelve hours felt like weeks. Exhaustion penetrated Katie's bones. Every time she closed her eyes, she almost fell asleep.

But she couldn't.

She had promised Laurefen she would be there when he woke up, and she would keep that promise.

The door opened. Mary-Lou peeked inside and frowned. "You haven't slept, have you?"

Katie shook her head. Forming words was beyond her at this point. Mary-Lou entered the small cavern and sat beside her. Sabart's rooms were little more than crude burrows, but the woven rugs, plush couches and jars of photonima showed at least some effort to make them comfortable. The woman John referred to as 'Warmistress' had done what she could to save Laurefen. Now, they could only hope for the best.

"Do you want to talk about it?" Mary-Lou asked. The woman appeared unperturbed by recent events.

"No," she murmured. "I'm just waiting."

"You don't have to stay here," Mary-Lou said. "Laurefen will understand."

"He almost died last night." Katie's insides crawled at the thought of how close they had come to losing everything. "If Declan and..." *John.* That hadn't sunk in yet. John was alive. *How? Why didn't he come find us?*

"Declan Moore saves our skin again," Mary-Lou agreed. "I think I'll bake him my famous custard slice when all this is over."

Katie tried to muster a smile, but the woman wasn't looking. A relieved grin split Mary-Lou's weathered cheeks as her gaze locked on the bed. "Laurefen?"

"Lou," Laurefen croaked. He looked older than ever, but his eyes sparkled as he considered them. "I take it I survived another brush with death? Where are we?"

Katie launched herself forwards. The man was a stubborn fool, but he—along with Mary-Lou and Michael— were the closest thing to family she had left. He winced as she hugged him and she leaned back. "I'm sorry I was so awful," she whispered. "I should have been more understanding, I—"

Laurefen squeezed her arm. "There is nothing to apologize for. You were right, Kate. About everything. I am sorry for not listening."

Katie wiped a tear away as Mary-Lou hid a smile behind her hand. "You'll never guess who put you back together again."

"Was it Declan Moore? You ought to make him your custard slice."

"I will bake that boy whatever he wants. But no..." Mary-Lou shook her head. "It was Helen Harcross."

Laurefen blinked. His cheeks paled further.

Katie looked between them. "What's all this about?"

"There is history there," Mary-Lou said. Laurefen cleared his throat and she chuckled. "But that's a story for another day."

"I'm surprised she didn't let me die."

"John was very convincing."

"John?" A cascade of emotions crossed Laurefen's normally controlled features. "I thought that was a dream. He's alive?"

Mary-Lou nodded.

"I suspect I have much to catch up on. Where are we? Is this Lombrives City?"

"Kind of," Katie said. "It's... lower. Another cave system. John calls it Sabart. They've got an army down here."

"One made up of a fair share of our old enrolments," Mary-Lou added. "Helen has been recruiting. No wonder nobody came when we called the alumni to Sabriva. They were all here."

"That is fortunate." Laurefen's smile faded. "They would have lost their lives responding to our foolish invitation."

An uneasy silence stretched between them. Katie broke it with a yawn. Mary-Lou turned a pointed gaze in her direction. "Horace may have outsmarted us, but we came out on top. Now, I think some rest is in order."

"He wants the Well," Laurefen said. "And I fear he will not stop until he gets it."

"Then we must be ready." Mary-Lou tossed her silver braid over her shoulders. "And the first step of preparation is being rested. Michael and I can run things for now. You both need sleep. Do you understand?"

Katie nodded. Her head felt like it was full of sand. *You kept your promise. You can't stay awake forever.* Yet before she could agree, the cavern door snapped inward and the raven-haired Warmistress entered. Her royal-blue eyes were like chisels as she took in the room. "Good. You're conscious."

"Hello Helen," Laurefen said.

"Dean Ember," she replied with a curt nod. "I'll make this quick. Do you have any idea why the Fatesmiths would be called back to Biscay?"

Laurefen shared a blank look with Mary-Lou, then shrugged. Katie pursed her lips. They had passed hundreds of Fatesmiths on their way down to Sabart.

"How many Fatesmiths?" Mary-Lou asked.

The Warmistress crossed her arms. "All of them." She scanned each of their faces. "You know nothing about this?"

"I do not." Laurefen shook his head. "Apologies."

Without so much as a goodbye, the Warmistress turned on her heel and stormed out. Mary-Lou rolled her eyes at the abrupt departure. "She is delightful."

A pit of anxiety formed in Katie's stomach as an unpleasant thought entered her mind. "Where would all those ironhands be going? You don't think it has something to do with Kingsbreak?"

"How?" Mary-Lou said. "Horace made it clear that he couldn't pass the Ancellum. The moon, the tower, it was all a ruse."

"The boy is an apt liar," Laurefen said. "My looptaps are gone since the fierisation. Can you ask Michael to check the college as a precaution?"

Mary-Lou nodded. "I can do that. You need to sleep. Rested is ready." Laurefen opened his mouth, but Mary-Lou raised her palm. "You are in no state to help. We will send for you if we must." Her attention shifted to Katie. "You too. You're beautiful, dear, but right now, you look like death in a cardigan."

Katie didn't doubt it. If she curled onto a bed, she would be asleep before her head hit the pillow. Still, anxious worries tickled her mind. She shook her head, hoping to dislodge the feeling. When it didn't budge, she sighed. "I'll come find Michael with you."

"You need to rest."

"We can make that decision after we've spoken with Michael." Katie squeezed Laurefen's hand. "I'm glad you're alright."

When she stood, Mary-Lou moved between her and the door. "I'll say this again. You need rest."

"Come on, Lou. I want to make sure everything's okay. I won't sleep well if I'm worrying about you."

Mary-Lou pursed her lips. "Fine. We will talk to Michael, and then you will go find somewhere to pass out until tomorrow morning."

"As stubborn as her mother," Laurefen said, smirking.

"As stubborn as *you*," Mary-Lou replied. "We will come find you if anything important comes up."

She exited the room and Katie followed. Photonima lamps built into the ceiling lit their path through the twisting tunnels. The air was frosty, damp, and smelled faintly of crushed stone. "Quartz Hall," Mary-Lou called over her shoulder. "Michael says he'll meet us there."

Ten minutes later, they emerged in an enormous cavern. A glowing crystal stalactite protruded from the roof, illuminating the cave in soft, white light. Hundreds of people moved between passages, most of them Katie's age —or younger.

"This is Quartz Hall, yes?" Mary-Lou asked.

Katie nodded, recalling John's rushed introduction of the place.

"Do you see him?"

Katie stood on her tiptoes to no avail. "Are you kidding?" She wasn't tall enough to see anything. As she searched her immediate surroundings, someone nudged her shoulder. She turned to find John—freshly showered, his hair combed in a wave—smiling at her. Katie's heart skipped a beat. *He's alive.*

"Michael's coming," John said. "He's finishing a *spirited* discussion with the Warmistress, then he'll be here."

"Goodness me," Mary-Lou said. "One day and they're already bickering."

"Can't say it's unexpected." Katie smirked at John. "Do you know what they're arguing about?"

"Michael's annoyed that Sabart stole half his students. Harcross is reminding him that every Sabartian is here by choice."

Mary-Lou groaned. As they waited, the mass of people moving between tunnels eased to a steady trickle. When Quartz Hall emptied, Michael entered through a side passage. A vein pulsed in his temple as he approached them.

"Have you heard about the ironhands?" Mary-Lou asked.

Michael nodded.

"Do you know what it means?"

He shook his head. "It's not a storm, otherwise they would hunker down here. It's not Vedmark, because that troll of a woman has scouts watching from afar."

"Troll?" Katie asked.

"Helen Harcross," Michael muttered. A sound escaped John's mouth. Katie caught a flash of a grin as he looked away.

Mary-Lou didn't seem to notice—or care. "Could they be preparing an attack on Kingsbreak?"

"I haven't ruled it out," Michael said. "I cannot imagine how, but I am not foolish enough to underestimate the Marley boy again." He nodded to John. "Has Declan contacted you?"

"He hasn't," John said. The amused expression faded. "And I have no way of contacting him. I have no idea where he went."

"He said he had a job to finish," Katie chimed in. "Horace is based in Biscay. I would bet that is where Declan's going."

"Let's hope he gets there soon," Mary-Lou said. She turned to Michael. "Laurefen wants us to return to Kingsbreak. Katie will remain here, and we can watch the college."

Michael nodded. "We can leave at once."

"I..." Katie trailed off as the words evaded her. She didn't want to stay in Sabart. She had to protect the Well. Michael would tell her to remain with Laurefen. Mary-Lou would say she needed rest. Neither satisfied the itch in her mind. "I have to pick up some items from the lab." Katie plucked the excuse from thin air, but now she rolled with it. "I've got the shield spikes, Oregin o Magi, and my crucible of..." she glanced at John. "And other stuff."

"We can bring it back for you," Michael said. "The best thing you can do is stay with Laurefen."

Mary-Lou nodded. "You're exhausted, Kate. We will

drop by the Imbusion Lab and get everything. You can continue your studies once you've had some sleep."

"No," Katie said. *Why are you pushing this?* "It's a mess. There are things everywhere. There's too much to sort through. Just let me come. I'll get what I need, and I'll meet you back at Cedrus." She fixed them with an unblinking stare. "Please?"

Mary-Lou exhaled through her nose and shared a knowing glance with Michael, who—after a long pause—sighed. "As you wish, but we should go now." He turned to John. "Is there a place to create an Opening?"

"Iron Hall will be empty until afternoon classes."

"Lead the way," Michael said.

They followed John through another narrow passage. As Katie opened her mouth to ask how much further, they entered a massive, octagonal cavern with smooth red walls. Blue plastic seats surrounded a dais in the cave's center. John gestured to the raised platform. "Is that enough space?"

"It will do."

A growing wave of anxiety smothered Katie's fatigue. Horace had told them straight that he could not breach the Ancellum. There was no reason to believe he would be there. Still, a curious mix of dread and adrenaline filled her body.

As Michael weaved nima into an elaborate tapestry, a triangular doorway rotated into existence ahead of him. Sunlight poured into the cavern. Through the Opening, Cedrus's towering trunk appeared, then its crown of leaves and finally, the sprawling lawns of King's College—covered in an endless mass of men and women in matching black coats.

The Opening stopped turning as Michael froze—

stunned—by the sight. The small window flickered and vanished. The four of them stood in shocked silence. Katie's mind went blank. Her heart nearly exploded in her chest.

"How?" Mary-Lou murmured.

The word opened the floodgates. In moments, Katie's head was spinning. *How did they get through? Is Horace with them? Is he already at the Well? Why did they bring so many? How much does he know?*

"It doesn't matter how they got there," Michael said. "They *are* there. We need to do something."

"Like what?" Mary-Lou said. "You saw them. There must have been ten thousand ironhands down there?"

Michael's eyes were frantic. "I... I don't know."

"What are they doing there?" John asked. "What exactly does Horace want with King's College?"

Katie opened her mouth, but Mary-Lou interrupted. "We don't have time for all the details, but the short version is that if Horace gets what he wants, magic will be destroyed."

John's jaw dropped. "What... why?"

"He thinks it will stop the storms," Michael growled. "We don't. We think it will erase magic itself. We have to protect Kingsbreak. It is the source of our power, of our ability to protect ourselves."

Protect. "Laurefen," Katie whispered. "Laurefen!"

Michael turned to her. "What?"

"We need to get Laurefen."

Mary-Lou shook her head. "He's too weak."

"Laurefen..." Katie didn't know how to explain herself without mentioning the Well. She glanced at John, then decided she didn't care. "Laurefen said there were protective spells in the Well. Something he could trigger with his key. We don't have to beat the Fatesmiths! We just have to activate the Well's protection!"

"Yes." Michael nodded. "That might work."

"Michael, go to Laurefen. Get the key and get to the Well." Katie pointed at John. "John. We need the Sabartians. If they really are an army made to fight Vedmark, they can't afford to lose their magic. Get whoever you can and get them to Kingsbreak. Now!"

John ran from the hall.

"What do you want me to do?" Mary-Lou asked.

Katie was surprised at how willingly they followed her commands. "You and I are going to Kingsbreak to buy time for the others." She waved to Michael. "Can you make an Opening? A small one we can slip through."

Michael nodded more times than was necessary. He remade the Opening; only this time, it pointed out towards the island's southernmost point and the glittering Mediterranean. "Good luck," he said.

"Get the key," Katie said. "The fate of Euryma depends on it." With that, she took Mary-Lou's hand. Together they ran through the Opening and into battle.

CHAPTER 41
KATIE

WHEN THEY REACHED King's College, they found it abandoned. Mary-Lou's brown leather boots echoed off the hallway tiles as they raced to the Imbusion Lab. Katie was supposed to be exhausted, but panic gave her strength she didn't know she had.

South of them, at least ten thousand Fatesmiths gathered into companies. Veiled by a curtain of bent light, Katie and Mary-Lou had slipped by the assembling army without trouble. Katie wanted to know what the ironhands were planning, but Mary-Lou insisted they keep their distance.

"We have plenty of nimrods," Mary-Lou said. "There are boxes of them in the administration building. We never put them back in storage."

"We don't need nimrods. Magic works here."

"Not to use. To break."

Katie raised an eyebrow. "How would that help?"

"You've never broken a nimrod?" The older woman stopped to face her. "Think of it like a flashbulb, but much less predictable. We wouldn't want to be there when they went off, but it would make a mighty fine distraction."

They continued to the Imbusion Lab. With the lights off, the crucible's orange glow illuminated the room. When Katie opened the door, Mary-Lou suddenly grabbed her wrist. "You have magic."

"I beg your pardon?" Katie didn't move. The words didn't make sense. *Or am I too tired to understand?*

"Magic. In the crucible." Mary-Lou's lips parted, as if she had just realized something important. "If Horace destroys the Well, there will still be... this." She nodded to the container on the stainless steel bench. "We might be able to begin again."

"I..." Katie eased her arm free of the woman's grip. "I don't know if it will work. Truth be told, I don't know anything about the magic."

"We have to get it to Sabart," Mary-Lou said. "When Michael arrives with the key, you need to leave with that crucible."

Katie's blood ran cold at the thought of moving the volatile substance, but Mary-Lou had a point. Horace might already be at the Well. Her capsule of orange power could be Euryma's saving grace. She squeezed her eyes shut. *No. Stick to the plan.* "I can get everything ready to move, but unless Horace reaches the Well first, we continue as agreed."

Mary-Lou frowned. "By the time we find Horace, it could be too late."

"No, Lou. We made a plan. We're sticking to it." Katie refused to lower her gaze until Mary-Lou sighed and looked away.

"Fine. You organize your belongings. I'll get the nimrods and meet you back here."

"Be safe," Katie said. "Wait." She plucked an invisible strand from her index finger and held it out to Mary-Lou.

"Looptap me if you see anything."

With deft fingers, Mary-Lou wound the nima around her left thumb. *I will.* She winked and left the room. The older woman's boots echoed down the hall as she rushed away. Katie scanned the Imbusion Lab. Everything was as she had left it. A half-full bag of shieldshards, a corner table littered with notes and a very old book.

Katie picked up Oregin o Magi. It could be the last record of the Well's creation, but every page was gibberish. The peculiar characters reminded her of the Cyrillic texts from the northlands, but as far as she could tell, the language was lost. A carpet of paper documented her failed attempts to decipher the words. It was no use. The author —J.W. Avonacas—had taken his secrets to the grave.

As she flicked through the pages, a series of small illustrations caught her eye. A crescent moon key, and something akin to a massive armored rat. The images—cramped between tight script—were the size of a postage stamp, but the key held Katie's attention. It was identical to the one Laurefen wore around his neck. "So you are about the Well," she whispered.

She wrapped Oregin o Magi in a sheet of fabric and stacked her notes in a neat pile. The paper went in the same bag as the shieldshards. The book went in her back pocket.

Katie flitted through the Imbusion Lab, finding bits and pieces as necessary and stuffing them all into the duffel. When it was full, she found a hot pink backpack in a tall cupboard. Another stack of paper went in there.

Finally, she considered the crucible. The magic inside glowed like molten stone. A shiver ran up her spine as she fixed the lid in place. As she prepared to lift it from the table, a looptap tickled her palm. *Fatesmiths are moving. I've got nimrods. Meet at the courtyard closest the east gate.*

Do you need help carrying the nimrods? Katie tapped back.

Probably. There was a momentary pause. *I'm at the admin block stairs.*

Katie put the pink backpack with the duffel underneath the crucible and raced from the room. As she dashed to the administration building in the campus center, she wondered what had happened to the rest of the staff. *Probably hiding in the Village.*

Mary-Lou waited for her at the top of the stairs with two stacks of yellow tubs at her feet. "This should be enough," she said as she began winding kinetic energy around the stack on her left. Katie copied her weave and together they carried sixteen containers down the stairs and into a hexagonal courtyard on the edge of the college.

"What's the plan?" Katie asked as she popped a lid off a tub. Hundreds of rods were stacked inside.

"Stab them into the ground," Mary-Lou said, gathering an armful. "Ten or so steps apart, heading out this way."

"How much damage will this do?"

Mary-Lou paused. "Enough to cause a distraction." She looked longingly at the ancient stonework surrounding them. "The buildings can be replaced. The Well cannot."

Neither spoke as they assembled a rough grid of nimrods. Katie drew on geonima, raising the brick tiles from the floor, while Mary-Lou drove the rods into the soft earth underneath. Soon, the courtyard resembled an enormous pincushion of multi-colored pegs. An alarm wailed in the distance, only to be drowned out by the Fatesmiths' shouts. They had almost emptied every tub when the head of the army appeared below the rise. "Throw the rest anywhere!" The rods tinkled like glass chimes as Mary-Lou upended her container.

The ground trembled beneath them. The Fatesmiths were coming. "That's not good," Katie said.

"We can't control that," Mary-Lou said. "Focus on what we can." She pointed to the gilded archway leading out of the campus. "We need to draw them through there."

Katie scanned the courtyard. It looked like some bizarre art installation. "This isn't going to work. It's too obvious."

"We could hide them deeper?" With that, Mary-Lou wound tiny spindles of kinetic energy atop of the nimrods. As she released the thread, kinima drove each one further into the soil, until only their colored tops were visible. She then took all the shattered tiles and compressed them into mounds of stone above the entry. "That might distract them," she said. "Though I do not know how we're going to get them in here."

The voices were close now, blended together in the indistinct mass of noise that only a crowd could make. "I've got an idea." As Katie ran to the entrance, she looped a braid of aeronima into a cone branching out from her mouth. The Fatesmiths leading the charge had already passed them, but the rest of the army followed behind. "Hey! Losers!" Katie shouted. Her amplified voice carried over the sloping lawns.

Almost as one, the Fatesmiths turned to face her. Some brandished iron batons, others raised shields. Katie coiled the air into a neat lasso. In one smooth motion, she launched it at the closest ironhand. The aeronima found the ankle of a woman with platinum blonde hair. Katie infused the weave with kinima and pulled.

The young woman screamed as the spell dragged her towards the arch. She clawed at the dirt while people rushed to help. Someone slashed below her leg with a baton and the aeronima broke. Katie let it dissolve as she wrapped three more ironhands in air. The Fatesmiths moved to encircle the entrance as Katie continued pulling men and women to the ground. *Got your attention now, haven't I?*

A familiar face pushed to the front of the group. Ophelia. Her auburn hair stuck to the sweat on her forehead. Her fingers danced like a pianist as she unraveled Katie's spells. With one two-handed push, Katie sent a blistering spray of kinima in her direction. Ophelia dropped to the ground as a staircase behind her crumbled. "Better luck next time," Katie shouted, dashing into the safety of the courtyard.

She looked around. Mary-Lou was gone. Katie's heart skipped a beat. "Lou?"

"Over here," called a phantom voice.

Katie squinted toward the sound. "Where are you?"

Mary-Lou's hand appeared—hovering like some eerie specter—and beckoned her to a faintly shimmering patch of air at the courtyard's edge. "Quickly!"

Katie vanished from view as the Fatesmiths arrived. Two young men tried to push past Ophelia, but she pulled them back. "Don't be fools," she hissed, pointing to the boulders perched atop the entrance. The pair paled as she unraveled the geonima.

"We need to draw them in," Mary-Lou whispered.

"How?"

In a blur of twisting fingers, Mary-Lou quilted a multi-layered braid of light at the far side of the courtyard. She attached it to the photonima strands hiding them from the Fatesmiths. "That should do it," she said.

"Do what?"

"Say hello." Mary-Lou waved with a jaunty grin. "They can see us."

Katie watched her jaw drop from the opposite corner of

the courtyard. Mary-Lou's spell was a masterful deception, bent light that made them appear somewhere they weren't. The older woman continued waving cheerfully to the Fatesmiths. Katie did the same.

"There!" shouted Ophelia from the entrance. The iron-hands rushed forward.

"Time to go," Mary-Lou whispered. She grabbed Katie's elbow and pulled her through the southern exit. They ran down the sandstone hallway. Katie struggled to keep pace until a deafening crack forced them to take cover. The walkway warped like an elastic band. When it snapped back together, it threw both women to the ground.

Cries and moans carried down from the courtyard behind them. Mary-Lou rolled onto her side. An open wound marred her hairline. Katie helped her to her feet. "Are you okay?"

"Better than our guests, I'm sure." Mary-Lou touched her head. Bright blood colored her fingertips. She swallowed. "We need to move."

They threaded their way through the alleys between buildings. As they reached a shaded walkway, Mary-Lou stopped. Katie almost ran straight into her back. "What is it?"

"Fatesmiths. They're everywhere."

She wasn't wrong. Blackcoats swarmed the campus footpaths like ants. Katie turned at the sound of footsteps as Ophelia and a dozen Fatesmiths rounded a corner. "Got you!" She thrust a finger at them. "Don't let them escape!"

Katie wrenched on the first thread she could find. Geonima. Clumps of brick exploded from the wall to form a crude barrier. Ophelia wrestled to pull the stone free. Mary-Lou shot a tempest of air towards her, but a cloud of dust absorbed the spell before it could do any damage.

"They have irofil," Mary-Lou said. "Come on. Up the stairs."

Katie abandoned the makeshift wall and pulled the roof down instead. Mary-Lou led them up a stairway to an elevated walkway. They climbed two steps at a time. Shouts filled the space behind them. When they reached the top, Katie lurched to her right and gripped the handrail. The floor quaked beneath her feet. A second group of Fatesmiths blocked their path ahead. With a violent thrust, Mary-Lou summoned a burst of wind and Katie added her own strength to the spell. Together, they pushed a gale force forward. It died against a cloud of iron.

Then the Fatesmiths were gone.

Katie squinted into the grey haze. "Where did—"

Movement threw her sideways. A thunderous groan filled the air as metal beams folded and snapped. For a moment, Katie was weightless. Below her, men and women in matching coats ran from the collapsing walkway. The ground rushed to meet her, and all went black.

CHAPTER 42

KATIE

KATIE HEARD the battle before she saw it. Cries of anguish, anger, the shriek of iron on steel. She flexed her fingers and wriggled her toes. Her muscles ached, but everything seemed in working order.

She lay in what remained of a narrow tunnel. Somehow, the fallen walkway had stayed together after it collapsed. Katie wiped her face on her shirt—blood smeared the fabric. *You must look terrible.* Disregarding the thought, she crawled towards the noise. She peered over the tunnel's edge. A seven-foot drop awaited her. With no way to turn around, Katie could stay put, or fall headfirst into a mess of broken concrete.

Beyond that was chaos. It looked like a historical reen-actment of the Founding. An army of sword-wielding teenagers pushed against a wall of ironhands fighting with batons and bucklers. Katie considered the dark clouds wafting through the air. The weapons made sense—the Fatesmiths' supply of irofil seemed endless.

"Kate?" John stood below the walkway with a sword in

each hand. Mud coated half his face; Katie couldn't tell if it was war paint or an accident.

A gargantuan man with two batons threw two Sabartians onto their backs and lunged at John. "Watch out!" Katie yelled.

John crouched, caught the man's torso on his shoulder, and straightened, swinging both swords as the man fell over him. Katie's stomach lurched at the sight. Keeping her gaze on John and not the body as his feet, she nodded to the crowd. "You brought them here."

"Not as many as I would like," John called up to her. "Are you okay?"

"I'll be better when I'm on solid ground. Eyes up. Here come some more."

John turned as three more Fatesmiths rushed him. "This is your fault!" screamed a squat man with a round face. Blood and spittle sprayed from his mouth. "Your magic has ruined us!"

They attacked as one, but their movements were sloppy compared to John's well-trained footwork. Katie averted her gaze as he dealt out death with militant precision.

The battle pushed out of the campus and onto the surrounding lawns. When the area cleared of irofil, Katie weaved a tunnel of aeronima and slid—headfirst—to the ground. John's chest heaved as he surveyed the bloody scene. Katie kept her eyes on her feet. The smell alone made her want to vomit. "What's happening?" she asked. "Where's Michael? Does he have the key?" she gestured back to the walkway. "What about Mary-Lou? She was with—"

"Mary-Lou is with Michael and Laurefen," John said. "They're off to activate the Well's protection. They told me to stay here and wait for you." John wiped blood from his lip. He stared at his hand, then waved to the shattered remains of the surrounding college. "I didn't realize you were buried in fallen buildings."

Katie snorted, then coughed. "Well, I'm here now. I have to go help them." She reached the edge of the campus before John caught her shoulder.

"No," he said. "Lou left strict instructions. She has a different job for you."

"What can be more important than protecting magic?"

"That *is* your job," John said. "They said you have a crucible of pure magic in the college. You need to take it back to Sabart. I've got fifty of my best here to help. We're not going to the Well, Kate. We're going to preserve what we can. Just in case."

"In case the Directive fails?"

John frowned as he surveyed the fight below them. A tight formation of Sabartians moved down the hill, pushing a line of Fatesmiths towards the lake. Before he could answer, a purple explosion stole the sky. Thunder shook the ground as a single bolt of lightning hit the water.

The cacophony of war fell silent as the lake drained into one gargantuan spinning cylinder. Ice filled Katie's veins as a towering liquid tornado formed before her. It roared like a thousand waterfalls and lumbered forward. The Fatesmiths split, but the Sabartians remained, frozen in shock.

"Call them back." Katie's tone was an octave higher than expected.

John weaved a cone of air around his mouth. "TO ME!" he shouted. The column surged over the lake's western bank. Fatesmiths retreated behind it while the Sabartians raced up the hill. "FASTER!" John yelled, a note of panic in his voice. "GET TO COVER!"

The immense spout was gaining on them. Katie could not fathom controlling such a spell. She felt helpless. "They're not going to make it."

"Then help me help them!"

John started down the hill, hurling long coils of aeronima to those in danger's path. Katie followed his lead. They dragged Sabartians to safety, but there were too many to save. Terrified teenagers screamed as they were swallowed in droves, sucked into a watery grave that touched the sky above them.

"PULL OUT THE WATER! BRING IT DOWN!" John shouted. With two hands, he drew hydronima free of the spout. The surrounding Sabartians did the same. Enormous bulbs of water formed around them. A girl with vivid red hair fell from the cylinder, arms flailing in the wind as she plummeted. Katie caught her inches from death.

Slowly, the massive column trembled and lost shape. With one awful lurch, it collapsed—dropping half a lake on top of them. It hit like a hammer, sweeping Katie off her feet in an instant. She gasped for air as the wave dragged her downwards. Tumbling backwards, she collided with something, or someone. Sore, scared, and confused—Katie pushed a burst of kinima into the ground that forced her free of the wave. She landed in a heap with a muddy splash. The water returned to the lake, and Katie lay sprawled in the dirt.

Sabartians littered the sloping lawns. Bruised, broken, but—miraculously—everyone seemed to have survived. The Fatesmiths didn't seem to care. They assembled on the other side of the lake, moving east—towards the Well.

Katie staggered to kneel over a young man. He lay curled into himself, soaked and crying. Blood stained his hair. "Are you okay?" she asked. The man flinched at her touch. Katie squeezed his arm. "They're gone now. Come on."

She helped him to his feet and they limped—boots squelching—up the waterlogged slope. John ran to meet her as she reached the college walls. "Where is the crucible?"

"The Imbusion Lab."

"We need to go." John gestured to a woman with hair as red as a rose in bloom. "Sephina, lead everyone back to the giant cedar tree. Take the injured back to Sabart. Stay with the rest to hold position. We'll be there soon." When he started towards the campus, Katie didn't follow. "Come on Kate," John said. "We have to hurry."

Katie shook her head. "I need to protect the Well."

"Protect the..." John gestured to the lake which still heaved like a stormy sea. "You can't stop that. None of us can. We need to preserve what we can, while we can."

Katie looked away. Every cell in her body screamed at her to go with him, but she couldn't leave Laurefen, or Michael, or Mary-Lou.

John took her hands. Despite the situation, Katie's heart skipped a beat at his touch. "You're not abandoning them," John said. "You're helping them. Come on Kate. We have to get that crucible to Sabart. Euryma needs magic!"

Katie knew she would be no more than a mosquito to Horace. John was right. Getting the last vestige of magic off the island would do more for Euryma's future than chasing a Reaper. "Okay."

As Sephina and the Sabartians went north, Katie led John through what remained of King's College. Between the broken nimrods and destructive Fatesmiths, the place was a mess. Shattered brickwork littered the ground, leaving gaping holes in the ancient buildings that once seemed impenetrable.

Fortunately, the ironhands appeared to have moved on. Katie shuddered to think where. They climbed the ruins of the staff library and scaled a fallen wall into the Imbusion Lab. The windows had blown out, but otherwise, things were as Katie had left them. One leather duffel, a pink backpack, and the lone crucible on the bench top.

"That's it?" John eyed the container as if it had teeth. Katie understood why.

"I'll carry it. You take the bags." She hoisted the crucible into her arms. It was warm, on the cusp of being hot, and heavier than she remembered. *A burnt hand is a small price to pay to save magic.*

John went through the window and Katie followed, now uncomfortably aware that she held the Dominion's future in her arms. When her foot found a loose tile, she started to slide. She cried out and John caught her before she went too far.

"Easy there," he said, helping her down to ground level. "Just pretend you're holding a tray of cookies. Slow and steady, yeah?"

"Right." Katie didn't mention that dropping these cookies would turn them to dust faster than they could blink, but she made the mental note to be more careful with her footing.

They snaked their way through an untouched section of the college. John's shoulders drooped, and Katie knew it wasn't because of the bag. Michael taught mimicry in this section of the college—with John's father... "Why didn't you come back?" she asked.

John stared at an ivy-covered lecture hall. He took a deep breath and shrugged. When he looked back at her, there was a shadow behind his eyes. "I needed something the Directive couldn't give me."

"John. We would have helped."

John shook his head. "Not help. Revenge."

The conversation died with that, but John's words struck a chord in Katie's chest. Her hands adjusted to the crucible's heat and soon, a different warmth burned in her chest. They exited the campus through the southern gate and soon met Sephina outside Cedrus. A dozen Sabartians stood guard around a small Opening. On the other side, an underground infirmary bustled with activity.

"Everything okay?" John asked.

"We saw some stragglers," Sephina said. "But they must have used up their irofil because they ran away as we approached."

"Good." He turned back to Katie. "Come on. Let's get you cleaned up and find a safe space for that jar of tricks."

Katie shoved the crucible into his chest. John held it tight. He raised a questioning eyebrow as Katie backed away from him. "Look after it." She turned on her heel.

"Kate! What are you doing?"

She refused to talk as she marched down the hill. Katie squeezed her eyes closed and let the flickering flame inside her building into a wildfire.

"Kate! Stay! Don't go!"

"Horace killed my mom!" she shouted, still not willing to glance back. "He killed Amber!"

"You can't beat him!" John called.

Katie turned to face him. John stood ahead of the Opening, arms wrapped around the crucible, his eyes round. She shook her head, letting the fire take her. "You should understand this better than anyone," she said. "I want my revenge too."

With that, she started running. Down the sloping road, away from Cedrus, and Sabart, and John. He didn't call after her. If he did, she didn't hear him. Tears streamed across Katie's cheeks as she raced towards the Well.

And vengeance.

And Horace.

CHAPTER 43
LAUREFEN

LAUREFEN, Mary-Lou and Michael waited for the Fatesmith host to pass by. Concealed in a bubble of inverted light, Laurefen held his breath as Horace led them through the shallow valley below.

The ironhands were less than a mile from the Well, though their current march tracked slightly too far north—if nothing else, it was encouraging to see that Horace was uncertain of the cavern's exact location.

"What's the plan?" Michael whispered.

"We need to get around them before they get too close." Laurefen shifted his weight; the wound in his chest ignited. He covered his discomfort with a cough. "There are too many to fight, and Horace alone could outmatch us with magic. Do either of you have an idea?"

Mary-Lou bit her lip. Dry blood caked her face and her left eye was swollen shut. "I might have something," she said at last. "But you're not going to like it."

Laurefen raised an eyebrow. "Go on."

"They're going the wrong way." Mary-Lou pointed to

the meandering army. "Look at them. They don't know where the Well is. Whatever information the Marley boy has is incomplete."

Laurefen nodded. He had come to the same conclusion.

"So what do you suggest?" Michael asked.

"If I dash past in plain sight, doing my best to look like I am headed somewhere with purpose, what are they going to think?"

"That you're rushing to the Well." Michael scowled. "That's an awful idea."

"If I can get Horace to chase—"

"He will kill you," Michael said. "There were seven of us at Sabriva. We didn't stand a chance."

"Then I'll make sure I keep my distance."

Mary-Lou's suggestion made Laurefen feel sick. It was a death sentence, but it did utilize their sole advantage— they knew where the Well was. Still, he could not let her die for this. "I will go," Laurefen said.

"You should be in bed, resting." Mary-Lou shook her head. "You're barely standing as is. Don't think we haven't noticed you pretending you're okay. No. You have the key, and Michael can protect you better than me. This is some- thing I *can* do. I will draw the army away." She smiled grimly. "You activate the Well's protection. If you can trigger the island's defenses before the Fatesmiths catch me, I'll be okay."

"This is ridiculous," Michael said.

"Do you have another idea?"

Michael scowled at her, but said nothing. Laurefen sighed. Every minute wasted gave Horace time to find the Well. Once he did, it would be over.

"We have to act now." Mary-Lou held his gaze, determination chiseled on her battered features. "You know I'm right."

Laurefen turned to Michael. A vein throbbed in the side of his temple. His lips were razor thin. He appeared as conflicted as Laurefen felt, but there really was no other way. "Okay," Laurefen said. "Circle back around them. When you are atop the next rise, make your presence known, and *run*. Use the hill for cover. Move north. Keep your distance. Am I clear?"

"Yes, Dean Ember." Mary-Lou's lower lip quivered despite her smile. "Don't you boys dilly dally. I'll be waiting for you."

Michael bowed his head. Laurefen gripped her hand. "We'll see you soon. Keep your distance."

"I will."

With a final smile, Mary-Lou left. The photonima bubble surrounding them made a soft popping sound as it separated into two shields of light. Laurefen kept his gaze trained on Mary-Lou's shimmering orb of air, afraid that if he looked away, he would lose track of her.

The minutes crawled by as the Fatesmiths moved further east. Laurefen's stomach tied itself in knots as he waited. *What if Horace can sense the Well?* He pushed that alarming thought away. *Focus on what you can control*, he told himself.

"There she is," Michael whispered. Shouts erupted from the Fatesmiths as Mary-Lou ducked behind a tree and disappeared down the opposite rise. Her act was convincing, one Laurefen would have believed, had he not known of the ruse. Orders travelled through the mass like ripples in a pond, and the army began its pursuit. In ten minutes, the last of the ironhands vanished to the north. Laurefen's heart thundered in his chest. "Come along."

Every step pulled at the stitches in his wound, but magic—and Mary-Lou's life—depended on speed. Michael fell in beside him. Everything became a frantic blur. They circled right and the small hill marking the Well appeared in the distance. His relief evaporated as a flash of purple crackled overhead and a shower of dirt engulfed them.

Laurefen stumbled, but Michael pulled him forward. Somehow, the photonima barrier remained intact. They were invisible, but Horace was nearby. The thought turned Laurefen's blood to ice.

"Where are you?" Haberdeen's voice floated through the haze. "I know you're there. Show yourself!"

I'll draw him out. Michael's looptap played against his palm. *You get to the Well.*

No. He is too strong. Laurefen tapped back. *Geokinima knots. If we reduce visibility, we can slip by him.*

Michael replied. *You take the left and back, I'll take the front and right.*

Go.

With deft fingers, Laurefen weaved kinetic energy and stone into loose braids. When he finished one, he started on the next. On his fifth knot, the first exploded. A geyser of earth rained overhead, and they rushed into it. Laurefen continued, using both hands to braid multiple ties. The cracks pulsed in his eardrums, but they were so close to the Well's entrance.

Stop!

The looptap arrived too late. Laurefen saw Michael's knot at his feet just before it unraveled. He felt his stitches split as reality turned upside down. An azure sky greeted him at his apex, then gravity took hold and his trajectory reversed. Laurefen braced himself for a hard landing that never came. A sparkling purple coil snatched him out of the air, wrapping around him like a warm tentacle made of light. It slid across his chest and drew him down to ground level. Horace considered him through Haberdeen's guise. "Why are you standing in my way? Don't you understand? I'm trying to save the Dominion."

"Destroying the Well won't stop those storms, Horace." Ire Tides forced the breath from Laurefen's lungs, transforming his voice into a desperate wheeze. "You don't know what you're doing."

"I know exactly what I'm doing," Horace said. "Euryma is built on a lie. Magic doesn't belong here. It is an artificial creation. I am returning things to the status quo."

"You'll destroy magic for everyone!" Laurefen gasped.

"People are more important than magic."

"Magic is our only hope to keep Euryma safe." Laurefen's head felt light. "If you do this, we will be helpless. You'll doom us all!"

An amethyst glow burned in Horace's eyes. "Magic never belonged to you." He raised a hand, then stared at his feet. Laurefen followed his gaze to the largest geokinima knot he had ever seen. Before either of them could react, the ground erupted with a deafening roar. The Ire Tides vanished, Laurefen fell backwards, and someone dragged him upright. "Come on!" Michael ripped him out of the haze. They stumbled through the cavern entry.

"Michael. That was..."

"Necessary."

"Amazing."

Michael didn't reply. Deep lines creased his brow.

"Did he see us?" Laurefen asked as they descended into the dim tunnel.

"I don't know."

The last vestige of sunlight changed from white to

purple. They rounded a corner and the light dimmed. Wet air filled heaving lungs as they raced downwards.

"YOU WON'T STOP ME!" Horace's scream echoed around them. Clattering footfalls chased them into the darkness.

Laurefen and Michael half-ran, half-slid down the final descent. They caught themselves before colliding against the stone door inlaid with seven dull gems. Laurefen reached into his coat pocket and fumbled for a key.

His heart stopped.

"Hurry!" Michael said, staring back the way they came.

Laurefen checked his other pocket with the same result. Frantic, he tried the hidden pouch inside his sleeve. It was empty. Despair diminished his voice. "It's not here," he managed in a strangled whisper.

Michael spun to face him. "What?"

"The key..." Laurefen shook his head as the reality sank in. "I've lost the key. I must have dropped it when I fell."

The approaching footsteps slowed as Horace descended the narrow tunnel. The Haberdeen facade was gone. Dirt caked the boy's sweat-soaked face. Laurefen swallowed as he stopped short of them. "Let me in," Horace said. "I will not ask twice."

Michael raised his hands. A beam of purple light poured from Horace's palm. It ran straight through Michael's stomach, throwing him against the Well door.

"Stop!" Laurefen shouted. "Stop this madness! We cannot open the door!"

The light vanished, leaving a burnt line in the darkness. Michael fell to the floor and Laurefen knelt beside him. Horace didn't seem to notice. He thrust out both hands and a blinding pillar of Ire Tides poured out of him. The extraordinary heat seared the hair on Laurefen's arms, but the door remained unchanged. Horace roared, pushing the power of a wildfire into the stone to no avail. When the passage darkened once more, he slammed a desperate fist against the lock. "WHERE IS THE KEY?"

Laurefen glanced up from Michael. "I don't have it."

"Where is it?"

"Here," said an unexpected voice from above them. Katie Hall stood at the top of the tunnel, barely visible in the dim light. In her outstretched palm, she held the crescent moon key.

No. Laurefen staggered forward. "Kate! Run!"

Katie disappeared from view. Horace roared and raced after her. As he vanished from sight, shouting after her, Katie stepped out of thin air beside them. Laurefen's breath caught as she handed him the key.

"What?" he stammered. "How?"

"A little spell I learnt from Lou. Get the door," Katie said, leaning down to Michael. "That trick of the light won't distract him for long."

Laurefen slid the key into the lock. It opened with a loud click. Ignoring the pain in his chest, he pushed it open. Katie seized Michael by his armpits and dragged him into the cavern. As Laurefen turned back, he saw a violet blaze hurtling towards them.

Laurefen dived inside. With a crunch, the glowing tentacle seized the door's corner. "Kate! Help!" Laurefen wrapped the door in enough kinima to move a bus. Katie joined him, and together they heaved. The magic glowed like cooling lava; it spread like cobwebs across the stone.

Laurefen gripped the geonima above and pulled the ceiling down. With a terrible noise, the passage collapsed, trapping them in darkness and breaking the Ire Tides' hold on the door. With one last heave, it closed. The ancient lock engaged, and Laurefen dropped to the ground. A flash of light and a thunderous crash sounded on the other side. Horace was here.

"OPEN THE DOOR, WIZARD!"

The cavern was dark, lit only by the Well's glow. Laurefen pressed a hand against his chest. The wound was wide open now. Blood pooled beneath him, but there was no time to stop. Painfully, he searched the floor—light-headed, yet determined—feeling for the telltale indent of the Well's protection.

"I WILL GET INSIDE! I WILL FINISH THIS!"

The seven gems in the door shone bright violet. The roof of the Well began to shake. Small fragments of stone dropped into the bore, flashing like sparks off a campfire.

"Laurefen!" Katie called, on her hands and knees. "Here. It's here!"

Laurefen crawled toward her. The crescent-shaped keyhole flickered in the light. With trembling fingers, he slid the key into the hole and words came unbidden into his mind. "Defenders of Kingsbreak, I release you. Rise and protect this place."

He turned the key.

A crystal chime echoed through the cavern. A pair of tiny dots flashed to life on either side of the keyhole. Two more appeared ahead of it. A line of lights blinked into existence, illuminating a path to the door. Once there, the seven white gems inlaid in the stone blazed to life. Laurefen shielded his eyes as molten sunlight filled the space, and the hum of a million beehives drowned out everything. The ground shook like an earthquake. Laurefen curled into a ball, and as the roar reached a crescendo, seven tremendous cracks thundered through his bones.

Laurefen rolled onto his back. Shimmering spots

hovered in his vision as the rock vibrated beneath him. Katie knelt over him, her mouth moving, but without a sound. All Laurefen he could hear was a high-pitched wail. He stared at the cavern's roof and hoped he had done enough.

For Mary-Lou. For Michael. For magic.

CHAPTER 44

KATIE

THE NARROW TUNNEL leading from the Well to the surface looked dreadful. Jagged lines marred the smooth walls, as if mammoth fingernails had clawed their way upward. Katie held a sphere of light as she ascended. Distant shouts grew louder when she reached daylight. Katie climbed atop the hill hiding the Well's entrance, and from that vantage point, she watched in terrified awe.

Seven crystalline spheres coursed through the Fatesmith army, which broke in all directions. The balls moved at incredible speed, herding the ironhands into groups before surging through them. They gleamed like enormous diamonds, dealing death at each turn.

What have we done?

Amidst the madness, flashes of violet light exploded from a solitary figure. Massive flares of Ire Tides glanced off the spherical creatures, bouncing away like water against glass. If Katie didn't despise the boy with every cell in her body, she might respect his persistence. She didn't. She wanted him dead, and she would watch until he was.

A battered figure appeared at the top of the hill to her

401

right and Katie felt a surge of relief. She was half a mile away, but Katie knew that silver braid anywhere. "Lou!" she shouted. "Up here!"

Mary-Lou limped at a steady pace while Katie watched Horace war against the defenders. The purple flashes of light grew less frequent. An exposed handful of Fatesmiths appeared to catch one of the defender's attention. As the sphere hurtled towards the group, a shimmering violet Opening appeared between them. Katie held her breath as the ironhands raced to safety. They leapt into the hovering doorway and the sphere followed after them. In a flash, the portal was gone—and the defender with it.

The battle froze. Katie felt like she'd been punched in the stomach.

Mary-Lou climbed the hill and collapsed at Katie's feet. Her breathing was labored, her face a mess of bruises, but she was alive. She lay on the grass, gulping mouthfuls of air. "You did it," she said between breaths. "Where are the others?"

Katie didn't answer. Her eyes never strayed from the distant conflict. Another sphere had vanished through another Opening. Horace couldn't hurt them, but he could remove them.

"Kate?" Mary-Lou asked. "Where is Laurefen?"

"He's..." Katie tore her gaze from the scene. "He's in the Well. He's unconscious, but I've bound his shoulder. Michael caught one of Horace's blasts through his stomach, but the Ire Tides cauterized the wound. If we can get them to Sabart, they should be okay."

"And what are *you* doing here?" she asked. "You were supposed to get the crucible and—"

"I did," Katie said. "John took it back. It's safe in the caves. I..." The sentence died in her mouth as an orb unrolled into a gargantuan armored beast—at least eight feet tall—with glistening white scales and the face of an...

"Is that an armadillo?" Mary-Lou asked.

The creature charged towards Horace, light streaming behind it like a comet on legs. It raised its claws and leaped as an Opening flashed to life. The defender tried to stop, but its momentum carried it through the portal and out of view. The doorway flickered away. The Fatesmiths cheered.

Katie and Mary-Lou watched in stunned silence. The remaining four spheres continued their attack. One by one, Horace removed them from the island. Katie's stomach turned to concrete as another vanished. *He just won't die! How do we stop this?*

Mary-Lou tugged on her shirt. "Come," she said.

"Where?"

"We need to get to the Well."

Katie grimaced. "Why?"

"It's not over." Mary-Lou's unswollen eye darkened as she cast a gaze towards the distant ironhands. "He hasn't won yet."

Katie knew they weren't enough. She had been so certain that the Well's protection would overpower Horace. That they would avenge her best friend, her mother, and everyone else he had killed.

"Come on." Mary-Lou gripped her hand and led her back into the dark passage. They didn't speak. At the Well door, Katie helped Mary-Lou climb over the deep mounds the defenders carved on their way out.

In the cavern's orange glow, Laurefen sat against the stone wall surrounding the bore. Relief washed the concern from his face as they stepped into view. "Lou," he crooned. "You're okay." He exhaled. "I worried we took too long. Did it work?"

"It bought us some time."

Laurefen's forehead creased. "I beg your pardon?"

"Horace couldn't beat the... the things... that came out of the Well. He didn't have to. He's using Openings to send them away from the island." Despite her efforts, Katie could hear the tremble in her voice. "He's coming back. We're out of time."

Laurefen breathed a deep sigh. Slowly, he nodded, as if digesting the news and not liking the flavor. Finally, he glanced up at them. "You should go. Get away from here while you can."

"I'm not leaving you," Katie said.

"I will remain to protect the Well."

"Laurefen Ember!" Mary-Lou snapped in a tone Katie had never heard before. "Do not be a fool! You cannot do this alone!"

"THIS IS MY LEGACY!" Laurefen shouted. He winced and pressed a hand to his bandaged chest. A shuddering breath broke the silence as he stared into nowhere, eyes glistening. "I am responsible for the Well. It is *my* charge. I will stay. You take Michael and get to safety."

Mary-Lou planted her fists on her hips. "No."

"You don't need to die."

"Neither do you!" she shouted. "Come with us Laurefen! We gain nothing by staying!"

Laurefen shook his head, his jaw set. "I will not leave the Well."

A distant sound echoed down the passage. Footsteps. White-hot hatred ran up Katie's spine, incinerating any sense of self-preservation. "We all stay," she said. "And we kill him together."

"How?" Mary-Lou asked. The unbruised sections of her face were pale in the flickering light.

"We don't have to best him with magic," Katie said. "We just need to toss him down there." She motioned to the Well's depths. "I don't care how powerful a Reaper is. *Nobody* can survive that."

Laurefen stifled a groan as he staggered to his feet. Sweat beaded on his forehead; his face was stone. He removed a dagger from his belt. Katie recognized it from Sabriva. It was the dagger Horace had put in his shoulder. "One last chance," he murmured.

As the footsteps grew louder, Katie and Mary-Lou dragged Michael to a dark corner on the other side of the Well. Once he was hidden, they took their positions.

Soft steps echoed down the passageway. Concealed in a stony crevice, Katie's heartbeat thundered in her ears. Ahead of her, Mary-Lou lay on the floor, half-buried in rubble, wearing Laurefen's coat. *This is it*, Katie thought. A cramp of pain bloomed in her shoulder, but she refused to move.

Someone stopped at the Well's entrance. There was a tired sigh and Horace stepped into the cavern. Katie pressed herself so hard into the wall, she feared she might become one with the stone. Horace knelt over Mary-Lou's motionless silhouette. "I told you that you couldn't stop me," he said. "You were a fool, Dean Ember."

He removed a torn piece of material from his pocket. Horace stared at it with a reverence that Katie did not understand. He held it out over the Well, as if completing some monumental task. *Is that it? Is that how he destroys the Well?* Katie's heart seized at the thought. She wound Mary-Lou's thread over her palm. *That scrap of fabric is important. I'll distract him. Grab it and run.*

Katie didn't wait for a response. She pulled every ounce of photonima from the Well into one spot. In a rush of light, a blinding flash filled the cavern. "Hey idiot!" she shouted.

Horace spun around and their gazes met. His eyes narrowed. "You!"

Purple light sparked in his eyes, but before he could move, Mary-Lou burst from hiding and snatched the cloth from his hand.

"NO!"

Mary-Lou did not take three steps before Ire Tides knocked her off her feet. She released the fabric square and Katie seized it with a flick of aeronima. Horace roared as she dashed to the cavern's exit. Vaulting over the shredded ground, Katie jerked back as something caught her by the neck.

Katie gasped for breath as a glowing purple tentacle turned her around. It extended from Horace's open palm. He drew her back and hung her over the Well. "Give me that," he hissed, and to her surprise, Katie saw desperation in his eyes. He didn't want the cloth, he *needed* it. Behind her back, Katie pulled a small coil of pyronima from the Well. She glared at Horace, knowing what she was about to do would cost her everything.

"Give. Me. That." Fury contorted Horace's sharp features.

Katie held out the piece of material. In the light of the Well, she could see it was stained with blood. She transferred the tendrils of flame from one hand to the other. She pictured Amber smiling by the lake, and her mother playing piano upstairs. *You'll see them soon.* As Horace reached out, Katie drew the cloth back and let the flames take it. The fabric sparked and sizzled. Pain engulfed her fingers as it charred to nothing. Outrage burned in Horace's eyes. Katie met them with a cool gaze. "You shouldn't have killed my friend."

"What have you done?" Horace's hand transformed into a long purple blade. He pulled Katie forward and ran it straight through her. The Ire Tides felt like a spike of molten glass. Katie stayed silent. She would not cry. Not now. He threw her aside. She smashed into the stone floor. It didn't matter. She had done something Horace couldn't undo.

Horace turned on Mary-Lou. "ALL I WANTED TO DO WAS STOP THE STORMS! YOU HAVE DOOMED US ALL!" A blistering violet orb formed in his hands. As he raised it high overhead, Laurefen shot out from behind an invisible shield and plunged the dagger into his heart. Laurefen gripped it with white knuckles and gritted teeth. "I believe this belongs to you."

It was the knife from Sabriva, now bound in a tight knot of kinetic energy. With a whip crack, the knife exploded. Horace arced backwards, moving in slow motion and tumbling down towards the swirling miasma. As Laurefen leaned forward to watch, a glowing purple barb rose up and wrapped around him.

"LAUREFEN!" Mary-Lou leapt after him. She wasn't fast enough. The Ire Tides pulled Laurefen downwards. One moment he was there. The next, he was gone.

Bright orange light filled the cavern. "No," Katie whispered. *He's not gone. He can't be!* Her mind refused to accept what her eyes had witnessed. With the last of her strength, Katie crawled to the Well. As she propped herself up against the bordering wall, she caught a glimpse of a figure hanging below her, held in place by merit of a dagger thrust into the stone. Katie's reeling thoughts jolted to a stop.

Horace had survived. Below him, the Well bubbled with the intensity of a volcano.

Katie turned to Mary-Lou. "RUN!"

Terror painted Mary-Lou's face as Horace climbed free of the pit. A grim smile plastered his face. "It is done," he said. "It is done."

A geyser of energy spat from the Well. Sparks of orange tore the cavern ceiling to shreds. Horace began to laugh. On the other side of the Well, a triangular Opening appeared. Immediately, it started to flicker. Hunched by the wall, Michael waved his arms in a complex pattern. Sweat poured off his forehead. The floating doorway trembled.

"Look at your magic!" Horace crooned. "Watch it unravel!"

The Opening quivered like a sheet in the wind. "Go!" Michael shouted. "Go now! I can't hold it!"

Mary-Lou flicked her hands and nothing moved. She stared at her fingers. "The kinima! It's gone!"

Horace clapped in ecstatic delight. He didn't seem to care what happened to them. His icy cackle echoed amidst the chaos.

"GO!" Michael's voice was frantic. "Now!"

Katie winced as Mary-Lou dragged her towards the Opening. One painful push and she stumbled into one of Sabart's empty caverns. She turned back to see Mary-Lou's wide eyes as the doorway dissolved, leaving her with Michael, Horace, and the collapsing Well.

CHAPTER 45

DECLAN

DECLAN JOLTED SIDEWAYS, grabbing the seat to steady himself as Haberdeen pulled onto the curb. The van skidded to a halt; Misha's skull hit the window with a bang. "What was that for?" he snapped, rubbing his head.

Haberdeen said nothing. She stared out the windscreen, then at her palms. Declan glanced at Ava for an explanation, but she appeared just as confused as he was. After a long silence, Ava touched her shoulder. "Is everything okay?"

Haberdeen twirled her fingers in small circles, creating an intricate pattern that—as far as Declan could tell—did nothing at all.

"What is it?" Ava asked.

The woman did not answer. Haberdeen's gaze never left her fingers, which danced in increasingly complex movements. After thirty seconds, she lowered her hands. "It's gone."

"What's gone?"

"Magic..." Haberdeen's voice was barely a whisper. "It's just... gone."

"What?" Declan could only think of one explanation, and the thought turned his stomach to steel. "How?"

"The nima... the threads..." Haberdeen waved a hand. "They do not exist."

"Could it be a storm?" Misha's pale face reflected in the window.

Ava unbuckled her seatbelt and climbed over Declan. There was a loud thud as she climbed onto the van roof. "None that I can see," she called down.

"It's not Remnant Magic," Haberdeen said. "Nima shrivels away when storms are near. No. This is something else."

"It's Horace." Declan pursed his lips. He considered the skeletal city streets. A nearby stoplight flashed orange. Beyond that, the scene appeared frozen in time. "It has to be. That's why he's not here. How though? How is this possible?"

As Haberdeen opened her mouth to respond, an enormous diamond orb rounded the corner. It moved with a chittering sound, tearing chunks out of the asphalt as it turned to face them. Somehow, the ball seemed to sense their presence.

"What is that?" Misha asked.

Whatever it was, it looked unfriendly. Declan banged his fist against the roof. "Ava! Get down from there!"

The thing hurtled in their direction. Declan braced himself, but a moment before impact, the sphere exploded into thousands of tiny fragments. They floated away like ash on the wind, leaving a vague smell of gunpowder. Speechless, Ava climbed back into her seat. Her blue eyes were like saucers. "What on earth was that? What is going on?"

Declan shook his head. "I don't know."

"It's the magic. Look there." Haberdeen pointed to a brownstone skyscraper on the other side of the block. It trembled like a reed in a gale before buckling under its own weight. The building collapsed with a deafening roar. Haberdeen reversed away from the massive plume of debris.

"There goes another one," Misha said, waving to the skyline. Through the haze, a distant tower tilted and fell. The horrific sound of its fall followed a second later. "Why are they falling?"

"Many buildings in Euryma are magically reinforced," Haberdeen said. "With those spells gone, there is nothing holding them up but bricks and mortar." Her knuckles were pale on the steering wheel. "We need to get away from the city."

As she pulled onto the road, a brilliant purple flash washed over them. Declan turned back. A beaming pillar of Ire Tides rose from Biscay's center. *Horace.* "Stop!"

"We can't." Haberdeen's head was level with the dashboard as she scanned the surrounding buildings. "Not here."

Frustration flared within him. Declan hit the door with a clenched fist. "Horace is back there!"

"If one of these structures falls, we'll be crushed."

"You said you were going to help me," Declan growled. Haberdeen glanced through her rear-view mirror and Declan held her gaze. "I'm here to finish this. Are you?"

After a tense pause, she spun the wheel once more. The tires screeched as the van navigated a tight circle. Haberdeen turned to Ava. "Does your Luck still work?"

"It does."

"Good. Tell me if we're about to be buried alive."

They hurtled through pure mayhem as the city fell into ruin. When they reached the top of Boundary Road, Haberdeen slammed on the brakes. Six enormous doorways filled the street, coalescing into one giant Opening. Thousands of Fatesmiths poured through it. Behind them, a distant cluster of buildings sank beneath a treacherous grey sea. Haberdeen—rather, a mirror duplicate of her—stood amongst the chaos. Crackling electricity extended from her outstretched hands to the colossal Openings.

"Kingsbreak," Declan whispered. "That's King's College." His axes jumped to his palms, unbidden. "He's destroyed the whole thing."

"How is he doing that?" Ava turned to Haberdeen. "I thought you said magic was gone?"

"He doesn't need to draw on magic," Haberdeen said. "He's a Reaper. His magic is stored within." She continued talking, but Declan stopped listening. Horace had sunk an entire island. He had likely killed the Directive to do so.

Sila sparked inside him, but the green flame did not catch. The power was somehow out of reach. *You're being soft, Declan. You cannot be soft. Not now.* He forced the voice away and focused on memories from the Void. He pictured his parents' final moments. Arman's final moments. Ava's final moments. He relived every terrible moment. With each second, the wall between him and Sila thinned. Someone shook his shoulders.

"Are you listening?" Ava whispered. Her face was inches from his. Concern filled her eyes. "We need to get Horace alone," she said. "Then you can approach him."

Declan held Ava's gaze. He imagined what life would be like without her. What would the world become if this girl was taken from him—like everything else he loved?

The wall broke.

An emerald haze clouded Declan's vision. The scene shimmered with a faint green tinge. Declan blinked and Biscay became clearer. Below him, thousands of blackcoats carried on their evacuation, oblivious to the monolith of power above them. Declan let Sila fill him, igniting every capillary in his body. He turned to Ava, Haberdeen, and Misha. "Stay here."

He pushed off the asphalt, and they were gone. Declan ran, but didn't run. More, he flowed towards the gathered army. At the edge of the Fatesmiths, he willed himself through them. They were grains of sand. He, a tsunami. Bodies tumbled aside in his wake; by the time they'd staggered upright, he was nowhere to be seen.

Veiled in Haberdeen's form, Horace stood at the forefront of the Openings. Concentration creased his face, then lapsed a moment before Declan reached him. A violet shield appeared between them; Declan hit it with the force of a meteor. With a blinding flash, Horace catapulted fifty feet backwards. The fizzling purple doors vanished as he was propelled through the glass windows of a nearby building.

Axe heads ablaze, Declan followed. Fatesmiths scattered as an angry stream of Ire Tides poured from the ruined lobby. Jagged fingers of lightning spread in all directions. Declan poured a torrent of Sila towards the source of the attack.

The tower groaned under its own weight as Horace—free of Haberdeen's guise—burst out of it, wielding a sword fashioned from Ire Tides. It crackled with a malicious glow. Horace lashed out, but Declan caught the blade against his axes. Horace glared at him. "Why are you here?" he hissed. "It's over! I did it. I stopped the storms!"

"At what cost?" Declan forced the sword down and attacked.

Horace dodged with blinding speed. As he retreated, his severed hand transformed into a glittering triangular shield. He pointed the blade at Declan. "It was worth the cost."

"You've lost your mind!"

"Isn't this what you wanted?" Horace hissed. "Remnant Magic is no more. Witches and wizards are gone. I leveled the field! We are all LAMPs now!"

Declan could not believe what he was hearing. "You've sentenced the Dominion to death."

"I have stopped the storms! I have saved Euryma!"

Declan's temper flared, and his axe heads with it. He leapt and swung down, hard. Horace caught the blow on his shield and every window within two-hundred yards shattered. Swarms of Fatesmiths ran for cover as a building overhead started to fall. Horace vanished in a flash of purple as a hundred-thousand tons of steel and concrete fell atop of them. Declan let Sila pour out of him.

Silence.

Screams.

Crying.

Thick black dust hung about the shredded street, muffling the shouts of the injured. Declan closed his eyes and focused on the individual particles surrounding him. With a thought, he gave them mass, and they fell. The air cleared, leaving a ravaged ruin. Metal pipes and bent bars protruded from the ground. Gaping holes scarred the buildings that still stood. Ahead of him, Horace brandished his sword.

"You short-sighted idiot," Declan shouted. "Vedmark marches on Euryma. Magic was our only chance to stop them. You've taken that away! You've turned our only hope into an army of defenseless LAMPs!"

"The storms will make our home a wasteland! What would Vedmark do with a Kingdom of burned blight?" Horace's eyes were bright with fervor. "The Dominion will survive because of *me*."

In a moment, Declan was on him. Axe heads sang as they pummeled Horace's shield. Every impact sent an explosive pulse through the brittle city street. Horace lunged forward. Declan stepped around him and delivered a clenched fist to the side of his head. Sparks skittered off Horace's face. When he came up, his false hand transformed unexpectedly from a shield into a hammer.

Declan caught the blow against his axe, but the force of it pushed him back. His boots left a line of tracks in the thick ash. His eyes narrowed on Horace. "What a mess you have become."

Horace tilted his head. A sad smile split his ragged features. "I am what you made me."

"The Ace I knew—"

"Is gone," Horace snapped. His eyes glittered like coals. "I am the steel hardened in the forge. The savior of Euryma. I *am* the chosen one."

"You are insane. This ends today."

Horace laughed—an eerie, high-pitched cackle. "You're going to kill me?" He shook his head, smiling without mirth. "You don't have it in you."

Declan attacked in a blast of green. Horace couldn't keep pace. His hammer became a shield as he sheltered beneath the hailstorm of axe heads and energy. When one shield proved too little, his sword transmuted into another. Declan pushed him backwards—denying Horace any chance of attack or retreat. Every blow roared through the city, each one strong enough to level mountains. Ire Tides cracked like static, then broke away. The shields shrank until—with the force of an avalanche—Declan put Horace on his back.

"Enough!" Declan shouted. He dropped his axes, withdrew Winterthorn, and pressed it to Horace's chest. "We are done. *You* are done."

Horace's ruined hand dissolved into a glimmering spike, and Declan pinned it beneath his knee. Horace strained to move, but Declan would not allow it. Not now. With that, he lay back. "Maybe you do have it in..." Horace trailed off. He squinted into the distance, then his face fell. "No." Horace's body went rigid. He shook his head as a frenzy overtook him. "No. No. No. No! NO! NO! NO!" The purple light faded from his eyes. Unadulterated panic took their place. "I... NO! You're tricking me! THIS IS A TRICK!"

Confused, Declan glanced over his shoulder. A vivid orange glow filled the horizon. The unmistakable tone of Remnant Magic. Declan's heart lodged in his throat. The Sila inside him vanished. Declan tried to claim it back, but it was gone.

"YOU DID THIS!" Horace shrieked. "THIS IS YOUR FAULT!"

Declan fixed his old friend with a level gaze. He looked pathetic, writhing beneath him. This was not the last memory Declan wanted of Horace, but that didn't matter. There was no time for merciful gestures. A storm was coming, and there was only one way to reclaim his Sila. "I'm sorry," Declan said, not daring to meet Horace's gaze. "For all of it."

He plunged Winterthorn downwards.

An iron grip caught his wrist. The dagger's tip stopped an inch from Horace's chest. Ire Tides held Declan's arm tight. With supernatural strength, Horace wrenched the hilt free. In a violet flash, Declan was on his back, coughing. Biscay's damaged husk gleamed orange as the wall of Remnant Magic grew closer, reflecting off glass and steel.

"This *is* your fault." Horace stood slowly. A burning purple orb formed in his hand. Madness flickered in the light of his eyes. "And now, I will make things right."

CHAPTER 46
DECLAN

DECLAN STAGGERED TO HIS FEET. Horace had Winterthorn, his Sila was gone, and a sky of Remnant Magic coursed in their direction. There was no time for second guessing. Twin axes rushed to his hands with a metallic hum.

Horace heaved the Ire Tides towards him. Declan crossed his axes as they exploded in a torrent of violet heat. He shifted his stance as Horace attacked. A bar of energy—thick as his torso—blasted the surrounding street. Declan stepped into the Armadillo form. Purple streamers flared off axe heads, melting glass and burning sharp lines through the remaining skyscrapers.

The spell died and Declan lunged for Horace. He alternated between Bull and Lion at random, always ready to move into Armadillo when Horace sent a column of Ire Tides his way. Adrenaline fueled his furious attack, but he knew he couldn't maintain it. If he was going to stop Horace, he needed to do it fast.

To his frustration, Horace pulled back. An endless procession of Ire Tides kept Declan at a distance. He appeared not to care that a Remnant Magic storm was minutes away. Horace had the advantage and—as far as Declan could tell—he knew it.

"You wasted your chance!" Horace shouted from atop a burned bus. "You've failed. Again. Like always."

Declan gritted his teeth and ignored his fatigue. The sky behind them was molten stone. *You're running out of time!*

Desperation took hold of his movements. With no regard for safety, Declan pushed forward—cutting through columns of Ire Tides and pushing Horace back towards a wall of fallen buildings. When Horace was cornered, Declan launched an axe at his chest. Horace blinked out of existence and the axe-blade lodged in the rubble.

Declan called his weapon back, but a beam of magic caught him off guard. He dived for cover as the ground exploded around him. Before he could stand, a second pillar sparked in the haze. Declan blocked the column with his remaining axe. He braced against the handle with both arms. Still, the force of Horace's power pushed him back.

The heat roiling off the Ire Tides scorched the hair on his wrists, creating a foul smell in his nostrils. Declan tried to angle the energy away, but it was like moving a mountain. An unexpected burst of power proved too much. His axe fell as the spell lifted Declan off his feet. It threw him into the wall of rubble. Biscay's broken streets spun as Horace stepped through the gloom.

He was trapped.

In a last ditch hope, Declan called his axes. A flickering purple barrier bloomed around them, like an enormous cylinder of light. The weapons sparked when they hit the shield, then dropped to the ground.

Gleaming violet tentacles poured from Horace's fingers, pinning Declan to the concrete ruins and burning his skin. Horace's eyes glittered, but his smile was gone. Behind him, streams of Fatesmiths fled from the oncoming storm. "Your grandfather is responsible for this mess." He drew Winterthorn free from his cloak. "Now, justice will be done."

Horace raised the dagger. A shadow appeared above, and a body crashed on top of him.

Ava!

She moved like a panther, lunging in and out with twin daggers. Horace lost his balance as Ava feinted. She slipped by and drove a knife into his side. The purple barrier and the glowing tentacles binding Declan's wrists vanished. Horace screamed in pain.

"ENOUGH!" Horace screamed. An explosion of gleaming tendrils erupted from his chest, wrapping themselves around Ava's arms, legs, and torso. She cried out as Ire Tides snaked up her fingers and forced the knives from her hands. With hate in his eyes, Horace drew her forward.

Declan froze. *No!* He knew this scene. He had lived it a thousand times in The Void's grip. Ava's gaze flickered towards him; he knew her words before they left her lips.

"Help!" she wheezed.

"He can't help you," Horace said. He brandished Winterthorn in her direction. This was it. The moment he killed her. "Declan Moore is well practiced in failing those he loves."

Time stopped. Declan's heart pounded in his ears. Everything he had done, every choice made, every attempt to protect Ava, had brought them to this inevitable point in time. He waited for despair to take him, to flood him with Sila. It did not come. There was only emptiness. Apathy. Resignation. Once again, someone Declan loved would die because of him.

The Sila would come after.

Declan would burn Horace to dust, and it wouldn't matter.

It would be too late. Ava would be gone, and the world would darken.

Then burn bright.

Those were Mrs. Winters' words. No, Arman's words. Carved by hand into his grandfather's final gift.

Burn. Bright.

One of Declan's axes lay in the rubble, visible through the tiny gap separating Horace and Ava. No longer hindered by a barrier of Ire Tides, it awaited his call. Perfectly positioned, as if by luck.

Horace raised Winterthorn until the tip touched Ava's sternum.

"BURN BRIGHT!"

The axe head flashed to life—stealing Horace's attention—as Declan called it forwards. The axe streamed to Declan's outstretched hands, threading the needle between the pair, knocking Winterthorn free. Declan caught the axe and threw it.

Horace blocked the blow on a glowing shield. Declan launched himself forward as Horace's hand melded into an angry purple spike. Declan saw it coming, but—mid-flight—there was no way to adjust. The Ire Tides passed straight through his stomach, burning like a sword of lava. Horace pulled him closer, smiling in triumph. "You lost," he whispered. "You—"

The scorching blade vanished.

Horace blinked. The glow in his eyes faded, and he tilted his head to peer over his shoulder. Declan leaned sideways to follow his gaze. Time crystallized.

Winterthorn was buried to the hilt at the base of Horace's neck. Ava held the grip with white knuckles. Her eyes flashed green as a millennium of memories poured into her.

A final breath escaped Horace's lips. The color fled from his skin until he resembled a waxy figure from the Void. Horace dropped to his knees, balanced for a brief pause, then collapsed. Skeleton pale. Dead.

Ava stumbled forward, and her hands trembled as she reached out to find solid ground.

"Ava!" Declan rushed to her side. "Ava! Are you okay?"

Ava squeezed her head. "There's... no time." She fell into Declan's arms. A fiery orange wall reflected in her blue eyes. "The... storm, Declan. The storm."

Declan turned to see a wall of light overtaking the city. A colossal wave sweeping from the east. He closed his eyes, willing himself down into the darkness of despair. It had worked before. He had done it when Horace appeared. He just had to focus.

"Declan!" Haberdeen's voice cut through his concentration. "Get in the van!"

They were parked in the middle of the ruined road. Misha rushed towards them but Ava waved him off. "There's no time!"

"Ava! Come on!" Misha took her hand, but she pulled away. Misha fell to a knee, then tried again.

"No!" Ava pushed him back. "We... can't outrun... it!" Long, gasping breaths punctuated her words.

Declan stared at the oncoming wave. She was right. The storm would be on them in less than a minute. The road was too damaged. They would never escape it. "What do we do?"

Ava took a shuddering breath. "We... need your... Sila."

"Okay." Declan closed his eyes again. He forced all thoughts from his mind, everything except the hope of despair. He focused on the worst part of every loss he had experienced. A piercing whistle picked up. A rush of searing wind roared past them. *It's not going to work.* "No!" Declan clawed to find the Sila within him. *You're all going to die.* "Not now!"

"Declan!"

He opened his eyes. Ava lay cradled in his arms, her face aglow.

"I can't do it," he said. "It's... it's not there."

Ava placed her hand on his. "So we do it together." Her brow furrowed as a single strand of trembling golden light pulsed in her wrist. It grew stronger, until tiny drops emerged from her skin, wobbling like rain on a windscreen and forming into larger beads. At the same moment, Declan felt a pulling sensation, like his emotions were being dragged downwards. He recognized the sensation. Ava was using Luck on him. Increasing the odds that he would feel enough despair to access his Sila.

"How?" Declan asked.

With her free hand, Ava tapped her temple. "It's... all... in the... memories."

Declan surrendered to the misery. An infinite darkness overtook him, empty except for a glowing green dagger. Declan took it, and a flare of emerald brilliance filled his soul. Sila returned like a flood on parched earth. Remnant Magic howled towards them. Haberdeen and Misha watched, stunned, as the storm closed in.

A globule of golden light danced around Ava's fingers. "Channel it... into... my hand," she whispered.

Declan nodded. He pictured the Sila as a river and redirected the flow down his shoulder. Gleaming sparks of green electricity wound their way down his wrists, coalescing in Ava's palm.

As the wall reached them, Ava gripped Declan's hand. Luck and Sila combined with a surge of power. Together, they raised their arms skyward.

The storm responded like they were conductors in an orchestra. Remnant Magic exploded upwards at their direction. A fiery cylindrical tempest that set the sky ablaze. A vertical burst that must have been visible for hundreds of miles, if not more. Declan stared in wonder as a pillar of pure magic coursed into the atmosphere, bathing the world in vivid orange. It was a sunset dialed to maximum. A wildfire amongst the clouds. He couldn't tell how long the storm lasted—seconds, hours, weeks—but when it finally faded, Ava slumped against his chest.

"We did it," Declan said. Tears streamed down his cheeks. He placed his hand under her chin and tilted her head towards him. "Ava, we did it!"

She answered with the slightest of nods. Then her body went slack. "Ava?" Joy turned to terror as Declan tried to shake her back to consciousness. "Ava? Ava?" A hole formed in his stomach. *No! Not now! Not after this.* Horace was dead. The storm redirected. She had lived through all of it, and now... *Not now!* He squeezed her hand as he turned to the others. "What do I do?"

"The girl has a thousand years of memories bursting through her brain," Haberdeen said. Her lips were thin, and the scar extending from them stood out in the dying light. "I'm not sure there is anything we *can* do."

Declan shook his head, refusing to believe it. "We need help! A healer!" His whirring mind stopped on the first idea that made sense. "We need to get to Sabart!"

CHAPTER 47
AVA

THE CACOPHONY of color and sound was overwhelming. A moment ago she was in Biscay, sending a storm skyward. Now, Ava felt as if she were in free fall. Tumbling through a million moments, a thousand lifetimes. It moved too fast. A screaming blur of pictures and noise. She tried to close her eyes, but she had none. She was not there. This was not a place.

It was all in her mind. The first memory—guiding her to redirect Remnant Magic—had come so easily. Now, she felt like a dandelion in a hurricane.

With gargantuan effort, she imposed her will on her surrounds. The exercise wasn't dissimilar to manipulating the bands of Luck, but so much harder. Yet as she did, she found her infinite descent slowed. She could make out faces, she could interpret voices, and then—at the sight of a familiar face—she hit the ground.

Ava was in an empty room, more a well-kept shed. A single lightbulb illuminated a concrete floor and metal shelves. She sat in a wooden chair opposite a hooded figure. A curious sensation overtook her as Ava glanced at her hands. Not on purpose, but as if driven by another. Chipped red nails trembled as she squeezed her pale fingers together. In that moment, Ava realized she was seeing this memory through another's eyes—Haberdeen's eyes.

Her gaze dipped downwards again. Winterthorn rested on her lap, sealed in the white-gold scabbard Ava remembered from her uncle's hall.

"What happens if I refuse?" she said, though the voice was not her own.

The hooded figure stroked a strong chin. A tense pause stretched between the pair, and the man spoke. The voice was deep—almost musical—and effortlessly dangerous. It sent a shiver down Ava's spine. She knew that voice. She knew this man. "I will find another," he said. "But they will not be you. They will be less suited to the task. If they cannot complete the task, you will bear the guilt of their failure."

Haberdeen breathed out a long sigh. She touched the dagger's hilt as if it might burn her. "What makes me so well suited to this task?"

"You have the requisite power to do what is required, both in magic and in will." The figure leaned forward. "Not just anyone can save the world."

"Flattery," Haberdeen said, but Ava felt the rush of confidence the answer inspired. "I... need time to think on it."

"There is no time left," the man said. A note of impatience played in his voice. "Euryma will not heed your warnings. Not at first. This I have foreseen."

The small shed fell silent. Ava's gaze darted—unbidden —about the cramped space. She could sense Haberdeen's uncertainty. The woman was making a show of considering her options. From what Ava understood, this memory was from before the Fatesmiths, before the storms. The man knelt in front of her and tossed his long hood over his shoulders, confirming Ava's worst fears.

A simple strip of leather tied Korvan's hair back. His expression was kind, but firm. Deep green armor was visible under the cloak's collar. "You know what you must do, Deena," he said. "I give you this blade so that you may see the truth in my words. Now, it is your duty to use it."

Ava knew that a white-haired wanderer had given Winterthorn to Haberdeen, though she had presumed the wanderer to be an old man. Never in her wildest dreams did she believe it came from her cousin—the heir to Vedmark's stewardship. The revelation felt like stepping off a stone into too-deep water.

"I have never taken a life," Haberdeen said in a small voice.

"Let me be your first," Korvan replied. "My memories are prepared for you. Take them, and learn what must be done."

Haberdeen nodded. Slowly, she unsheathed the dagger. "I don't want to kill you," she whispered.

"You are not killing me," Korvan said. As he spoke, he thumbed a brilliant ruby set in the ring on his finger. "I will live on within you. You will carry my memories and save our Dominion."

"Our Dominion?" Suspicion rippled through Haberdeen, and her eyes narrowed. "But you hail from Vedmark? You are not—"

Korvan stood, and his looming shadow cut her short. "We will be as one. A nation united to stop the coming storms." He took Haberdeen's hands. Ava flinched at the touch. Korvan wrapped them around the dagger's hilt.

"Every moment wasted in indecision is folly. The storms are coming, Deena. Let me show you."

"I..." Haberdeen tugged her hands free and put Winterthorn down. "I... can't."

While the lightbulb remained the same, the room somehow darkened. Korvan's jaw tensed. Without warning, he slapped Haberdeen—hard. Exquisite pain erupted in Ava's cheek, as if she too had been hit. Haberdeen fell from the chair, landing awkwardly on the concrete. Blood dripped onto the floor. Ava touched her lip—Haberdeen's lip—and felt a deep cut running from the left corner of her mouth. Korvan's ruby ring had left its mark.

"You are being weak," he spat at her. All signs of kindness were gone. "You have wasted my patience too long." He unsheathed the sword concealed beneath his cloak. "You will take my memories, or you will take leave of this life."

He kicked Winterthorn towards her. Haberdeen scampered to the edge of the room. Ava felt a boot in her back and she sprawled forward. She rolled over as Korvan raised his weapon. "Draw your weapon!" he commanded.

Through muffled sobs, Haberdeen obliged. Blood mixed with tears as it streamed down her chin. She drew the dagger free of the white-gold scabbard. Her hand shook like leaves in the wind.

"Now decide," Korvan said in a voice like a winter storm. "Your life, or mine."

He eased his sword towards Haberdeen's chest. With white knuckles, she knocked the blade aside. Korvan knelt and placed his sword to her neck. "I will count from five, then I will take your head." He closed his eyes and smiled. "Five. Four. Three. Two."

Ava couldn't tell if the bloodcurdling scream belonged

to her or Haberdeen. The memory was so real. She lunged forward and thrust Winterthorn into his chest. Korvan's smile widened as his skin paled. The hilt vibrated. Green light clouded her vision. Ava did not see the memories that Winterthorn took, but she felt the pain as they clawed their way into her mind. Screaming, Haberdeen stumbled back and curled into a crying, bloody mess.

Korvan's body fell hard on the concrete beside her. His corpse unmoving while the ruby on his finger swirled with crimson clouds.

CHAPTER 48
SAMANTHA

SAMANTHA LAY on the cold floorboards, her mind trying—and failing—to grasp the sudden change that had enveloped Vedmark's travelling court. It wasn't Remnant Magic. When the storms arrived, the surrounding nima lost their integrity—shriveling like cotton in fire. This was something else.

Her ruined hands could not manipulate, but she could still see nima. She had watched it transform from vibrant colors to nothing. Every strand around her had stiffened, then vanished.

Now, she saw none.

Magic was gone. *How?*

There was a commotion of activity outside, and Korvan burst through the door. The last remnants of the sunset—an artwork of magenta and gold—poured in after him. His face burned with a manic fervor that made Samantha's stomach turn.

"What do you see, witch?" The directness of the question seemed lost on him. The two servants in the room glanced at each other before their gazes dropped to the floor. "What do you see?" Korvan asked again.

"I see you."

Korvan barked a laugh. "What do you see of your magic?" He kneeled by her iron cage. Madness smoldered in his skull. "What do you see of the threads my brother forged?"

The question hit Samantha like a fist. Her jaw fell open. Her spinning mind jammed to a halt. Nothing made sense.

"Tell me," Korvan hissed.

Samantha blinked as her lips formed the words. "Magic is gone."

Korvan clapped his hands together. The ruby on his finger glimmered in the dying daylight. "Gone. Destroyed. As intended."

"Intended?" The one-word question was a slip, and Samantha braced for the inevitable punishment. It did not come.

Korvan knelt in front of her. His smile was the gaping maw of some hideous monster. "A thousand years of waiting, of planning, of weaving. An intricate tapestry to undo his threads. The puppet strings have been cut. Euryma's magic is destroyed. Now I can feast once more. Now, I can regain my power."

"Who..." Samantha barely heard her voice over her racing heart. Korvan had either lost his mind, or something else was wrong. *Very* wrong. "Who are you?"

"You know who I am."

The hairs on Samantha's arms stood on end. She swallowed, shaking her head. *It cannot be. He is dead.* "How?" she whispered.

The monster in Korvan's flesh smiled. "The witless Steward sent his witless son into my Void. The imbecile brought my dagger right to me." The monster's face split further. The grin made Samantha's skin crawl. "They freed me to enact a plan, millennia in the making."

A clay pot shattered behind them. A servant had dropped their water jug. Beside him, a middle-aged Knight with a grizzled chin of stubble stood, frozen in shock. The servants exchanged glances, then both rushed to the floor. A terrible flame engulfed them as they reached their knees. When the fire subsided, the bodies were gone.

The Knight stepped back in concern. "My King, what is the meaning of this?"

"You are not supposed to be here, Uldrock." Korvan's visage seemed to grow a foot taller as the creature towered over the Knight. "Find peace. Your Sila will not go to waste." Before Uldrock could respond, the monster clenched its fist and the Knight stiffened. He grasped at his throat, word-less, as a pulsing cloud of green light spewed from his mouth. Samantha watched in horror as the sparkling haze arced across the room and into the monster's waiting maw. She didn't believe what she was seeing. When the sickening display finished, the Knight fell to the ground and—like the servants—vanished in an emerald flame.

The monster licked its lips. "My brother's foolish magic barred me from feasting. No more. Now, I will take Sila as needed.

Fear wrapped its hands around Samantha's neck as the reality of it set in. She stared at the spot where the Knight had died, unwilling—unable—to look at the creature ahead of her. She felt like crying and vomiting and passing out at the same time. "But..." Her breaths were shallow as she struggled not to hyperventilate. "But Arman killed you."

The thing that was not Korvan tilted its head. For a

moment, Samantha expected green flames to swallow her too. Then it laughed. A sound that made Samantha retreat in terror.

"I am reborn." It inhaled deeply. "I am returned to reclaim what is mine. Magic is gone, and I will feast on the Sila of all who oppose me. Euryma is mine. The world is mine. None can stand against the power of Morkurik."

- The End -

THE STORY ENDS IN 2025

facebook.com/ntaylorwrites

amazon.com/stores/Nathan-Taylor/author/B0CG649CZD

About Nathan

Nathan Taylor is an outstandingly distracted author with a penchant for imagining wizarding worlds and magical storms that could knock your socks off.

He gravitates towards ice baths (or rather the dopamine hit that follows), milk chocolate, and issuing stern warnings to his muggle children about the consequences of leaving dirty laundry on the bathroom floor.

Nathan lives in rural Queensland, Australia, which is the perfect place for snake bites, spider bites and picturesque sunsets.

Want More?

Join the Wintersmiths for a free short story collection at www.nathantaylorwrites.com

facebook.com/ntaylorwrites

amazon.com/stores/Nathan-Taylor/author/B0CG649CZD